The Snake and the Serpent

SM Humphreys

Published by Clink Street Publishing 2023

Copyright © 2023

First edition.

ISBN:
978-1-915229-18-2 - paperback
978-1-915229-19-9 - ebook

To Laraine and Peter (Mum and Dad), thank you for helping me see the things I see, hear the things I hear, and think the way I think, without which the way I work and the way I create would not be what it is today.

To my sister Cherilee, thank you for encouraging me when needed and pushing me when needed. You are amazing and I draw courage from the faith you have in me.

Olwyn, thank you for being you, being supportive and all that you bring to our family

To Lynley, Taylor and my Grandparents, you have all affected my life in ways you will never know and helped me to become the person I am today. I miss you all but feel that you are still with me.

To all of those who have and will in the future, put their lives on the line, to support, and protect others. Who may never be given the recognition they deserve, but do it, as they feel it is their duty, to not sit on the side-lines and watch injustice to others, but to make a difference. You inspire and humble me, for the sacrifices you make in this quest. The words thank you seem insignificant, yet it is all I can say.

CHAPTER 1

Munich 1932

Even the oxygen felt like it was on hold, waiting. The waiting had driven the girls outside. Having escaped the house, they were now relaxed on the sloping lawn, basking in the sun. Helene wanted to be outside with her girls, free, not suffocating, waiting for him. She shook her head and clenched her teeth.

Laughter broke her thoughts; she refocused. The girls were chalk and cheese. Her youngest, Michele, the tomboy, was playing with the gardener's dog. Tug of war. Who'd win? Tough call. The dog was bigger, but that wouldn't stop her. You could see the determination on her face, as she dug her heels into the ground. In contrast, Natasha was sitting on the grass, leaning on one of the old trees. Her eyes closed as if asleep or relaxing. Helene's hand pushed against the lead trim of the window, opening it more. She sat on the bay window ledge and managed to lean out so that she could feel the wind on her face.

Natasha's eyes opened. She sat upright. Her head flicked to the right. Helene followed her eldest daughter's gaze. Nothing. What was it? A car appeared between the trees that lined the driveway, followed by another and another.

He was here.

Helene shot a look at Natasha. Had she noticed her glare? You could never tell with that girl, far too alert for her age. If the eyes are the windows to your soul, Natasha's were fortified, no one could penetrate them. Helene got up. She wished she had Natasha's skill; it would come in handy sometimes. It would come in handy now.

***

If he were honest, Friedrich felt sick. He hadn't been able to eat all day. Saliva flooded his mouth, but he couldn't swallow, he was trying, but couldn't. This was stupid; there was nothing physically wrong with him, just nerves. Everything was how it should be. Helene had organised that. The only thing that could go wrong now was. The nausea came back. Maybe that was the problem. Could he ruin it? He wanted so much to be in this, to be part of it, but if he felt like this now, could he?

Friedrich looked towards the photograph of his men in the trenches, all smiles in the chaos. It calmed him. The new Germany would be for them. He glanced around his study. It was too grand for his liking, the war had changed things, changed him. The dark oak sideboards and panelling felt oppressive. The literature, which lined the walls, amplified the divide between him and his men. Why should there be a difference, they had given all they could, all we could. But Germany had lost so much with the Treaty of Versailles and now the depression. Everyone needed a win, to be led out of this darkness, to feel the pride, to realise what made Germany great. It was the German people; they knew how to right the country, how to make it strong. Europe had no right to tell them what to do, to keep them small, in debt, not allowing industry to grow. He looked back at the photograph. There was no class system in the trenches and there would be no class system in the future and the future Germany would reclaim what was theirs, what was ours. He smiled. Enthusiasm came back, followed by the nerves. They would accept him, they would understand.

***

Helene walked down the stairs as the butler collected the guest's coats. She didn't recognise most of the group. Her old university professor hung back from the main group with another tall military man. Both acknowledged Helene and then analysed the others. Although confident and proud in their official uniforms, the rest of the group stepped aside to allow a shorter man in a beige overcoat through, lining an imaginary path for him to follow. His dark hair looked like it was patchy as he incessantly tried to smooth it over his skull. A small, squashed moustache rested on his lips. Alert eyes roved around the area and finally moved up the staircase to Helene. There was a challenge in the stare, a nod, and then he moved through to the study. Yes, thought Helene, change had arrived. She didn't like him. She didn't trust him, and she definitely didn't want him in her house.

***

Friedrich had been busy since the meeting. His life seemed to consist of working at the Party headquarters and then working in his study. It felt endless; so much to do. So many reports to assess and proposals to review.

Michele burst into the study. 'Papa, I want to play.'

'I'm busy.' Friedrich said. 'I'll play later.'

'No, you never play later. You never play at all.'

Michele's bottom lip curled, she stood with her arms crossed, her eyes defiant as ever, staring up at her father. He kept working. She grabbed a book off the shelf and dropped it on the floor. He ignored her. She did it again, and again, until there was a little line of books along the floor.

'Michele.'

She walked up beside him and started poking his arm. Then she grabbed his jacket and started pulling at it.

'Michele.'

She didn't stop. His patience was running out. He couldn't focus, the noise, the interruption, the constant barrage. That was enough. He threw down his pen and turned to her, his anger about to explode.

Michele looked at him; her eyes glazed and a tear spilling down her cheek.

'I miss you, Papa.'

The image melted his anger. He lowered his hand, and wiped away her tears, then lifted her onto his knee. She snuggled into his chest, and he hugged her.

'I love you; you know.'

He stroked her hair.

'I know,' she said. 'I love you too, that's why I miss you.'

'I've been busy.'

'You're always busy, always working.'

'I have a new job now. It's very important. I'm the boss of the police.'

'I know, but don't forget about us, don't forget about me, Papa.

He glanced at his desk. His head was spinning with population statistics and location reports. He looked into Michele's eyes, they were glistening, her eyelids were swelling and there was a quiver in her bottom lip. No, the reports could wait. The work was to make a better country for his family after all.

He stroked Michele's cheek. 'I have a very important job for you.'

She smiled and nodded.

'You need to go and get your mother and sister and tell them that we're going for a–' he paused, '–picnic.'

Michele's eyes lit up and she jumped off his knee and skipped out of the room singing.

'We're going on a picnic; we're going on a picnic.'

***

Helene sat out on the blanket watching her family. This was what she missed. Friedrich was running around the field with Michele and Natasha, playing tag. He looked younger than normal. Out here, there was no stress; it was as if there was no one else in the world but them. Helene closed her eyes to plant the image firmly in her mind. She opened her eyes to mass laughter as Friedrich fell over and the girls attacked him with tickles. Helene smiled, oh how I miss you Friedrich.

He managed to wriggle free and ran over to Helene.

'Now it's your turn.'

He started tickling her and the girls joined in.

'Stop!' she giggled. 'Stop, I can't breathe.'

They all stopped to catch their breath.

'Oh, Papa,' said Michele, 'I miss this, I miss the fun! When can we do it again?'

'Soon,' Friedrich said. 'Soon.'

CHAPTER 2

'Wake up,' Anneliese said, as she drew the curtains.

Michele shielded her scrunched up face with the blankets and muffled, 'I don't want to.'

'Come on.' Anneliese jumped on the bed and started bouncing on it.

The covers came down to reveal a grumpy face and folded arms. Anneliese stared grumpily back, but neither could keep a straight face for long and they both laughed. Michele tried to snuggle into Anneliese for a hug and a little extra sleep.

'I know what you're doing,' Anneliese smiled as she got off the bed, 'you have to get up.'

Anneliese walked out of Michele's room and to Natasha's. She gave a soft knock before entering.

'Are you awake?'

'Yes,' Natasha replied, looking up from her book.

'Breakfast is ready downstairs.'

'You really do spoil us,' said Natasha as she put the book on the bed. 'Sometimes you act like a servant, and you know you aren't.'

'Your Mother does pay me.'

'Don't be silly' Natasha said. 'I get paid for chores too, does that mean that I'm a servant? I go to the parties like you, and my family joins in for dinner and—'

'Stop' Anneliese said, 'you've made your point, and I've made breakfast, so go eat.'

Anneliese closed the door laughing. Natasha was right, she didn't have an official role. Anneliese met Helene just after the war when Anneliese was six. Her mother had just died, and her father struggled with her headstrong personality. Helene took her under her wing. When Michele was born, Anneliese helped and slowly became more and more involved with the family. Now she felt like the older sister, even though she still lived with her father.

After taking the children to school, Anneliese walked along the road to the local bakery. Just ahead of her she saw some brown shirts standing outside a Jewish shop barring people from entering. They smiled at her as she approached. She was lucky. The way she dressed, and her look allowed her to pass as a German rather than a Jew. But she didn't want to get too close, just in case. She crossed the street to the local bakery. She could never go past it without stopping in. The scent of baking was enticing, and before she knew it, she'd been drawn inside.

'Hello, Anneliese,' said the short, plump man behind the counter. 'What will it be today?'

'Hello, Herr Schmidt.'

Anneliese looked at the small cakes, her tastebuds started to water. 'The pink one please.'

She felt like a little kid in a confectionary store.

'This bakery is a bad influence on me.'

'Me too,' he replied, laughing.

She headed to meet her brother in the local square. Was that yelling? She ran. There was chaos. Police were surrounding a group of people, there was yelling and pushing. Others trying to run away, some trying to fight their way out. She could see Yosef in the group.

A chill rose through her body.

'Yosef.'

Yosef turned around searching for his sister. He looked confused. He tried to get out of the mob, but people were pushing him back.

'Anneliese.'

There was terror in his eyes: she froze. Slowly her brain caught up and saw who was in charge. Friedrich. She started running towards him.

Friedrich yelled, 'Go home.'

'He's my brother, Friedrich. Let him go.'

Her shock turned to fear, then anger, and a rage fired through her.

Yosef tried to reach her, but they pushed him into a truck.

'He's done nothing wrong.'

Friedrich looked through her. Anneliese scanned the crowd for her brother again. Her breath caught in her throat. Everyone was moving. Just glimpses.

'Let him go,' she shouted, not at Friedrich, but everyone, anyone, anyone at all. 'Let him go.'

'I'll talk to you later,' Friedrich said, pushing her out of his way.

The push caught her off balance and she fell to the ground. He turned and got into a truck. Anneliese was frantic; there was a scream. It made her shudder. Then she realised she'd made it.

'Anneliese.'

'Yosef, what's happening? Where are you going? Where are they taking you?'

The truck started to drive away, 'I don't know, I don't know; help me, Anneliese, Anneliese.'

'No, no, no,' was all she could say.

She stared at the trucks after they had vanished. Silence, confusion, and emptiness, both she and the courtyard felt, empty. The only sounds heard, was the steady fall of water from the fountain and her sobs. She was dizzy and stunned.

Scared of going home, alone, Anneliese got up out of the dirt. Her hand smudged the tears across her face. She rinsed her hands in the water.

What? Why? Her brain was fuzzy, can't focus. Can't think. I need. Talk to someone. She turned and staggered to the bakery.

Anneliese collected the girls after school, trying to act normal. Michele beckoned Anneliese to her room.

'What's wrong?'

Michele indicated her to sit.

'Nothing.'

'That's an awful smile, what's wrong?'

A tear ran down Anneliese's cheek, she loved the girls they were like family. She didn't want to lose them too.

***

Friedrich was home early today. There was something he had to do. Something he'd been putting off for some time. He took a deep breath. Anneliese was like a daughter. But she wasn't, no she was not. She was not a daughter. The party constantly reminded him. He looked up and saw Natasha coming down the stairs.

'Get Anneliese.'

He turned and walked into the study.

Natasha walked back up the stairs towards Michele's room. There was sobbing. She paused and listened.

'It's Yosef,' Anneliese said. 'He was arrested today in town.'

'Why?'

'I don't know?'

'Well, I could ask Papa to…'

'No.'

'Why?' said Michele. 'He's a big boss; he may be able to help.'

'I don't want you to talk to your Papa.'

'Why?' Michele asked. 'That's silly, why not talk to him?'

Anneliese just shrugged.

'Why?'

Anneliese hesitated.

'He arrested Yosef.'

Michele looked at Anneliese for a minute, confused.

'Why?'

'I talked to Herr Schmidt, and he said that groups of people are being arrested.'

Michele looked quizzically at the bed, then to Anneliese.

'I still don't understand. Why arrest Yosef? What has he done? What groups?'

'Different types of people, but,' Anneliese paused. 'most are Jewish or Communist.'

The door opened.

'I'm sorry,' said Natasha, coming inside. 'Father wants you.'

Anneliese caught her breath and looked at them both.

'Wait,' Natasha said, pulling them together. 'I want a hug.'

They all huddled together.

Natasha joined them, 'We'll always be family, you do know that; we're here for you.'

Michele whispered, 'sisters forever.'

They all nodded.

'I love you both,' Anneliese said.

Then she turned and walked out of the room.

Michele turned to Natasha.

'I don't understand, make me understand.'

'I don't think I can,' said Natasha.

***

Helene walked upstairs to Michele's room. Opening the door quietly she found Michele on her bed crying.

'What's wrong?'

She gave her daughter a hug.

'Anneliese, I miss Anneliese.'

'Why, where's Anneliese?' Helene said.

'Papa sent her away,' Michele said, 'because Papa said she was bad and that I shouldn't talk to her.'

'What?'

'Because her people aren't good, shouldn't be here and she was telling lies about the people Papa arrested yesterday. But – I miss her.'

Helene pulled her daughter towards her.

'Why doesn't Papa like Anneliese anymore? It's not fair.'

Michele's eyes betrayed her anger.

'I don't know, I don't know.'

She stroked Michele's hair until she was asleep. Helene quietly made her way out of the room and downstairs. Then she walked straight into the study.

'What – you don't knock anymore?' Friedrich said, although he didn't look up from his papers.

'It appears the rules of this house have changed,' Helene retorted. 'Talk to me about Anneliese. Why was she dismissed?'

'She's a bad influence, putting ideas into their heads,' he said leaning back in the chair.

'Better than someone else, putting ideas into their heads. Why now?' said Helene.

'I cannot have someone like that, on my staff.'

'Like what?' said Helene, 'A Jew?'

'Well. Yes. If you want to put it like that.'

'I cannot believe you. Your politics are not to come into this home.'

She was shocked. What was happening? She could feel her temper building up. It took all her willpower not to cry, slap him, shake him, or something, anything.

'The children will be educated in the true ways of Germany, like the true breed they are,' Friedrich stated and looked back at his papers.

'Like hell they will,' she said as she stormed out slamming the door.

Friedrich looked up. He didn't like it either. But why could she not see that, not support him. There couldn't be one rule for him and one rule for everyone else. He sighed, he'd had to do it, he just had to, damn it.

***

Helene had to get out of the house. She went to the car and drove. Thoughts were racing in her head; how did this happen? What had happened to Friedrich? I don't even know him anymore.

She was driving on autopilot, until suddenly she recognised the area. A two-storeyed house stood before her, small but impressive. Bordered by old trees, it had a small stream running through the back of the property. She couldn't see it, but she knew. Helene parked and made her way to the door. She paused, then pressed the doorbell and waited. Nothing. She pressed it again, no reply. She pounded the door with her fist to knock, but instead of making a sound it simply opened.

'Hello.'

Light filtered through the doorway into the foyer.

'Anneliese?'

There was eerie silence. She walked up the stairs to Anneliese's room. It was chaotic: the furniture was out of place, papers and clothing were on the floor. Helene tried to make sense of it all. She ran out of the room, pushing doors, screaming, and the more she ran the more she felt a cold chill creep through her. Suddenly she stopped, and gulped for air, she couldn't breathe. Helene pushed the back of her hand over her cheek and across her eyes, to wipe away tears.

'Anneliese, Anneliese.'

Slowly she lowered herself on to the bottom steps and leaning her head against the wall and cried. What's happening?

After a while, she sat, slightly dazed and then got up and walked to a small table in the foyer. Things were askew but sitting peacefully in the mess was a photograph. It was Anneliese, Helene and the girls.

Why can't it be as it used to be before, before that man? Everything has changed, it was good before. Not perfect, but it was getting better. We used to be good. Damn you Hitler, you wretched man. She picked up the photograph and threw it at the door.

The smash jolted her out of her thoughts, and she immediately ran over to where it had landed on the floor. Shattered glass surrounded the frame, but apart from a small scratch, the photograph was undamaged.

She turned it over to take it out and noticed the word open on it. Sliding the clips back, she opened the casing and both a note and the picture fell out. The note read, 'We're fine, we just have to hide. Love you all.'

Helene clutched the picture.

'Ouch'

Her finger was cut, stupid glass, stupid me.

She didn't care. Anneliese was safe. A weight lifted. But now – now there was work to do.

After the girls came home from school the next day, Helene called them.

'We're going Grünwalder Forst, get your coats.'

They looked outside. The wind was whipping up the leaves and torturing the trees, by blowing them in circles. They looked quizzically at each other, then at their mother. Helene rolled her eyes and then raised an eyebrow.

'Now.'

She trusted no one in the house and wanted no one to overhear.

Twenty minutes later, they were on the sheltered bank of the stream that ran through the wooded area.

'Whatever we speak about here cannot be repeated at home,' Helene said. Natasha smiled, 'Father cannot hear about it.'

'Yes,' replied Michele.

Helene looked at her youngest. The anger was showing on her face, she was no longer the easy-going tomboy. Natasha however had her calm façade, which always hid her emotion.

'Anneliese's house was empty,' Helene said, 'but they're safe.'

'How do you know?' Natasha asked.

'I found a note behind a photograph of us.'

Helene raised her hand to stop more questions.

'Anyway, I want you both to think of places or people she may have gone to.'

'She knew everyone,' Natasha said, 'but I don't know who she would trust.'

They all tried to think.

'Um um,' Michele broke the silence, her hands flapping and then cupping the top of her head, 'Anneliese talked to someone.'

Michele was getting annoyed with herself.

'I know, I know, just let me think, I know it, I know it. Ummmm.'

Natasha and Helene were both leaning forward, staring at the flustered Michele trying to will the information out of her.

'Um oh, oh, that's it, I remember.'

Michele smiled excitedly.

'Herr Schmidt.'

'But the baker is in the city, why go all the way there?' Natasha queried.

'I think we should find out,' said Helene.

***

When they reached the bakery, it was busy. A rally had just finished and the excited feeling of the customers, only acted in heightening the stress that Helene felt. The bell on the door rang behind them.

'I thought it was you,' said a familiar voice over Helene's shoulder. 'Why are you here?'

Helene turned around to face Friedrich and smiled.

'Getting something special for dessert, what would you like dear?'

'Special? What's the occasion?' he interrogated.

'To cheer up the girls, they're sad since you fired Anneliese.' Helene held his stare.

Friedrich's smile vanished. Grabbing her arm, he pulled her towards him and said, 'We've talked about this. Don't make a scene.'

'You, are making the scene,' she said, 'now what do you want?'

He let go, stepping back.

'I'm not hungry. Be careful Helene, look around you, the world is changing, you have no idea what or who you are dealing with.'

He turned and walked out.

Helene felt cold and a little shaken. She looked at the floor to compose herself, and then turned. Eyes darted away.

'Are you alright, Mama?' Michele asked.

'I'm fine.'

Helene looked at Natasha. Her jaw was set and eyes glaring after her father. Then Natasha looked back at her mother, face blank, back to normal.

They pottered around the bakery until they were the only customers.

'I have a message for you,' Schmidt paused, 'I was confused when I was told that you were the only ones that I should give it to, but now – are you alright Helene?'

'I'm fine,' she replied, 'I just want to know how she is.'

'No,' he said, 'you want to know is where she is.'

Helene nodded.

'Do you know Mittenwald?' Schmidt asked.

'No,' she said.

'It's a small village on the German-Austrian border southwest of here. There's a house, outside the village on the road to Innsbruck, called Der Kampfgeist,' whispered Herr Schmidt, 'but be careful.'

'We will. That's a very patriotic name, *fighting spirit*,' she remarked.

'I know. I wouldn't have chosen it. Now, what will you be bringing home this evening?' he asked.

Helene looked confused.

'After all, now the acting has begun, you must continue the show.'

He was right and they all knew it.

***

Helene picked up the children from school the following day. She'd promised them they'd go together. Natasha was *lookout* for the two-and-a-half-hour journey. Friedrich had not talked to Helene all day, but she knew he would work late.

They drove down a small avenue bordered on one side with a little bubbling brook and on the other with trees that had spread up one of the foothills to the Alps. This opened to an entrance of a rather large building on the side of the hill.

Helene had got used to the flatter landscape of Munich, but now she was here, she felt the homely feel she knew from her childhood. This was the in-between land, a little bit of Austria and a little bit of Germany. The dramatic landscape gave a sheltered feel from all angles. And it reminded her of home. The Austrian alps were like the Swiss and she realised it had been a long time since she had seen them and felt this protected.

The two-storeyed cube house was almost baroque in style, with ornate decorations on the balcony and attic windows. Flowers spilling over their edges. A scene from one of Grimms' fairy tales was painted to the right-hand side of the front wall. There were smaller buildings slightly to the left, with what looked like stables. A stately property. It made Helene wonder, whom she was going to meet.

'What exactly are we going to say?' Natasha asked. 'Hello, you don't know who we are, we don't know who you are, but can we please speak to Anneliese?'

'I don't know,' snarled Helene.

She parked the car near the entrance, and they all climbed out and headed towards the door. It opened before they got there, and the Butler welcomed them to the front room. A woman served refreshments, but no one else came to the room. Natasha looked at her mother. Helene kept sipping coffee, hiding behind the cup; she had no idea what to do. Michele was looking around the room. On one side there was a large bookshelf, almost wall to wall. She walked over to it. She was bored.

Michele pulled a book off the shelf.

'Be careful.'

'Yes.'

Michele opened the book. It was full of animals, of all sizes. She sat down and started looking through the pages.

'Look at all the animals,' she said.

She got up and grabbed another book. It was all about myths. She looked through it. She was enjoying this bookshelf; it had some wonderful books on it. Large drawings of mermaids and phoenixes filled the pages. She turned the page and saw a picture of a serpent. She was confused. Then she looked at the other book.

'Mama, what is the difference between a serpent and a snake?'

Helene looked at her, 'I don't think there's much of a difference, except one is generally a myth and one is real. There are some real serpents, that are very poisonous.'

Natasha smiled, 'The serpent is supposed to represent knowledge and deception, and the snake, people often associate with cunning or even protection, as it strikes down its enemies. But I think they're really the same, they just appear to be different.'

'So, people only think they are different,' asked Michele.

'No,' Helene said, 'regarding those books, the snake is real, and the serpent is made-up.'

Helene shook her head at Natasha, who looked down smiling, 'Stop, she will believe you'.

The door opened and an elderly woman walked in.

'I apologise for the delay,' she said. 'How can I help you?'

Helene knew this was a formality. 'Can we please speak to Anneliese?'

The woman smiled, 'Yes my dear. And I'm so sorry about the wait, we just had to be sure you weren't–'

'I understand,' Helene cut in.

Michele put the books back on the bookshelf and returned to the group

The woman left the room. Five minutes later the door opened again, and Anneliese rushed in. She ran to the girls and gave them a hug. A tear was running down her cheek.

'I didn't know if I'd see you again.'

'Don't be silly,' Helene said. 'We were always going to find you.'

'What happened?' Natasha asked.

Anneliese looked at everyone, and then started to explain. She'd gone downstairs to Friedrich, who had told her that she was no longer needed. She wasn't allowed to say goodbye.

'He told me to leave the country, quickly,' she said. 'Not to tell anyone what he'd said and that he'd miss me.'

Helene thought for a moment, maybe deep down somewhere there was a little hope.

Anneliese explained 'I got Papa and went to Herr Schmidt. He recommended coming here. When we went home the door was open and the house…'

She paused and took a deep breath.

'We grabbed a few things; I left a message for you and then came straight here.'

The woman came in with some sandwiches. Anneliese turned around and smiled.

'This is my hero,' she said. 'Her name is Hilde.'

Hilde blushed and sat down. Helene looked at her.

'Yes, I am fully German,' she said, 'but I disagree with what's happening to my Germany. Mind you, never thought I'd say that to the wife of one of the commanders of the police. But

Anneliese assures me that you're quite the opposite of your husband.'

Helene smiled and then looked at Anneliese.

'Why are you still in the country?'

'I'm not,' said Anneliese. 'The woods to the back of the house are about a mile away from the Austrian border. Papa and I are staying there for now.'

'Because I'm German, no one investigates my property and because the woods are so dense the area is not patrolled, at the moment anyway. But there are rumours that Germany may move into Austria soon,' said Hilde.

'I walked through the woods to get here,' Anneliese said.

'What would've happened if you were home,' Natasha asked.

Hilde and Anneliese looked at each other.

'I don't know,' said Anneliese. 'Jewish people are being taken into custody for being political opponents, and no one knows what happens to them.'

Helene looked at the girls and wondered just how sheltered from reality they all were.

Natasha looked at her mother then back at Anneliese.

'Is there anything you need; is there anything we can get you?'

'No,' said Anneliese, 'no we're fine, I'm just glad to see you.'

Helene handed Anneliese a piece of paper.

'This is the address of my sister in Austria; if you need anything contact her.'

'Thank you.'

'Where's Yosef?' Michele asked.

Anneliese's breath caught in her throat, and she looked down.

'We don't know where he is' Hilde said, 'But we're trying to find out.'

'Is there something we can do?' Helene said.

Anneliese looked up at Helene, her eyes watery. 'No, but if you hear anything?'

'Of course. I'm so sorry.'

Anneliese managed a smile.

'Thank you for finding me.'

'Come' said Helene, 'we must be going.'

It was almost eleven when they arrived home. Helene opened the door and walked into the foyer.

Friedrich walked out of the study.

'Where have you been?'

'Oh,' Helene replied slightly startled. 'How are you?'

'Fine. Where have you been?'

'Thank you so much, Mother,' Natasha said. 'That's going to help for school.'

'What?' Friedrich asked.

The usually quiet Natasha stepped between her parents. 'Well, I never knew how much natural flora and fauna was around. It's for biology. Father, I still don't understand, and maybe you can answer this, but how do we know what's German and what's Austrian or is it just native to the area.'

Michele didn't want to be left out.

'And what about bugs Papa, when they go over the border, do they realise?'

Friedrich stood bewildered, 'I, I don't know.'

He paused, 'well hopefully soon it won't be a border and they won't get confused.'

Helene sighed as she walked away. Where would she be without those girls?

The charade had begun; it was like living a fantasy. The girls were good at the act. Meanwhile Helene began her research.

***

Helene was walking against the flow of people to get to the bakery. A Nazi rally had just finished. It was an uncomfortable mix of euphoria and hatred. Excited people were waving flags and grouping together cheering about the future.

'We must stop the Bolsheviks,' a lady said to her companion.

'No, it is the Jewish that are the problem' he replied.

'They both are–' she continued as Helene walked out of earshot.

Conspiracy theories, so many seeds of hatred and blame were being sown.

Helene felt sick. How could this be happening, to her friends, her neighbours; they were intelligent people, they were smart, but how? Helene bumped into a girl whose bag fell on the floor. Pens, books, and pamphlets scattered on the ground.

'Sorry,' Helene said as she bent to help the girl get her things.

The young girl smiled to her as she grabbed what appeared to be her prized possession. *Mein Kampf.*

'He's going to save us you know,' her eyes sparkled in awe, 'he is going to make Germany great again, for me, for us.'

Helene felt herself turn cold as she stood up. She could feel her eyes moisten. She reached out to the girl to say something, to warn her. But the girl turned before the connection was made and then was gone.

People pushed past Helene as she stood still, in their way. Was she missing something? Could all these people really be wrong, or was it her, was she the one missing some vital information. No. She knew more. She knew more than them. They were untouched, unaffected. For now.

She moved against the flow towards the bakery. The crowds were thinning out. As she pushed through the door Schmidt acknowledged her presence but continued to serve until the bakery slowly emptied.

'This is madness, it can't be happening, it cannot possibly continue,' she said with a mixture of frustration and disbelief, 'people must start to realise.'

Helene looked out of the window as the stragglers wandered away.

'I fear this will not continue, I fear something worse is coming,' Schmidt said. 'I think this is building momentum now and that worries me.'

'What do you mean?' she said turning to him. 'This has to pass soon.'

'I don't think so,' Schmidt replied. 'He learnt from last time. He is putting structures in place. He's crazy, but clever.'

'But the Beer Hall Putsch was a disaster. He was imprisoned.'

'Yes, but for how long? Nine months? It fuelled him, he took the time to write a book, gain more followers, and consolidate. He was made a martyr for the people,' Schmidt said, shaking his head.

She looked around the bakery.

'Any news about Yosef?'

Schmidt wiped the counter.

'No. There are possibilities though. There is a detention centre that we are trying to get information from. I hope he's there. They released some people yesterday.'

'Jewish?' Helene asked.

'No.' Schmidt was scrubbing the same bench again. 'No, they were political opponents and a priest. They have been released after a few months. They were forced to sign documents stating that they would not take part in any more civil disobedience activities and that they could not discuss the centre. But they have. Some said that they were forced to build structures. Large complexes. I think they were building bigger prisons.'

Helene had never seen Schmidt so sad, his eyes showed so much pain.

'Are you sure you can get no information from Fried–'

'No,' she said swiftly. 'We hardly speak.'

She turned away to compose herself.

'It's…' she paused, '…difficult.'

'Be careful,' he said.

Then he continued to clean in silence.

***

The house no longer felt like a home. Friedrich was systematically replacing all the old staff. There was a constant edge in the air, an unease.

One evening Friedrich called Helene into the study.

'Hello, dear,' he said, 'I feel like I never see you anymore. I feel like I'm neglecting you and the girls.'

'That's because you are.'

Friedrich's smile vanished, but he recovered quickly.

'I intend to spend more time at home shortly. Until then I thought you might need help, so I employed a nanny and tutor for the girls. She's lovely and will go everywhere with the girls apart from school.'

'No,' said Helene.

'She starts tomorrow,' he stated and then continued with his paperwork.

***

Olga arrived early the next morning and it was obvious that they would not get along. More of a Matron than a Nanny, she immediately set up a schedule. She supervised the little time Helene could spend with the children. All through the Christmas holidays Olga also tutored the children about Germany and the superiority of the Aryan race. Helene knew her children were strong, but she felt like any opportunities to teach them about what was really happening, were being taken away from her. Both girls were already part of the Jungmädelbund. Helene wouldn't let the girls be moulded that way, to make them little Nazi clones. Hitler became Chancellor and Friedrich was more involved with the party. He needed to groom the family for his role. But Helene wouldn't allow it.

***

The day started as any other. Friedrich left for work and Helene snuck into the girl's rooms, instructing them to pack what they could. Then they quietly went downstairs to the car. As they climbed in the car, the new Butler came outside.

'Good Morning. Where are you going?'

Helene smiled. 'To town, I have a surprise for Friedrich.'

She was sure that his real job was to spy on her. He smiled and then disappeared back inside. She didn't have much time.

Helene slowly drove down the driveway, to the street, and then quickly headed towards the Austrian border. The drive was long, her hands were shaking, and it took all her strength to control her breathing. When they reached the border, they got out of the car, while guards checked it and their papers.

'Mother,' Natasha said, 'Mother, it's father's car.'

Helene turned around to see Friedrich's car approach in the distance.

'I am sorry about the inconvenience Frau, I didn't realise who you were,' said the embarrassed guard handing back the papers.

'You're just doing your job.'

She glanced at the border, they were about 200 feet away, and the car was fast approaching. The few cars that were in front of them were ambling to the border.

'Girls get your suitcase, Papa is taking the car back for us,' Helene said as calmly as she could.

Both the girls picked up the bags and started to walk towards the border. A horn sounded and brakes screeched. Someone yelled and then there was chaos, shouts, guards running, doors slamming.

'Run,' screamed Helene.

Natasha ran ahead, but Michele was struggling, Helene grabbed her suitcase and pushed her forward. It felt like it took forever, but she eventually crossed the border. Helene hugged Michele with relief.

A scream pierced the noise. She froze. Natasha, where was Natasha? A chill rippled over her skin. Helene frantically looked around. Natasha was struggling with a guard. Her suitcase was slightly in front of her. The guard's arm locked around Natasha's torso and her arms stretched towards her mother. Helene turned and started towards her daughter.

A hand grabbed her shoulder.

'Don't leave this one,' an Austrian accent commanded.

A flicker of fear, wide eyes, then Natasha shook her head at her mother and stopped struggling, 'Auf Wiedersehen.'

Natasha needed them to be safe, she would survive; she always did. She forced herself to smile. However, she couldn't watch, not as she saw her mother crumble, not when she couldn't help, couldn't change anything. She looked away and she never looked back.

Helene dropped to her knees, her eyes filled and overflowed. Numb, she felt numb. Arms wrapped around her as Michele tried to comfort her. Helene could barely feel them. Slowly the shock started to fade, and they both sat sobbing, at the border, together, divided and alone.

CHAPTER 3

Munich 1940

The hairs stood up on his arm, his back rigid and his head snapped to attention. The interrogator's steady footsteps echoed down the corridor. She wasn't coming for him. She was coming for who he guarded. But he held his breath anyway. Someone screamed. His muscles tensed. But she didn't falter as she glided towards him.

Everything about her was not as it should be. She was handsome, someone that you could imagine on the silver screen, or as a model. Her black hair framed her defined cheeks. But her eyes pierced through you. She wore black shirt and trousers, under her long flowing black coat. Her shoes had a low heel, not the fashionable higher heel.

She was elegant, sophisticated and scary and she stopped right in front of him. Dropping her head slightly to the left, she looked up at him, then raised an eyebrow. He was wasting her time.

He quickly turned and opened the door. The interrogators inside looked up, then put down the equipment. They had failed. Heads down they walked out, and she walked in.

He closed the door and let out his breath. They all looked at each other, then the interrogators left him at the door. He stood shuffling, waiting, and thankful that he did not have to see what was happening on the other side.

**

Half an hour passed, a knock at the door, indicated for him to open it.

'Prepare the van,' she said.

He called another guard as they scampered in, grabbing the prisoner by his arms. They dragged him unconscious along the corridor, his broken ankles scraping the ground behind him.

A trail of blood smeared across the floor. She glided ahead. Hungry, yes, she was hungry. What to have for lunch? She walked down the street to buy some pastries from the bakery. Today some lemonade and a Bienenstich. Then she walked back to the headquarters, to collect her prisoner.

Three hours later the van was back. It was empty as normal, no other soul in it apart from her. There was only a little blood in the back. The guards could clean it if they wanted. Natasha opened the door, and alighted, before handing the key to the guard.

'Did you enjoy your lunch?' said the guard.

'Yes,' replied Natasha, 'very much.'

He smiled back, not a real smile, more of a grimace. No one ever returned. What happened to them? Only she knew.

She walked past. So, you don't like me, I won't lose sleep over it. The fewer people I must associate with, the better. She strolled around to the office.

'Hello,' Friedrich said. 'Any luck?'

'Luck?' Natasha said. 'The prisoner is of no further use to us. The resistance is organising an attack on trains. We caught him too early. He didn't know much.' She paused 'It may pay to step up security checks along the main rail routes and…'

'Thank you. I'll organise it from here.'

She turned to leave.

'Natasha,' he said, 'we have the function this evening; you will need to be ready by seven.'

She looked at him. 'I would prefer not to go.'

'I'm still your father, and you will be attending.'

'Because my treacherous mother cannot accompany you,' Natasha said, knowing it was a sore point.

'She is imprisoned, for crimes against the Reich,' he retorted, 'and making me mad will not mean you will not attend.'

She grunted and left the office. These events are so boring. So ostentatious, why do I have to go? It's not a good use of my time. She took a deep breath. Maybe there would be some trinket of interest tonight. Please let there be some solace.

***

Anneliese sat on the couch, her head in her hands.

'It's going to be fine,' Hilde said, 'we'll get him back.'

The door opened and Michele walked in, 'Schmidt just called.'

'I'm going too,' Anneliese said.

'No. Stay here… Actually, go back to Switzerland.'

Anneliese tried to protest.

'No.'

Michele turned and was gone.

Hilde's grandson Oskar, had already started the truck when Michele got in. The drive through the countryside only took about half an hour. They parked the truck in a little clearing and walked into the woods. As they walked, they heard a shot. It made Michele jump. Oskar smiled.

They waited patiently as they heard a vehicle drive away. Slowly they moved to where the sound had come from. Twenty yards away they could make out a body. When they were sure no one else was there, they crept towards the spot. Oskar was holding a medical kit. Michele's eyes focused on the crumbled body. It stole her breath and made her pause, while she tried to compose herself. It was always harder when it was someone you knew. Someone, well, he had always been there, always, like a brother that never was. Stop it. Stop it. He's here, he's alive and he's now in your care. Michele was glad Anneliese wasn't here.

They strapped up what they could, used a few splints, and then pulled him to the truck. He lay on his back covered with blankets. Michele looked at him and clenched her jaw.

'He's bad' she whispered.

Oskar looked around uncomfortably.

'Thanks for being here,' Michele said. 'I know this must be hard.'

'I just don't know what to do,' Oskar said looking at Yosef. 'What would he do?'

'He'd do what you're doing now.'

Michele looked away, looking at the sky trying to regulate her breathing.

'Are you alright?'

'Fine' she said. 'You?'

'Fine' he said, getting into the car.

***

Yosef opened his eyes slowly, blurry. Everything was blurry. He could just make out the white walls. Suddenly an intense pain ripped up through his side. He felt tears on his face. His hand, someone was holding his hand. He tried to move his head to see who it was. Everything hurt. He gently squeezed his hand. A movement just out of eyesight. Slowly Michele's face appeared above him.

She started to stroke his forehead and she whispered, 'It's okay, you're safe now.'

The intense pain came back and then black.

'Keep him under,' she said as she left the room.

***

Natasha snarled. She did not want to go. It wasn't a party; it was a party event, and they were two different things. Natasha was the expert of fake, if she had to be, but not just for the sake of it. She closed her door. She knew she had to go. No one else could accompany her father. Then there was the fact that she was one of the best interrogators in the area. Unofficially of course, she was a woman after all. Although there had been rumours of a change in policy, which did excite her. However, her job tonight as far as her father was concerned, was to look good and assess possible suitors. He believed it would strengthen both their positions to, what did he say, 'Get a boyfriend.' The next step would be breeding. She had no interest; they were all sheep. She zipped her long black formal dress, adjusting the oversized collar and put on her black low-heeled shoes. It took a few moments to get use to them. Natasha dabbed her cheeks with her lipstick and rubbed it in as much as possible, then bit her lips before putting a little Vaseline on them. She let down her hair, which fell into a slight wave that only just reached the collar. Natasha lifted her dress up to attach her Walther PPK thigh holster, before lowering and patting the folds of her skirt in place. Would this pass her father's inspection of what a respectable single girl should look like? Probably not, but it would do. She grabbed a shawl, it was cold, and fur was a not acceptable at these functions. Hitler didn't like it, cruelty to animals. He was such a contradiction.

She was ready. Well, as ready as she'd ever be.

Friedrich and Natasha drove in through the main gates to the entrance. The door opened, and she stepped out of the car. Friedrich was soon at her side. They walked up the main steps through the doorway and into the foyer. A white and pink marble grand staircase dominated the room, with two large Nazi flags hanging from angled flagpoles attached to the wall. At the top, doors opened to reveal a grandiose ballroom. Flags hung from the roof in couples, tables surrounded a dance floor, and people were mingling in their finest, dripping with jewels and champagne. Typical, thought Natasha, over the top theatrical. She wondered if anyone truly liked these events. Hitler was theatrical though. You could tell when he got in front of the masses. His adrenaline rushed through his veins, and he lit up. That euphoria wore off on the crowd.

His speeches were like a patient fisherman. Slowly he would let the bait, the idea's, engulf the people until they identified and felt comfortable with them, agreed with them, insisted on them, and then he reeled in the line and sent them on their way, preaching his vision. Clever. He was one of the most uplifting and the greatest orators that Natasha had ever heard. He was also one of the most irrational, uneducated, arrogant men that Natasha had ever met. However, she didn't have to like him; she just had to believe in her work.

***

Michele tucked her hair under the cap. She was dressed in black, to blend into the darkness. She signalled for the group to split. They had been watching for the past hour. The guards had a circuit and passed by every fifteen minutes. The real problem was the tower light. It shone over a large area. She knew that since Yosef's interrogation, they would step up security along the tracks. She just hoped that their arrogance would stop them from giving her any surprises this evening. After all, who would be stupid enough to hit a building with forty SS on duty?

She looked at her watch: it was almost time. Slowly she moved down the bank to a little stream. There were four members in her group for the south side and three on the north. They crawled up to the tracks and started unloading their bags. There was a noise behind them. She made a silence gesture and ducked to the ground. Two guards walked up to where they were and stood laughing for a moment. Michele was lying flat on the ground, and she slightly lifted her head. There in front of her was the heel of one of the soldiers. Oskar was just to her left. Another guard shouted over to the two, to stay in the area. Damn. Michele heard the third guard turn and walk back. The heel in front of her moved past Oskar. One of the guards finished his cigarette and flicked the still burning butt. Before it had fallen past his shoulder, two figures were standing behind the guards. As it dropped past his hips, hands clasped their mouths and synchronised blades slid across their throats.

Henri and Rolf continued the laughs and chatter as the guards dropped to the ground gurgling, drowning in their last breaths. Henri caught the smoke butt just a couple of inches above the dynamite. Thankful that the blasting caps were not in place.

Michele bent down and shut their eyelids 'I'm sorry. God speed your soul and give us forgiveness, amen.'

'Put on the coats and hats,' she ordered.

There was no time for guilt; they had a job to do.

This made their job easier. Rolf and Henri posed as the guards while they organised the explosives and ignition caps.

Michele nodded, and Rolf put on the timer.

They hid the dead guards in the bushes and the group headed back to the pre-designated area. There was an explosion and silence, then alarms and shouting. Soldiers came from everywhere. Someone shouted commands and guards started to comb the area.

Michele heard footsteps behind her. She rolled over and pointed her gun at those approaching, although she knew it was the other group.

Werner crouched beside her. 'Two minutes.'

Dogs were barking. Two minutes was a long time. Some of the guards were getting very close. The group all waited patiently. Michele was looking at her watch. A single guard was walking towards the group, only a few yards away. Werner moved to get up. Michele grabbed his hand to restrain him. BANG. The second lot of explosives went off. The guard turned and ran back to the depot.

'Go,' said Michele.

The group got up and went back to the depot. Two soldiers were on guard and Rolf and Henri still dressed as officers went to talk to them and then rendered them unconscious. The group went through the wall of the building to the armoury; they filled the empty dynamite bags with weapons and then set more charges before running back into the forest.

***

Natasha was smiling and standing next to her father. He was engaged in a discussion with one of the regular attendee's, Albrecht Haushofer. The man talked too much, too much of a gossip for Natasha's tastes. She had little time for it. Although sometimes little gems of information emerged.

'And is Karl, joining us this evening?' Friedrich asked.

'Yes, he's around somewhere. Probably talking to Hess and Hitler about boundaries for–'

Natasha had lost interest already. An observer would have thought she was like any of the other daughters that had accompanied their parents or fiancée. To all intent purposes, she looked like and acted like a spoilt brat. The major difference was, while they were at home being coached on how they should act, how many children they should have for the Reich and generally people making every decision for them. She was in total control of her life and could do what she pleased. She smiled. 'You idiots.'

She scanned the room and its groups. Always the same. Most of the women floated around a small group of wives, the elites. Magda, Margarete, Emmy, Ilse and of course Eva. They would not widen their group no matter how many times they were approached. In fact, Natasha thought a few of them secretly wanted to make it smaller. But even they knew Ilse and Eva were untouchable. The only real power they had, was through their husbands. How unsatisfying that must be.

She stepped aside and took another drink from a passing waiter.

'Bored?' enquired a voice.

'Dreadfully,' she said turning to look at the speaker.

He chuckled.

'Natasha, you never could suffer fools.'

'No, I can't,' she said, 'but that's why you're here, my knight in shining armour.'

It was half-true. It was always good to talk to Wilhelm. He was interesting; he had a job in the strategic side of the air force. A different side to the war, something she knew little about. Wilhelm was a pleasant guy, handsome, okay, not handsome, maybe a little more. Always well presented. His blond hair clipped at the side, exaggerated his chiselled face. However, his eyes drew her attention, so blue, clear, innocent. No wonder he was easily led. Most of the people were. Although sometimes, Natasha caught herself wishing circumstances were different, but they weren't. She had no intention in settling down with anyone. It was not in her best interests.

The conversation moved on to chitchat for a while. He was overseeing many projects, but the current focus seemed to be in rockets, rockets that could fly themselves. He had mentioned it previously, but it was interesting to hear of the progress.

'You're not like the rest,' he said changing the subject.

The comment took Natasha off guard.

'What do you mean?'

'Nothing,' he said looking slightly embarrassed.

He looked off to her right. She could see in his eyes that something was troubling him.

'Here comes the Pied Piper,' he said.

Natasha glanced to her right. A tired looking man was walking over. Even then, he was still as charismatic as the first time she'd met him.

'Natasha.'

'Adolf.'

There was a flinch in his face. As they both looked at each other for a moment.

'You remind me of your mother.'

'How unfortunate.'

He forced a smile.

'Good work on the resistance interrogations.'

He turned to Wilhelm.

'I must talk to you, urgently.'

They walked off and Natasha suddenly felt lonely in the crowd of people. She was used to feeling that way. Being alone was a skill she thrived in; it kept her focused.

She could see in the distance a group of people surrounding Hitler. Something had happened. Natasha was sure it was the resistance.

***

Michele let the water wash her muddy arms. A stream of water ran down her cheeks, but it wasn't from the shower, it was from her eyes. She was scrubbing her still shaking hands. The shock had set in. She couldn't get the dirt off, she felt that there was a layer that couldn't be removed. Just get off. As head of the resistance in her area, she couldn't show weakness. It would jeopardise everything, everyone. Her suffering was not to be seen by others, not the ones she had to protect.

She felt dirty and disgusting. She always did after taking someone's life. It was a necessity, for the greater good of the country, she kept telling herself. Although Hitler was saying the same thing. It was lies, all lies. When it boiled down to it, they were both murderers and that was something she just had to live with.

When she finally got out of the shower, she quickly dressed and went to Yosef's room. He was asleep. Walking over to the bed, she nudged him slightly and he stirred a little.

'We have to move you' she whispered.

She grabbed the needle beside the bed and injected morphine into his arm. His eyes closed again. It was for the best.

It took three hours to drive and an hour to get him through the woods, but now Yosef was in a Swiss bed under a doctor's watchful eye. Anneliese was sitting on the lounge with her head in her hands. She looked up at Michele, but every time she tried to speak, she burst into tears. Michele walked over and put her arms around her.

'He'll be fine,' Michele said.

She took long deep breaths to calm herself down. Anneliese needed strength now, not someone to cry with.

'We got him back,' Michele said.

The door opened and the doctor walked in.

'He'll recuperate, he won't be able to walk for at least a couple of months, and after that it'll be a slow process. Basically, he has two broken ankles and concussion.'

'Is that all?'

Anneliese stopped crying.

'That's enough,' said the doctor. 'There are scratches and bruises, but they'll heal.'

'Thank you,' Michele said.

'Yes, thank you,' Anneliese said absentmindedly as she disappeared through the doorway.

***

Natasha sipped her drink as she looked around the room for some way to escape. She spotted her father walking quickly towards her, which could only mean one thing. She turned in time to greet Hitler and Hess.

'What happened?' Natasha asked.

Friedrich was by Natasha's side.

'The resistance,' Hess said.

'We need to crush the resistance, I don't want these internal problems,' Hitler raved. He took a deep breath to calm himself.

He turned to Friedrich.

'Eva is organising a dinner party and I wanted to invite you,' he paused as he looked at Natasha with contempt, 'and your daughter.'

'I can't make it,' Natasha said.

Her father cringed.

'Why not?' Hitler asked with a note of sarcasm.

'I'm busy.'

'You don't even know when it is.'

'I'm always busy.'

Friedrich was trying to pull his daughter aside, but Natasha stood firm. Hitler looked at Friedrich.

'I only tolerate her because she's your daughter.'

'Correction, you tolerate me because I'm good at what I do,' she said.

Maybe the champagne was getting the better of her.

He looked at her with disdain.

'No one is indispensable!'

'You're right' she said. 'No one is indispensable.'

They both stared at each other, and then Natasha added with a smile.

'Some people are just better at the job.'

Natasha casually looked at Hess, while Hitler took his frustration out on Friedrich. Hess was looking at her as if trying to work something out. He gave a gentle smile and redirected his gaze to Hitler.

She analysed him. Imposing in stature, yet quiet; he'd never really interested her. Hitler's right-hand man didn't say much and was unassuming. Normally his eyes were blank, brainwashed most likely. Natasha watched him, perhaps it hid something far more dangerous than she'd originally assumed.

Suddenly she felt a little scared of this unassuming lap dog.

Friedrich brought her back from her thoughts.

'Come, I think it's time for us to leave.'

'Oh,' said Natasha, 'And I was just starting to enjoy myself.'

Natasha smiled at Hitler, and then she shot a quick glance to Hess. He smiled concealing a laugh. Friend or foe, she would be wary of this man until she knew him a lot better than she did now.

CHAPTER 4

The shadow concealed Michele as she sat back in the chair. The room was empty and barren, with paint peeling off the walls. It had been a warehouse but now it was nothing. Deserted. Michele was early; she needed time to think, to collate her thoughts.

Her contact had many ideas, many ideas, and the problem with ideas is when they are suggested, they have to be done, not because she's told she has too, but because Michele has to prove she can do it, because that is what she is, a doer. Deep breath.

Five minutes later. There was a noise; she quickly jerked her head in its direction. Her eyes caught a shadow; slowly she stood and edged around the room until she was right up behind him.

'Oskar I'm so glad you're first. Help me organise the place.'

He jumped, eyes almost popping out of his head.

'Don't do that.'

Within ten minutes, everyone was there. Michele's main group. They mulled around, confused not knowing what was happening.

'Everyone, settle now there's lots to get through,' Michele said. 'Berlin, was bombed earlier this month, as some of you know.'

The room was quiet now and people were nodding their heads in agreement. Michele took a deep breath and continued.

'My fear is, that it will only get worse. We are here, we know what's happening around us, and so far, we've done what we can.'

Michele was walking around the group now.

'We bomb a train, steal some weapons, forge papers, free prisoners, and that's good,' she paused and stood in front of them once again, 'but it's not enough. Not anymore.'

There was a murmur around the group. Oskar looked at Michele; she smiled and focused back on the group.

'Now is the time to change this part of the resistance group to an intelligence group.'

There was a slight chuckle before people realised that she was being serious.

'What exactly do you mean?' asked Henri.

Michele smiled.

'Until now Germany has blamed everything on the Jews, the Bolsheviks. These people have been made into the enemy, someone to blame everything on. Slowly these groups of people are being moved. The cities have less and less in them. The Germans, or should I say Aryans are getting the treasures of this, the houses, the furniture, the businesses, the wealth. It has kept the German people settled, in line. They may not like things, but it does not affect them enough to make things change. In fact, they prosper, so they can still look away.' Michele paused for a moment.

'They are losing their husbands, sons, fathers in battle,' said Jean. 'They are not happy.'

'No, but they are proud,' Michele said. 'Dying for the Motherland. Hitler constantly says what an honour it is. They are fighting for their country. That continues the war. It doesn't stop it. We need a lot of civil unrest. The British will bomb military targets and supply links. Rationing will take its toll.'

She kept talking through the gasps and whispering that was filling the air.

'Goebbels fights his war with his telling of the truth, of information. The only way to fight him is to use his tools against him. With the information he receives, with the information he bases his plans on. We need to win at his game.'

'We have to be careful now. So many resistance groups are being compromised. Is now the right time?' said Henri.

'You're right, we must be careful. But we are not allowing anyone else in this group. I trust the people in this room, you are a small group, but I trust you with my life and more importantly with the lives of the other members of this group.'

'Why don't we just kill Hitler?' Ernest said. 'Get rid of him. We have opportunity.'

Michele shook her head. 'Unfortunately, it's not that simple. We kill Hitler and several things happen. First, he becomes a martyr. His followers will rally in his memory. Or those that have been schooled in his ways will have a power struggle and could potentially be worse than him. I know that is hard to imagine. But imagine Himmler as your leader. Or no one takes leadership as there is no collective group who are organised to lead a country, which was where we were before Hitler was elected. This open door would allow both the English and the Russian's in. Killing Hitler would not be the answer, it would cause more problems. It needs to come from within.'

'Umm, excuse me for interrupting.' Jean raised her hand to get attention. 'I'm confused about what you said before, about information, Goebbels and winning at his game?'

'Good point,' Michele said. 'Goebbels is the head of the propaganda division. His main job is to keep the German spirit motivated and to put a spin on things so that the German people are controlled. If we can give him information, the wrong information regarding what the public think, he will aim the "spin" too far in the wrong direction. People will start to question him. Hopefully. We need to be subtle with encouraging distrust, but have his messages more overstated, or uncredible.'

Jean sighed but nodded.

'We need to enhance the negatives that are bound to happen. Feed information to the British to ensure raids are targeted and successful, causing lack of luxury goods and maybe some of the basics. We need their support to help undermine the faith people have in the government. We also need to branch out further to get more information on what is happening and try to sabotage messages to the people. To do this we need to know what propaganda is being planned and when it's happening before it happens.'

'You have done some *extraordinary* things, in a time when no one can safely do anything. But this is big undertaking, even for you, for us,' Jean said.

She was looking around the group; they were all silent.

'I know. I know it may seem impossible. This war is happening, things are still happening in our society that shouldn't be, because people accept it. It's the little changes that are introduced and people don't mind them. They aren't affected enough to make a change, to take a stand. And it happens so slowly, until finally society has changed so much, that people are both horrified and scared, and they don't see how they can make a change, make a difference. We are on that precipice. We have to try. If we don't, no one else will.'

Silence filled the room.

Michele said, 'and I have you, you are all so smart and have many skills. So, make some groups and work on the smaller tasks that can work towards our end goals.'

Michele allocated the groups tasks. She smiled; it would happen.

***

Anneliese gritted her teeth. Nauseas, her stomach was physically nauseas. Why her?

'You tell her.'

'Oh no, you tell her,' said Hilde shaking her head, 'you answered the phone.'

Why did she answer the call? Michele was a rational person, right? Who was Anneliese trying to fool; she wouldn't be rational about this.

Michele walked through the door and flopped down in the chair.

'Hello' she said, 'I think that went well, I feel like…'

She looked up at her audience.

'What is it?'

There was silence. Then Michele did her thing, you know that thing with her eyebrow and the stare that made people break under pressure.

'Alright, it's your mother, she's being moved,' Hilde said looking at Anneliese.

'Where to?'

'Auschwitz,' Anneliese said.

'When?'

'A month on Friday,' said Hilde.

Michele got up and walked out.

'That went better than I expected,' said Anneliese.

'No,' Hilde said, shaking her head. 'That my dear is the calm before the storm.'

***

Michele looked out the window. She missed the feeling of innocence, but had she really ever had it, or was it a dream of what she thought it should be like? Oh, to be young, and silly and to have no responsibility. Michele bit her lip, but she still felt a tear. It was too late. It was there. The image. As if it was happening all over again. The feeling of guilt came back, no not the guilt, the shame. She took another deep breath and then looked up and did a little pant. Stop it. It was the walk, she remembered walking along a corridor and watching Gestapo haul her battered mother from the apartment they had rented in Berlin. Blood running down her mother's bruised face as they dragged her, with her hands tied behind her. She could still see her mother's eyes rise to meet hers as she called out to the guard, 'Keep looking if you want, but there's no one else here.'

In that moment, Michele had mastered her sister's blank expression as she walked by. She hadn't even flinched as she continued walking down the corridor to the stairs. Even now with all she knew, she still felt like she had betrayed her mother, by not attacking the guards, not trying. She wouldn't have won. She knew deep inside that wasn't what her mother wanted. But now. Now, she could do something. Wiping her eyes, she thought, I need more information. Her brain had been thinking subconsciously. She jumped up off the bed, and walked downstairs as her normal calm, collected self.

'Sorry about walking out, it was rude.'

'It's quite understandable,' Hilde said, watching her suspiciously.

There was silence for a moment, before Michele casually asked, 'what other information do you have?'

Anneliese was shaking her head and looking at Hilde.

'No no,' Anneliese pleaded. 'You can't.'

'I can, I will.'

'The resistance shouldn't be used for this. I love Helene, but you can't jeopardise it all,' Anneliese said.

'This is not a resistance mission,' said Michele, 'I'll be going by myself.'

'No.' Oskar had slipped into the room to hear what was going on. 'I'm going too.'

'Oh, don't go saying that. That means me too,' said Anneliese. 'We can't have you two being the only heroes. Damn you two, damn you, you know I'm not brave.'

'Then don't do it. It's going to be dangerous,' said Hilde.

She was looking at Oskar. Oskar's eyes flicked away from his grandmother's.

'I'm in.'

'Thank you,' said Michele. 'We have a lot of planning to do.'

She was back to organising things, which helped her control her emotions.

Hilde got up, shaking her head.

'I have a bad feeling about this, a very bad feeling.'

She left the room and slammed the door.

**

It had been just over a week since the meeting.

The sun was beating down on Michele's face and a slight breeze rippled through her hair. She was pedalling down a country road. She sighed and thought that just for a moment she could pretend that there was no war, that everyone was friends. The area felt so peaceful. Then as if to remind her of reality an army truck rattled by choking the air with dust. One day she thought. One day.

She turned off the road and pedalled up a dirt track, which led to an old farmhouse. On the porch was an elderly woman on a rocking chair. She looked up from her sewing and smiled as Michele cycled by. The track rounded the house and ended at an old shed beside a barn. Leaning her bike beside the barn, she opened the door. It creaked slightly and some hens scattered. A few gates divided the room and an old rickety ladder led to a second level well above Michele's head. Hay covered the floor and as she walked in the aroma of manure hit her. She winced. This was to be the new headquarters; she just didn't know where exactly. She walked over to a harness that hung on the wall. Michele slid her hand across the wall to just under the hook that it sat on. Her finger felt something like a nail, which she pushed down. A hay bale moved slightly to its left. She smiled as she walked down the stairs into a room that was almost as big as the barn.

Ross was sitting in a chair.

'What do you think?' he said.

'The room is great,' she said, 'but what are we going to do about transport?'

'That I haven't worked out yet.'

He'd heard about this place when he was growing up. Ross's grandfather had made the room during the First World War as a bomb shelter and a place to hide if they needed it.

'Can we trust the owners,' Michele asked?

Ross laughed, 'Um, yes. They are my grandparents.'

'I know, but we have to be careful, families are not always—'

'They are trustworthy,' Rolf interrupted. 'My parents, not so much. But my grandparents, they were the ones that taught me the truth about Hitler, they hate him and what he stands for. They will not betray us.'

Michele smiled and hoped he was right.

Ross went over some of the other security that he'd put in place. Animals stayed in the barn each night, their smells and manure would confuse any dogs. Dynamite was in the corners in case they needed a quick destruction and an emergency exit led out to the stables. Michele was quite impressed, but bikes or another mode of transport was still a problem.

'I'll do something about the bikes. I just don't know what yet,' he said.

'It doesn't have to be just you; everyone can think about it,' she said, 'well done, I mean it, really well done though, this is wonderful.'

Having a headquarters was risky. Transport was going to be a problem, if the Gestapo found a group of bikes or cars with no people, they would get curious and they would thoroughly search the area. A dull noise broke her from her thoughts, and she looked at him.

'It's the alarm, everyone's arrived,' he smiled.

The door soon opened, and they all piled in. Within a couple of hours, the room looked like an operations room. They put up a pinboard on the wall, which showed the different categories including Goebbels, propaganda and tactical. A large map was also on the board with pins to show where the German army was advancing or attacking.

There were two major tasks left to do. One was to let the allied forces know what was happening and the other was to infiltrate Goebbels office. She looked around the group. So many different skills, which was why it worked. There were two ways she could infiltrate Goebbels' office. She walked over to Oskar and Jean, who were pinning up a map. Jean was wearing baggy trousers and a jersey, which completely hid her petite frame. Her long blonde hair was pinned back, revealing defined cheekbones and a sophisticated but cheeky looking face. She was stunning, but also tough and often underestimated because of her looks, which could be very helpful.

'Jean,' Michele said, 'I think that you should be the one to work with Goebbels.'

Jean smiled.

'He's a bit of a ladies' man isn't he; sure, I will try. But I thought he preferred actresses.'

'I'm sure you can act, if need be,' said Michele.

Oskar said, 'And I thought I was going to have that mission.'

They all chuckled, and the girls pushed him.

'Don't you worry, I may put you in the Munich office Oskar,' Michele replied.

Jean looked at her. 'So where will I be based?'

Michele took a deep breath.

'Berlin.'

Jean looked up at Michele and then turned to Oskar.

'Can you excuse us for a moment?'

Oskar walked away.

'Michele really, I'm not sure. Berlin is so far away. You know what happened last time we tried Berlin. I'd be completely isolated.'

Jean's face was pale.

'I'm not leaving you. Last time, well I didn't want to trust anyone up there. It was…' Michele's voiced trailed off for a moment.

'This time it'll be done my way. I won't lose you.'

'Thank you.' Jean looked straight at Michele. 'But you can't promise me that. We all know the risks.'

'You'll be just as safe up there as down here. I'm going to put a network in place. People travel between Munich and Berlin constantly. You'll not be alone. I promise you. But it is important that you're there. Goebbels spends hardly any time down here. You need to be near the heart of it.'

Jean nodded and looked away; her hands had a slight tremble in them. Michele would let her think and calm herself down. She would be fine. Jean was right, Michele couldn't guarantee anyone's safety, she just hoped for the best and planned for the worst.

It was decided that Henri would travel to Spain, to try and make some contacts. He had a friend there in the British Embassy and hoped he would help introduce him to people that may be interested in or linked to British government. The idea was to eventually get links into London. Michele wanted him to leave as soon as possible. She needed it set up before she could go after her mother. Although she thought it best to keep that bit of information quiet. Henri was to leave before the end of the week, which gave them four days.

Transport was still a problem, and it was something they had to address soon. For now, people just got as creative as possible when it came to hiding vehicles. The ultimate test was whether they would survive an inspection from the Gestapo. It would be better if the inspection came sooner rather than later though.

***

Natasha walked into the office and saw her father reading a report.

'What time are you coming home this evening?' she said.

He looked up 'I don't know, probably around six. Why?'

'Just wondering.'

He looked at her, she never just wondered.

'What's on your mind?'

'I'm just curious,' she said, 'What do you know about Hess?'

Her father put down his pencil and looked at her.

'Why?'

'He has slowly been moving in here and I like to know who I am working with.'

'Officially you're working with nobody.'

Natasha rolled her eyes.

'He's trustworthy.'

Friedrich turned back to his report.

'Is that comment from first-hand experience or because that's what you've been told?'

'He's the Deputy Führer, the Führers right hand man.'

'So, you know nothing about him then?' Natasha said and stormed out of the room.

Friedrich tried to focus on his report, but his mind had begun to wander. She was right; he knew nothing about Hess at all. Even in the initial stages of the party, Hess hadn't said much. However, when he had something to say it was important. Friedrich wondered if it was time to get to know him a little better or at least understand what he was doing in Munich when so much was happening in Berlin.

***

Michele put her coat on and grabbed her hiking bag. She snuck out of the back of the house towards the truck.

'Excuse me, where are you going?'

The voice came from near the stables.

Michele turned her head, 'I'm going for a walk.'

'Oh good,' Oskar said, reaching down to pick up his bag, 'you can keep me company.'

Michele pulled a face and rolled her eyes; Oskar made a good second in charge while Yosef was recuperating. Oskar and Michele drove along the back roads past the old border and along the mountain range. They didn't want to go into the major city so parked along an off road and they both disappeared into the forest that bordered the estate. The forest wasn't too dense, but in places the ground was steep. Michele enjoyed it and felt peaceful walking by the trees, which gently swayed in the breeze. It was a place to absorb, not make sound. After about twenty minutes, they came along to an alpine chalet and went inside.

Michele sat down in a chair opposite the fireplace. There was no fire lit, but the room had a warm feel. The walls were red, and the furniture was traditional, but comfortable. She always felt at home here, safe, even though they were still in enemy country.

'Can you do it?' Michele said.

Her Aunt looked back at her 'It is going to be difficult. Austria is part of Germany remember.'

'Anita, I know you can do it' Michele said.

Oskar just sat watching.

'I'll need to contact some people,' Anita replied.

'They need to be trustworthy. And I don't want them to know where he comes from or ultimately where he's going.' Michele said, 'Oh and this is going to be a regular track, hopefully.'

Anita smiled

'You're always so demanding, is there anything you don't think is possible?'

'I'll let you know when I find it,' Michele said.

Anita said, 'I shall look forward to my guest. How long are you both staying?'

'We'll leave shortly,' Michele answered.

'Why?' Anita asked.

'I have a lot to do in the next few weeks.'

'Like what,' Anita said, 'What's so important it couldn't be put back twenty-four hours.'

Oskar interrupted 'You have no idea how much we have to accomplish and now we are on a short timeframe because of her mother, we just don't have much time, sorry.'

Anita looked at Michele.

'Your mother?'

Michele looked down and then across to Oskar.

'Sorry I didn't properly introduce you before. Oskar this is my mother's sister.'

Oskar looked sheepishly at them both.

'I am sorry I–'

'You weren't to know,' Anita said. 'Now what's happening? Maybe I can help.'

Michele explained to Anita what was happening with Helene. Then she added 'You can't be part of it. You're her sister. Knowing things would not just put yourself at risk, but Helene as well. You'll know how it goes though. I promise.'

Tears rolled down Anita's face, 'Even if I disagreed, I don't have a choice, do I?'

'No.'

Michele gave her aunt a hug.

Oskar and Michele left before dusk, for the leisurely journey back.

'Thank you for coming along,' Michele said, 'but you realise what this means don't you?'

Oskar looked at her. 'What?'

'You need to oversee this now.' Michele paused. 'If something happens, you need to look after Jean and Henri especially. Don't leave them by themselves.'

'Nothing's going to happen.'

He pulled her arm, turning her to face him. Momentarily, Michele had lost her composure.

'It's just…' Michele paused, '… Oskar, you have to promise me, you'll look after them.' She was back to her normal self.

'I will,' he said.

'The three of us are the only people that know about how Henri is getting to Spain and my aunt doesn't even know why he's going. But just in case.'

'I promise' he said.

***

Friedrich summoned Natasha to the headquarters. She hated being summoned. Natasha walked into the room and nodded at her father. Behind her father's shoulder stood Hess.

'Finally,' Friedrich said.

She ignored the comment and sat down amongst the other Gestapo, Kripo and SS in the room.

Hess stepped forward.

'We've received some information that the resistance is getting stronger in this region and that they may have set up headquarters. This is a disconcerting rumour, as it means they would be organised, more committed in their resolutions, harder to monitor and harder to infiltrate. You'll each take an area to search.'

Friedrich said, 'If they're as organised as we believe, they'll be well hidden. Search thoroughly.'

They divided the region into six areas and allocated those present to groups. Natasha oversaw the southern side of Munich countryside.

She sat in the passenger seat of the truck and stared out the window. The countryside seemed unaffected by the war. There was a peace here that she hadn't felt in a very long time, so long she could hardly remember it. They turned into a gravel road lined with trees. The trucks pulled up outside a two storied farmhouse. A Nazi flag fluttered in the wind to the left of the main entrance. Natasha got out of the vehicle and walked to the door, sharply knocking a few times before announcing, 'Gestapo, open the door.'

A man in his forties opened the door. He stumbled with his greeting, unsure how to address a female but eventually decided on Fraulein.

'We are doing inspections in the area,' she said walking into the house. 'We would like to look around.'

The shock left the man. He realised he had not made the right greeting.

'Heil Hitler,' he said raising his hand in a salute.

Natasha returned it with as little effort as possible.

'Fraulein, please search as much as you would like. Is there anything I can do for you?'

Natasha sighed, as she indicated for the guards to begin their search. 'Is there anyone else here?'

'My niece, she is staying here before she starts her new job,' he replied.

Natasha raised an eyebrow.

Misunderstanding the meaning, the man called out, 'Sophie, come down please.'

Sophie appeared at the top of the stairs, paused, and looked a mixture of annoyed and flustered. Then she walked down the stairs to her uncle, with a touch of defiance. She must have been in her late teens, but there was a challenge in her stare, a harshness. It reminded Natasha a little of herself.

Natasha smiled as she looked around the room. On the mantle was a picture of Hitler, a copy of *Mein Kampf* and some other trinkets that were common among supporters.

'Are you a member of the Nazi party?'

'Yes,' he smiled, 'would you like to see–?'

'No,' Natasha dismissed him, 'that will not be necessary. What job are you going to start?'

'Kindergarten teaching,' Sophie answered.

'Hmm,' Natasha said, 'it is important to start young. I am

sure you will teach the children correctly, what they should know about the Aryan race.'

'Yes,' said her uncle. 'She is very dedicated.'

'We are searching the area for resistance. You have an important duty to report suspicious activity. Have you seen anything...' Natasha paused but looked directly at Sophie, '... suspicious?'

Sophie's eyes turned piercing. 'No, nothing at all.'

'Thank you,' Natasha said. 'Please make sure to be alert, it is your duty. Sophie, can we search your room?'

'Yes'

Natasha walked up the stairs to Sophie's room and looked around it. It was sparse, there were some books in the corner that were dangerously close to those that had been banned, but they were legal technically. Natasha looked back at Sophie. But there was nothing else, nothing untoward.

When Natasha ascended the stairs, the guards were waiting for her.

'Anything?' she asked.

'No.'

'Thank you, please report anything you may see, also keep up your good work,' Natasha said. 'Sorry, what was your name?'

'Herr Scholl,' he replied, 'and Sophie Scholl. Heil Hitler.'

'Heil Hitler,' Natasha replied and then strolled back to the truck.

She could soon see her next stop, a farm just down the road. The whole area was dirty and old, and seemed uncared for. They drove down the dirt drive to the farmhouse.

***

Michele had left early in the morning; there was a lot to do. She needed to be at the new headquarters for a last-minute briefing with Henri. Pulling up at the farmhouse, she hid her bike behind a pile of wood, and then proceeded inside. They set about introducing codes and authentication names.

'What if I need to contact you?' Henri said.

He was smiling.

'You need a codename. How about, phantom or the boss or…'

Michele shook her head.

'Stop, stop it. Snake is my codename.'

He looked at her, 'what, you already have a codename?'

'Yes, I do. Snake. That was the name Mama gave me. It's from a conversation I had a long time ago and a book and, it's a long story.'

'Snake,' Henri said pulling a face, 'I would not have thought of that.'

The bell rang; Michele looked at Henri. He shook his head; he didn't know who it was. Michele indicated to be quiet. They just had to wait now. Michele crossed her fingers and said a silent prayer.

***

Natasha walked up to the farmhouse and greeted the elderly woman. Again, she explained that they were searching the area as a routine exercise. The old woman grumbled an agreement but looked a little annoyed. Leaving her door open, she sat back down to finish her food. They walked around her simple home and found nothing. Using the dogs, they combed the surrounding area, including the stables. Next, they looked around the barn. Light was filtering through some of the windows. The smell that she caught first was hay followed by manure. She smiled, country smells. She stood at the back of the barn near an old ornamental harness and barked orders at the soldiers to do a thorough search.

The dogs sniffed around but seemed distracted by the different smells. She sighed nothing had been found. She didn't think they would find anything in their searches anyway.

***

Henri and Michele froze on the spot. Michele could feel sweat on her forehead. They heard boots walk into the barn and pause. The sound continued over their heads to just beside the trap door and paused again. Henri looked around nervously at the entrance. He was white and looked like he was going to pass out. Michele could not afford for that to happen, they had to be completely silent. She indicated for him to lower to the ground so he would be more stable.

A woman's voice ordered the men around. Michele smiled; it was Natasha. No other female had any authority like her in Munich. Michele had to admit that she admired what her sister had accomplished, although she would never say that to anyone.

There was a last-minute scurry.

'There's nothing Fraulein.'

Two pairs of footsteps left. Michele sighed. They had survived the inspection, now the serious work could begin.

Henri turned to Michele. He looked like he was about to throw up.

'How do you keep calm, Snake?' He said as he sprawled out on the ground.

She smiled.

CHAPTER 5

The sound of the bedroom door opening made Michele look up quickly. Her eyes blinked as they adjusted from looking at the maps to the shadow in the doorway.

Hilde stepped into the room.

'It's suicide you know.'

'I can't let it happen, she's all I have.'

'She's not,' Hilde said.

'Sorry, but it's not the same. Don't you see, everything is organised so it could run without me,' said Michele. 'Anyway, I have a plan. I'll just hijack the train and drive it to the border.'

Hilde frowned and shook her head as she left the room.

Michele looked at the maps. She'd joked about a plan with Hilde, but it wouldn't be that easy. It was a very secure route, very well thought out. Unfortunately. Different scenarios went through her head, most she could counteract easily, and if she could, then they would too. Where were the weak points? That's what she wanted a weak point. I'll find you. But nothing came to her. She gave the quest to her subconscious and moved on to her next task.

How was she going to put Jean in Berlin? How to set up this intelligence support network when there was currently no network. Now they needed it to reach right into Goebbels' office. Michele looked at the map. If she chose small towns then there would probably be resistance, however the downside would be that new people would raise suspicion. In larger cities people tended to not notice new people, but it meant less protection. You can't rely on protection anyway.

Michele drew her pencil down from Berlin and stopped at Leipzig. That would be a good point. There were Gestapo headquarters there as well, so surveillance was an option. She circled it and then continued south. She had a friend that lived in the countryside just out of Lichtenberg who could be trusted. It was the halfway point. She circled it and continued south. The next likely spot was Nuremberg. Now all she had to do is place people there. But then there was the bigger problem of getting Jean on Goebbels' staff, or just even in his headquarters to start with.

***

Natasha couldn't resist Herr Schmidt's bakery. The windbeutel with a little bit of chocolate were her favourite. She picked up two this morning and then dashed out the door to the headquarters. She bumped into someone on the way out, almost pushing them over.

'I'm so sorry,' she apologised as she looked around to see who it was.

'It's fine, I don't mind you pushing me around,' Wilhelm said.

'Oh, it's you.'

'Do you really need to go to work in such a hurry?' he said.

She thought for a moment.

'No.'

Natasha glanced down the street to the old palace, they used as headquarters. Her eyes connected with someone looking straight at her. It was Hess.

'No, I don't think I do.'

'Let's walk,' he said.

They walked together down the street idly chatting.

'What were you going to say the other night?' Natasha said.

Wilhelm looked at her warily.

'What do you mean?'

'You know,' she said, 'when you said I'm not like the others.'

She stared at him. It looked like he was analysing her. What was he thinking? Then she wondered why she cared.

His face softened.

'You're not a follower, yet you're being led.'

She looked at him again. Was that a question? He had chosen carefully what he said.

'Who said I'm following? Just currently most people are going in my direction.'

Natasha gave him a cheeky smile.

She knew she would get no more response on that subject. They both sat on a park bench on the edge of Königsplatz.

'What do you think of Hess, what's he like?' she said.

He let out chuckle as he shook his head.

'Quite inquisitive, aren't we?'

'What do you expect when you talk to an interrogator?'

Wilhelm nodded and sighed then looked straight ahead.

'He's good, he's fair.'

The smirk came back.

'He's a leader, a very intelligent man.'

'And yet he's being led' she said.

Wilhelm got up and leaned forward grabbing the back of the bench, so that he was just over Natasha's head. It made her look up, so that she could keep eye contact. He was so close that his breath glided past her lips and across her cheeks and he whispered.

'Maybe you two have more in common than you think.'

He gently pushed off the seat and turned. Natasha blew a long breath out. She felt a little flustered. That was not good. As he walked across the Platz, she could still feel Hess's eyes burning into her. Hess walked over to Wilhelm and then they both started talking to each other and walked off. Natasha pulled out a windbeutel and took a bite, she didn't enjoy the windbeutel; she chomped it. Wilhelm was nice, he was her knight in shining armour, well not hers, but could he be hers? Stop it. The point was, he was not his, not Hess's. Hess, she didn't know and yet they were walking away as if they were the best of friends. She hated not knowing and she hated not being in control. A little growl made its way through her clenched teeth. In a single moment, she'd become completely disorientated. I don't like that one bit. Natasha got annoyed with herself. I want to know what game this Hess is playing.

She got up, crossed the street, and entered the headquarters: wondering what else would be on today's agenda.

***

'I have something to tell you.' Friedrich paused. 'There is a train load of prisoners going to Auschwitz very shortly.'

Natasha shrugged, there was always a train of prisoners going somewhere.

'Your mother will be on it.'

Natasha turned to her father.

'I haven't had a mother for a very long time. It was her choice to leave, she must live with the consequences of her choices.'

Friedrich recoiled in his chair with shock, as his daughter turned and left. He knew Helene was a traitor, but he still loved her. He had a contact who had given him the information. She was well monitored, not just because of his connection to her, but also because of what she was, what she had done. She was a senior member of the resistance. They thought eventually she would talk, be broken. But she didn't, and she wasn't. Her character was the only reason he knew she was still alive.

Sitting down at his desk Friedrich opened his drawer and pulled out a photograph, it showed the five of them in happier times. His finger traced over Helene's face, across Anneliese to Michele and stopped at Natasha. Well, it mattered to him. A tear ran down his cheek and he cradled his head in his hands.

***

Michele quietly opened the door and looked inside. Yosef looked like he was sleeping. She crept around the bed and sat down.

'Hello,' he said, 'I think you've seen me more recently than I've seen you.'

'True' she replied, 'I thought I'd visit as I'm going to be busy for a little while.'

'You never were a visitor, so what's changing?'

'You know most of the time I try and make it so that the senior people in the resistance are not at the same place at the same time,' she said.

'It makes sense.'

'Yes well, I am changing that for one particular mission. This isn't really a resistance mission as such. I mean I won't be in exactly the same place as Oskar, but in very close proximity. I–'

'Michele,' he cut in, 'I've never heard you speak this much useless information in my life. And I've known you a long time.'

'You're right,' she said.

She leaned forward in the chair. Michele was back and focused.

'I'm going to tell you what's being organised, just in case we don't come back, you can fill Mama in on everything.'

'Okay,' Yosef said.

Michele sat down and talked Yosef through everything. She told him everyone's responsibilities and how she intended to get intelligence on German tactics by putting Jean in Goebbels' office. She also gave him all the addresses of the network to Berlin. She mentioned Henri and the messages he was taking to Spain Then she mentioned that when Helene came back, she was to go to Egypt. There are operatives there who would look after her.

'Is there anything else?'

Michele paused for a moment.

'I have to do this,' she said looking at Yosef.

'I know,' he said. 'I haven't tried to talk you out of it, have I?'

'No.'

She squeezed his hand and then stood up and walked to the door. Michele paused and then turned slightly. There was sadness in her face.

'Yosef, I need you to know something, I really appreciate everything you've done for me; you've been my strength.'

'See you next month,' he said.

She gave a quick smile and left.

***

Opening the door to the headquarters, Natasha walked down the corridor. She was heading straight for her father's office, which made her pass the office that Hess had commandeered while his new office was being renovated. Casually Natasha looked around; there was no one in the corridor. She walked over to the door, turned the handle, and then slipped into the room, closing the door behind her.

It looked like her father's office. There was a dark rosewood desk at the back of the room near the window. It faced towards the door. The desk was clear, apart from an ink bottle, pencil and eraser. Natasha walked around towards the chair. As she looked at the desk, she noticed there were two small drawers under the desk. One had a lock. She opened the unlocked one first. It was empty. Natasha ran her hand around the drawer and under the desk. Underneath the drawer, her fingers ran over a key. She peeled it off and tried the locked drawer. It didn't work. She took a hairclip out of her hair and bent down, so the lock was at eye level. Within a couple of minutes, the drawer was open. Inside were papers. One was a draft document, titled Extermination Camps. The original document was well presented and signed by Himmler. There were notes on the papers and a line crossed out the title with Concentration and Work Camps written on top. She put it back but made a mental note. Sorting through the other papers, she saw what looked like a diagram of a plane. She didn't know what type it was. It was strange, completely out of place. She looked closely at it, there were some comments, 'Weight?, seats removed, radio.' There were also maps of Europe. The paperwork seemed unrelated, but confusing. She closed and locked the drawer.

Natasha looked around the room. It was a temporary office and sparse. A cupboard and filing cabinet were along one wall. She tried the key in the filing cabinet. It worked. Opening the top drawer, she found personnel files. They were not just of the staff based in Munich, but of senior staff of the regime. She flicked through the names, Himmler, Göring, Goebbels. She stopped when she got to her fathers. Pulling it out, she read the file. It was very comprehensive, starting from childhood and going through to the beginning of the year. She flicked through the pages and then stopped as her eye caught something. At the bottom of one of the pages, printed in capitals, was her name with 'Under investigation' written beside it. She closed the file and returned it to the drawer. Flicking through she tried to find her file, but she couldn't. Footsteps sounded in the hall, and she could hear Wilhelm's voice. She closed the filing cabinet and locked it. She walked towards the door but saw shadows. Damn, damn, damn. She turned around. He eyes moved from the window to the cupboard, and back again. She didn't have time. Taking a deep breath Natasha dived into the cupboard and then realised that she still had the key in her hand. She slowly tried to open the door but could see the front door to the office opening. She quickly closed the door and hoped that no one would notice anything.

'I need you there. It's important.'

'Fine,' Wilhelm said, 'but it's going to be hard to keep my opinions to myself.'

'Well, you have to,'

A drawer opened and closed. There was a rustling.

'Have you got everything?'

Footsteps walked around the room, some felt very close.

'Don't worry' Hess said 'anyway, I think that you're just procrastinating. Come, let's go.'

The office door opened, and then closed. Natasha slowly opened the door and stepped out of the cupboard. She opened the filing cabinet again. There was no file with her name on it. If Hess had her on file, it wasn't here. She closed and locked the cabinet and returned the key to its hiding place. Now all she had to do was break out of the office.

***

Jean sat on her bed. She had a sinking feeling about Berlin. This is stupid. It'll be fine. Her feet dangled over the side of the bed, and she swung them, like a child, who couldn't reach the floor. She knew Munich like the back of her hand. She knew the people, the good, the bad and here she had friends, people she could trust. People she fought alongside, people she went on missions with. She took a deep breath. She wasn't a child anymore. Slowly she eased off the bed and stood. Michele was her pillar of strength and now she was the one that was sending her away. She looked around her room, she'd miss it. Everything she knew, everything she had confidence about, was here. All she wanted to do was to remember as much as possible before she left. There had been a change in the timetable, and she was leaving sooner, than they had expected. She hadn't had time to prepare. Michele had said to trust her, and she did, she just hoped that Michele's luck would last.

There was a knock at the door.

Jean opened it saying hello, and then paused. Michele walked in carrying a suitcase.

'What are you doing?' asked Jean.

'Going to Berlin.' she said. 'Are you going that way?'

Jean smiled. 'Yes.'

Her safety blanket was going with her, even if it would only be for a short time.

The trip to Berlin wasn't the most comfortable journey they'd ever made. But it was nice to look out the window and see the world go by. Jean and Michele had agreed not to mention anything to do with the resistance on the train. You never knew who was listening and the train was crowded with uniformed staff. They just talked about old times.

It took most of the day before they arrived in Berlin and headed to their hotel room. Michele and Jean ran through last minute arrangements. Michele had information on some of the staff and regulars of Goebbels circle. Jean began to read up on them and discussed possible scenarios. They identified a target, along with a back-up plan. She couldn't just go and introduce herself to Goebbels, she had to manoeuvre her way in. Michele's contacts had told her there had been a sudden vacancy on his secretarial team, which was why they had come to Berlin earlier than expected. Jean sat back formulating a plan, while Michele had to find an apartment. They went to sleep early; tomorrow was going to be a big day.

***

Jean glanced in the mirror of the bar. Yes, she was still presentable. Her hair was up, and she had a low-cut blouse on, with a slight frill. She crossed her legs so that the top of her stocking was just below her short black skirt. She casually smoked a cigarette in one hand and sipped Vodka in the other. Her prey was a man on the opposite side of the bar. She glanced his way then looked back at her drink and played with the straw. Another drink appeared in front of her; the barman indicated that the man across the bar had bought it. She looked up and mouthed a thank you, raised her glass and then looked down as if she didn't know what else to do.

Her target was high up in the press division governed by Goebbels. A senior member, but not at the top level within the organisation.

He walked around the bar to her and offered her his hand.

'Hello, I'm Hans.'

'Jean.'

She gave him a little smile.

'Thank you for the drink.'

'I don't mean to pry,' he said, 'but you haven't been smiling much.'

Jean looked down.

'I haven't had a good day, I went for an interview, and I didn't get the job, I just don't know what to do. I really need a job... I'm sorry I shouldn't have said anything. Forget it.'

'No, no.'

There was concern in his face.

'I may be able to help. My boss is looking for another person for his secretarial group. Have you done any secretarial work before?'

She nodded.

'I can't guarantee anything, but I can introduce you to him.'

'You'd do that for me?' she looked surprised. 'You don't even know me.'

'Yes, but I must confess, I'd like a favour?' he queried.

'Yes?'

'Go to dinner with me?'

She looked at him coyly and nodded again.

They finished their drinks and Hans led her down the street straight into the Reich Ministry of Public Enlightenment and Propaganda.

The head of the secretarial teams took her to a small office and instructed her to type and do some dictation, while her papers were checked. Jean was using her actual papers as she had no record on file. The lady then walked her upstairs to Goebbels office and with an icy stare, looked Jean up and down.

'Oh, I'm sure he'll like you,' she said, almost pushing Jean through the door.

Goebbels looked up from behind his desk. His taunt oval face looked over her figure and then his thin lips curled slightly at the corners. Jean stood coyly in front of him, trying her most innocent smile. He indicated for her to sit. She did.

After a few questions, and a lot of flirting, Jean was ushered out of the office and told that she would start the following day.

***

The landlord opened the door and there was a flood of light from a large window opposite, followed by the smell of damp stale air.

'How long ago did the last tenant leave?' Michele said.

'Two months.'

She walked in, past the small kitchen, into the front room. Furniture was minimal. There were a few chairs, a table, and a sofa. Some of the floorboards were a little loose. She walked past the bathroom, which looked very clean and almost new. In the bedroom there was a bed in the corner and a wardrobe. Sparse to put it mildly. Some of the skirting boards had rotted through and Michele saw a mouse scuttle through a hole in the corner.

'Can you fasten the floorboards in the front room?' Michele said.

'I can have that done this afternoon.'

He looked slightly shocked.

'Is there anything else?'

'No, it's fine,' Michele said. 'Its fine for the money you are asking, and that's basically my budget.'

'I need a bond and this week's rent up front,' he said.

'Fine,' Michele said. 'It will be here as soon as the floorboards are fixed.'

She started opening the windows. He turned and left. Michele knew Jeans tastes. If she couldn't provide her with friends, she would provide her with a sanctuary. Michele got to work.

***

Michele stirred her coffee and looked out the windows just watching. Her back was to a wall, covered with art from Germany. Some of the artists were not famous, some were dead, and others still painted, while one controlled the country. Not many people noticed a small picture amongst many others, in the centre of the wall signed Adolf. On the opposing wall were more pictures with their centrepiece being that of a bulldog. The owner of the café was in the resistance, and this was his little way of hitting back.

He didn't know her, but she knew him. In fact, she knew most of the resistance contact points. That's where Michele and her mother had disagreed. Michele hadn't wanted to open their network to the rest of Germany. She just hadn't trusted them. Helene had, although she never linked them together, which was good, because someone that she trusted had betrayed her.

Jean leaned forward. 'Hello.'

She sat down with a smile. 'I'm in.'

Michele replied 'Good.'

'What's the plan? I'm only doing some copying and filing.' Jean said, 'I'm on teas and coffees.'

'Well,' said Michele, 'I think you're exactly where you should be, and those coffees may be a lot more important than you realise. Are you working directly for Goebbels?'

Jean smiled, 'Yes. Although, there are a few of us, and I am the lowest level secretary obviously, but yes.'

Michele sat back for a moment while her head started to formulate a plan. 'Let's go.'

They got up and walked out of the café. Smiling she outlined what she thought would be the best method. Jean needed to use the soft approach. She would need to copy any important documents and send them through to Munich. One of the most important things Jean could do was watch and listen. If they could find out internal politics of the Nazi party, then maybe, just maybe they could build rifts, maybe turn some against each other. It would be good to also make friends with secretaries in other ministries, but that was a secondary objective. They both looked at each other and smiled.

Michele said, 'I've found the perfect apartment for you.'

'I hope it has a view,' Jean smiled.

'Sort of,' Michele giggled.

The apartment was on the second floor of a building just north of the river. It was within walking distance of almost everywhere. The view was a wall, but it was a large one-bedroom place, clean. In fact, the colours and the fabrics were almost the same as her old room.

Then Jean noticed the smell of paint.

'Did you decorate this?'

'Yeah, don't touch the walls till they dry.'

Michele pulled her into the bedroom.

'I didn't do the skirting boards, and you have mice.'

'I'll get rid of them,' Jean said.

'Well,' said Michele, 'I don't want you too.'

Jean looked confused.

'I want you to hide any copies, in the mouse hole,' Michele said.

'But I don't need mice to have a mouse hole.'

'It is all about covering yourself,' Michele said.

'I guess we all make sacrifices.'

Michele smiled and looked at her.

'There are some things I need to tell you.'

Jean nodded.

'Trust no one. No new people will contact you; it'll just be our group. If there are people that say they are resistance don't–'

'I know,' Jean said.

'And don't,' Michele said, 'get emotionally involved with anyone.'

They looked at each other and smiled. Jean felt like she was talking to her mother.

'I feel a bit like I've been sent to a boarding school.'

Michele grabbed her hands and smiled as she looked at her.

'I have to go' Michele said. 'I'm going to set up your links home.

If you have a problem, phone me, and talk to me about mice in the apartment.'

She grabbed her case, gave Jean a hug, and walked out the door. Jean sat on her bed again and looked around the apartment. She sighed. She had a lot to do.

CHAPTER 6

Friedrich was tired; too tired to finish reports. It had been a long day. It was time to go. He walked down the corridor and noticed another light on. He knocked on the door. He opened it slightly

'I didn't realise you were here,' said Friedrich.

Hess looked up.

'I arrived this afternoon.'

Hess looked at the clock, then cleared his desk.

'I'm going for a drink; do you want one?' said Friedrich.

'I don't drink.'

'I'm having dinner too,' smiled Friedrich.

Hess nodded and they both left the building and headed for the restaurant.

'I like this place,' Friedrich said, 'it always feels so cosy and welcoming.'

'You don't always get that when you go out in uniform,' Hess said, 'do you?'

'Is that a general observation?'

Hess looked down at his plate.

'I haven't been out in Munich for a while. It's changing, there's an atmosphere.'

'You're spending more and more time down here, maybe you just need to give it time,' Friedrich said. 'Are you planning on staying or are you going to make your escape soon.'

'My escape?'

'Back to Berlin,' Friedrich said.

'I've always liked it down here. It's the heart of everything.' Hess relaxed. 'My home. They're decorating offices here for me.'

'What are you doing down here if you don't mind me asking?' said Friedrich.

Hess put his knife and fork down and looked straight at Friedrich to watch his reaction. 'I'm just putting in place my network. Doing a bit of intelligence gathering.'

'Anything I can do to help,' Friedrich said, 'just let me know.'

Hess smiled.

'I will.'

***

The taxi pulled up outside the station. Michele got out and paid the driver. She bent down, grabbed her suitcase, and then walked straight into someone. Falling sideways, she tripped on the curb and landed on the pavement.

'I'm sorry,' said a male voice with an outstretched hand. 'Can I help?'

'I'm fine, it was an accident, don't worry.'

She looked up; the man helping her up was dressed in full uniform.

'Are you going into the station?'

'Yes,' she said.

'Well at the very least, as a way of apology, may I carry your suitcase?'

She was standing now and brushing herself down. The suitcase was already in his hand. She quickly thought about what was in it.

'Thank you' she said. 'Do you normally knock girls off their feet?'

He chuckled and they walked inside.

'Let me introduce myself,' he held out his hand. 'My name is Wilhelm.'

She shook his hand, 'Margot. Thank you for carrying my bag.'

Margot had been the first name she could think of. She took her bag and sat down on the seat on the platform. He looked at her and then looked away. Sitting down he looked at her again, slightly confused, he looked straight ahead at the train tracks.

'What?'

His cheeks went crimson.

'It's just, you remind me of someone. No matter how I say that it sounds wrong, but do I know you from somewhere?'

Alarm bells went off in Michele's head.

'I don't think so. Are you based in Berlin and what do you do?'

'No, I only come to Berlin at the end of each month for meetings. I sort of do' he paused, 'administration, for the air force. Most of the time I'm based in Munich.'

'I don't think so then. Everyone is supposed to have a doppelgänger, aren't they?' she smiled.

'Maybe you're right.' he said. 'Where are you off to?'

'Leipzig,' she replied. 'You?'

'Munich,' he answered.

She looked at him and smiled. She'd taken him off guard. His uniform was immaculate and the way he held himself showed confidence. He was no administrator. He'd downplayed his role, not shown off, must be senior. She wondered who he really was and whether his name was really Wilhelm. Then she began to analyse her own behaviour and wondered if she'd given anything away.

She looked at him, he seemed a little more guarded now, almost embarrassed, what was he hiding? Curious, she reminded him of someone. That wasn't good, had they met before? She looked at him, he smiled, but his eyes were deep in thought. Who was he?

The train pulled up, and they boarded. It was a two-hour journey to Leipzig, and they talked most of the way. It was nice to talk to someone different. The journey was over in no time and the train slowing down brought her back to reality. Saying goodbye, she disembarked and focused on her mission to secure an apartment for the links up to Berlin.

***

She was sure that Michele had managed to look around most of the flat, but Jean just wanted to double check. She looked in the cupboards, and along the walls, the ceiling and in the light fittings. It looked as if this apartment was clean of any listening devices.

Jean brushed her hair and put some lipstick on. She really didn't want to go out tonight. The apartment still smelt of paint. It was almost dry, but the smell would be there for the next few days at least. It made her feel lightheaded and she needed some fresh air. Also, a deal was a deal, and she had promised Hans dinner. She sighed and grabbed her bag and coat, then walked out the door.

The restaurant was a lively, busy place, where everyone seemed to keep their distance and not notice anyone. Hans poured some more wine into her glass.

'So,' Jean said, 'what do you actually do?'

Hans enjoyed talking, 'I help with press, but my real love is radio. You'll find out soon enough, through work. You'll enjoy the team.' He grabbed her hand, 'I'm glad you got the job.'

She giggled. 'So am I. Thank you so much for all your help. I do appreciate it.'

Jean looked across the table at him. He came across as quite a confident man. But he was not giving away any information. She would have to try a little harder; she didn't like not getting her own way.

***

Wilhelm got off the train and headed straight for the headquarters. There was a lot that needed doing. He walked through the main foyer and headed to Hess's office, he needed to talk to him urgently.

'I will not go,' stated a female voice from an office further along the corridor.

'You will, and you will enjoy yourself,' was the male reply.

'I hate these functions, they're boring,' retorted the female. Natasha stormed out of the office, slammed the door, and strode down the corridor.

Wilhelm smiled, 'You're a spoilt brat.'

'I just want to be in a bad mood,' Natasha replied.

'No, you just want to get your own way like you normally do,' Wilhelm said.

'Don't make me laugh,' she started to smile. 'I'm warning you.' She looked up. 'Sometimes I really hate you.'

He smiled and looked back at her. His face dropped and he felt like he'd been winded. It was the smile, the eyes, different colour hair, but those eyes.

'What's wrong?' Natasha rushed over to him, 'You look like you have seen a ghost.'

'I feel like I have,' he looked back at her and sat down. He recovered his composure, 'I'm sorry, it's been a long day.'

'How can I be angry with you when you look like you're about to faint?'

He tried to laugh it off; the last thing he wanted was Natasha's curiosity.

***

People were scattered around the room, mingling in groups. Hess and Wilhelm were talking in one corner on a small collection of chairs. The room opened out into another room, dominated by a long table, which was set up for the night's dinner.

Natasha walked in with her father at her side. 'I won't get into any trouble tonight, Father,' she commented, 'Adie's not here.'

'Adolf, Natasha, his name is Adolf. Actually, no, to you, Herr Hitler,' her father sternly corrected, 'and I'm sure that won't stop you.'

'Please smile,' he added, 'you look like you don't want to be here.'

She leaned towards her father and spoke through gritted teeth, 'Because I don't.'

Slowly they were ushered to the table. Natasha ended up sitting opposite Hess and Wilhelm much to her relief; the others at the table bored her.

'Are you feeling better?' she said.

Wilhelm looked at her. 'Feeling better?'

'Yes,' she replied, 'remember the other day when you almost fainted.'

Wilhelm nodded, 'That's right. Yes, I'm fine. I don't know what happened there.'

She looked up, to see Hess looking straight at her.

'Hess,' she started, 'how are you enjoying being back in Munich?'

'Fine, thank you,' Hess replied.

'Anything new in the air force?' she asked Wilhelm.

'No,' he smiled, 'I seem to be stuck in meetings.'

He looked up at Hess and then looked back at Natasha. It was a private joke, and she wasn't included.

Natasha looked at them both, 'I'm a little bit confused, do you two work together, or are you related? You always seem to be organising things together.'

Hess and Wilhelm looked up and there was silence.

Wilhelm answered first, 'Just friends.'

Natasha looked at Wilhelm, 'How did you both meet each other?'

Wilhelm looked down at the table quickly and took a deep breath.

'Flying,' he answered. 'Hess is a pilot, as well as deputy to Hitler. We met through flying.'

Wilhelm's facial muscles relaxed, but Hess leaned back in his chair just observing, no, he was analysing. There was a lot Wilhelm wasn't telling her.

'Flying,' Natasha commented, 'how wonderful, I didn't realise that. How long have you been interested, or involved with flying?'

Hess replied, 'A very long time. Since I was injured in the First World War, in fact.'

Natasha nodded, remembering the plane drawing in the drawer.

'I must confess, I don't know much about flying,' Natasha continued, 'in fact I don't know anything about planes. I think it is remarkable that they actually fly at all, harnessing the air.'

Wilhelm took over the conversation after that. He tried to teach her what type of plane did what, what their pitfalls were and how some planes were superior to others. Natasha looked interested, but there was no way that she would be able to remember all this.

'That's a lot of information, Wilhelm and it's really fascinating, have you got any books I could read on planes and some of the things you mentioned?' She asked. 'I love to learn new things and flying is such a big part of the war effort.'

'Sure,' said Wilhelm, 'I'll bring one to the office tomorrow.'

Wilhelm seemed happy with her interest. Natasha smiled as innocently as she could manage. Hess looked at Natasha. His eyes still watching, analysing. She tried to act as if she didn't notice. Hess leaned back in his chair but stayed quiet.

***

Anneliese opened the door to see Oskar standing on the doorstep.

'Can I come in?' Oskar asked.

'Yes, I wasn't expecting you.'

'I know,' he said, 'I need to talk to Yosef. Do you mind?'

'No, of course,' said Anneliese.

Oskar walked up the stairs and knocked lightly on the door.

'Come in.'

Yosef was looking so much better. He was sitting up on the bed and smiling as if nothing much had happened.

'What's wrong?' Yosef asked.

Oskar closed the door and sat down, 'I'm worried about Michele.'

Yosef sighed, 'I gave up worrying about her years ago.'

'She's stubborn and pig-headed. She's going on a suicide mission.'

Oskar cupped his head in his hands and then pulled them down, so he was leaning his chin on them.

'She needs to do this,' Yosef looked at Oskar. 'And you need to support her.'

'It's different this time' Oskar said. 'The other day she let her guard down, it was only for a second, but it was down, and I saw, fear, well not fear exactly but a knowing, I can't describe it.'

Yosef looked at Oskar. 'You shouldn't have seen that. Don't let her know,' He sighed, 'I think to a certain extent Michele blames herself for her mother's imprisonment. She has to do this, no matter what the outcome.'

Oskar looked at Yosef, 'No matter what the outcome. You can't be serious.'

Sometimes Yosef felt like Oskar's father, 'don't you see if anything happens to her mother, she'll never be free. I love her like a sister, but she'll be caged. She may be good at making things happen, but she's also realistic.'

'I don't accept that,' Oskar said.

'Well make sure she comes back then. There's something you don't know but for as long as I've known Michele, she's always had a Guardian Angel looking over her.'

Oskar got up, 'I thought that maybe you'd have better advice for me than believe in Guardian Angels.'

Oskar stormed out of the room and raced down the stairs past Anneliese and slammed the door.

'You should believe Oskar,' Yosef said under his breath. 'You should believe.'

***

Wilhelm had given the book to Natasha, and it was full of aeroplane information and plans, but she could only vaguely remember what she'd seen. She needed another look.

Natasha walked down the corridor to Hess's office. Just before she entered, she heard voices, so she kept walking to the end of the corridor and pretended to read. Twenty minutes later, Hess and colleagues walked out of the office to the exit. They disappeared out of view. It was lunchtime and the corridor was getting extremely busy. She needed to get into his office. But how?

Walking up to one of the people in the corridor, she asked, 'Sorry to bother you, but do you know which office is Hess's?'

The man indicated the office and Natasha thanked him and knocked on the door. She pretended that there was someone inside and proceeded to enter.

Natasha went to the desk, bent down, and started to pick the lock. Opening the drawer, she flicked through the papers trying to locate the plane. Once she had located it, Natasha grabbed a piece of paper that she had put in the book and a pencil off the desk and traced its layout. She put the document back and locked the drawer. She looked through the filing cabinet, although she knew it was highly unlikely anything would have changed. No, her file was somewhere else, but why? Stop it, focus on the information you do have. Natasha walked to the door and took a deep breath. She boldly walked out to the corridor, saying goodbye as she shut the door and then left the building.

At home, Natasha sat in the chair and had a drink of coffee. She compared the plane plan that she had traced to the ones in the book. None of them matched exactly. The one closest to her drawing was a twin-engine ME110. Her drawing had more fuel tanks and no navigator's seat. She sat back and thought. Why would Hess be interested in this plane?

***

Jean walked into the office. 'Herr Goebbels, there is a man here to see you, shall I send him in?'

'Who is it?' Goebbels replied.

'He wouldn't give his name.' She was only half lying, he wouldn't give his name, but she knew who he was.

'Send him in,' Goebbels said. 'Next time get the name.'

'Yes,' she replied and showed the man into the room.

'Ah Himmler, what do I owe this pleasure?' Goebbels sat back in his chair,

Jean walked out of the office and raced to get a drink. The pot took forever to boil on the stove. She returned to the office.

'I want him to listen to you and not Hess,' Himmler finished.

'It's hard. He has his ear,' Goebbels said, 'but I am working on it.'

'Work faster.'

She placed the drinks in front of them and then walked out of the room.

Five minutes later Himmler exited, and Goebbels called Jean into the office. 'When is the meeting with Hitler and Hess scheduled for?'

'Next Thursday,' she replied.

'Phone Himmler's secretary and let her know,' he looked down at his papers.

***

Friedrich opened the door to the house. It wasn't the same as their home in Grünwald. The countryside on its doorstep. The house had just felt too big. There was so much travelling into town, it had made sense to get a town house. It was in a nice area, and close to the office.

He heard Natasha come walking down the stairs.

'Hello, Father.'

'Hello dear,' he said walking into the parlour and sitting in his favourite chair.

'Oh,' he called, 'I didn't tell you, did I? I had dinner with Rudolf Hess at the beginning of this week.'

Natasha stopped.

'Did you?'

A smile came across her face, finally some information.

'Yes,' he called back. 'Nice man and that's from my experience of him.'

Natasha walked into the room and sat in a chair opposite.

Friedrich looked at her.

'I would have told you before, but last time we ended up having an argument.'

'True,' she answered. 'I'm listening now.'

'He's here doing intelligence work,' revealed Friedrich. 'He seems to be under a lot of pressure; I do feel sorry for him.'

'He's doing some intelligence work is he?' she said trying to hide a smirk, 'what on, exactly?'

'I don't know,' he commented, 'he mentioned some network, but I didn't ask.'

'Some interrogator you are father,' she smiled.

***

Michele walked into the operations room. There were maps spread out all over the table. Anneliese and Oskar were looking over them.

'We just don't understand what you're thinking of doing,' Anneliese asked as she saw Michele approach.

'We'll break them out on the border,' Michele replied.

'Where, in Russia?' Anneliese asked.

'No,' Michele replied, 'the forest, on our old border.'

Oskar looked confused, 'Right in the middle of enemy territory.'

'Yes,' Michele replied. 'The train will run through the forest and bottom of Poland to get to Auschwitz. They will not expect anyone to try anything on German soil; it would be a suicide mission. But that is what will work in our favour, the forest is the place where we can cause the most confusion. An attack on train would never be successful because you cannot save all the prisoners. But that is not the objective for us, we want to save one, and if others escape, then that is good.'

They both looked at her.

'You're crazy,' Anneliese said

'Yes,' she replied, 'and that's why it'll work.'

They looked at each other and then back at her.

'What are we going to do?' asked Anneliese.

'Right,' Michele started. 'The train itself is where most of the guards will be stationed. One guard between each carriage while the train is moving. Most of the soldiers will be in the first two carriages. You will be between the second and the third carriage Oskar. This is the division between the guards and the prisoners. It's important that you know which carriage Mama, I mean Helene is on, to find her. There is a tunnel located here. Just as we go into the tunnel, you need to unhook the carriage and obviously be on the side closest to the prisoners. There will most likely be a lookout on the carriage so make sure you disarm that guard first. The carriages will keep moving so be careful. There are normally about ten carriages. I need you to get rid of the other seven guards. Remember the object is to retrieve Helene, not save all the passengers.'

'What about the guards in the two carriages?' said Oskar.

'Don't worry about them.' Michele replied, 'Anneliese you need to be on this road. You'll be in a first aid truck with a spare nurse's uniform. Helene is to change into a uniform as fast as possible. Oskar you'll pretend to be wounded if you're stopped.'

'Where will you be?' Anneliese asked.

'I'll meet you in Nuremberg,' Michele answered. 'We'll need explosives and guns. Can you organise that, Oskar? Anneliese, you need to organise the nurse's uniforms and a vehicle. That's the plan.'

***

'Have you got much more?' Goebbels enquired as he put his coat on.

'Not really,' Jean smiled back, 'I should be finished in about half an hour. Why is there something that you want me to do?'

'No,' Goebbels replied, 'just don't stay too late.'

'Yes Herr Goebbels,' she said and continued typing.

He turned, spoke to some of the other secretaries and then walked out of the office.

She wasn't completely alone. There were few secretaries finishing their work. She wasn't sure if they all worked for Goebbels or if they supported others within the surrounding offices. The office was always busy, but no one really knew what she was supposed to be doing. All they saw was her typing and filing, nothing out of the ordinary for a secretary within the secretarial team. She finished typing her page and placed it on the pile of papers. Then she crossed the room to the filing cabinet. Goebbels didn't really keep anything of great importance in this cabinet. But Jean did. She opened the drawer and pulled out her file. In it were copies of documents that Goebbels was organising for the public. But they did not focus on the war; they were more information, and indiscretions of people within the Nazi party. There were also past smear attempts that dated as far back as Rohm through to the current personnel, some of which had been very successful. But one, had constantly failed. For the past two years, it had been evident that Goebbels had wanted Hess out of the picture. Although he had not found anything that could be used to topple the Deputy Führer.

Jean looked around. No one was looking. She rolled the papers up and put them in her thermos. She added the page that she had just typed and closed the filing cabinet. Her work completed for this evening. Tonight, the mice would have company. She grabbed her coat and thermos and walked out of the office.

***

Hilde walked into the room. Michele paused her packing and looked up at her. She didn't know what to say. Michele was going no matter what, and she was taking the two most important people in her life.

'I'll look after them,' Michele said.

Suddenly she was angry with Michele. So angry that she was almost crying. 'You better.'

Michele was shocked but understood. 'I didn't ask them to help me,' she said.

'But you knew as soon as you said something that.' Hilde's voice broke, and she looked away.

After a pause, Hilde looked back to Michele, 'Are you sure this is the right thing to do?'

Michele closed her bag. 'If it were Oskar, would you do it?'

Hilde stood. Of course, she would. Michele threw the bag over her shoulder and walked out of the room. Hilde followed downstairs.

'Michele,' Hilde paused for a moment, 'I want you all back, alive. All of you.'

Michele smiled back at her and walked out the door.

Michele and Anneliese were waiting in the car for Oskar. Hilde hugged him and didn't want to let go. Eventually Oskar pulled away and kissed her on the forehead. They were all Michele's responsibility now.

CHAPTER 7

Natasha saw Wilhelm ahead of her, so she quickened her pace to catch up with him. He looked distracted. Natasha didn't want to interrupt, but he soon became aware that there was someone beside him.

'Sorry,' he smiled, 'I was focused on something.'

'I could see,' she replied, 'I didn't want to interrupt. Thank you, by the way for the book. It was really interesting.' She handed it back to him.

They were walking up to a café.

'Natasha, do you want a coffee?'

She nodded and they both went inside.

Natasha looked at Wilhelm. 'Do you miss it?'

'Miss what?'

'The air force,' she replied, 'I mean, I know that you are still in the air force, but the flying side of things, being out and about.'

'Oh, believe me I get out and about,' he answered, 'but I guess, yes a little bit.'

'What made you go into the tactical side of things?' she enquired.

'The girls, they love all that spy and strategy stuff.' He laughed, 'Honestly, I just want to make a difference. When you're flying, you do what everyone else tells you. I want to be able to influence the people that give those instructions.'

'And do you?' she asked.

He smiled at her.

'Sometimes.' He paused. 'Luckily, I don't have you as a boss. I couldn't do much influencing there.'

She smiled. 'What was your favourite plane?'

'I like them all. They were all good and bad depending on what you're doing.' Wilhelm started flicking through the book.

Natasha stopped him on one of the pages, 'I just don't understand how some of them can fly. Don't they need quite a bit of power to get off the ground? For example, this one just looks too small, but I guess that means it needs less power for take-off, is it faster but for small distances.'

He smiled. 'The ME110. It is a good little plane, deceptive; you can fly quite a way with that plane. You could reach the Mediterranean in that.'

'Wow' she replied, 'I wouldn't have guessed that.'

She asked other questions concerning planes so that no one plane would stand out. They finished their coffees.

'I have to go,' Natasha said, 'but Wilhelm we have to do this again soon. Just have a talk, the two of us.'

He smiled at her, 'I'd like that.'

She got up and walked out of the café. When she looked over her shoulder, she saw Wilhelm staring at her with a puzzled look. She pretended not to notice and crossed the street.

***

Oskar drove them to Nuremburg, which had been one of the safe houses that Michele had organised. Erna, their contact, was working at the Red Cross Headquarters. It was the perfect base for Anneliese's cover and her use of a Red Cross truck going in and out of the city wouldn't alert anyone of anything.

As dusk fell, Anneliese and Oskar went for a walk to check out the area. They walked past the Red Cross depot. High gates surrounded the area, although there was a road that went in and out of the depot with minimum security. The two of them acted as if they were on a romantic stroll. They walked around counting the vans. Only a couple were in use at night, the rest were in the garage around the back. They casually walked to the back. No one stopped them as they walked by.

'Here we are Anneliese.' Oskar stood beside the door. 'I'll time you.'

'Doing what?'

'Unlocking the door,' Oskar said.

'Can't you do it?'

'No, I won't be here.'

'But I've never done that.'

Oskar smiled, 'I'll teach you.'

Oskar bent down to the locks height with Anneliese and handed her a couple of tools. She raised an eyebrow but took them. He talked her through it step by step. She gently slid one of the tools into the keyhole and pressed it down. Then the other she lightly dragged along the top of the key lock prodding trying to make it move slightly. After a few groans and much frustration, the lock opened. Anneliese smiled.

'Great,' Oskar said closing the lock, 'now again.'

Not impressed Anneliese started the process again and then again until she could pick the lock within two minutes.

'Are you confident with that?' Oskar asked.

Anneliese nodded.

They slipped into the garage. There were eight trucks inside.

'Have you ever started a vehicle without a key?' Oskar asked.

'Look, you give me a gun and I could shoot you between the eyes from 300 yards, I know cryptology and navigation, but no, I have never broken into a building and stolen a car before.' She stormed off behind the trucks.

'I'm sorry,' Oskar said, slightly taken back by her outburst. 'I was only going to teach you.'

When he finally found her, she turned to him and said, 'I would prefer to use a key.'

She pointed towards a wall full of hooks with keys on them.

He smiled, 'Are you alright?'

'Yes.'

They soon understood the system of what keys belonged to which trucks. At the far end of the building, a door opened to the petrol filling area and then the road followed around to the gate. Anneliese and Oskar walked towards the main gate. They milled around pretending to talk to each other as a romantic couple would. Eventually a first aid truck came out of the depot. The guard just waved it through. They smiled at each other and headed back.

***

Michele marked where the van had to be on the map for Helene's escape. She put it in cupboard in the room Anneliese would be staying in for the next two nights.

Michele was analysing another map when Anneliese and Oskar walked in the room.

'Anneliese, do you know where you're going?'

'Yes,' Anneliese said turning to Oskar while pulling a face, 'that I know.'

Oskar laughed. Michele was slightly confused, but let it go.

'I guess it's an early night,' Oskar said and turned to leave.

'No,' Michele replied, 'I think we should go out for a drink.'

They didn't need much encouragement and were soon heading out.

***

Wilhelm walked into Hess's office and sat down.

Hess looked up, 'What's wrong?'

Wilhelm took a deep breath. 'You know how you asked me to tell you if Natasha did anything out of the ordinary?'

'Yes,' Hess answered looking intently at Wilhelm.

'Well, it might not be anything.'

'Go on,' said Hess. 'I get the feeling there's always something connected to Natasha's actions.'

'She's developed an interest in planes,' Wilhelm continued. 'I lent her this book and she even asked me questions regarding different aeroplanes.'

Hess grabbed the book and flicked through the pages.

He looked up at Wilhelm a little concerned, 'Do you remember what she was interested in?'

'Oh, there were lots,' Wilhelm replied.

Hess opened the book to the page that contained the ME110. He handed it to Wilhelm.

'Did she ask about this one?'

Wilhelm looked down at the page in astonishment.

'Yes.'

'What did she ask about it?' Hess questioned.

Wilhelm thought for a second. 'How far it would fly, she seemed to think it was too small to…'

'Damn,' Hess yelled and jumped out of his chair.

'What's wrong?'

He'd never seen Hess react like this before.

'I want to talk to that girl.'

Hess was fuming; he looked out the window while he calmed himself. After a moment he regained his composure, he smiled and turned back towards Wilhelm.

'Thank you,' he said, 'that information was very important.'

Wilhelm got up.

'I'll organise a meeting,' he said and then left the room.

Hess looked back out the window. Wilhelm frustrated him sometimes, the boy seemed observant but didn't follow through. He couldn't put things together himself, take that next step. A follower, and a follower cannot be trusted, as they are easily led. Natasha was different, she was a very clever girl. Pragmatic. Clinical and efficient. If things were to go as planned, he'd have to step up his game.

***

Michele and Oskar had set off early for the long drive to Berlin. Although they took the back roads, they were always on the lookout for other vehicles

When they arrived, they met up with Jean, settled into her flat and started to organise things.

'I don't have a lot to tell you,' Jean said, 'but there is some interesting information coming to hand.'

She had copies of the reports on the table.

There have been no alterations in the propaganda campaigns at the moment. But this might interest you,' Jean said as she handed the papers to Michele.

Michele looked at the papers briefly.

'Jean, this looks like information on some of the major Nazi decision makers.' Michele kept reading the papers.

'No,' said Jean, 'it's propaganda on some of the major Nazi leaders. Goebbels is trying to discredit them for some reason.'

'I don't remember some of this. Has it all been used?' Michele asked.

'Some has, but not all,' Jean replied, 'it's like he's waiting for something.'

Oskar looked at the papers, 'It looks like a real power struggle, and it even includes Hess.'

'Hess is one of the main figures in the campaigns. This is not the first time he's been in the list. It's all through the files. But it is basic compared to the others. Trivial. Nothing that would really make a difference. There is another filing cabinet I am trying to get into, but it is almost guarded by two of the secretaries. I'm working on it though.' Jean continued, 'The people he does seems to be trusting are Himmler, and Bormann. I don't understand what he's trying to do.'

'I do,' Michele said. 'He's trying to eliminate the competition. Reports not used, could be blackmail material.'

'But Hess is not competition, he has no real power,' Oskar replied.

'No especially not now that Goebbels has been given total control of the media. He controls the public, and Goering is Hitler's successor,' Jean cut in.

'And yet neither have Hitler's ear,' Michele said, 'that's the goal. But we all know Goebbels, if he is really trying to get rid of Hess, there will be something bigger. And it will be hidden. You need to get into the locked cabinet.'

Michele thought for a moment.

'Do any intelligence reports come through you to Goebbels,' Michele questioned.

'Yes,' Jean answered. 'Why?'

'Oskar, after we finish here,' Michele started, 'I want you to discuss with Henri what sort of information we want Goebbels to receive.'

'We're going to give Goebbels information?' Oskar asked.

'Yes,' Michele replied, 'we want him living in a false world. It puts us on a more even footing.'

They both nodded in agreement.

It was dusk by the time they arrived in Fürstenberg/Havel. They waited until it had gone dark before they approached the train in the station. The station was about a 15-minute walk from Ravensbrück prison camp, but it would be a struggle for the prisoners and a walk that would be full of dread. There were only a few guards around the station, but most were at the prison, in fact most lived just outside the prison gates. Trains passed through the station and the lights were bright, so they had to be careful. Slowly Oskar ducked into each carriage. He put small amounts of dynamite strategically near the rails of the doors. The fuse ran through the frames to the underside of the carriage. Jean ran the fuse down the centre of the train, under the carriages and Michele attached the two fuses together. It all ran from the third carriage. Oskar put a thick plank of wood on the side of the doorframe on the second carriage.

Jean smiled, 'Do you know Michele. I feel safer doing this, than going to the office. How silly is that?'

Michele looked at her, grabbing her shoulders, 'Doing this, you know what to look for. You know the enemy and where they're likely to be. At the office, you never know who is watching. I hope you continue to feel this way, it's safer for you.'

A shiver ran down Jean's spine. She was right, don't get comfortable, that's when you'll get caught. They got back and went straight to sleep; tomorrow would be a long day.

***

Anneliese looked in the mirror as she pinned back her hair into a bun. She slipped into the Red Cross uniform jacket. Then she stopped. She stared at herself in the mirror. The reflection that she saw showed her just how scared she really was. Now, calm down, breathe deeply, in, then out. I can do this. It was her first mission by herself, even though she wasn't truly by herself. There was no one else here to distract her nerves. She focused on the thought of how good it would be to see Helene again. She smiled; it was worth it just for that.

***

Michele walked into the room. She was wearing baggy black stokers' uniform that managed to disguise her athletic frame. She used a black cap to hide her hair. Oskar had put on his uniform.

'Don't get too comfortable in that,' Michele said.

Oskar smiled. 'Definitely not.'

'Ready?'

'As ready as I'll ever be,' he replied.

Jean was up. 'I'm not really a morning person,' she said, a little dishevelled. She was dressed in village style clothes and had worked hard on looking scruffy to say the least. Soon they were all heading out.

There was chaos at the train station. Different groups of soldiers were hanging around waiting for direction. But no one really seemed in charge. Most were just trying to keep warm as the mist was starting to clear. Drops of rain seemed to be chasing it away and no one really wanted to be there. It was easy for Oskar to offer to stand between the box cars. Another was put in the lookout and a few scattered along the train. But most were going to stay in the front carriages and swap out later. Most were hoping that the day would warm up before that happened. Anyway, the prisoners were not going to do anything, there were squashed in the box cars, locked from the outside.

The under carriage was inspected for sabotage. Oskar hoped they would not see the fuses. They were mainly looking for explosives, and those were inside the carriages. The check seemed to clear.

Michele had been near when the coal had been emptied into the tender and had been slightly covered by some of the dust. But the rain was not helping her cause. She managed to grab a piece of coal and rub her face and hands with it. She met up with the other stoker, who although confused, was happy that he would not need to do all the work

***

There was a group of Germans on the platform watching the prisoners. The prisoners were slipping and sliding all over the place with the rain. Most of them were not fully clothed. Bones protruded through saggy skin, and yet a crowd had gathered to ridicule them. Jean stood in the crowd that were yelling at them. She felt physically sick but couldn't let it show. Her eyes scanned the crowd for Helene, finally she saw her. She looked frail, weak, and scared. Her normally beautiful long hair was ratty and had been gathered under a scarf, her eyes almost dead and it was hard to watch for Jean. But she would not cry.

She was frantically trying to think of abuse she could yell to get Helene's attention without raising alarm. But all she could do was keep calling out and hoping that she might be seen.

***

Helene walked along the platform, guided by the female guards, who she had come to realise could be far more horrifying than their male counterparts. Although weary of her captors, she was becoming numb to the normal ridicule of the brainwashed public. She felt sore, numb and tired, but she had survived better than others had. She slightly slipped in the mud and while regaining her balance she aimlessly looked around. Her eyes passed something familiar, and she looked back at it. It was Jean. She made eye contact and Jean winked at her and then disappeared in the crowd.

The person beside her grumbled, 'What are you smiling about? Do you not know where we're going?'

'I think it's going to be an interesting journey,' she replied.

It was as if someone had woken her, she felt more alert. Her skin tingled and Helene felt something that she had not felt for a long time. She felt hope. She looked along the train and wondered what exactly Michele had planned. All she knew was Jean had done her job, and now she had to wait and be ready.

***

Jean walked to the front of the station and just as she passed Oskar, she turned to the person beside her and said, 'It feels like every three days they're taking people from here, where do they store them all?'

She shook her head and walked off. The person she had talked to looked confused but kept walking. Oskar smiled, thank you Jean. Helene was in carriage three. All the variables were working in their favour today.

***

Wilhelm walked towards the train. A confused German woman walked up to him and mentioned something about three days then continued walking. He hadn't really been listening. He was still confused as to why he was there. Hess had been quite definite about it, although he'd not elaborated. It wasn't Wilhelm's job. He disagreed with it. In fact, he hated it. However, an order was an order.

Wilhelm wasn't like Hess, he couldn't just think of people as objects, to help do things with, like chess pieces, to be part of an overall strategy. It wasn't just about Jewish people or Communists. Sometimes he thought Hess just didn't like people in general. But then there were so many other things that Wilhelm agreed with, could learn. He found Hess a constant contradiction.

He boarded the front carriage and sat down. Getting out his newspaper, he didn't know what to do. Hess had told him to do nothing. I'm never told anything. It is like being back in the damn air force. So, he read.

Most of the guards had crammed into the front carriage. It had the nicer seats. However, because of this, it was stuffy and after a couple of hours, smelly. After three hours, Wilhelm couldn't take it anymore. He looked around for a window to open. Nothing. He felt for the prisoners, most of them were so squashed, they wouldn't be able to move, to breathe. He got up and pushed his way to the door. It was raining outside, but it was fresh air, and that's what he needed. He opened the door and stepped onto the main engine. He took a deep breath and sighed. The breeze through his hair felt nice and refreshing. It stopped raining, so he decided to take a walk.

Wilhelm lit his cigar then he walked along the narrow walkway to the front.

***

Michele had taken the water from the lad and poured some for everyone. This was it, there would only be the four of them now. She managed to slip a sleeping drug into the drinks. The train driver drank away and so did the other stoker but the not the guard.

'Thirsty?' Michele asked.

'No.'

There was a knife and gun hidden in her overalls, but she didn't want to use them. Michele put some more coal in the fire. She paused. She could hear something, footsteps. Her heart started to pound. The footsteps got closer and rounded the corner. She peered up from under her cap, and gasped and then looked down again. It was Wilhelm. What was he doing here? He was one of the few people who could recognise her.

'Good morning Gruppenführer' the guard said.

'Good morning,' Wilhelm smiled back.

The rest of them replied and smiled back, apart from one lad who was busy feeding the fire.

'Are you joining us for a while?' the guard asked.

'Yes, I need the fresh air,' replied Wilhelm.

Michele kept looking down. Any moment the drug would start to show some effects. She had to get rid of him. The guard had not drunk anything, and she would have to deal with him, but not Wilhelm.

She said, trying to keep her head down and in the deepest her voice would go, 'Very shortly we will be coming up to a tunnel and in the tunnel, you'll get completely covered in soot.'

She continued putting fuel into the fire.

'I don't mind,' he said.

She forgot herself while she tried to think about what else to do. When she snapped out of her thoughts, she realised she was staring straight into his eyes.

Wilhelm did not mind a little soot. He looked at the lad, thinking that it was nice that he was concerned. The lad looked up at him, with the most memorable eyes. Those eyes were the same ones that he had seen not so long ago at the Berlin train station. His face dropped and then he smiled. Now he had an inkling of why Hess had put him on the journey. What was happening on this train?

Michele looked at him. She didn't really know what to do, but she saw the look of recognition on his face.

The person helping her with the coal had dozed off. The train driver was starting to get drowsy as well, although the guard hadn't noticed. Michele looked ahead of the train. The tunnel wasn't far away.

'May I suggest you sit down?' she said in her normal voice to Wilhelm.

He moved toward the furnace and sat quietly. She added more fuel and then headed towards the driver, who had now fallen asleep at the controls.

'What are you doing?' the guard asked as he looked around and realised the other two were unconscious.

'I really wish you'd drunk your drink,' Michele said.

The guard grabbed his gun and Michele blew the whistle as she turned and shot the guard's forehead. They all disappeared into darkness.

***

Oskar looked around the corner, the tunnel was about ten minutes away. He picked up the wooden plank that he had attached to the carriage and ran it through the handles that were on either side of the door. It effectively locked the guards off from the rest of the train. He climbed up the ladder to the watch tower. Smiling at the guard on duty, he pretended to stretch his legs. As the guard turned to look at the rest of the train, Oskar, punched the back of the guard's neck and he crumbled. Then Oskar climbed on to the top of the train and crawled across the roof. On the other end of the carriage, he leaned down and quickly wrapped a rope around the guard's neck. The guard tried to grab the rope, struggling, and kicking as he was slightly lifted from his ledge. His hands flying between the rope on his neck and Oskar trying to defend himself. The wet rope slipped slightly in Oskar's hand, but he regained his grip and with all his strength pulled the guard up. Slowly the resistance stopped. Oskar attached the guard to the carriage. He crawled back to his end of the carriage and lit the fuse. The tunnel was approaching. Reaching down he unbolted the train and grabbed hold of the carriage on the prisoner's side. Both were going quite fast, so they continued moving but the carriages were slowing down. The third carriage managed to stop just inside the tunnel. He crawled along the top of the carriages. There were three more guards on the train. One guard was now walking beside the train. Oskar leaned over the side and shot him. Another guard spotted Oskar and shot back. The first carriage side exploded. The prisoners started pouring out.

The guards stood in shock as one by one the sides of the box cars exploded. Oskar managed to get down to the ground and crawled under the train. He had to find the two other guards.

***

Helene had felt the motion of the train slow down. She smelt the lit fuse and just wondered what was going to blow. She looked around for a sign and then tried to bend down a little, but it was useless, you couldn't move. The side doors blew out. Not a big explosion, but because so many people were in the carriage, she knew not everyone would have survived. None of them had time to think, they just saw freedom. She'd already put her resistance cap on. The possibility of most people escaping outweighed the death of a few. Harsh as it was, this train was sending them to their deaths anyway. Some of the prisoners were screaming, some were in shock; others were already scrambling to get away. People were being trampled, pushed, it was chaos. She had to get out.

Helene helped people out of the carriage. She had to find some guards. Preferably, dead. Where there were dead guards, there would be guns. She got out of the carriage and looked towards the front of the train, but it wasn't there. Slightly confused she headed to the back. At the back of the first carriage was a soldier hanging from a hook. She took his gun and knife and slowly she climbed to the train's turret. The guard was starting to rouse. Using all her energy, she whacked the guard's temple with the butt of the gun, and he went quiet. She had a good viewpoint, but she could only see two guards. They did not seem too interested in the prisoners but looked like they were hunting something. Helene placed the muzzle of the gun on the wooden ledge, looked down the site of the gun, took a deep breath and pulled the trigger. She was rusty and shaky, but she had to do it. The front guard of the two went down. There was another shot, as Helene was looking for her next target. The other soldier went down. Helene kept looking. She spotted a soldier come around the end of the train. She kept him in her sight, gently her index finger rested on the trigger. Then something made her focus on the face, it was Oskar. She slowly, climbed down the carriage.

'Oskar,' she yelled.

He came running over.

'I nearly shot you.'

'How would you have got home?' He smiled, 'This way.'

***

The front of the train came out of the tunnel.

Wilhelm looked confused, 'It's still going.'

'Yes,' said Michele. She had placed the sleeping people in safe places. 'I didn't want to kill him,' she said. She walked over to Wilhelm and reached inside his jacket. She pulled out a revolver. 'Why didn't you shoot me?'

'Because then you would've had to shoot me,' he replied. 'I'd prefer to live.'

She turned and grabbed the iron rod that had stoked the fire and jammed it into the controls so that the train was stuck in acceleration.

'What are you doing?' Wilhelm asked.

'Look behind you' she replied.

He turned and looked down the track. There were only two carriages attached to the train.

'Margot, or should I call you Michele?' he said. 'What's so important about this train?'

She looked at him, he knew her real name. Not wanting to let her surprise show she said, 'It's a family thing.'

'Your family is almost as screwed up as mine.'

She smiled. 'I have to go. I want you to know that what I'm about to do is for your own good. Thank you for not shooting me.'

Wilhelm looked at her confused. Michele lent on his shoulder slightly and pinched the nerve at the base of his neck. Wilhelm crumbled within seconds. She dragged him to rest his head against the others. Then she walked to the first carriage. There was another tunnel in the next ten minutes. If she could get to the back of the train, she could simply jump off.

Michele climbed the first ladder onto the carriage roof. The young lad walked out and saw her, as she was halfway down the carriage. She heard a scream from the front and the young boy started shouting. She stood up and started to run. Michele leapt onto the second carriage, sliding slightly but managed to keep her balance. Soldiers were pouring out of the front carriage and a couple had managed to get out of the second. Michele flattened herself against the roof as she heard gunfire. She slid along to the ladder, and then climbed down. It was time to jump. This was going to hurt.

Michele almost made it onto the grass area but caught her foot on the way down. It twisted when she landed. She stood up.

The pain ran straight up her leg. 'Pain is just in the mind,' she kept saying to herself, in between her panting. She had to move. She started to hobble, and then to run. The pain increased, but she had to push on. Guards had jumped off the train now. She tried to make for the river. She could hear gunshots. Her running was erratic because of the pain, and she was stumbling down the hill.

'Stop or I'll shoot,' said a voice from behind her.

She turned around; the guard was only a couple of feet away. There were about ten others' coming down the hill towards her. She was in trouble. Damn. There was no way she'd get out of this, not here, not now.

He came closer. She waited, waited, waited and then when he was less than an arm's length away, she grabbed his rifle and then kicked him in the groin. He collapsed to the ground. A couple of other guards came at her. She managed to knock one of them out completely and hit the other, so he was dazed.

Wilhelm came down the hill still a little groggy from his forced sleep. He stood watching as a group of trained guards tried to arrest one female. Three of them were on the ground by the time he was close enough to do anything. Finally, four guards managed to hold her down. Only four, he chuckled, and she was still giving them a hard time.

One of the guards loaded his gun. 'We have right to shoot you on the spot for treason against the Third Reich.'

'Halt,' Wilhelm said. 'Tie her up and bring her to Munich.'

The guard turned to him and said, 'I'm the senior guard here, what right, do you have to tell me what to do?'

Wilhelm looked back at the upstart. 'Kill her if you want, but then you can explain to my boss why you killed someone who may be able to give us vital information about the resistance.'

The guard laughed, 'And who's your boss?'

'Rudolf Hess,' Wilhelm said stone faced.

The guard looked at him, 'Tie her up.'

Michele looked straight at him and smiled. For some idiotic, irrational, illogical reason, she felt calm and safe when Wilhelm was around. This will get you bloody killed if you don't watch it. However, going back to Munich was good.

As they dragged her up the hill beside him, she said, 'Administration, was it?'

Wilhelm smiled. 'Not exactly a boring person yourself, Margot.'

***

Helene and Oskar made it down to the road. It took them about twenty minutes. Anneliese was waiting in the Red Cross van. She saw them and ran over to Helene. She paused when she saw Helene but forced herself to continue. After giving her a quick but soft hug, she beckoned Helene to a nearby stream for a quick wash. Helene quickly got into the nurse's uniform. It was loose on her, her bones showed through her skin and the material. Anneliese gave her a cardigan to try to hide her frame. Anneliese just wanted to cry, but now was not the time

As Oskar was about to get into the van, Anneliese came up behind him. 'I'm sorry Oskar.'

'About what?' he said as he turned around.

'About this,' she said as she shot him.

'Ow, you shot me?'

'I grazed your leg,' she said. 'It will bleed, but you'll survive.'
She helped him into the van. Helene got in the back with him,
and they set off.

There was a checkpoint along the road out of the forest.
Anneliese pulled up to the guard as he flagged her over.

She made herself hyperventilate.

'Are there more people coming? Please tell me people are
coming because I'm not going back, you can't make me, that.
I mean, I–'

'Calm down, calm down, breathe, what's wrong, coming for
what?' he asked.

'There's all this shooting in the forest. The guard in the back
was crawling to the road. I was just driving by. I don't want to
get shot. You should call for help,' she continued.

Helene put some of the rags that had been on Oskar's leg
by his shoulder. The guard went to see to look. Oskar looked
badly injured.

'Go through,' the guard said.

He looked back at Oskar. 'You'll be fine. Get him to hospital
quickly.'

Anneliese sped away.

On the outskirts of town Anneliese, pulled up beside another
car. She took off the top layer of her nurse's uniform and put on
a jacket. Helene put on a dress and cardigan and Oskar bandaged
his leg and tidied up his uniform. They drove to the flat, and
finally felt they could relax.

'Welcome back,' Anneliese said, 'it's good to see you.'

Helene smiled and gave them both a hug.

'It's good to be here,' Helene smiled, 'but where's Michele?'

'You'll see her soon,' Oskar said. 'Food anyone?'

'A little, I don't have much of an appetite these days,'
answered Helene.

Anneliese looked at the time. They were supposed to leave
the flat in two hours. She hoped everything had gone as well for
Michele as it had for them.

***

It was late afternoon when Erna came home from work, unlocked the door and walked into a crowded apartment.

'What are you doing here?' she asked. 'You're not supposed to be here.'

'What?' Helene asked. She looked around. 'Why?'

Anneliese looked at Erna and then Helene and walked into Erna's bedroom. Erna walked in after her. Helene looked at Oskar. She'd gone completely white.

'We were waiting for her,' she said. 'She was supposed to meet us here, wasn't she?'

Oskar didn't know what to say. Helene looked stunned; tears started to run down her cheeks. Oskar came over to hug her.

She punched him and struggled, 'Get off me.'

He just held her tighter, but she felt so fragile, he didn't want to break her.

Erna and Anneliese came back into the room. Helene broke free of Oskar's hold and slowly slid down the wall and curling into the foetal position, crying. She couldn't bear to lose another daughter. Anneliese ran over to comfort Helene.

Erna looked at Oskar.

'You're in charge now.'

Oskar stood in shock, no, no he couldn't be. No Michele, no Yosef, it was just him. What would Michele do?

'We have to go,' he said, 'we have to go now.'

They looked at him. Inside they knew he was right, but they wanted to stay, just in case.

'Now.'

They got up and dried their eyes. They had to continue with their plan, no matter what happened. Helene had to get to Switzerland to get some rest. She wouldn't make it to Egypt in the state she was in.

CHAPTER 8

Natasha pushed the door to the corridor open. All eyes diverted to her, including her father's. She walked steadily along passing guards that looked at her with fear. There was no sound apart from her footsteps along the wooden floor.

She paused outside to look at her father.

'You can't do this,' her father said.

'Yes, I can.'

'No,' her father retorted, 'she's too close to you. She's your sister.'

'She's the enemy,' Natasha factually replied. 'Remove Friedrich. He has a parental bond with this prisoner.'

Friedrich looked at her in disbelief. He walked towards the door.

'Guards,' she said.

After a confused pause, hands wrapped around his arms pulling him backwards down the corridor.

'What are you doing? Somebody, stop her,' he shouted, 'She can't do this. You can't, don't, don't–'

Natasha paused and turned to the guards raising an eyebrow to those who might think to oppose her. All stood fast except those dragging her struggling father away. Friedrich's face looked at her confused, then stunned and finally with anger and hatred.

She turned back and continued to the door. It opened and those inside walked out knowing they'd failed. Half of them felt sorry for the girl within, she hadn't told them anything. She knew nothing. However, they knew the interrogator would work her badly, not for information but because of who she was. They all looked at each other and then stared at the door and waited.

The door closed behind Natasha. She took a deep breath, stretched her neck, rolled her shoulder blades and relaxed. To a certain extent, this was her sanctuary, an interrogation chamber, so ironic. She looked at the figure before her.

***

Michele's head was resting on her chest, she could taste some of the blood from her lip and her face felt a little numb in places. She'd heard the door open, and people leave. Slow, controlled steps came in as the door closed. Natasha had arrived. She tried to raise her head slightly, but only managed to bring her eyes up to look for her sister. There was a bright light shining towards her. She squinted slightly, as she made out the tall figure that stood before her.

'Hello,' she managed to mumble. 'I've been waiting for you.'

'Well, I'm here,' Natasha replied. 'Are you ready?'

Michele forced a smiled.

Natasha reached forward. She took a syringe from her pocket and grabbed Michele's arm.

'What are you doing? You can't.'

Michele's heart pounded fast with fear. She could feel the drug creeping through her body. Her arm was numb, and it slowly moved through her limbs. She was aware that Natasha was talking to her and that she was answering, but she wasn't aware of what she was saying. Michele realised that Natasha wasn't in front of her and then she passed out.

***

Friedrich paced up and down the room. He couldn't let this happen.

'Get me Natasha now.'

'I'm sorry, but she's unavailable,' his secretary said.

He knew she was busy; he could see her. He walked towards the window that looked out over the Platz. Natasha was standing behind a soldier. Opposite her a newly erected wall and a post. Two guards were struggling out of the main entrance with a girl between them. They tied her to the pole. They offered her a blindfold, but she declined. Michele stared at her sister, who stared directly back. Michele held her head high. She was going to be defiant until the end. No, this couldn't happen. This wasn't happening. Friedrich couldn't watch, he turned away and walked to a corner to hide.

***

Wilhelm looked around. He could see no one; he quickly opened the door and slipped in, closing it quietly behind him. He paused, he didn't think he could watch, but he had to. Wilhelm leaned on the windowsill and looked down at the Platz. He couldn't believe what he saw. He knew Natasha, she wasn't like this. People said she was, but she wasn't, not for him, there was a softness he would occasionally glimpse before she hid it again. But this confirmed all the rumours, it confirmed everything. The contradictions were fighting in his head, and he couldn't comprehend what was in front of him. His hand pressed against the window, as if it would make everything stop, but it just slid down to the ledge. As he looked at Michele, a tear fell down his cheek. All he wanted to do was protect her. But she was the enemy, even if he really didn't want her to be. This was all wrong, this was wrong. Suddenly he didn't want to be there. He punched the wall.

'It's hard to fathom really isn't it, two sisters, so different and yet. Well, here we are,' came a voice.

He turned around and tried to compose himself.

'It's fine,' Hess said, 'what's one more secret between friends?'

Wilhelm just looked at him and Hess smiled back.

'So how close are you and Michele?'

'What do you mean? Nothing's happened between us,' Wilhelm was taken off guard. 'I've only met her couple of times, and I didn't really know who she was.'

'Of course,' Hess said and walked towards the window. 'Join me.'

'I think I'd prefer not to, actually.'

Wilhelm replied and started heading towards the door. He didn't want to see this. He didn't want to see Natasha this way.

'No,' Hess said. 'Anyway, if you have no emotional interest it doesn't matter. I want you here, with me. You will stay.'

It wasn't a request; he was being made to watch, but why? He walked towards the window and stood by Hess. Now was the time to put his shield up. He pulled himself up, lifted his chin, and set his face.

Hess smiled.

***

Natasha could feel the eyes of the public and her father burning into her. She knew what this would do. It would cement her reputation; it would confirm what she was truly capable of to the public. She would be completely isolated, no father, no Wilhelm. Everyone looked on in disbelief as one sister prepared a single guard to shoot her own sibling. She felt like all her insides were shaking. She wouldn't let it show, she couldn't.

'Aim.'

Natasha instructed, lifting her hand. It did not matter what Natasha was feeling on the inside, this was for the greater good. She clenched her fist as she saw a hint of terror behind Michele's defiant eyes.

There was a shot. The soldier standing in front of Natasha yelled, dropping his gun and fell to the ground, clutching his wrist. Another bullet grazed Natasha's arm, which instantly went numb. She staggered and clutched her arm but remained standing. Natasha looked around the Platz. The sound had bounced off the concrete buildings that surrounded her. It was impossible to work out where the shot had come from.

***

Wilhelm looked through the window. A wave of relief hit his body as he saw the scene unfold. He sighed as all his muscles relaxed; he could barely stand.

Hess smiled as he looked at him and then looked back out the window to watch the courtyard.

Wilhelm's face set, Hess had known. That bastard had known.

If he had any energy, he would have punched him, but he looked back out of the window.

***

There was chaos in the Platz, locals were running for cover, people were screaming. Guards were pouring out of the headquarters, looking for where the snipers were located. No one noticed a figure cut Michele free. By the time Natasha's eyes caught up with Michele, she was climbing into a truck.

'Get her,' yelled Natasha.

The guards had seen nothing, and by the time they started looking for Michele, it was too late.

'You imbeciles,' screamed Natasha. 'How could you let this happen?'

None of the guards could look at her. They were all scared because they all realised something. The resistance had received inside information, and they did not want her to think it was from any of them.

***

Anneliese quickly drew back from the window, so her back was to the wall beside it. Reaching towards the window and she slid it down slowly till it was closed. Then she put the Mauser back in the cabinet she had taken it from and patted down her hair and dress. Taking a deep breath to calm her nerves, she opened the door to corridor and asked as a guard ran by 'what happened?'

They looked at her annoyed, shook their heads and continued. They didn't know where the shots had been fired from. She tried to look flustered, she was using the fact that the guards would assume they were looking for a male sniper, not a female, in a dress with a handbag. Right now, she had to blend in and look as scared as all the other girls. Which was easy, she was scared, but for a very different reason. So, she followed the crowd down the stairs and out of the building and disappeared onto to the street.

***

Friedrich sat at his desk crying. Two shots had occurred. Was one not enough? She was the enemy, but she was also his daughter. He couldn't help but think about the mess that had happened since he had joined the party. Uniting families, what a sham, his family was broken, unfixable and now part of it was gone forever. He sat down struggling to breathe.

The door swung open. Friedrich looked up. Natasha's sleeve was soaked in blood.

'I want a full investigation,' Natasha said. 'There has to be a leak. I scheduled this an hour ago. How could this happen?'

'What?' Friedrich queried. 'I don't understand?'

'You had a perfect view,' Natasha barked. 'She escaped.'

She paced the room ranting and then walked out the door.

Friedrich looked at the door in shock; he'd stopped listening after the word escape. Everything had happened so fast, it hadn't really sunk in. Michele was alive. A smile took over his face. Now, there was a lot to do. A shiver went through his body; he had to make this right. He had to correct everything.

***

They knew that it would take the Gestapo approximately fifteen minutes to control the Platz, organise teams and get vehicles out to join in the search. They needed to get rid of the truck within twenty minutes. The truck drove less than ten minutes from the Platz before Michele climbed out. She limped quickly to the terraced house as the truck drove away. Reaching into her pocket, she grabbed the key and opened the cellar door. She had a few bruises and cuts, but it looked worse than it was. As she hobbled down the stairs, army trucks rattled by.

The basement was barren to say the least. There was a pile of rugs on an old mattress in one corner. On a table nearby was some bread and cheese and some orange juice. She lit the candle in the corner. Shafts of light found their way through the boards and Michele lay down enjoying the peace and waited.

When Michele awoke, she noticed that her empty plate and glass had been refilled. She sat on the edge of her bed. She had to lie low, and she hated it. The light filtered through, and her eyes were gradually adjusting to the darkness. She was going to go insane. Michele relit the candle. On the desk were a few maps and notes. She sighed, good, something she could do.

***

Friedrich knocked on Natasha's door and opened it. Natasha was reading on her bed.

'We have been summoned to headquarters,' Friedrich said. 'Hess has asked for both of us.'

Natasha got up and walked out of her room slamming the door. Summoned, again!

They both walked into the meeting room. Hess was at the front of the room.

'We all know why we're here, so let's begin.' Hess paused.

'Natasha, tell us what occurred yesterday.'

Natasha got up and walked to the front of the room. 'In short, an execution was organised. During the execution, the guard and I were both shot, and the prisoner escaped. Now…'

Hess interrupted, 'Why did you want to publicly execute your sister?'

The room went silent.

Natasha was surprised. She paused before replying, 'I wanted to show the public that there is no mercy given to traitors, no matter who they are.'

'Why do you think that the resistance wanted her back?' quizzed Hess.

'I don't know.' said Natasha. 'She didn't really give us any useful information during interrogations. Maybe it was more of a statement. So…'

'Thank you, Natasha, that'll be all. You can go, rest, heal, we'll take from here,' Hess stated.

'I can help.'

'No, go home and heal your wound. It's under control.' Hess smiled, as he leaned forward and locked eyes with her, 'I will get her.'

Natasha clenched her jaw, but Hess held her stare.

She turned, walked past her father and out the door.

'Natasha,' Wilhelm closed the door behind him.

She turned around.

'The searches are starting on the outskirts and moving to the centre,' he said.

'Good,' Natasha said turning to go.

'Natasha,' Wilhelm paused and grabbed her hand. 'Your house will be searched at about 5 pm.'

Natasha looked confused.

He continued, 'West of your house is the first area to be searched, which should be completed by twelve.'

'In case you didn't realise, I'm not involved in the search, so I don't need to know this,' Natasha stated.

'Hess said I was to keep you informed,' he replied.

'I'll see you later then, during this afternoon's search of my house, will you be stopping for dinner?' she asked pulling her hand out of his.

'Is that a date?' he smiled, but it was a sad smile.

'I can't make sense of you,' he paused and looked at his shoes, 'I want you to be the girl I thought I knew. Not the one….'

There was silence, but the silence hurt Natasha. She knew what he meant, and it hurt. She turned and walked out of the building before he could see her eyes water.

Natasha got home and closed the door. This wasn't what she'd expected.

'Hello is anybody home?' she called.

She took off her coat and hung it on the coat rack. She shivered; it was cold. Opening the door to the basement, she walked down the stairs.

'So, how are you?' Natasha said.

'Not as bad as I thought I'd be,' Michele replied. 'You scared me.'

'I scared myself.'

Natasha took a deep breath. There was silence for a moment; it felt like they were both holding their breath. As if one more word would bring everything down, like a house of cards.

'I'm so sorry,' Natasha looked at the roof and had a few light pants of breath, 'I should've been able to protect you more.'

'You tried your best and I'm stubborn,' Michele was trying not to cry but it wasn't working.

Natasha just sat down; she couldn't fight back the tears anymore. 'I'm so sorry, what sort of big sister am I? If anything had gone wrong, I just.'

'Nothing went wrong.' Michele interrupted as she came over and they both hugged each other crying.

It had been an impossible situation. The only way for them both to continue what they were doing, was for her to escape. What Natasha had felt from the moment she knew they captured Michele was unbearable. Now that it was over, she could feel the shock set in. She just shook and cried.

'When a bug crawls over the border does he realise?' Michele commented randomly.

Natasha looked up.

'You always had to add something' she smiled.

'Well, the positives are that Mama's okay, they still think you're a heartless bitch, and I'm alive and kicking,' Michele giggled. 'What more could we want?'

There was silence as both sisters looked at different walls.

'How do you survive?' Michele asked. 'You're so isolated here.'

'No,' Natasha replied, 'I have Father. You're the one by yourself.'

'I have the entire resistance to support me,' said Michele. 'Father doesn't count.'

'He's getting better,' Natasha said.

'I don't believe it.'

'He tried to save you.' Natasha grabbed Michele's chin so that she looked at her. 'That must count for something.'

'I'll believe it when I see it,' Michele said. 'Do you ever feel like no matter how many friends you have around you, there's just no one you can talk to, there's no one you can be yourself with?'

'Yes,' Natasha seemed lost in thought momentarily, 'but not needing, that's what makes us strong.'

'No Natasha, I think we've just lived like this for so long.'

'That we think that's the only way to live,' said Natasha. 'Well at least we have each other. Shall we schedule another talk like this in the same place in another five years?'

It wasn't that funny but it was nice to laugh and so they did.

'You have to get ready to go,' Natasha said.

'Why?' Michele queried. 'I thought that it would be best to lay low for a little while.'

'The house is getting searched at five. I know where you need to go. Let's clean up and get out of here.'

'How do you know?' Michele asked.

'My source told me, although that scares me a little.' Natasha said. 'Does anyone you know live west of here?'

'Not anymore,' Michele replied, 'but they use to, it's still their place and I have the key.'

'Good,' Natasha said. 'Think you can walk?'

Michele thought for a minute. 'I don't think I can make it.'

'Fine, put this on and let's clean you up.' She threw a uniform to Michele, 'I'll help you.'

***

Everyone dispersed from the office with duties.

Hess pulled Wilhelm aside, 'Did you tell her?'

'Yes.'

'You're not wrong about either of them you know,' Hess commented. 'What is Friedrich up to?'

'Searches,' Wilhelm said, slightly confused.

'Organise for him to do paperwork or anything but keep him here.'

Hess started to walk off, 'Oh and Wilhelm organise a meeting with Natasha for me please. I'll not be back for a couple of days.'

Wilhelm asked, 'Who's coordinating the searches?'

Hess laughed. 'You are. Don't worry, you won't find her.'

'What?'

Hess paused, turned, and walked back towards him. When he was close enough, he whispered, 'Oh Wilhelm. Use your brain for once. Who knew about the execution and how would you have saved Michele in a way that would protect both of you? There's only one person, who was in control of this. Sometimes what you see is an illusion, a myth. Not all legends are real. You really need to start questioning things yourself.'

Hess turned and walked out the foyer doors, leaving Wilhelm confused, trying to process the information. Then it hit him, 'No, really, no it couldn't, could it?'

Dazed, he turned and walked towards Friedrich's office.

**

Friedrich was getting his coat from his office. He picked up his bag and turned to leave. Wilhelm was standing in the doorway.

Wilhelm cleared his throat, 'Hess and I have discussed the searches today and believe it would be best if you could co-ordinate them from here. We'll get all the teams to update you on anything that they may find.'

'If you don't want me involved,' Friedrich replied, 'I have other things to do.'

Wilhelm smiled. 'That would be best.'

Friedrich nodded and Wilhelm turned to go.

'Wilhelm, did you get to talk to her?' Friedrich asked, 'because you were there, on the train.'

Wilhelm closed the door and walked towards Friedrich. 'Yes, I did.'

Friedrich took a large breath, then asked, 'What's she like? Off the record.'

Wilhelm looked down at the floor and then back at Friedrich. He was a broken man, who couldn't show any feelings for one of his daughters, and it was eating him up.

'Friedrich, if she was on our side,' Wilhelm commented, 'I would think she was a lovely girl, very intelligent and enchanting.'

Friedrich turned away quickly and looked out the window. 'Thank you that'll be all.'

Wilhelm left the room; he made a mental note. Hess may be wrong about Friedrich.

Friedrich looked out the window. Enchanting, he smiled. He composed himself and sat down at the desk. He had a lot to do. He called his secretary in to the office.

'Can you please contact Berlin and find out what prisoners are unaccounted for, from the attack on the train,' Friedrich asked.

'Anyone in particular?' she asked.

'Yes,' he replied, 'a lady called Helene.'

She didn't need to ask any other questions. She knew who Helene was. Everyone knew.

Friedrich went to his file and took out his old address book and a few maps. He turned to Anita's address and looked over the map to locate where exactly she lived.

Ten minutes later, there was a knock on the door.

Friedrich called out, 'Come in.'

His secretary popped her head through the door.

'You were right, she's unaccounted for. There were some people killed during the attack on the train though.'

'Thank you,' Friedrich replied.

She closed the door. He smiled. They hadn't attacked the train. It had been a rescue mission. She wouldn't have been blown up; they were too clever for that. He would let Wilhelm look for Michele. He had a good feeling about Wilhelm. Friedrich was going to search for Helene. He put his address book and the map in his bag and grabbed his coat.

Friedrich walked out of the office and down the corridor. His secretary came running out of the office.

'Where are you going?'

'Out,' Friedrich replied still walking. 'Phone Natasha. Tell her I won't be home for dinner.'

***

Goebbels, Himmler and Bormann had been in Goebbels' office for over an hour. It was a secret meeting, which Jean had not been privy too. The door to the office opened and Hess and Hitler walked in. Jean and another secretary grabbed their notepads and opened the doors for them before sitting in the corner to take notes.

The meeting was pleasant enough to begin with, discussing the advancing fronts, covering wins and losses. Goebbels looked at ways that the losses could look more like victories or strategies. The scheduled propaganda was also analysed. They decided that Hitler should make some more speeches to the business sector and soldiers.

Then the discussion changed tack.

'Führer,' Goebbels started, 'we've been discussing earlier what we are hearing from the public it's still very anti-Jewish. They want rid of these people entirely.'

'Isn't that what we tell them to think, Goebbels?' Hess asked.

'We are not fulfilling our mandates to the people,' Goebbels said.

'What do you recommend?' said Hitler.

Goebbels smiled, 'Work and extermination camps. There are whispers of other solutions also.'

Himmler smiled.

Hess didn't look surprised. Jean looked around the table. The other two contributors were laying all these facts in front of Hitler who looked confused. Hitler took a breath as if to say something, but Hess started first.

'Although it is a good idea, have we forgotten something? True Aryans should not have to do the menial jobs of our country. The people that you want to kill are the people who save our kind from the embarrassment of doing jobs that are below their station. If we don't look after them to a certain extent, yes, they will die. When they're all dead, who will do that work? Will you Goebbels, or maybe you, SS Himmler?'

Goebbels glared at Hess. Jean noted that Hess had won that round.

CHAPTER 9

Just after three o'clock Michele and Natasha made it to Jean's old apartment. Dressed in uniform, and with a lot of makeup, Michele managed to blend in with the crowds, hiding in plain sight. They walked up to the front door. Michele bent down and moved a flowerpot to reveal a key.

Natasha opened the door, 'Who are you?'

Oskar and Natasha stared at each other for a few seconds.

'Oskar,' Michele interrupted.

'Michele?'

He lunged for her, and Natasha helped her into the room.

She barely made it to the apartment. She had tried to look normal when she walked but it'd been a struggle.

'Right,' Natasha said taking control. She closed the door behind her. 'I need the uniform back.'

'Sorry, who are you?' Oskar asked.

Michele replied, 'This is my sister.'

'The bad sister, who wants to kill you?'

Natasha just looked at him with astonishment.

'You don't want to kill her?'

'Obviously, or she'd be dead.'

Oskar just kept silent, he felt stupid.

Michele went to lie on the bed.

Within a couple of minutes, Natasha had the uniform back.

'I'm sorry I have to go, but I need to be home when they search the house. Look after her for me.'

Natasha smiled a goodbye, gave her sister a kiss on the forehead and left.

Oskar sat on the side of the bed and smiled shaking his head. 'So that's your Guardian Angel?'

Michele smiled, 'That's a nice way of putting it.'

Oskar shook his head. Did he really know anything that was happening? Yosef must think that he was an idiot.

***

Natasha walked along the cobblestone street. People were carrying on with their lives as if everything was normal. And it was, at least, it was the new normal. There were a few differences. People queued for some items that were hard to find. Younger girls and older women were resorting back to the dirndl. Whereas most of the men, what few of them there were, wore SS or Hitler youth uniforms.

She walked past the cinema. A matinee was about to start. Excited couples stood in line to get tickets to the latest film, Carl Peters. Natasha couldn't remember the last time she had been to the pictures. She didn't understand the appeal. If she were to pay to see something, she wanted to feel happy afterwards, not sickened. Her father had stopped trying to encourage her to go last year, just before *Jew Süss* came out. She felt her skin crawl just with the thought of it. He now left her to her books.

Goebbels was clever. He had visually saturated everything, movies, newspapers and posters, with lies to divide everyone. To make people think of others as less, as disposable. And people accepted this, slid into it, because they felt helpless. Because it is easier to follow than not. Previous movie posters still hung in the little display windows, making Jews into scary monsters and disabled people into hideous creatures. Natasha winched and then looked around hoping no one saw. Just stop it, black it out. Ignore it. There was so much. If she absorbed it, allowed it in day in day out, then she was scared it would paralyse her, devour her. And she would end up like those in line. Aryan clones that did and thought what they were told. Accepting it as truth. Natasha wiped the tear before it could fully form and then walked away as quickly as she dared.

***

Wilhelm stormed into the building. He headed straight for Friedrich's secretary. 'I asked you to do one thing today, just one thing, and that proved well out of your capability.'

She stood there shaking, 'I'm sorry. I couldn't stop him.'

'Where did he go?'

'He said,' she paused, 'out.'

'Out?'

'He did say that he wouldn't be back till late,' she added. 'He made me call Natasha and let her know.'

'Really?' he said, amazed at the fact that no one knew where Fredrick was.

'I'm sorry,' the secretary looked down at the floor.

Wilhelm sighed and looked at her. It wasn't her fault. No one could have kept him in the office without arousing suspicion.

'Fine,' Wilhelm stated. 'Is there anything that you can think of, that may help me find him?' He tried to seem as sincere as possible.

'Just before he left,' she said, 'he asked me to find out if Helene was accounted for, from the train.'

'And was she?'

'No,' she replied.

'Thank you,' Wilhelm said then turned and left.

He smiled, so Friedrich was going after Helene. That meant one less job for him. He walked out of headquarters. He had to get to Natasha.

***

Natasha was sitting in the parlour reading a book. She kept looking at the clock. It was quarter past five. They were late. If they were going to search the house and let her know about it, they could at least be punctual. She'd made sure there was no trace that Michele had been there. In fact, the basement had turned into a mini office. This did two things. It successfully hid the mattress and any idea that someone may have slept down there and gave Natasha a space to work in. After all, if Hess had a file on her, she needed a file on him. Over the past few years, she had copied information on the staff that worked at headquarters. Previously she had kept it in a few folders in her room. But now, she needed to use the basement space and make it look authentic. At first glance, people would see the general staff and not the main targets such as Hess, Göring, Himmler and Goebbels. She'd coded those files to disguise them even more. The bell rang. Finally, she thought as she put her book down and walked into the foyer.

She opened the door.

'Welcome to my house.'

Wilhelm smiled as a group of guards walked in. The guards looked at her with a bit if astonishment.

Natasha said, 'You must treat everyone as a suspect until proven otherwise.'

Wilhelm directed the still confused guards around the house. Natasha followed one group around. They cautiously looked around the rooms.

'I hope you're more thorough with other houses, look in the cupboards and in the attic.'

She went downstairs to Wilhelm.

'They're not very good at searching.'

'They are,' Wilhelm said, 'they're just petrified of you.'

A guard came up to Wilhelm and hovered, not wanting to interrupt the conversation.

'Can I talk to you please?' said the guard indicating for Wilhelm to walk with him. 'There's an office in the basement,' said the guard, 'I didn't know if you wanted to know or not.'

Wilhelm looked back at Natasha. She was smiling. He walked down the stairs to the basement. In one corner was a bookshelf filled with books on a range of different subjects ranging from languages to chemistry. Beside the bookshelf was a three-drawer filing cabinet. He walked over and tried to open it. It was locked. There was also a desk with some papers on it. Wilhelm flicked through them but saw nothing of importance.

'Natasha,' Wilhelm called, 'we need to look in the filing cabinet.'

The guard walked towards Natasha who had already walked into the room. She was leaning against the wall. The guard asked for the key.

'No.'

Wilhelm looked up.

'You can look in the filing cabinet Wilhelm,' she said, 'but no one else can. I can assure you I haven't hidden anyone in it though.'

She walked past the guard over to Wilhelm and handed him the key. Wilhelm opened the filing cabinet. He flicked through the files. They were personnel files from the office.

'Why are these not at headquarters?' he asked.

Natasha calmly answered, 'Because I don't have an office there.'

He looked straight into her eyes. It didn't make sense. He closed the drawer and locked it, then handed the key back to Natasha.

'Have we finished here?' Wilhelm said to the guards.

The guards all nodded with relief.

Wilhelm walked back towards Natasha and leaned close to her ear, 'May I join you for dinner around eight.'

'Yes,' she said.

He walked up the stairs and out the door. The rest of the guards scuttled out of the house. All was quiet. Natasha sat back in her chair started to read her book again. She tried to settle. Settle. She couldn't focus on the book. What did Wilhelm want? Dinner was that a date or was it do with work? Seriously, stop acting like a child. Focus. She turned the page and started again. It didn't work; banging the book shut, she looked out the window at nothing in particular.

***

Helene sat in the chair next to the fire. The soft material of the chair felt so gentle, so soft, so foreign.

Anneliese was pleading. 'You have to go now.'

'No.'

'That's the plan. There are people waiting for you,' Anneliese continued.

'No.'

'You stubborn mule,' Anneliese said. 'Now I know where Michele gets it from.'

'You can't be serious, Anneliese,' Helene questioned. 'I want to see Michele. I'm not going anywhere until I see her, and I am not going to Egypt at all. It's too far, too much needs doing here.'

'Fine, do whatever you want. You will anyway.' Anneliese stormed out of the room and slammed the door.

Helene was surprised by Anneliese's outburst. She looked out the window at the Swiss Alps and wondered how her daughters were.

***

Friedrich pulled up outside Anita's house and turned off the engine. This was a long shot, but it was worth a try. He got out and walked up to the door. It opened; Anita stood in the doorway.

'Can I come in?' Friedrich asked.

Anita looked over his shoulders at the black car with the little swastika flags floating in the breeze. She grimaced but nodded.

He walked into the house. She indicated to the front room.

'It's been a long time,' Friedrich commented.

He felt very awkward as he sat down in the chair.

'You're a long way from home Friedrich,' Anita responded. 'Why are you here?'

'Helene is free,' he replied.

Neither spoke for a moment.

'I was wondering if she was here?' he asked.

'No.'

'Where is she?'

'I don't know.'

'Anita.' Friedrich replied, 'I need to see her.'

'Why?' said Anita. 'So you can capture her again. So you can send her back to that prison, to the concentration camps you Nazis are so proud of. You're all animals, animals.'

She was shaking with anger; tears were rolling down her face. He could see the hatred in her eyes. Her fists clenched and for a moment, Friedrich did not know if she would hit him. He didn't care. He deserved it and then suddenly, he couldn't see. His eyes were so wet his vision was blurred. He cried hunched over like a child.

'I know. Don't you think I know,' he looked at her. 'You may not believe me, but I love her. The thought of her in a place like that eats at me. It tears me apart,' he continued, 'but I couldn't do anything about it.'

'You, expect pity, from me. There is always something you can do. Always.'

'You don't,' he said 'you don't understand. You grow into your life, trying to do what's best. And before you know it, you're not in control anymore, you're following a direction and it doesn't matter if it's right or wrong. It's just the way it is. I don't expect you to understand. I barely understand myself.'

'You don't know what it's like, to see someone that you love go through, what you've put my sister through.' said Anita. 'How dare you come here.'

'I woke up from a nightmare yesterday' Friedrich started, 'I watched one of my daughters try to kill the other. I saw two people that I helped to make. How they had turned out. The one that I had no influence on, was a caring creature. The one that I had influenced had no conscience. I can't let that happen again.'

They sat in silence for a while, watching each other.

'Are you staying this evening?' she asked.

Friedrich looked confused. 'I don't know.'

'If you decide to, there's a room made up upstairs. I'm going to bed, I've had enough for this evening,' she turned and left.

Friedrich looked at the clock; it was midnight. He was tired and confused. Where was Helene? He took a deep breath and walked up the stairs. Tonight, he would stay.

***

There was a knock at Jean's door. She opened it. Hans was standing in the doorway with a bottle of wine in one hand and some flowers in the other. Jean smiled.

'I thought maybe we could stay in this evening,' he said.

'That's a bit presumptuous,' she replied.

He grabbed her around the waist and gave her a kiss. She kissed back, she wasn't really interested, but she was learning a lot by seeing him. She remembered what Michele had said about emotional involvement. No problem. He closed the door behind him and put down the bottle of wine and flowers on the table.

'Oh, I've missed you,' he said and led her to the bedroom.

Talking to Hans wasn't very informative. Jean found out most information when he was asleep. It's surprising how much information you can get if you talk to someone's subconscious at the right moment. She kept notes about things he mentioned. They were mostly around his work with the press, and in fact he oversaw a press division. A lot higher up the ranks than Jean had imagined. They were aware that their newspapers would be analysed by the enemy, so they were not just aiming propaganda at the German public but also the British, Americans and Russians to alienate them from each other. They were trying different strategies for this, while also trying to make any losses that Germany had, into strategic wins. These nightly accounts she sent down to Munich at the end of each week. She just hoped they were helpful.

Her main concern was Michele. Where was her safety blanket? She knew she'd been captured. Had she escaped? This is what made her nervous, not knowing, no, it wasn't, it was not having Michele, she was the protector. Where was she?

***

Natasha wasn't much of a cook. She never had been. After very long conversations on the phone to Hilde she managed to barely scrape through enough food for two. The doorbell rang and she opened the door. Wilhelm was there with a bottle of wine.

'Thank you,' she said and indicated for him to come in.

He wasn't wearing his uniform. Natasha looked at him and thought she'd never seen him dressed in civilian clothing before. Surprisingly, he looked quite dapper.

'I hope dinner is palatable,' she said, 'I'm not much of a cook.'

He laughed. 'There's a restaurant down the road. I never really took you as a home body.'

They walked into the parlour. Natasha indicated for Wilhelm to sit down.

'Let me get some glasses,' she said and disappeared into the kitchen.

'Do you have a corkscrew?' he asked.

She walked into the kitchen feeling a little bit warm; her heart was racing as well. Natasha got two glasses out of the cupboard and then grabbed the corkscrew. She started to carry it to the bench the glasses were on. It slipped out of her hand. She picked it up. This was stupid she thought, she was acting like a schoolgirl. Natasha felt nervous. She took a deep breath and looked at the bench. She'd known Wilhelm for many years, and she'd never felt like this around him. It had hit her unexpectedly. She tried to rationalise her thoughts. It was an emotional time. Her mother was free and so was Michele. Yet she still was finding it hard to keep her guard up. She was angry with herself; this was stupid. She picked up the glasses and corkscrew and walked back into the parlour.

Wilhelm was sitting relaxed on the lounge. He looked up at her with a lovely smile. Natasha could feel herself beginning to thaw.

'Here we are,' she put the glasses on the table and gave him the corkscrew. 'I'll leave that to you.' She didn't trust herself, but she wasn't going to admit it.

He opened the bottle and poured some wine into the glasses.

'How's your arm?' he asked gently lifting it to look at the bandage.

Natasha felt her skin tingle and it made her blush. 'Fine.' She looked away before he noticed. 'Are you hungry?'

'Can I make a toast?' he asked.

'Yes,' replied Natasha.

He raised his glass, 'To a job well done and everyone's safety.'

'What do you mean?' Natasha acted confused.

He put down his glass, grabbed Natasha's glass, and put it down. Natasha followed the movements of his hands until they stopped by cupping hers.

'Hess has always been one step ahead of me, and it took a while to understand, why I should tell you how we were going to do the searches. Now I understand. Can we stop pretending,' Wilhelm said, 'you're the leak, you're the one that let people know about the execution.'

Natasha went to pull away. 'Me? I don't know what you mean. What are you talking about?'

'Natasha it's okay,' Wilhelm reassured. 'I know, we know.'

'We know?'

He brushed a lock of hair from her face and gently brushed her cheek. She could feel herself naturally tilt her face towards his hand. She stopped and clenched her jaw. His hand dropped and he sat back. 'Hess and I.'

Natasha felt her stomach drop.

Wilhelm said, 'Believe me, it's alright. If it wasn't, you would be at headquarters now, in an interrogation room. Or dead.'

Natasha relaxed; he was right. But it did make her wonder why she wasn't and what plans Hess had for her and Michele.

They soon moved into the dining room to have dinner.

'If you don't like it, you don't have to eat it,' she said.

'It's actually quite nice,' Wilhelm replied. 'I must confess I did not have high expectations.'

Natasha laughed, 'Thank you, I think.'

'Can I ask a question?'

Natasha nodded, took another bite of dinner, and then sipped her wine.

'Why were you asking about ME110s?'

'I asked about a lot of planes,' she replied taking a sip of wine.

'Yes but, that was the one you were very specific about,' he pressed. 'Why are you interested in it?'

'I'm not,' Natasha looked at him. 'Hess is.'

'How do you know?' he looked surprised.

'He's the one who started my interest in it,' she continued.

'It's in one of his files.'

Confused Wilhelm asked, 'How do you know that?'

'I can't reveal my sources,' she said. 'Anyway, when you find out why he's interested in it, can you let me know?'

Wilhelm paused.

'Maybe,' he smiled. 'Hess would like a meeting with you.'

'Tomorrow?'

'No.' Wilhelm responded. 'He's away for the next two days.'

'Just let me know when,' she smiled.

Interesting Natasha thought. They idly chatted for the rest of the dinner. Natasha cleared the table and Wilhelm moved back into the parlour.

'Would you like another drink?' she called out from the kitchen. 'The wine is finished.'

'What do you have?' he asked.

'Gin, brandy, whisky or a beer?' she replied.

'Whisky please.' Wilhelm answered as he relaxed back into the lounge. She brought him one and sat next to him.

He turned and looked at her. 'Do you know, when you are not acting, you look beautiful,' he smiled.

She could feel his arm so close to her shoulder, but not quite touching.

He was a little drunk. Natasha blushed again.

'Thank you.'

He was making her feel like a schoolgirl again.

'You remind me so much of her right now.'

Slap, it felt like a door had just slammed in her face. Natasha couldn't believe what she was hearing. She froze.

'How is she?' he asked. 'I kept thinking about her, since I first met her in Berlin.'

Natasha wasn't really listening; she was trying to fight back the tears. Natasha had fallen into this false feeling that he liked her, but it wasn't her at all. It was Michele. There was a quick stab of jealousy. She wouldn't let him see her reaction.

'She introduced herself as Margot though,' he continued, 'not Michele.'

He sipped his drink. 'How is she, is she well?'

At least he had saved her from making a fool of herself. What had she been thinking? She had worked so hard to make people not like her. To protect her from the world, isolate herself. What did she expect?

'She's fine,' Natasha was back. 'When she's fully recovered, I'll try and organise a meeting if you like.'

'That'll be nice.'

Natasha changed the subject, 'Hess seems to be travelling quite a bit. I do feel sorry for his family, down here all alone.'

'Oh,' Wilhelm replied, 'they're not, they're up in Berlin, not down here.'

How convenient Natasha thought. The conversation went from subject to subject and eventually Wilhelm left. Natasha sat on the lounge, cuddling a cushion feeling all alone, again.

CHAPTER 10

Helene was walking to her bedroom when she noticed a light shining under a door. She lightly knocked and pushed it open. Peering inside she saw someone packing a bag.

'Excuse me,' she said.

The man turned around. She didn't recognise him at first and looked more closely, he was so familiar.

'It's me,' he said, 'it's Henri.'

No, it couldn't be. He was a teenager with baby fat, not a muscular grown man.

'Oh,' she said grabbing his chin and inspecting the now chiselled cheeks, 'of course. Oh my, you've changed a bit since I last saw you. Look at you.'

He laughed.

'I didn't even know that you were here,' she continued.

'It's just a stopover, I've just come from Spain and am on my way to Austria, this morning,' he replied.

Helene looked confused. Henri started to tell her about some of the things that the resistance had accomplished since she left. 'You must be very proud of Michele, she's a great leader. I mean she was while you are away.' He said, realising who he was talking to.

Helene smiled, 'you're right the resistance is in very capable hands, it's moved on much further than I could've taken it.'

'Oh, I'm sure that's not true,' said Henri. 'Anyway, it's good to see you, Helene. We've all missed you.'

Helene smiled and walked out of the room. She was tired and it was time for her to go to sleep. There were far too many things happening here for her to leave for Egypt. The sooner she talked to Michele the better.

***

Clang. Metal on metal sliding. It was a bolt. The door opened slowly. Hess could feel the cold, the blanket didn't shield him.

As the silhouette against the corridors light walked forward, its Russian uniform takes form. The guard puts a tray on Hess's table and then walks back closing the door behind him. Hess struggles out of the bed; everything is taking longer and by the time he reaches the door he can hear the metal slide along. Enclosing him in his gaol. He tries to open the door, to peer out the little peep hole. But nothing. Now there is no light. His energy is draining, is seeping away and he slides to the floor. 'Noooo.'

Hess sat up and gasped. He looked around. Where was he? His mind took a few moments to adjust. He was in his apartment in Berlin. The cool breeze came through the window, making the net curtain dance in the moonlight.

But Hess was still gasping for air, steadying himself. His forehead was clammy and his shirt wet.

He didn't dream much. But lately when he did, half his dreams would be a nightmare like this. Being held prisoner by Russians. And the other, well the other was better. His dreams were trying to guide him, to help him. If he didn't do this, if things continued as they were, he would become a prisoner. Worse a Russian prisoner. He lay back down but couldn't get back to sleep.

**

Natasha closed the door. She'd only had a couple of glasses of wine. As she started to clean up, a tear ran down her face. Natasha felt so lonely, even more than she had before. Wilhelm had been her knight in shining armour. Just for a moment, there was a possibility. But it was gone. It had never really been. Being a loner was what gave her strength, right? The thought just made her cry.

She needed to change her focus. Natasha looked at some of the maps. Hess's house was about twenty minutes from hers. Natasha went upstairs and changed into her black trousers, a blouse and jacket. She took a small bag, put paper, pens and tools in it, and grabbed a black hat.

It wasn't long before Natasha was outside Hess's house. She parked just out of sight. Flicking her hair up under her hat, she looked at the house. It was behind a large fence, half bricked and half cast-iron. Natasha was just about to scale the fence when she saw a flashlight coming around the side of the house. Great. Security. She ducked behind the bricks, barely peeking over them. Waiting another twenty minutes she discovered the patrol patterns. She had a ten-minute window between each sweep of the house. The security guard walked out of view. Natasha climbed the bricks and looked at the fence's iron spikes on top. How the hell, am I going to do this? Where's a foothold? She took a deep breath and clenched her stomach muscles to pull herself up. Her arm started to twitch. She had only been grazed by the shot, but it still hurt. Why do I do this to myself? Pulling herself up, she managed to slide a knee in between the spikes. Exhale. Another deep breath. Natasha swung her foot up and hoped she wouldn't impale herself. When she was on top, she dropped to the ground. A light was coming around the side of the house; she lay flat on the ground. The guard passed, then she ran to some bushes by the house and ducked behind them. The guard walked past her, and before he had turned the corner of the house, she made her way to the door. Taking off her bag, she grabbed some tools and started to pick the lock. She was concentrating so much on the lock she forgot the time. Out of the corner of her eye, she saw the light come around the building. She looked around for shelter. There was no time to hide. She dropped to the ground and lay perfectly still. Don't breathe, quiet, keep walking, go on, keep walking. The guard ambled by not noticing anything. She got up and finished picking the lock. Natasha opened the door and slipped inside.

The entrance foyer was almost empty except from an antique oak sideboard with a bronze female figurine art deco oil lamp. To the side of the door was an empty coat rack. The door was open to the front room, but Natasha was looking for a study. There was bound to be one, in a house like this. The stairs were functional as opposed to grandiose, and a simple polished wooden banister complimented the décor. Sophisticated, but not pretentious. She walked upstairs and followed the corridor, which had several dark panelled doors along it. Each one she gently opened and peered into the room, before closing and going on to the next.

One was a little boy's room. It had model aeroplanes in it. Was that a ME110 sitting on the windowsill? What was it about that plane?

She opened a door near the end of the corridor, which led to the master bedroom. It was dark. The heavy flower-patterned drapes were not fully drawn, and the dark green rope tiebacks were hanging from their hooks. Natasha looked around the room for a safe or a locked drawer. She opened the wardrobe and had a look at the top shelf. It seemed normal. Looking at the bottom, she saw a few old boxes. Natasha opened one. She found photographs of the Olympics and a group of men that she didn't recognise. One photograph caught her attention; it had Hess and a man that had been in a few of the photographs. She put it in her bag and replaced the box. Closing the wardrobe, she left the room.

Natasha continued down the corridor to the end room. She opened the door. Dark oak bookshelves lined three walls and a large desk faced the window. Finally, she thought as she walked towards the desk. The desk was clear and had no drawers. She looked around the room, no filing cabinet. Where would his information be, where would it be stored? Berlin? She continued to look around the room. Any one of these books could have something hidden in them.

There were some boxes on top of one of the shelves. Natasha walked over to them, but even on her toes, they were out of reach. She looked around for something to stand on. Perfect, there was a piano seat in the corner. Her hands tested to see how sturdy it was, and the seat wiggled a little. She bent down to have a look at it. Just below the cushioned seat was a very small keyhole. Natasha picked the lock and opened the top of the seat. Inside were three files, labelled Natasha, Michele and Wilhelm. Natasha's heart began to race; he was watching everyone, including his friends. She picked up her file; it was heavy. It started from when she was young and continued through to just before Michele's capture. It detailed all the people that Natasha had 'interrogated' and what ones had been relocated. It was not exact, but very close. She took the list of resistance contacts from the file and then closed it.

Natasha opened Michele's file, it felt lighter; maybe it was her imagination. The file covered the same period, but it did not include the new division of the resistance. There was a note mentioning a possible move for Michele, from Natasha's town address to Jean's address. He had known where Michele was going before they had, and then had organised the searches accordingly. He manoeuvred them to Jean's apartment. What did he want? Damn you Hess. She quickly grabbed all the addresses from Michele's file.

It would be dawn soon. She looked at the file labelled Wilhelm, that file would have to wait. She closed and locked the stool, then walked downstairs to the door. Looking out the keyhole, she waited until the guard had passed. Natasha opened the door, double-checking to see that it was clear. She had to work faster this time the shadows were decreasing. She quickly managed to lock the door and then hid in the bushes. The guard passed her and rounded the house. She got out of the bushes, sprinted towards the fence, and dived behind a tree just as the next guard rounded the corner. The fence was going to be a problem. She needed some form of cover. There were some bushes further down. She would just have to risk it. Waiting until he had walked past, she moved to the bushes and tried to climb over there. She was halfway up as the guard rounded the corner. He didn't seem to notice, but she froze till he had passed before she jumped down the other side. It was time to get home.

Natasha snuck into the house; she did not want to wake her father. She walked upstairs and crept past his bedroom. She paused. His door was open. He wasn't there. She walked back downstairs and searched around the house. There was no sign of him. She walked back up to her room. Confused, she had a wash and then climbed into bed. Maybe he had left early for the office. Her head hit the pillow and she was asleep.

**

It was still dark when they left the house. They took Henri to the outskirts of the wood. He turned on his flashlight and started walking through the forest. It wasn't a long way to go, but it would take him about an hour. The light was just starting to creep over the horizon as Henri made it through the last trees and ran across the field to the house. The group had decided it would be too risky to drive to the house and approaching from the forest at the back of the property provided more cover. The back door was unlocked as planned and he went inside. He felt tired, so he headed straight up to the room that Anita had put him in last time. He opened the door and walked in. Henri took a step towards the bed and noticed a movement.

**

A noise woke Friedrich. His eyes adjusted to the light and managed to focus. There was a figure standing just inside the doorway, and it wasn't Anita. Both froze for a moment. Friedrich sat up and reached for his gun. Henri dropped his bag and pulled out his gun. Both guns were poised towards the other's head.

Anita woke up to hear a thud. She blinked a couple of times and then jumped out of bed. Friedrich had distracted her so much that she'd forgotten about Henri. She grabbed her dressing gown and ran to the room.

'Stop.'

Friedrich and Henri were looking straight into each other's eyes; they had not flinched. Anita stepped between them. Now they couldn't shoot each other. They relaxed their guns.

Anita ordered. 'Put them away.'

They placed them in their bags.

Anita picked up the bags. 'Downstairs now.'

136

Henri walked into the parlour first.

'How could you do this?' he asked. 'Michele trusts you.'

'I'm sorry, I didn't exactly invite him over,' Anita replied angrily.

'Why is he here?' Henri asked.

'He wants to know–?' Anita paused as Friedrich walked in the door.

Friedrich sat down. This wasn't going to plan, he might have got information from her, but not now there was support. Her guest had training; the quick reaction he showed in getting the gun was something that he'd only seen in the Special Forces. He looked at him. He was relatively nondescript, which would be perfect for missions. Two possibilities went through Friedrich's mind.

'Who do you work for?' Friedrich asked.

'The Third Reich, and you?' Henri replied.

Friedrich ignored the question. 'What department?'

Henri wanted to look at Anita for support but knew that as soon as he flinched it would all be over.

'The Air Force, in Berlin,' he answered.

'You're a long way from home,' Friedrich smiled. 'How's Berlin these days?'

'Good,' Henri answered, 'you know the same as normal. Sorry about almost shooting you.'

'Don't worry,' Friedrich laughed, 'I'm sorry about almost shooting you.'

He offered his hand for a handshake. Henri shook it.

'I'm going soon,' Friedrich replied, 'I didn't know it was your room.'

Anita was looking nervous.

'Does anyone want a drink?' she asked.

Henri said, 'I'd love a drink thank you.'

'I'd love a drink too,' Friedrich replied.

They both sat down in chairs opposite each other.

Friedrich thought for a moment. 'You guys are always busy up there?'

'Yes, we definitely are.'

'Anything in particular?'

'Not much really, a lot of training.'

'What would you be training for?'

'I don't really know, not privy to all the information.'

Henri desperately wanted to change the subject and tried to think of something else.

Friedrich looked at him, he was distracted so he casually asked, 'By the way how's Helene?'

Henri was trying to think of what subjects he could talk about and started to reply without even thinking about what he was saying.

'Yeah, she's fine, she…'

He stopped as he focused on what his mouth was saying. He looked up at Friedrich, who was looking straight at him. Anita froze in the doorway with the drinks. Henri went white, he felt sick. He'd been interrogated before and hadn't broken. But now, he'd confessed with no pressure.

'Where is she?' Friedrich asked as he got up and crossed the room.

'I don't know,' Henri replied.

'I think you are lying.'

'Friedrich,' Anita yelled. 'Leave him alone.'

'Friedrich,' Henri repeated. 'You're Michele's father? Why do you want to know? What are you doing here?'

'Is a man not allowed to see his wife?' Friedrich asked.

'You haven't wanted to before,' Henri yelled back. 'In fact, weren't you responsible for keeping her in there? You helped keep her in that prison.'

'It was a concentration camp,' Friedrich corrected him, he was white. 'It's worse than a prison.'

Friedrich looked out the window trying to compose himself. Then he looked back at him. 'Look I don't care where you've been, what you're doing or where you're going,' Friedrich said, 'I want to see my wife, I want to make sure she's okay, and I want to tell her how sorry I am.'

His eyes started to well up and he turned away again.

Stunned Henri turned and indicated for Anita to follow him. He walked out into the kitchen area.

'Don't tell him where she is,' Henri whispered. Friedrich quietly moved close to the door to listen to the conversation.

'I haven't said anything,' Anita replied. 'You're the one with the big mouth.'

'I need my bag,' said Henri

'Why'

'He knows too much. My gun.'

'No,' Anita looked horrified. 'I know my sister, and she will never forgive you for killing him. Only she or the girls get to decide his fate.'

'But he could destroy everything.'

'No.'

Henri's cheeks went red. 'I'm going back then; I need to talk to Helene about this.'

Anita nodded, 'I'll keep him busy here.'

Friedrich sat down. Henri walked up the stairs, he returned within a couple of minutes.

'I need some fresh air,' he said to everyone and walked out the door.

Friedrich walked over to Anita. 'I just want you to know that I'm sorry. I'm sorry for everything.'

Anita turned away 'I don't kno—'

Anita felt a pinch in her neck, making her wince in pain and then she collapsed.

***

Natasha slept solidly for three hours, and then woke up. She couldn't go back to sleep. She looked at the papers that she'd taken the previous night. Hess knew where Michele was. He knew everything, but why, to what purpose? Why was he so interested in Natasha and Michele and why had he not arrested them? And how did he know? Was there a leak in the group, was there a few? She couldn't make any sense of it. Natasha quickly had a shower and changed into some civilian clothing. She packed her bag with some clothes for Michele and headed out the door. It was time to move.

***

The phone rang disturbing Wilhelm's sleep. He opened his eyes and squinted. His head pounded and he grabbed it with one of his hands. Slowly he got up and walked over to it.

He picked it up and said 'What?'

'Good afternoon Wilhelm,' Hess said down the phone. 'My, aren't we in a happy mood?'

'What time is it?' croaked Wilhelm.

'It is one o'clock in the afternoon,' Hess answered. 'Why are you not at work?'

'I'm not feeling well today.' His stomach was feeling delicate to say the least.

'How did yesterday go?' Hess asked ignoring the last comment.

'We found nothing,' Wilhelm said.

'Fine,' Hess said. 'How are Natasha and Friedrich?'

'Natasha may be feeling a little unwell today,' Wilhelm answered, 'and Friedrich is missing.'

'He's missing?' Hess said. 'What do you mean? He isn't at work or…?'

'No,' Wilhelm said, 'he's not at work, he's not at home, and no one knows where he is. I think he has gone looking for Helene.'

'Hmm. Interesting. I need you to do me a favour,' Hess changed the subject, 'there is a parcel I need you to pick up. If you could deliver it to my house and put it in the basement, I'd be grateful.'

'Is it heavy?' Wilhelm asked, there was no way that he could carry much today.

Hess laughed.

'No, but you need to pick it up in the next couple of hours. You must get into the apartment, and you may have to break in to get it.'

'What does it look like?' asked Wilhelm.

'You'll recognise it.'

Wilhelm wrote down the address. Now he had become Hess's deliveryman. That wasn't in his job description.

***

Michele opened the door to Natasha.

'Do you think it's wise visiting this soon?' Michele said.

'You have to move,' Natasha replied.

Shocked she let Natasha in and shook her head.

'I think it's best to lie low, which means not moving every day,' Michele said.

Natasha sat down. She didn't need to explain herself. Her sister was a clever girl. She handed Michele the pieces of paper.

'You need to tell me what addresses are not on these pieces of paper.'

Michele fell into the chair and flicked through the pages, 'there are no others. This is all the resistance addresses.'

Natasha sat back in the chair and then lent forward and put her head in her hands. What was she going to do?

'Where did you get this from?' Michele said, standing up. 'Where?'

'Hess's house,' Natasha said, 'he can't know everything; he can't, how many years of work has it taken. Everything is in his little file. Everything.'

'We have to warn them all,' Michele said.

'No,' Natasha replied, 'if he wanted to destroy the network, it would have been done already.'

'The only places that are not on this list are the new intelligence network apartments,' Michele volunteered.

'I don't want to jeopardise the network,' Natasha said, 'but we have to go, now.'

'Why?' Michele said. 'I could be at any one of these residences. They don't know.'

'Michele, Jean's flat is named as your next stop after my house,' Natasha said. Michele was dazed, how could this possibly happen?

'Let's go,' Natasha said. They packed up and were about to go.

'One minute,' Natasha said grabbing the clothing Michele had worn when she'd escaped. Folding them, she put them on the table.

Michele smiled, 'It's just like chess.'

Natasha smiled back, 'And now he knows we're playing.'

She closed the door but left it unlocked.

***

Henri walked through the door. He was drained. He just walked straight past Anneliese to sit down.

'What are you doing here?' she asked. 'What's wrong?'

Helene walked into the room, 'Can I get you a drink?'

Henri nodded, 'Yes, a cold drink would be lovely.'

Helene went to the kitchen but stopped. Anneliese looked at her and then followed her eyeline. Helene saw a figure walking towards the house. She couldn't move, her feet felt so heavy and yet her mind was trying to get her to move. The figure stopped and looked straight at her. Everything paused. She'd never forgotten that face. His features never seemed to age. He started to move again, slightly jogging. Helene didn't know how she felt. There was anger, resentment, and frustration, all sorts of feelings.

Anneliese came over to Helene. 'Quick come out the front.'

'It's too late.'

'But you can't trust him,' Anneliese said.

'He didn't come here to kill me, it's not the way he would do it.'

Friedrich walked to the door.

He looked at Helene. 'You look beautiful.' His eyes welled up and he took a step forward but held back. 'Can I walk with you?' he asked.

Helene nodded. They walked out of the door towards the wood.

'I know this is stupid,' replied Friedrich, 'but I'm sorry.'

Helene had her face set; she kept walking.

'Nothing I can ever say is going to be enough. I know,' he stated, 'but I'm so sorry.'

Helene didn't say anything. Friedrich turned to go.

'I can't say that I spent a lot of time thinking about you Friedrich,' she said. 'Sometimes I did, but not always. I was more concerned about my children. I'd given up on you a long time ago. You died to me.'

He looked at her; she was unemotional.

'What do you want?' she asked.

'To make sure you're alright,' he said.

'Is that it?' she asked. 'I'm fine.'

She turned to leave.

'I've made so many mistakes, I know, and if I could turn back time. I would. But I can't,' he said. 'I guess I wanted to know if I could help or if I could change anything.'

She looked at him; she hated and loved this man at the same time. No matter how much she tried to deny it. How could she? She did not know what to do, so she walked back to the house. She needed time to think. Friedrich sat down in the field.

She turned around, 'It's cold out here, come inside, but leave me alone.'

He silently followed her in.

***

Anita tried to open her eyes. Blurry, everything was blurry. The floor came into focus and slowly her vision extended to the ceiling. Her head was thumping, and she felt like she was going to vomit. She wasn't the adventurous type. That was her sister's side of the family. As she rolled over, she recognised her room. Slowly she tried to rise to a sitting position. Dizzy, dizzy. The room was moving. She slowly got off the bed and went to the door. She had to warn her sister. She turned the handle; the door wouldn't open. She tried again, pulling at the door. But it would not budge. It was locked. She sat on the bed and looked at the window. She was going to have to climb out the window. She waited until her head stopped spinning. Taking a deep breath, she walked towards the window and opened it. The room was on the second floor and although there was a little ledge, she was not sure how she was going to get down to the ground. Anita climbed on the dresser and opened the window. She swung her leg out the window. Straddling the window frame, she looked for somewhere to put her foot.

'Fraulein what are you doing?' called a voice.

Anita looked around and there below her was the maid.

'Can you unlock the door please?' Anita called down.

She climbed back inside and waited for the door to open. The maid was confused when she unlocked the door but did not question anything as Anita raced down the stairs to the phone in the foyer.

'Anneliese, Friedrich is on his way, he's following Henri.'

'He's here,' Anneliese replied.

'I'm sorry,' Anita said, 'I was a little locked up down here.'

Anneliese smiled, 'I heard, I'm glad you're not hurt. I was going to come over and see if you needed help.'

'I'm fine, of course,' Anita said quickly.

Anita hung up the phone. That was quite enough excitement for one day. No, actually for a week or so at least.

CHAPTER 11

'Where are we going?' Michele asked Natasha.

'Well, as you have no bright ideas, I thought we would go looking in the countryside.'

They drove out of the city. Michele started looking at different things out the window. 'This looks so familiar.'

Natasha smiled. They kept on driving past a few houses and then down a small road that ended by a stream.

'Well,' Michele said, 'now I'm really confused, me. Am I staying in the woods? I don't have a tent.'

'We're walking,' Natasha said.

She grabbed a bag of Michele's clothing out of the trunk of the car.

'Follow me,' she said.

Michele followed behind and they walked along the stream for about five minutes and then through a small, wooded area. They came across an old, abandoned house. The back door was unlocked, and it creaked open. The house had not been lived for a very long time. Rot had started in several different places.

'Do you remember it yet?' Natasha asked.

Michele shook her head. Natasha cleared a path through the cobwebs to the front of the house. Most of the valuable things were gone. But there was still some furniture. Rats scuttled around the floor, it looked like the wildlife had taken over. They walked up the stairs and into one of the rooms that had been a bedroom.

'I would stay up here,' suggested Natasha. 'There's a good view and access to the attic as well.'

Michele sat on a chair, 'I would feel more at ease living in Hitler's basement. You know how I hate creepy crawlies.'

'You always exaggerate,' Natasha replied. 'Do you know where you are yet?'

Natasha walked over to the corner and pushed back some wood. Brushing the dust from the wall revealed a little drawing. Natasha beckoned Michele over. 'You know you were a naughty child.'

Michele looked at the little drawing and started laughing. 'It was a present for Anneliese. I worked a long time on it for her. You're clever, I would never have thought of Anneliese's old house,' she said to Natasha, nodding her approval.

'Well let's hope Hess doesn't.'

***

Wilhelm looked at the address and then checked it with the one on the piece of paper. It was the same building. He entered, walked up the stairs, and looked at the numbers on the doors. He was looking for Number 8. Wilhelm was confused. What was so important about this parcel. Why me? Really why me? Anyone could pick it up. He got to the door. Knocking he called out. No one answered. He turned the handle and it opened. Edging slowly through the door, he pulled out his gun just in case. He couldn't see anyone. Quietly he closed the door. The apartment itself was very small. He slipped into each room, with his gun barrel pushing the doors open. There was no one there. He walked back into the kitchen. There had been nothing anywhere. In the kitchen he found a pile of clothes on the table. Surely this wasn't what Hess had wanted. He walked over to the clothes and picked them up. They looked very familiar. He rolled his eyes and smiled. They were the clothes that Michele had worn when she escaped. What was Hess up to? It wasn't a small parcel he'd wanted. It was Michele, but someone had moved her first. He put the clothes in his bag and walked out of the apartment. He needed to talk to Hess.

***

Jean was typing a copy of the minutes from the previous day's meeting. Hess walked in and looked at the secretary.

Jean looked up, 'Sir your meeting isn't for another half hour.'

'I know,' Hess answered. 'Are the three of them in there?'

'Yes,' she said.

'How long have they been in there for?'

She finished typing and put it on the pile beside the typewriter. 'They've been in for over an hour,' she replied, 'and I don't know what they are talking about.'

Hess smiled; she was a clever secretary.

'Not even a hint of an idea?' he pushed.

'I should think it's about trying to stop another crucifying like the other day,' she said. 'But I will deny saying that.'

'I try my best.'

He paused for a moment and then looked back at her. 'So how long have you worked here for?'

'Very inquisitive, aren't you?' said Jean, 'Just over a month.'

'Oh, that will be why I haven't seen you much before,' he said.

Jean nodded, 'Do you know what happened to the last secretary?'

'I think she was shot,' he said casually. 'She wasn't as clever as you are though.'

Jean looked at Hess a little confused and looked around the rest of the team for any responses. They were all busy doing their tasks.

The meeting started the same as the last. It soon changed to the previous subject of extermination camps.

'I think very valid points were brought up the other day by Herr Hess,' Goebbels started.

Bormann interrupted, 'I had a look at some of the studies that have just been completed, and unemployment appears to be slowly creeping up.'

Goebbels continued, 'It would be good for some German people to do these jobs to employ them. We could help society and fulfil our mandate at the same time.'

'I think we need to push ahead with the termination of this vermin from our country. They are still influencing people and they are not popular with society,' Himmler added.

Hitler thought for a little while. Jean looked around the room. Hess was relaxed and didn't seem concerned. In fact, he did absolutely nothing at all, except smile. This seemed to infuriate Goebbels, who beforehand had seemed quietly confident.

'It's always a concern when unemployment starts to rise,' Hitler started. 'It is after all one of the important things that has made this government work.' He pondered for a moment, 'Hess, what do you think?'

Hess looked at Goebbels as he leaned into Hitler and said something to him. Smart thought Jean, very smart.

'That's a very good point,' nodded Hitler. 'Don't worry about unemployment gentlemen. I have another job for the German people.'

Goebbels leaned forward. 'And what's that?'

'Don't worry about it,' Hitler said. 'What I need you to concentrate on is making the German public accept the Jewish as work people. Slaves, for the lack of a better word.'

'Well,' said Hess, 'as always, it's been a pleasure. I do look forward to our next meeting.'

Hitler and Hess got up and left the room. Goebbels was fuming; he had just had his meeting dismissed for him. This had not gone to his plan at all. Jean looked down to conceal her smile. Hess was good; he was really good; no wonder he was Hitler's confidant.

***

Natasha got home. She would go back tomorrow with more food. No one would trace her to the abandoned house. At least not until Hess got back. That meant she had another twenty-four hours. She wanted to get back to Hess's house and find out more information.

She walked around the house.

'Father,' she yelled.

There was no reply. She walked up to his room. It was empty. She wanted to check in with him and make sure he was okay. It had been a tough couple of days for him and he was starting to act strangely. Sometimes she wished she could let him know everything, but she couldn't trust him. She had left him for long enough though. She decided to go to the headquarters to talk to him.

***

'This is too much for me to work through,' Helene said. 'I can't think.'

Friedrich just looked at her.

'I can't make it go back to the way it used to be just like that,' she said. 'I don't know what you expected really.'

'I don't know either,' he said. 'I think I should go.'

'Maybe you should.'

He looked at her, 'I wish the three of us could just run away to England and start all over again. But I know it's not possible.'

'The three of us?'

'You, Michele and me,' he said.

'What about Natasha?' Helene asked.

'She's been in the Nazi mindset for too long,' he replied. 'It wouldn't work.'

'She's had less time in it than you.'

'I know but it's different.' Friedrich seemed forlorn. 'It's different for her, it's too late.'

'You're asking for another chance Friedrich,' Helene said. 'Don't be so hypocritical, you need to see if you could give her one.'

Friedrich looked at her, she didn't understand. She didn't know what Natasha was capable of.

'It was good to see you,' he said. 'Remember above all, I do love you, Helene.'

He turned and walked out the door.

Anneliese walked over to Helene. 'I don't trust him, and I don't think I ever will.'

Helene looked at her, 'The person you just saw is the old Friedrich; I just don't know how long he'll be around for.'

'Or what exactly he wants,' Henri said.

They all stared out the window as his silhouette disappeared into the woods.

***

Natasha walked into headquarters to her father's office but found it empty. Confused she entered the secretary's office.

'Where's my father?'

'He's not here,' the secretary answered.

'Really,' Natasha said, 'I didn't notice. Where is he?'

'I don't know,' the secretary said. 'I haven't seen him since yesterday. People are continually asking where he is. And I don't know.'

She pushed past a stunned Natasha, who paused before returning to her father's office. She had a look around; there wasn't anything she could see that was out of the ordinary. Father, what are you doing?

***

Wilhelm walked into the foyer, towards the corridor. Friedrich's secretary stormed past him. He walked towards Hess's office. Inside he used the phone and called Hess's house in Berlin.

'Hello,' Hess said.

'Um I don't know how to say this,' Wilhelm started, 'but when I got to the apartment for the parcel, there was only a pile of clothes there.'

'What?' Hess yelled. 'Watch the apartment.'

'I don't think there's much of a reason to actually.'

There was a pause.

'Are you questioning my orders?'

'Yes,' Wilhelm replied. 'The clothes were folded and put on top of the table. The flat is immaculate and has nothing in it and the door was unlocked. They're not coming back.'

'I'm going to come back on the next train,' Hess said. 'I should be there by ten.'

Wilhelm put down the phone. Hess, this is what it feels like when you don't know what's happening. It was nice to know that even Hess couldn't control everything, or everyone, all the time.

CHAPTER 12

Jean poured another drink.

'Hans?'

He walked in with two plates. 'Yes?'

'What happened to Goebbels last secretary?'

'Why do you ask?' Hans put her plate in front of her and then sat opposite and started to eat.

'Hess said she was shot.'

'What were you talking about?' he asked her.

'Filing.'

He laughed. 'She wasn't shot due to filing.'

'She was killed?' she said, 'I thought he was joking, it's just I never thought being a secretary was a hazardous job. But if she was killed, maybe I should look for another job.'

He reached over and grabbed her hand, 'You have nothing to worry about. She was a spy for the resistance. She got caught handing over information.'

'Oh,' said Jean taking a deep breath, 'that's a relief. I'm really not that exciting.'

Concentrate, concentrate, try and look relieved. Don't look scared, act normal. Just normal, that's right, normal.

'Oh, but dear,' Hans said, 'I think you're very exciting.'

She smiled but she really wasn't in the mood tonight. Quick note: be extra careful, they already got rid of one spy. You never know who is watching.

***

Natasha parked in the same place. It was easier this time she knew the routine. She was still nervous about the fence but was soon back in the library, but she was in a lot faster than last time. She had left early tonight so that she could have more time.

She was curious about Wilhelm's file, so started there.

She quickly flicked through it, nothing jumped out. She started from the beginning and read each document. First there were school records. They were impressive; he had excelled at school especially in the sciences and mathematics. She carried on looking through the school and university reports, then through to his career. His birth certificate was in the file, along with his parent's marriage certificate, and a family tree. Wilhelm's father had died a few years ago. Natasha then progressed to his mother's side. Wilhelm's mother was Ilse Hess's sister. Hess was Wilhelm's uncle. Now it all made sense. Hess had obviously taken Wilhelm under his wing when his father had died.

Natasha continued looking though the different reports, they included psychological reports, military career, and manuscripts of conversations that Wilhelm had been involved in. Natasha had known that he oversaw some projects but hadn't realised that they were with some of Germany's top physicists. And he was a member of the Reich Aviation Ministry. Busy boy. Natasha made some more notes and then put his file back in the stool. She locked it and then proceeded to look around for more hiding places. There was more information here she could feel it.

She again went to look in the boxes on the top shelf. It seemed too obvious, but there must be something in there. She reached up and slowly, slid the box along with the tips of her fingers. The front door slammed shut. Natasha froze. She held her breath. Don't be silly, it might just be the guard. She tried to push the box back in as fast as possible. She jumped off the chair and placed it in the corner. Natasha slightly opened the door so she could listen.

'You're back early Herr Hess,' the guard remarked. 'May I take your jacket?'

'I've had a change of plans,' Hess commented. He did not seem happy.

A deep inhale. Damn. Where to go? She grabbed her bag; there were two places he was likely to go, either his room or the study. She heard him coming up the stairs. Natasha slipped out of the study into the child's bedroom and slid under the bed.

She heard Hess's footsteps go into the study and then the door close. After about five minutes, he walked out of the study to the top of the stairs.

'Who's been in this house?' said Hess.

'No one Deputy Führer,' the guard replied.

'Someone's been in this house,' Hess commented, 'and I want to know when and how.'

'Yes, Deputy Führer,' answered the guard and then walked out and closed the door.

Stunned, Natasha wondered how he knew. Maybe it was the list of addresses. No, too bad, he shouldn't have them anyway. How to get out? It was quiet. She carefully looked out the window. Hess's car and chauffer were at the front door. He was going to go out again, and soon. A smile crept over her face. Natasha crossed the hallway into the bathroom. She closed the door slightly and walked over to the window. Looking out the window, she saw the guard disappear around the front of the house. She opened the window and climbed out of it. This was going to hurt. She dropped to the ground just clear of the garden. She crept back into the bushes that bordered the house. The rose thorns scratched her skin, but there was no other shelter. She crawled along between the house and bushes to the corner of the house. She watched the chauffer. He was leaning against the car, watching the front door. Natasha flattened herself against the ground and rolled under the car. Now, what can I hold onto?

***

How dare they, how dare they play me. Hess was annoyed. I control; people do what I want, or what I know they'll do. They don't make the rules. He wasn't used to this; someone had turned the tables and he was sure it was Natasha. Michele's file was the last one he had looked at, not Wilhelm. Yet Wilhelm's was on top. He'd not updated Wilhelm's file for some time, yet it was on top. He grabbed Michele's and flicked through it, then Natasha's. All the addresses were gone. Hess threw the files on the floor. That had taken years. That was it. Even though he was upset, he believed the guard. No one would know she was here. That was a protective strike, she didn't need the addresses, but he did. Maybe, just maybe she was as angry as he was. He put Wilhelm's file back in the stool and put the other two files in his bag. Hess headed down to the car and he began to smile. How refreshing it was to have a challenge, it would keep him on his toes. In fact, he would have to step up a gear to take back control.

The car drove through the gates and paused before turning on to the road. Natasha dropped to the ground. The car drove off and Natasha rolled into the grass. She waited for the gates to close and then she crawled to the brick base and lay down on her back. Well at least she didn't have to climb that fence again. After a few moments, Natasha walked to the car and drove to her house going the long way around.

***

Hess knocked on Wilhelm's door. Wilhelm opened the door and indicated to come in.

Hess walked in asking, 'Have you found Friedrich yet?'

'No.'

'Have you found Michele yet?' Hess questioned.

'No.' Wilhelm replied, 'but it would have helped if I'd been given all the facts and then your little parcel might have been in your basement by now.'

Wilhelm was fuming.

'You know I have things I'm supposed to actually be doing,' he continued 'and I don't mind helping you, but you have to trust me enough to let me know what exactly your master plan is.'

Wilhelm sighed and stormed into the parlour.

Hess stood stunned for a moment. What was happening to his world? He walked in and saw Wilhelm pouring himself a drink.

'You shouldn't be angry, I don't tell anyone everything,' Hess dismissed.

'I've noticed.' Wilhelm looked straight at Hess. 'While you were up in Berlin, I had a chance to think about something. Uncle.'

Hess sensed a change in tone.

Wilhelm paused trying to build up the courage, but he had started now. 'You put me on a train, knowing full well it would be attacked. You didn't tell me so I could prepare. I could have been injured or worse.'

Hess dismissed it with a wave, 'It was not their objective.'

'But anything could have happened.'

'I needed someone there to protect Michele if something went wrong.' Hess sighed.

'Michele is that important, that I should be put at risk? Is she really more important than me?'

Hess looked at Wilhelm and paused. He was considering who would be more beneficial.

'Your silence speaks volumes, Uncle.' Wilhelm took a step back. He felt he had just been winded.

'Don't be like that,' Hess replied. 'Everyone has an important part to play.'

Wilhelm shrugged. He had expected more from his uncle, a man he looked up to and yet now he felt used and manipulated.

As if sensing this Hess interrupted the thought, 'I may not share everything with you, but you are in my extremely small group of confidants.'

Wilhelm knew that was as close as he would get to affection with pragmatic Hess.

Hess left an appropriate pause and then continued.

'I need your help,' Hess said, and he threw the two files onto the table.

Wilhelm looked at Hess, 'What's this?'

'All the information I currently have on the girls,' said Hess.

Wilhelm grabbed the files; they were heavy. He started looking through the file and paused, 'What do you mean currently? Is it being updated?'

'No,' Hess replied. 'Some of the information was taken while I was away. That's why the parcel wasn't there.'

Wilhelm was looking through the files. There was a little bit more on Natasha than Michele, but it still wasn't very detailed.

Wilhelm looked confused, 'How strange.'

'What?' asked Hess, 'What's wrong?'

'Well, if Michele is based in Munich,' Wilhelm asked, 'why did I meet her in Berlin?'

'I don't know,' Hess smiled. 'Maybe she was preparing for the rescue of Helene.'

'Maybe,' Wilhelm replied.

He kept reading and then closed the files.

'Where's mine?'

'What?'

'My file.'

'You don't have one,' said Hess. 'Anyway, it's all in here.' Hess pointed to his brain and smiled.

Wilhelm laughed, 'No, seriously where is it?'

'I only keep files on my opponents,' Hess answered, 'and unless there's something you're not telling me, you're on my side.'

Wilhelm looked at Hess and wondered if that was just a simple comment or if it was a threat.

'Don't take this wrong but, I don't believe you. Anyway,' Wilhelm asked, 'what do you want me to do?'

'Well since I've been raided,' Hess began, 'I have no idea where Michele is.'

'I don't understand why Michele is so important,' Wilhelm said. 'Natasha appears to have the information that you need, and you know where she is.'

Hess smiled and shook his head, 'I don't want to turn them in; I could do that right now if I wanted to. I want to work with Natasha. But Michele is an intricate part of Natasha's network. So, I need both, unfortunately. But I need leverage, I need a lot of leverage. It's a big gamble, they are technically the enemy. Both should be shot. And if I work with them, then technically I would be deemed the enemy.'

Wilhelm corrected him, 'Them work for you, don't you mean?'

'I used to think that.' Hess continued smiling. 'Have you met Helene?'

Wilhelm shook his head.

'Well, all the women in that family are leaders,' Hess was almost talking to himself, 'they're intelligent, calculating, and manipulative.'

'Helene got caught,' Wilhelm remarked, 'so did Michele.'

'Helene wasn't raised in this environment. She taught the girls everything she knew, but they learnt more. She's the weakest link, maybe...' Hess paused. 'Michele took a calculated risk. It was the only way she could get her mother back, and she knew she'd probably end up with Natasha.'

'Natasha's the only one that hasn't been caught,' Wilhelm commented.

'Natasha has the upper hand. She's used to trusting no one and having no one.'

Wilhelm felt hurt again, he was Natasha's friend, she did have someone, she had him. Or was it the other way around? Wilhelm looked up at Hess.

'Did you know that Michele was not going to be shot?'

'I assumed.'

'But if she had of been shot, would you have been upset about her loss?' Wilhelm asked intrigued as to what the answer might be.

'It would have been unfortunate. I really don't know how that would have affected Natasha's competency.' Hess stated. 'Or yours.'

Wilhelm paused, he was finding it hard to digest what had just been said, although deep down it didn't surprise him. It was just a means to an end for Hess.

Wilhelm took a deep breath, 'What about Friedrich?'

'He's a follower not a leader, I do pity him, he had no chance in that family,' Hess replied.

'If that's the case, who's he following now?' Wilhelm asked. 'He's still missing.'

'I don't know,' Hess replied, 'I really don't know. It's not supposed to happen this way.'

CHAPTER 13

Friedrich walked into Anita's house.

'I'm sorry,' Friedrich said.

'It's fine.'

Pause.

'I had to see her.'

'I guessed.'

'Are you–?' he asked not knowing the right word to use.

'Yes,' she replied. 'How is she?'

'Good.'

Another pause.

'Should I pack up my house and hide?' Anita said.

Friedrich was momentarily confused.

'Anita of course not, I would never'

But he understood where the comment had come from and looked down.

Anita nodded an acknowledgement.

'Goodbye,' he said and was out the door.

It was a long drive ahead of him. Seriously, what had he expected? Trust? How could he expect trust? I'm the enemy. Maybe time will heal the scars. Maybe they are just too deep. Please no. Friedrich hoped not. He rolled his eyes, now he had to deal with Natasha and all her questions about where he'd been. He had no energy for that. No energy at all.

***

Natasha sat down on her bed. All she knew was that Hess knew about the resistance and her. She knew nothing about him. She needed something, something she could use as leverage. The only bit of information she had was on the plane and now Wilhelm's connection to Hess. Natasha went downstairs to the study and looked along the books on the shelves. Her father had never been interested in planes, but he was interested in business. She pulled out a book and took it upstairs. The book was the Bavarian

Business Directory. Flicking through the pages, she found several factories that made fighter planes. She noted the company names, addresses and phone numbers. She would have to do some research. She tapped the book with her pencil. But what am I looking for?

He had mentioned taking out seats. Why would he need to take out seats? It's not the kind of thing he would do personally. He would need it professionally altered or built. That's what she needed to find. Who was altering it?

***

Helene looked out the window and took a sip of coffee. Anneliese walked into the room and sat down. Today they all moved, Anneliese back to Germany and Helene to Egypt. She looked at Helene, who seemed miles away in thought. Helene broke her gaze from the window and looked towards Anneliese. Anneliese knew that look, she hadn't seen it for a long time, but it told her something. Helene was back, and that meant trouble. Helene took another sip of her coffee and then smiled.

'I'm going back.' she stated.

It had been the smile; Anneliese had known what she was going to say as soon as she smiled. She knew it was pointless, but she protested anyway.

'You can't. The plan—'

'Screw the plan,' Helene interrupted, 'it's changed. I guess I should get ready.'

She got up and left the room. Anneliese looked down at the ground. 'Michele is going to be so angry'.

Helene sat in front of the mirror. She was ready. But was she really? She needed to get back; she needed to do something. She needed to stop thinking.

It was strange that now, when she was free, she felt so trapped, so confined in life, being told where to go, what to do. Everyone was well meaning, talking about taking time to heal, and she'd offered the same advice before, before she knew better. In hindsight, it was wrong, it was so wrong.

In the camp, there was hopelessness, an uncertainty about life, a resignation to death just being around the corner. The small things brought hope. The big things brought, well, what did they bring? She looked down. Numbness, or no, it was worse than that, it brought nothing, a nothingness that ate away at your brain, then your soul and finally all your feelings. It taught you to help others, but to stay detached, because they or you would disappear at some point. It taught you to be numb to life. And death. People didn't die from starvation, they died because the guards killed them and because they lost all hope, and without hope, there's no point to life.

A tear had rolled down her cheek. Others had suffered so much at the camps. Not her, not Helene, she'd been numb, she'd not felt at all. Not in camp, well not after the first six months anyway.

Now, things were coming back, things she hadn't noticed, that had passed by the numbness, they were coming back. The images, the names, the scenes, the people. The children. What she needed was something else to fill her brain. Something to stop the memories, before they came flooding back, before they ate away at her. All over again. She needed change. She needed a focus. That would be the only way to heal if it was possible at all.

A small bag on the dresser had a few bits of her old jewellery in. Anneliese had left them for her. Not much. Mainly trinkets. She sorted through them. Her ruby engagement ring that she hadn't wanted to wear, but not had the heart to sell. It still felt too heavy for her fingers. Another smaller ring, that had been crudely made. Yet it was one of her prized possessions. The soft band wound around her finger where two snake heads crossed to complete the circle. She knew they were two snakes, but they were her Snake and Serpent. Her two girls who were the same but appeared so different. Neither ring fit her fingers now. She took a necklace and linked it through both rings, before putting it around her neck. Patting them for comfort, they belonged with her.

She picked up her brush and began to brush her hair. It was long and over the past few days a little shine had come back. It was amazing the resilience of the body. She'd always had long hair; it was her trademark. She couldn't afford to have trademarks now. It is just like a plaster; you must get rid of it fast. She wanted to start again, be new. She grabbed a handful and cut it, just above her shoulder. She quickly continued until it was all the same length. She looked at the hair she had placed on the dresser. It all went in the bin except for one lock, which she packed. Helene closed the suitcase people had filled with clothes for her and walked downstairs. Anneliese turned and looked at her, surprised by the new hairstyle.

'I'm ready.'

Helene grabbed her by the arm and dragged her out of the house.

Today was going to be a new beginning.

***

Michele woke up with a start. She had heard something. She folded her blanket, placed it a cupboard, and then crept over to the window. There wasn't anything outside, but someone was here. She knew the stairs squeaked and were far too open. She had discovered that she could crawl into the chimney and make it downstairs. Slowly she lowered herself down to the ground floor. She stood in the shadows of the fireplace and looked around the room. A shadow passed one of the windows. She crept over to the window. She saw no one. Michele quietly snuck into the kitchen to be near the door. She grabbed a knife off one of the benches, it was blunt, but it was all she had. Then she hid behind the door. It slowly opened and a figure walked in. She went to grab them. The person took the hand with the knife, twisted it behind her back, pushing Michele face first against the wall.

'For goodness' sake, you're supposed to be head of the resistance and you can't even recognise your own sister,' Natasha whispered.

She let go.

'That was good,' Michele said turning to Natasha. 'Can you show me how to do that?'

Michele was going over the move in her mind to understand it. She started trying to move her hands to work out how Natasha had done it. Natasha grabbed her and pulled her upstairs.

'Later,' Natasha giggled.

It was one of those times, when Natasha really did feel like the older sister. Didn't happen that often nowadays.

They got upstairs and Michele crumbled onto the bed.

'So,' Natasha said, 'are you bored yet?'

Michele rolled her eyes and mimicked putting a noose around her neck and pulling it tight.

'Do you have access to a telephone?' asked Natasha.

'Not here.'

Natasha looked at her.

'Yeah, I do,' Michele replied. 'You're no fun today.'

Natasha handed her a couple of pages. Michele looked down at them. It was a list of names of companies and their phone numbers. She looked up at Natasha.

'So, what are we doing?' Michele asked.

Natasha explained everything she knew including the Wilhelm connection and the plane.

'I've got a meeting with Hess tomorrow,' Natasha stated. 'I need to know as much as possible before then.'

Michele sat in thought.

'How far did you say it could fly?' Michele asked.

'Well technically speaking it could fly to Norway and back,' Natasha commented.

'That's if it was a return trip,' Michele enquired, 'what if it is a one-way trip to say Russia?'

'He would barely get there let alone to somewhere of importance.'

Natasha looked out the window. The sun was coming up; they would have to go soon.

'Okay,' Michele was still thinking. 'What about London?'

Natasha looked back at her, 'That's a possibility, but he would still have fuel spare.'

'I wonder why?' Michele spoke to herself.

'We have to go,' Natasha said, and they both left the house.

Walking through the wooded area Natasha said, 'We need to find out where they are making the plane, and what is being adjusted before we will know where he's going.'

Michele stopped and turned Natasha around. 'Why are you so focused on this plane? It might not be that big a thing.'

'You're right, maybe it's nothing. But I have nothing else. I can't go into a meeting with the Deputy Führer, knowing nothing other than the fact he knows everything about us. But highly classified information was kept in the same kind of place as a sketch of a plane and some maps. That's strange. You have to admit that is strange. And if strange is all I have; it is what I'm going to go with. But honestly, I'm not sure of anything.'

Michele nodded. But agreement was not what Michele was thinking about. She was worried. She was worried about her sister and what plans Hess had for them.

***

Friedrich waited until he heard Natasha leave, before heading to the office. He sat down at his desk and grabbed his head. It was spinning. What to do, what to do first? Papers on the desk, notes, messages and then there was Helene. His focus was gone, direction, what direction? Everything I wanted, everything I aimed for wasn't real. It was supposed to be real; this was supposed to be a good thing and now I'm so far away and I don't know if, can I, can you…'

Wilhelm knocked on the door and opened it enough to squeeze through. Friedrich looked up from his desk.

Wilhelm sat in the chair, 'Good morning Friedrich how have you been?'

'Good,' Friedrich replied. 'How are you?'

'Friedrich,' Wilhelm asked, 'we were just wondering where you were?'

'Do you know how many people asked me that this morning? I should have a sign on my door saying that I took a couple of days off,' Friedrich replied.

Wilhelm relaxed in his chair and decided a different tack. 'Did you have a nice relaxing time?'

'Yes,' Friedrich lied, 'I did thank you. You know sometimes I need to get out of the city and get some fresh air,'

'Where did you go?'

Friedrich paused, 'To up near the Thurgau National Park. It was refreshing.'

Wilhelm looked at Friedrich. He was lying. He would have picked a place opposite to where he had been. This meant Friedrich must have been south near the border, maybe Austria or maybe even Switzerland and he must have found Helene.

'It's good to have you back,' Wilhelm smiled.

Friedrich relaxed, 'Thank you.'

Wilhelm walked out; he needed to talk to Natasha.

***

'Nice,' Natasha said, 'very nice.'

She walked into the main room. Michele walked over to the pinboard. Not much was on it.

'Hello,' a voice called over.

Michele turned around and smiled, 'Hello, Oskar.'

He gave her a hug. 'Good to have you back.'

Natasha studied the map. It showed all the fronts Germany was fighting and where English troops were. On the pinboard were details of English government, their connections, and estates. No in-depth details, just names.

Natasha turned to Michele. 'You have the foundations of a good network here.'

Oskar walked over, 'Look at this.'

He took Natasha by the wrist and dragged her over to two filing cabinets. He unlocked both and indicated for her to look in them. It was full of files on the English people who were on the pinboard. She closed the drawer and opened the other filing cabinet. That was full of Nazi personnel files.

She flicked through. 'You don't seem to have any information on Hess, Goebbels or Himmler. They are debatably the most important figures in Germany. I will see what I can get for you.'

'No,' Oskar said. 'I have files.'

Both girls looked at him.

He put them on the table. 'I just don't know what they mean.'

They all looked at the paperwork. Jean had provided a lot of information, but none of it seemed linked. A majority revolved around the fact that Goebbels wanted Hess out of the way. Natasha picked up Hess's file. It was a lot lighter than the rest of them.

'There's a surprise.'

Michele smiled.

'This is very anti-Jewish, and they want to take it to the next level with extermination camps.' Oskar was trying to summarise the findings.

'Not all of them,' Michele replied, 'or it would be occurring.'

She continued reading. 'It says here that each time it's been brought up Hess has recommended other things.'

Michele looked at Oskar.

'Yes, he wants to use the Jews as slaves. I think that's what Jean said. It makes you wonder what goes through their heads,' Oskar answered. 'In the back of your head, you know things are happening, but you just don't see it, it doesn't hit home, until it effects someone you know.'

Oskar was so angry; he'd grown up with Jewish friends and seen them disappear one by one. It made him sick. But that was the life that he lived in, day in day out, anti-Jews, anti-Roma, anti-disabled, anti-everyone that was not deemed Aryan. What was worse was, he was deemed part of the superior race. There was so much it was numbing him, making him angry but numbing him, like he'd been bombarded so much with this hate, he couldn't absorb any more.

'I know you're angry Oskar,' Natasha commented, 'but you know slaves still have their lives. I'm not condoning this, don't get me wrong. But maybe…'

Oskar looked shocked, 'You're defending him? Are you trying to tell me that he's protecting them, in some crazy way?'

'I don't think he would actually protect anyone, but he finds them useful,' Natasha said, 'which inadvertently protects them.'

'The problem is,' Michele interrupted, 'he's running out of excuses.'

They all looked at each other, the silence was deafening.

Natasha broke the silence. 'Let's see just how good your little intelligence network is.'

Michele smiled, 'Is that a challenge?'

'Maybe,' Natasha said. 'I need all the information you can find on Hess. I want his family links, information on his wife, contacts before the war, subjects he studied, everything.'

'I'll get it for you,' Michele replied.

'No,' Natasha interjected. 'Oskar you can do that. Michele, I need you to learn about aviation and our aeroplane. Use the details that I gave you to start with. I need to know that by tomorrow morning and I want to find out who this is.'

Natasha handed Michele a photograph of Hess and another man standing in front of a plane. She needed as much information as possible if she was going to survive the meeting with Hess.

Michele looked at Natasha, 'You've got demanding in your old age.'

Oskar looked at them both; you could tell they were sisters. Assertive, focused and both believing anything was possible.

CHAPTER 14

Natasha knocked on her father's office door.

'Come in,' he called.

She walked in and then sat in one of the chairs near his desk. He looked up at her and waited. As Natasha looked at Friedrich, she knew something had changed. He seemed at peace, yet deep in thought.

'How are you, father?' she said.

'Good.'

'I haven't seen you for the past couple of days,' she said. 'I was worried.'

'I very much doubt that.'

'Doubt?'

'That you are worried.' He looked at her.

Natasha stared back. Could he really hate her that much?

'Why do you think that?'

'You probably had other things on your mind...' he said, '... like killing your sister or whatever is your latest ambition.'

'You talk to me about being ambitious,' Natasha snapped before thinking. 'How dare you be so hypocritical?'

Friedrich sat shocked by her outburst, for her lack of control. For her accuracy.

'Get out.'

She got up, leaned on the desk, 'Where were you?'

'Get out,' he yelled again.

'Where were you?' she yelled back.

He jumped up. 'Get out now.'

She stared into his eyes, they were wild. She'd get no further information. Natasha turned and walked out of the office. She slammed the door, hard. The glass shattered. Walking down the corridor, she could feel everyone looking at her. She just needed to make it out of the building. Natasha had never relied on her father, but he was there, just in case. There was hatred in his eyes. She held her breath as she stormed past everyone. Natasha didn't even notice Wilhelm come out of Hess's office. She kept her eyes looking up and tried to control her breathing. She would not cry in public, which wasn't her image, it would destroy everything.

***

Wilhelm was looking at Hess.

'What is it you need exactly?' Wilhelm asked, 'You must have a plan. You just haven't included me in it.'

'I'm reformulating my plan, or rather how they fit into my plan,' Hess replied and looked out the window.

'What's the goal?' Wilhelm said. 'There must be a goal.'

'You're right,' Hess smiled, 'the goal is to end the war with as little as possible loss of human life and to make Germany into a great nation again through the vision of Lebensraum.'

'Is that all?'

Bang, then silence. They looked at each other and then ran to the door just as Natasha walked by. Wilhelm nearly pushed Hess over as he grabbed his coat and raced after her. He finally caught up with her as she reached her house. Natasha tried to close the door on him, but he forced it open and walked through, closing it behind him.

'Go away,' Natasha said.

She was close to tears.

'No, what's wrong?'

'Go away,' she yelled. 'Leave me alone.'

'I'm your friend.' Wilhelm didn't know what to say. 'You can trust me.'

'I can't afford to trust anyone,' she snarled.

'Well in different circumstances I think I'd be devastated by that comment,' Wilhelm was almost talking to himself, 'but I don't blame you, personally I don't trust anyone either, not you, not Hess, no one.'

'Are you trying to change the subject?'

'I'm not, you feel upset because of your father,' Wilhelm continued. 'I feel let down by Hess. He doesn't trust me; no, he doesn't have faith in what I can do. It's similar.'

'You don't understand.'

He appeared confused and angry.

'Try me,' he challenged. 'I'm sick of this. I'm here, I'm right here, for you. Try me.'

She looked at him.

'He despises me,' she whispered. 'No, he hates me.'

'I'm sure he doesn't,' Wilhelm tried to console her.

Ignoring him, she continued, 'And I didn't think that would matter to me, but what annoys me the most, is that it does.'

Wilhelm didn't know what to say.

She took a few deep breaths and walked over to the cupboard and poured herself a drink.

'Do you want one?'

'Yes,' he said.

'So, what's happening between you two?' she asked handing him the drink.

'He won't let me know what's happening. He's almost as bad as you. I'm merely a pawn that well, never mind.' Wilhelm continued the thought. Just a pawn that could be sacrificed for the greater good.

'You're sulking. I swear you guys are like a married couple.'

Wilhelm looked distressed, 'We're not, well you know. We, I mean I, I mean…'

'I know you're not gay,' she replied, 'although people do wonder about your uncle.'

'He's not gay,' Wilhelm sighed, 'he's just married to his work. He's not really a relationship kind of–'

He stopped short and threw Natasha a look, 'How did you know, no, actually, don't answer that. I need you to do something for me.'

'What?'

'I need you to get my file.'

'I don't have it,' she said.

'From Hess.'

'Get yourself,' she said. 'You have easier access to his house than I do. It's in the study, in the piano stool.'

Wilhelm looked down at his glass. 'Why does no one trust me?'

Natasha looked at him; he was so forlorn, like a little boy lost and it was good to focus on someone else.

'No one trusts anyone.'

He looked straight into Natasha's eyes.

'Think about it though; think about the possibility, of maybe trusting me at some stage, please.'

She didn't know what to say. There was a part of her that wanted to hold him so badly or have him hold her, but she couldn't. She would crumble.

'Well, I must trust you a little bit, I've just admitted to going through your uncle's files. Think of that as a first step.'

He smiled as he got up, he didn't feel as used being Natasha's confidant. Then headed towards the door and paused. 'Your father went to see your mother. He's swapping sides Natasha. That's why he can't like you. He will in the end though. I know he will.'

He closed the door as he left.

Natasha sat in the parlour. She put the glass on the table and tried to wipe away the tears, but there were too many. Instead, she sat, sobbed, and wondered when it would all be over. Will this ever end?

***

'Hello' Michele said, 'I don't know if I am calling the right place, but are you involved with the production of ME110s?'

'No,' said a voice, 'phone the Messerschmitt factory in Augsburg.'

'Thank you,' Michele replied.

She ran her finger down the list of factories until she found the number of the Augsburg factory. She had called so many places that she was bored already. Fingers crossed that this would be the place. She was running out of time. She dialled the number.

'Hello,' she started, 'I don't know if you're the right place to phone, but are you involved with the manufacture of ME110s?'

'Yes, we are,' came a proud male voice down the phone, 'why?'

'I'm phoning on behalf of my brother who is studying at university, and he's looking at the ME110 as a thesis.'

'Yes,' said the voice, 'how can I help?'

'Would it be possible for him to come and visit the factory, to ask some questions?'

'Certainly,' he said, 'I'm Martin, just ask for me.'

'Thank you very much,' Michele said and then hung up.

She heard a noise. Michele paused for a moment. She wasn't expecting anyone. The trapdoor opened, and a voice called out.

'Hello.'

It was Henri.

He came over to hug Michele and said, 'I have a present for you.'

Anneliese and Helene walked down the stairs. Helene rushed over to Michele as she saw her daughter's jaw drop.

'You're supposed to be in Egypt,' said Michele.

'I know,' said Helene. 'I didn't make it.'

Michele turned towards the others.

'It wasn't their fault,' Helene said, 'I belong here.'

There was no point in fighting with her mother; it wouldn't get her anywhere.

Michele changed her focus to Henri and Anneliese. 'I need you two to do things.'

'I can help,' Helene interrupted.

'Fine, Anneliese and Helene can you please research Ilse Hess her maiden name is Pröhl, and I need you to find out who this is.'

She handed Anneliese the photograph.

Henri peered over Anneliese's shoulder.

'I know,' he said. 'It's the Duke of Hamilton, he's based in Scotland. RAF I think. He was in one of the papers from London the other day, I can't remember what the story was about now. My contact in Spain, has a cousin that works for him, that's why I remember. I don't know what they do exactly, I didn't ask, didn't think it was important at the time.'

'Thank you,' Michele smiled, 'now I need you to act like my brother. I'll fill you in on the way.'

She looked at Anneliese, 'Find out about the Duke of Hamilton too.'

Michele turned to her mother.

'It's good to have you back.'

She gave her another hug and disappeared up the stairs.

'It's good to see you too,' Helene whispered back.

***

Helene and Anneliese sat in the corner of the Munich University library. They were reading old school yearbooks, studying university rolls and newspapers. Helene rubbed her eyes.

'Is everything alright?' Anneliese asked.

'Yes,' she said. 'I haven't read much recently.'

'Take a rest.' Anneliese gave her a hug. 'You're expecting too much of yourself.'

'I know, I really hate it,' she whispered, 'I've lost so much time, I feel like I…'

She paused.

'I'm just being silly,' Helene said. 'Don't worry about me.'

Helene looked better than the day of the escape, but still wasn't her old self.

'Maybe it's too soon to come back to all this,' Anneliese said.

Helene shot a look at her that made Anneliese recoil in her chair.

'Or not,' Anneliese said, and turned her head back towards the book.

By the time they left the library, they had quite a dossier on Ilse. All documented information tended to promote the fact that she was a loving wife, mother, and devoted Nazi. However, the further back they had researched, the more she seemed to be involved within the Third Reich. It was as if Ilse had removed herself from politics as soon as she married. In one of the books, it said Hitler himself had been a bit of a matchmaker in her relationship with Hess. This of course in the Nazi kingdom was the ultimate seal of approval.

They pulled up at the farm. Anneliese walked into the farmhouse and handed the keys to the old woman.

They both proceeded to the barn and soon spread all their information out on the table.

Helene looked up at Anneliese. 'Something's not right.'

'I know. It's annoying me too,' Anneliese agreed.

'I used to know Ilse,' Helene commented.

Anneliese looked up at her.

'It was a long time ago, but I do remember her. She was so ambitious,' Helene said. 'It just doesn't make sense that she would change so much after getting married.'

'I just…' Anneliese paused '… I don't think we can trust any of this information.'

Anneliese looked depressed and disheartened; she started to collect all the information and walked over to the rubbish bin.

'Don't throw it out,' Helene said.

'Why?' Anneliese asked. 'We don't believe it.'

'I know,' replied Helene. 'Often fact is mixed with fiction. Some of this may be true, and until we know what is and what isn't, we'll have to keep it all. Anyway, sometimes you can find out more about someone because of the documented lies. They're all put there for a reason.'

Anneliese smiled; it was good to have Helene back

***

'I need you to do this filing,' Goebbels pointed to a pile of records on his desk. Jean went to grab them, Goebbels continued, 'and write a letter to the SS commanders and accidentally leak it to the press section, I'll approve it first.'

He smiled to himself. That was the normal way he fed information to the German people.

'The memo should be along the lines that we will be attacking England soon and are keeping all our supplies near Russia to ensure their safety. Expand on that a little, but you know what I mean.'

Jean nodded.

'When will this be happening?' she asked.

'Just say soon,' he replied.

She picked up the pile of paper.

'Oh sorry,' he said, 'not that bottom file.'

She placed it back and walked out.

Sitting down at her desk, Jean typed out the letters. She rolled her eyes and took a deep breath; filing was something she found very monotonous. Jean started to put the paper in piles that related to each other. They covered a range of things from opinion polls to weather reports. She picked up the last piece of paper and started to read it. One line caught her eye. 'No start time for Operation Barbarossa, as weather research is not yet concluded.' Jean thought for a moment. She picked up the weather reports. They were all for Russia. There was also information on transportation links and geography. She sat back, looking around quickly. Hitler didn't intend to attack England; he was going to attack Russia. She filed all the information in the cabinet and then picked up the last page.

Jean walked into Goebbels' office.

He looked up, 'What's wrong?'

Jean smiled back, 'I don't know where you want me to file this.'

He looked up at the paper and then grabbed it out of her hands.

'I'll look after it for you.'

'Okay, thank you,' she said innocently, 'and here is the draft for approval.'

He read the draft and nodded approval. She walked out of the office and sat back at her desk. She needed to talk to Michele.

Jean walked into her apartment block and went over to the communal telephone. She called Hilde's house. Oskar answered the telephone.

'Hello, its Jean,' she said down the phone. 'I have some rats in my house.'

There was silence for a minute, and then he replied, 'What do you expect me to do about it?'

Jean let go a frustrated sigh.

'Michele knows,' and then she hung up.

She walked up the stairs and hoped that the message would get through to Michele.

***

Michele took her hair out of her ponytail and ruffled it, so it fell loosely around her shoulders. She reached into her bag and grabbed mascara and lipstick. Henri smiled. She never wore makeup.

She saw him smile and asked, 'Do you think I look like there is not much between the ears.'

She smiled and fluttered her eyelids.

Henri nodded, 'And I thought you are making yourself look beautiful just for me.'

He pulled up outside the Messerschmitt factory and they both got out. The only person-sized door that they could see was to the left of the building. They walked through it ducking slightly due to the height of the door. There was a small office to the left and to the right a group of workers sat smoking and having coffee. They turned and looked at the strangers and started smiling and elbowing each other as their eyes followed Michele and her little swing as she walked. Henri smiled to himself. Michele went to the office and knocked on the open door.

'Yes,' said the woman behind the desk as she peered up over the rims of her spectacles.

'Sorry to disturb you,' Michele replied, 'but is Martin here?'

The woman sighed and pulled herself up out of the chair. Shuffling over to the door she yelled, 'Martin.'

A young man at the back of the smokers got up and walked over to Michele.

'Hello,' he said holding out his hand.

Michele shook it and introduced herself, 'Hello, I'm Michele, and this is my brother, Henri.' She paused. 'I spoke to you on the phone about my brother doing a project.'

'Oh yes,' Martin smiled. 'I remember.'

He looked at Henri, 'So how much do you know about planes?'

'On the building side, not much,' Henri confessed, 'but I thought this would be the ideal place to start.'

Martin led the way into the main factory. He started talking to Henri about the process. Michele looked at him; he was very passionate on the subject, almost ignoring her, which was perfect. The room was full of machinery. This was obviously where the parts of the plane were stored. There were three doors to the room, one of which they had just walked through. She kept scanning the room; there wasn't anything that looked out of the ordinary. The door opposite her burst open, as two men carried a box into the room. It let sunlight into the room and Michele could see a bit of a delivery truck.

They slowly walked through the area. Henri tried to look as interested as possible. He took notes, to make it more authentic. Internally he had no interest whatsoever. They walked into another large room where they were assembling the planes. Michele scanned the room. At the end of the building were two large doors, which allowed the planes out. She was a little confused; she couldn't see any fully made planes.

She came bouncing up to Martin, 'Where are all the planes?'

Martin smirked, 'They're in the other building.'

'Okay,' she smiled and settled back behind.

She'd have to wait.

***

Wilhelm sat back on the seat. He looked out the window as the world flashed by. He hated this train journey, especially now. So much had happened over the past few days that it felt like his life ripped apart. Now it was up to him, as to which parts he wanted for his life from today and which parts he wanted to discard. He looked down at his satchel. This little bag had the key to the death of hundreds of thousands of people. It contained the plans to Barbarossa, the attack on Russia. He wished he didn't have to be a part of this, but he was, whether he liked it or not. Hess kept on telling him that it was for the greater good. Wilhelm just wondered what Hess' grand plan was. But Wilhelm wasn't convinced. He could understand defending territory, defending people and he was proud of the work that he did at the ministry. But there were certain things he disagreed with, and this was one of them. He struggled with the thought that you could not have one without the other. There must be a way.

Wilhelm took a deep breath, walked into the entrance foyer and started to ascend the stairs. He went through all the information he knew, trying to think of questions, they may ask. He walked into the reception area of Goebbels office and approached a girl at one of the desks.

'Excuse me,' he said. 'I have an appointment to see Goebbels. My name is Wilhelm.'

Jean looked up and smiled. 'Will you please take a seat; I'll let him know you're here.'

She called through to Goebbels, 'Wilhelm is here to see you.'

'Thank you,' Goebbels replied. 'Tell him I'll be about ten minutes.'

She hung up and spoke to Wilhelm, 'He'll probably be about ten minutes. Can I get you a drink?'

'No,' Wilhelm smiled. 'I'm fine thank you.'

She busied herself with typing, while Wilhelm took a seat. He looked at the secretary. She looked vaguely familiar.

Before he even thought about what he was doing he asked, 'Do I know you?'

She looked up, 'I don't think so.'

She looked genuinely confused. He went to dismiss it, but then remembered the last time he had felt this way and decided to trust his judgement. He sat back and tried to think. He closed his eyes. He could visualise her face in a crowd of people. Where was that he thought? He tried to push his memory, but he just couldn't place it. He knew it would really annoy him all day. Goebbels phoned through and the secretary indicated to the door.

**

They walked through the doors that lead outside.

Martin explained, 'That's the main production area. We store all, planes and spare parts in the buildings on the other side of the runway.'

Before this Michele had thought that they were standing on the edge of a delivery road.

Henri asked, 'Can we have a look at some completed planes?'

'Sure,' said Martin.

The boys started talking about plane specifications. Michele just followed. They walked into a much bigger hangar than the previous one. Martin indicated for them both to walk around. He leaned back on the plane and watched Michele.

Henri needed to divert the focus back to him, 'Can I climb into one?'

Martin stopped leaning and walked over to give Henri a hand. Michele took the opportunity and dashed to the side. She looked around; no one was looking. She took off her shoes so that she wouldn't make a sound. There didn't appear to be anything on her side, but the wall was extremely long. She ran along it. Her eyes spotted a door. Turning the handle, she quietly opened it. It was a cupboard. She continued. There were several cupboards along the way. She reached the end and listened for a moment. The boys were still talking. Keeping an eye on them, she sprinted across the back wall. She reached the opposite wall and again ran along it. It also had several cupboards. She stopped at one halfway along and quietly opened it. It was a door. She climbed through the tiny doorframe. The room was smaller than the other one. It still had quite a few planes in it. Michele couldn't find a plane that looked like the one Natasha had drawn her. Again, she scanned the room. There were two large doors at the end for the aircraft. However, there was also one to the left of her. Where was this damn plane? Maybe it wasn't here at all, maybe it didn't exist. She couldn't risk it. She could hear voices and she ran to the door, opened it, and climbed inside.

CHAPTER 15

Martin was a very patient tour guide Henri thought. He'd been asked every possible question about the plane, its controls, capabilities, and development.

Martin looked around, 'Where's your sister?'

'I don't know,' Henri tried to fob it off. 'She's not that interested in planes.'

'Oh,' said Martin, 'anyway we better make sure that she doesn't get lost.'

They both climbed down from the cockpit. Martin started looking around. He got on his hands and knees to see if he could find her. There was no sign of her.

'She must be in the adjoining hangar,' he said, and walked to the open door.

'Just like my sister,' Henri said.

Martin turned. 'What?'

'If there is a door,' Henri replied, 'she'll walk through it.'

Martin looked a little upset and ran through the door. He continued to the other door not even looking around.

Michele heard footsteps and started to run, but it didn't matter, because the plane was right in front of her. She ran up the steps beside it, putting on her shoes and peered through the cockpit window, just as Martin climbed through the doorway.

'You're not supposed to be here,' Martin said nervously looking around.

Henri climbed through the doorway after him. He looked at Michele, and sighed, he was sick of planes.

Michele looked at Martin and smiled, 'Why?'

She was very good at looking angelic.

'It's just,' Martin was a little flustered, 'you're just not supposed to be in here.'

'Oops,' giggled Michele.

Henri walked over, 'This is a bit different from the rest.'

'It's an, um, an experiment,' Martin replied.

'What for?' Henri questioned.

'Come on get down,' Martin called to Michele.

Michele looked down the steps and then back at him. 'Can you help me?' She paused. 'Please?'

He smiled and started walking up the steps. He was near the top when she leaned slightly forward and whispered, 'What's this?'

She turned so her back was to him. He stepped onto the top of the platform.

'What?' he said over her shoulder.

She slowly leaned her neck away from him and then turned her head towards him, saying 'This?'

She grabbed his hand to point to a radio system inside the cockpit.

Henri smiled. He felt sorry for Martin. He was a handsome man, and to all intent purposes, Michele was looking very interested, but he had no hope. Interrogation had many forms.

Peering over her shoulder he said, 'It's a radio.'

She could feel his body relax. His voice was comfortable, not flustered and he was getting closer and closer as they spoke. She turned towards him again with her head slightly down, so she could peer up from under her eyelashes.

'What a large radio it is. Are they normally that large?'

He smiled back, 'No, not normally. They're normally that size.'

He pointed to the front of the cockpit.

'So why has this plane got two, a small one and a large one, what would it do?' she enquired.

'With this you can hear for miles around,' he said. 'You'd be able to hear information in Austria from here.'

'Why is this plane so different?' she asked.

He looked at the plane, 'This baby is going on a very long trip.'

She turned to face him, 'I thought they all did?'

'No, this one needs to travel across water, and fly into windy extremes,' he smiled.

His hand was leaning on the plane, and he was only a couple of inches away from Michele. That's all she would get out of him.

He leaned forward. She gently raised her right hand with her thumb pointed up, while looking straight into his eyes.

Henri saw her raise her thumb. Surely, he deserved a kiss. Then he thought, no, no, she'll kill me.

'Um,' Henri called out, 'sorry to interrupt, but I think it's time we go.'

Martin stood upright quickly; he'd forgotten about her brother.

'Let me help you down,' he said.

'Thank you for showing us around,' she said and gave him a kiss on the cheek.

Henri dragged her out of there as if she'd been a naughty girl but thanked Martin on the way.

They drove down the driveway.

Henri started laughing. 'You're a tease, you're so cruel.'

'I thought you were never going to save me,' she giggled. 'But seriously, what's your take on the plane?'

'Well first,' he started, 'I'm impressed you found it.'

'I almost ran out of time.' She sat back in the seat.

'I think,' he paused for a moment, 'that it is going to fly a long way.'

'Really,' she said.

'Point taken,' he nodded. 'Russia, maybe.'

'No,' she said, 'it needs to fly over water.'

Henri looked at her confused, 'How do you know that?'

She smiled, 'It was part of the sweet nothings that he whispered into my ear.'

Henri smiled, shaking his head. 'So that would mean Egypt or Great Britain.'

'Why would Hess want to go to Egypt,' she asked.

'He was born there, maybe it's an escape route,' Henri offered, 'in case they lose the war.'

'You're trying to tell me that Hitler is not only forward thinking, but he can also fathom defeat,' she said.

'Unlikely I know,' he agreed, 'but why Great Britain?'

'I don't know,' Michele answered, 'it makes no sense at all, but that's what my gut is telling me.'

Michele watched the road roll by. Her head was full of scenarios. Her first thought was with Hitler. The way that Martin had reacted made her think that the plane was a secret. Why would Hess want a special secret plane for either country? Why would it be secret? Nazi officials could easily travel to Egypt. They had forces within Africa, but why? Hitler was trying to let people know that although he didn't want to attack Great Britain, he would if he had to. There was just no point in having a secret plane. In fact, planes flew between both countries all the time as first aid planes. What was the need? Did Hitler know? Maybe that was it. Was it a secret from Hitler? Or did Hitler need deniability? Michele couldn't wrap her head around it, just what exactly was Hess up to?

Henri parked the truck outside a café and walked inside. He knew what to order. Michele walked down the street to the local telephone booth and placed a call.

Hilde answered.

'Is Oskar there?'

'Yes,' she replied, 'just one minute.'

Using the telephone system was always dangerous. You never knew who was listening. So, they used code that could be manipulated, speaking as if someone was at veterinarians' school, as complicated as that sounded, was a subject that made it easier to describe things and actions.

'Hello,' Oskar said down the line.

'Hello,' she replied. 'Hey just phoning to see how you are.'

'Good, thanks,' he replied. 'How was your day?'

'I learnt all about this bird today,' she said 'my tutor said that it didn't just fly in Germany, it could fly over water, even to England if it wanted to. It also has excellent hearing. It can hear a lot further away than other birds. Isn't that exciting?'

'Exciting, yeah,' said Oskar sarcastically, 'can fly over water, wow, even to England.'

'Only if it wants to though,' cut in Michele excitedly.

'Okay,' resumed Oskar, 'and it has great hearing. What fascinating information.'

'That's right,' Michele smiled.

Oskar managed to sound completely bored while confirming all the information.

'I'm actually glad you phoned,' he changed the subject. 'I was wondering if you could help my friend Jean. She has a rat problem and you're learning to be an expert on animals.'

'Oh,' Michele replied, 'I'll call her.'

'You take care,' he said. 'Enjoy the rest of school.'

'Bye,' she said as she hung up the telephone and wondered what exactly Jean wanted.

***

Wilhelm walked through the doorway into the office. It was a private meeting and Jean was not privy to it. The telephone rang, and Jean answered it.

A female voice down the other end of the line said, 'Hello, I'm the exterminator; I believe you have a rat problem.'

'Oh, thank you,' she said recognising Michele's voice instantly. 'Do you have the address? It's near the bridge.'

'Yes,' replied Michele, 'Is six o'clock okay?'

'Perfect,' Jean said and then hung up the telephone.

She sat back. It was good to hear Michele's voice again.

***

The meeting itself wasn't that interesting. It was mainly to give information to Goebbels and Himmler. Plans were scattered over the tables and Wilhelm went through all the technical details. There were a few standard questions. Himmler suggested alternating trains of prisoners with military supplies. They were less likely to be attacked. They would launch the attack from Poland, Hungary and Romania and the main targets would be Leningrad and Moscow, which they would try and cut off from the rest of Russia.

Wilhelm felt sick as he remembered the prisoner's train that he'd been on. He remembered the cries from the prisoners, and could visualise the jeering crowd, the woman who was talking to herself. He looked up and thought for a second. That was where he knew her from; Jean was the woman.

Himmler looked at him. 'Are you alright?'

'I'm fine.'

Confused, Himmler continued with the meeting. As the meeting adjourned, Wilhelm asked if he could use the telephone, which Goebbels agreed to and indicated that Jean would be able to assist him.

Wilhelm came out of the office and walked over to Jean.

'Jean isn't it?'

The others disappeared out of the office.

'Yes,' she replied, a little confused.

'I have seen you before,' he stated.

'Oh, I don't…' she started.

He cut in, 'Just north of here. I think we have a mutual friend.'

She smiled, 'I really don't think so.'

'You may be surprised,' he smiled. 'Look after yourself.'

He turned and walked out of the office. Jean made a mental note to do some digging on Wilhelm. Just in case.

CHAPTER 16

Goebbels opened the door, two employees came out, and he said, 'Thank you. But I want that report tomorrow.'

Goebbels grabbed his coat and put it on.

He turned to Jean, 'Have a nice evening.'

'Thank you,' she replied, 'you too, sir.'

He looked sad and walked towards the door, then turned back to look at her. 'Take care.'

He turned and then was gone.

Jean stared at the door. The hair on her arms tingled; a feeling of unease crept through her. He had never said that to her before. Why, why this evening?

She looked around. Could they know she was meeting Michele? Was it Wilhelm?

The only other people in the office were the men who had just had the meeting. She had half an hour to go before she had to leave. She typed another letter and finished her filing. Opening the filing cabinet, she went to her copies file. She took it out and closed the top drawer. Opening the bottom drawer, she put the file behind the drawer, letting it fall underneath the drawer before she closed it. She stood up. The only information she felt comfortable carrying this evening was in her head. Jean tidied her desk and put on her coat. Picking up her bag, she walked out of the office.

***

Wilhelm sat in the café across the road from Goebbels office. He was intrigued. He finished sipping his cappuccino and watched the street. Goebbels walked out and got into his car. Wilhelm sat back and looked at his watch. He called the waiter over. She took his cup and he asked for a glass of water.

About half an hour later, Jean came out of the office. Wilhelm had his suspicions about her. He'd remembered her as a crazy, deranged, chaotic lady near the train that Michele had hijacked.

She wasn't crazy, far from it, in the office she was calm, collected and focused. So, it was one of three things, she had a twin, she was a schizophrenic, or she was very good. But for Wilhelm, if you combined her working for Goebbels and the train incident it only led to one conclusion. He just wished he had taken more notice about what she had been doing or saying that morning.

Wilhelm pulled some money out of his pocket, left it on the table, and walked to the door. He put on his gloves and thought let's see just how good this girl really is. Two agents came out of Goebbels building, Kriminalassistents possibly. They followed Jean. Wilhelm smiled; there were few people interested in Fraulein Jean this evening.

Everyone knew the Berlin resistance tried hard, but they weren't trained to the level of the German Secret Service. The Nazi regime knew about them, who they were and what they did. It'd been accepted that there would be groups of resistance and one that they could keep their eyes on, was better than one they couldn't. They would surveil Jean because she was new. Perhaps they had little information on her. But they would expect her to either be a normal civilian or a new member of the Berlin resistance. Newer and inexperienced were easier to turn, to scare.

This was different. He believed Jean wasn't Berlin resistance, she was part of Michele's group, and if he was right, she may surprise her followers a little. It would also answer something that had really bugged Wilhelm; why did he meet Michele in Berlin?

**

The wind whipped Jean's hair around her face. It was a cool wind, but she found it refreshing. She had walked more than a block before she noticed her tail. Jean sped up her pace to a jog until she got to the shopping area, where she stopped dead and used the window as a mirror. A man came running around the corner and then realised she'd stopped, so he walked slowly by. Jean saw his reflection; he was one of the men from Goebbels' office. She smiled, but it wasn't a happy smile. Now she knew who they were, all she had to do was lose them. Why of all days, had they decided to follow her today and now?

***

The two men split up and one crossed the road to Wilhelm's side. They walked along following Jean who appeared oblivious to it all. Wilhelm stepped onto the pavement and started to shadow them.

After a block Jean appeared to look at her watch as if she was in a hurry, she started running down the street and turned out of sight. Her two pursuers ran down the street after her. Wilhelm walked normally down the street. He turned the corner and saw one agent a couple of feet away from her and the other trying hard to look inconspicuous. Jean was looking in a shop window. Wilhelm crossed the street, bought a paper from a lad, and quickly flicked through it. His back was to her, but he too was watching the scene behind him in a reflection.

***

Jean turned and walked slowly down the road, dragging her feet almost. She only had five minutes before she was supposed to meet Michele. Damn it, they were quite good at their job. What am I going to do? Come on, really, I have no time for this. Just leave me alone. Now she was getting annoyed.

She walked into a department store and started looking at shoes. She watched in the mirror as her pursuer quickly looked around to analyse the area. She ducked behind some dresses and still crouching moved towards him. He ran to where she'd been. This gave her time to duck out the other exit. Jean started walking down the road to the bridge, she could see Michele in the distance, but there was still a long way to go.

Jean strode along the bridge with Michele was in her sites. She could see her turn to greet her. Jean put on a stone face and walked straight past her. She just hoped Michele would understand why.

***

Wilhelm watched Jean enter the shop. It was on a street corner. He could see that there were many exits on both streets. Both her pursuers entered the department store. Wilhelm smiled and shook his head.

'Amateurs.'

He stood on the corner and looked down both streets. Down one street were some bombed out buildings, which would be perfect to try to hide in, and the other street led to a bridge, which wasn't sheltered and completely out in the open. It made no sense at all. He went to cross the street for the warehouses, but then stopped. His head was telling him to go that way, but his gut feeling was the bridge. She was trying to lose them in the shop. Why go to the bridge, why? This is stupid. I hope I don't regret this. He crossed the road and walked along the path to the bridge on the opposite side of the road to the department store.

***

The agents ran out on to the street. They looked around; she couldn't be seen down the street where they'd come from so, they started running towards the warehouses to catch up. One of the pursuers tripped over his shoelace. His colleague hurried ahead to try to catch up to Jean. He bent down to tie it up. As he stood up and took a quick sideway glance down a side street and then turned back to continue. He stopped for a second and looked again. He could see Jean halfway down the bridge. He called out to his colleague and then started to run after Jean.

***

Wilhelm didn't want to walk too far down the bridge just in case he had to double back. He scanned the area, but he couldn't see Jean. He continued walking slowly but then stopped dead in his tracks. On the opposite side of the bridge leaning on the rail was Michele. He smiled and pretended to look at the view. He felt relieved and scared. He was right, but he didn't want Michele caught again. Could he warn her? No, he couldn't, but he was there, and that was the main thing. He would just have to wait and see.

***

Michele saw Jean approach. Jean's face changed and she walked right past. Michele kept facing where she had come from. It could only mean one thing. Someone was following her. A man in a suit came running past. Michele watched him. Jean went to the side of the pavement as if to cross and so did he. How obvious could he get? Idiot. She looked around, there must be someone else supporting him. She couldn't spot anyone. She saw Jean coming to the end of the bridge and then turn off it. Michele looked around one last time and still couldn't see anyone. She took a deep breath and looked at the ground for a second. She'd promised to protect Jean. Michele turned and hurried to where Jean had turned off. She started to walk down the steps and hearing a struggle she sped up.

Michele saw the agent over Jean with his hands around her neck. She was kicking him and trying to grab his fingers to loosen his grip. Michele could see the colour draining from Jean's face as she raced down the stairs. Her kicking was becoming less violent and there was less force in her fight.

'Who do you work for?' he kept asking.

As Michele approached, she saw Jean go unconscious. Michele stood just to the side of him.

'That would be me,' she said kicking him off balance and he let go of Jean and turned to face Michele.

He swung a right hook and she ducked and kicked him in the shin.

***

Damn thought Wilhelm, Michele had moved too soon. If only she had waited another couple of minutes. But he knew why. She hadn't been able to see a second agent and Jean was out of sight. Oblivious, the second agent was still going after Jean. Wilhelm saw him stop when Michele turned off the bridge, as if he couldn't comprehend what exactly was happening. Wilhelm crossed the road and followed a short distance behind him.

***

A lucky punch found Michele reeling backwards against the wall. She could taste blood from the impact. Ducking she managed to move out from another fist and sliced her palm up under his ribs to try to wind him. He was quite a heavy build and could easily overpower her, but she was more agile. While he was turning, she managed to kick straight into his other side. He turned to face her and rammed his hand straight through one of her punches to grab her throat. She felt his hand surround her windpipe and he slowly squeezed it. He was enjoying this; she could see it in his eyes. She tried to gulp for air. She couldn't get any.

Blurry, blurry, spots. No, I will not go out this way. Not by a lucky chance. You're amateurs. Darkness. Go away. Air, air. Gasp. The darkness was closing in.

Close eyes, focus, focus. Energy. Come on. Energy. I just need a little. With all the force she could muster, she punched through the side of his arm. Crack, crack, cracking of bone. Grunt. Release. Gasp, gasp. Air, air, focus. Open eyes. Michele crumbled to the ground and started to gasp for air. She saw Jean's bag to the right of her and made her way towards it. She needed more time, more air. It wouldn't be long before he would recover. No energy. Something. Everything was spinning. She felt in Jean's bag, for any, anything. She could hear his footsteps coming towards her, but she couldn't really make him out. Her hand came across something metal, something sharp. She closed her eyes and listened. Her eyes were useless now. Tight grip on an arm, breath on cheek. She had a bit more strength, focus. Focus on the breath, and all her strength, she pushed as hard as she could. Push more, hard and turn. He fell beside her, and she lay on her back and gulped for air.

Air, more air. Michele turned over and got on her hands and knees. She had to get to Jean. Something hit her, crashed against her ribs. The pain went straight through her, as she flew across the path, against a wall. The pain helped her focus. She blinked, and then made out a man lunging towards her. She managed to move out of the way. She tried to punch back but she had no energy. Get it together; get it from somewhere, from anywhere. You're losing.

**

Wilhelm started running down the steps. He could see the first pursuer lying on the ground and the second was fighting with Michele. She seemed almost sluggish in her movement. He raced down the steps. Michele received a punch that sent her reeling onto the ground. The attacker went to step over her, and she kicked straight up, there was no real power in the kick, but it did the job. He doubled over falling back slightly. He hadn't noticed Wilhelm. He went for Michele, but Wilhelm caught him around the neck and crack. His neck snapped instantly.

Wilhelm looked at Michele; blood covered her. Her face had started swelling and her clothing had ripped. He leaned over her, and she punched him, but her energy had gone.

'Hey,' he yelled, 'it's me, it's me Wilhelm. It's alright.'

'Jean,' she struggled, 'Jean.'

Wilhelm had forgotten about Jean. He looked around. Jean was in one corner. She was motionless. He ran over to her, kneeling, he held his ear over her mouth. There was a faint breath from her. He started slapping her face gently to try to wake her. She jerked her eyes open and gulped down some air. There was terror in her eyes as she recognised Wilhelm.

'Stop,' Wilhelm said, 'we have a mutual friend.'

Jean looked relatively unscathed, except for bruising around her neck. Wilhelm took off his jacket and placed it over her.

He walked back over to Michele. Her eyes were rolling to the back of her head, she wasn't well. He scooped her up, so she was leaning against him.

'Don't you leave me now,' he whispered to her, 'don't you dare leave me now.'

She tried to smile, but her whole body was numb. She had only just recovered from the interrogations. Now she felt broken. Jean slowly raised herself up on one arm while holding her throat and looked over at Wilhelm. She saw Michele and a tear strayed from her eye. She crawled over to them. Wilhelm leaned down and kissed Michele on the forehead. He just wanted to protect her and cradled her rocking back and forward. She was the only thing in his life that felt real, and he didn't want to lose her. Don't you leave, don't you dare leave me. He could feel her body relaxing, as if her life was draining. Her hand slid to the ground.

Jean grabbed his arm and removed it from Michele's body. He looked at her indignantly.

She pulled Michele onto the ground.

'Damn it, woman,' she said and slapped Michele across the face.

'Where's your pride, where's your conviction,' Jean yelled at her, 'is it that easy, that two idiot Nazi thugs can take it? You pitiful excuse – I thought you were made of more than that.'

Jean continued the diatribe, her voice was hoarse, it hurt to speak, but she couldn't give up, not now.

Michele couldn't fight anymore. Broken. But she could feel Wilhelm next to her. No energy. Her ears were starting to work though. Jean was speaking. What was she saying?

Then she heard, 'Because of you, Hitler will win, you hypocritical bitch.'

With all the energy she could muster Michele whispered, 'Shut up.'

Jean continued.

'I said shut up.'

Jean gave her a hug. Michele tried to smile, but it hurt.

Jean grabbed Wilhelm's coat and placed it under Michele's head.

Then she turned to Wilhelm, 'We have to get rid of these bodies.'

Wilhelm dragged the body that he had killed and rolled him over the side of the barrier into the river.

Jean rolled the other over and recoiled in shock.

'What's wrong?' asked Wilhelm.

'That was my favourite letter opener,' she said, pulling it out of the guy's nasal cavity.

'Well, that's an original way to kill someone,' Wilhelm commented as he started to drag him over to the river and threw him in.

She threw the letter opener in the river, 'I can't use that now, can I?'

Michele was sitting against a wall. She was trying to wipe the blood off her face. She was still dazed.

Wilhelm helped her up, 'I think it is time to get you back to Jean's.'

'No,' Michele said, 'there's things we need to do.'

They looked at her confused.

'You said the men had a meeting with Goebbels?' she stated.

'Yes,' Jean said.

'The likelihood is, they're working for Goebbels, and may have left a message,' whispered Michele.

'So, I guess we need to make a little trip to the office,' Wilhelm suggested, 'how are you?'

'I'll be fine,' Jean said tracing her fingers around her neck, 'I just need a few minutes.'

Wilhelm nodded and they all sat in silence.

CHAPTER 17

Natasha walked over to the chair in front of Hess's desk. She didn't sit down. Not because she was waiting for permission, but because she wanted to talk somewhere neutral, not in Hess's office. Hess looked up at her and leaned back in the chair.

'Natasha.'

'Rudolf.'

Hess paused looking at her inquisitively and then indicated the chair to her.

She shook her head.

He nodded, stood up, grabbed his coat, and they both walked out of the office.

The park was quiet with only a few families around. Hess and Natasha were sitting on a wooden bench.

'You asked for a meeting?' Natasha said.

'Correct,' Hess said.

They sat in silence.

One of the first things you learn in interrogation is people feel compelled to talk, in silence. Natasha knew Hess used this tactic, so she just watched the people passing by. No one spoke. After about ten minutes, Natasha turned to Hess and smiled. Slowly a smirk spread across his face.

'Interrogating, interrogators.'

'Yes,' smiled Natasha.

'I know about you,' Hess said, trying to regain a bit of control.

'Same,' Natasha said. 'So please let's stop playing games.'

'You only know what I allow you to know,' he said.

'Of course, so how about I ask a question and you answer it and then you can do the same,' she replied.

'Fine,' he said.

She saw him relax. Normally you wanted to do as little talking as possible. Interrogation was about listening, watching. He thought he had the upper hand; she could see it in his body language. Natasha sat back. I have one chance at this. Please let this be right, or I lose the game. I lose it completely. This was a huge gamble.

'Where do I start?' she said as if she was unsure.

She looked at him; he was pretending to be open and willing to be helpful. Butterflies, she had butterflies. That bit she didn't have to fake.

'What do you intend to wear?' she started.

He looked at her nodding as if listening intently.

She continued, 'When you fly to Britain.'

Hess's face dropped.

Yes, she thought, jackpot.

Now she felt no butterflies, just sweet satisfaction. Relief and smugness, yes it was her time to feel smug.

Hess was in shock, he couldn't speak. By the time he'd regained composure, it was too late, the damage had been done. Natasha looked at him and raised her eyebrow. She had a smirk on her face, but she didn't want him to know that it was just a lucky guess.

'Now shall we start again?' she stated. 'What do you want to talk about?'

'I'm rusty.'

'I see,' she said, 'but I get the feeling that we may want the same type of thing.'

'You know you shouldn't reveal all your cards at once,' Hess said, 'but well done.'

'You know you shouldn't try to manipulate me,' Natasha replied, 'and thank you, for the compliment.'

'I need someone I can trust,' Hess spoke, 'and I think I can trust you.'

'Why?' Natasha asked. 'Why am I so trustworthy?'

'You trust no one,' Hess stated, 'not even your father. Which makes you the kind of person, I am.'

She shrugged; he was right. She wouldn't dispute it. Natasha had worked hard to isolate herself, and not trust or rely on anyone's support. There was even a distance with her sister, but that was for her safety.

'What do you need doing?' she asked.

'I need someone to reason or balance ideas with Hitler while I'm away,' Hess said.

She smiled, 'I don't know if you realise but we're not exactly friends.'

'I know, he respects you, but, well you're a female. Anyway, you know there's more than one way to influence people.'

'What are you planning?'

'Don't worry about that,' he dismissed.

She looked at him. 'Seriously, we're back to this again?'

Hess looked at her, and then looked around. 'He doesn't know about the mission.'

'Really?'

There was a pause.

'I feel like, the goal has been changed,' Hess stated, 'that my vision has been corrupted, I mean the Reich's vision of where we should be heading as a nation.'

'And you want England's help,' she concluded.

'He thinks he's invincible,' Hess paused. 'He's going to attack Russia.'

'Barbarossa,' Natasha nodded.

She looked at him; not a hint of surprise that she knew about Russia.

'I'll not work for you,' she said. 'I'm not a follower.'

'I'm not asking you to do that,' he stated. 'I want to work with you.'

Natasha took a deep breath, 'How long will you be gone?'

'I don't know…' he said. 'No one knows what I've just told you, not even Wilhelm.'

She nodded and leaned back on the bench.

She didn't know why she believed him, but she did, and for a man who didn't trust anyone, he'd divulged a lot.

***

Jean looked at Wilhelm. 'How did you know?'

He pushed the door open for Jean to walk through.

'I recognised you,' he sighed, 'from Helene's great escape.'

They both walked up the corridor to Goebbels' office.

He smiled, 'And believe me, you're far too clever to be involved in Berlin resistance.'

She laughed, 'So I've heard.'

'Pardon?' Wilhelm asked.

'Hess said something like that, sort of,' she said. 'He was joking about what had happened to my predecessor.'

'That sly old dog,' Wilhelm murmured. 'He doesn't joke.'

Jean's face dropped, 'He knows?'

'If he was your enemy, I'd know about it.'

'Why would you know about it?'

'I arrange things for him,' he said.

She stopped walking. 'You kill people?'

He stopped stunned; then turned to her and grabbed her by the shoulders.

'I would know, and this shouldn't be a surprise…' he spoke to her as if she was a stupid schoolgirl, 'You know I've killed tonight. I'm not saying I'm an assassin, but I would know.'

'Sorry,' she blushed, 'of course.'

He turned back and started walking, 'And don't you try and act all sweet and innocent.'

'Okay, point taken,' she growled and stormed off past him to the office.

Jean walked over to the men's desks and started rummaging through the drawers. Wilhelm went straight to Goebbels' office. Jean soon appeared with a piece of paper that had a list of names. A couple crossed off. The writing looked familiar, but Jean could not quite place it.

Wilhelm came around to her side of the desk. 'What happened to these people?'

'They work here,' she replied.

Wilhelm had an envelope in his hands.

'How good are your forgeries?' he asked.

'Mediocre,' she replied. 'Why?'

He handed her the note that was inside the envelope. There was an asterisk against one name that Jean didn't recognise, and she wondered if that had been the secretary she replaced.

'I don't think I need to forge this' Jean said. 'There are two names left on this. Mine and another of the staff.'

'Who's this guy?'

'He is a graduate of Munich University,' she said, 'he's only been here for a month or so.'

'Okay,' Wilhelm answered. 'Find out where he lives and cross off your name on the list. Make sure you use the same pen.'

Jean left the room to look for his address and return the pieces of paper. Wilhelm pulled an address book out of his pocket. He flicked through to find the name for an old friend at Munich University. He dialled the telephone and waited for someone to answer.

'Hello,' said a tired voice.

'Kurt, it's Wilhelm,' he said.

'How can I help you?'

'I need some information on a student of yours, quite urgently,' he answered.

Jean walked back into the office and gave Wilhelm a piece of paper with the boy's address on it.

'Thank you,' Wilhelm said. 'Now check on Michele.'

Jean looked at him with surprise.

'Go,' he said.

They both left the office; Wilhelm had a busy night ahead of him.

***

Jean walked into the office the following morning, hung up her coat, and sat at her desk. She had to keep reminding herself not to touch her face which was layered in makeup to disguise a bruise. She just kept thinking, it's a normal day, just like any other. But it wasn't. The next hour or so could be the difference between life and death for Jean. The door opened and Goebbels walked through. He paused when he saw her.

'Good morning,' he said.

'Good morning, sir,' she replied, with a puzzled look on her face.

He never said anything for the first hour or so.

'Are you alright?' she enquired. 'You look pale.'

She went to get up.

Goebbels assured her and then smiled, 'I'm fine.'

Jean took a deep breath and started typing.

***

Wilhelm sat on the bed next to Michele. She was still asleep. Bruises covered her body. She had a cut on her swollen lip and black surrounded her eye. Wilhelm stroked her hair and watched her sleep. She was still beautiful to him. If only he could protect her, but she would never let him. He got up and walked to the door.

'Don't stop,' she whispered, 'please don't stop, it takes away my headache.'

He walked back to the bed and started stroking her hair again. She looked up at him and smiled.

'Thank you.'

Then she closed her eyes. He smiled back at her; maybe she did need him, just a little.

***

Friedrich was sitting at his desk. Hess peered through the office door at him. The last few weeks had taken its toll. He looked tired and stressed and his black hair was changing to grey.

'Hello, Friedrich.'

'Hello.'

'How are you?' Hess said. 'You've been acting differently lately.'

'I've had lot on my mind,' said Friedrich.

'It's time you left for the evening,' Hess said grabbing Friedrich's coat.

'I can't, I have too much to do.'

Hess grabbed all the papers off the desk, bundled them into the drawer, locked it and put the key in his pocket.

'Look now you have nothing to do,' he said. 'Let's go.'

Friedrich followed Hess out of the building. He couldn't be bothered fighting. They wandered down the road and soon found a small restaurant that was almost deserted. Hess and Friedrich sat down at the bar. The bartender asked what drinks they would like.

Hess turned to Friedrich, 'What would you like?'

'A vodka on the rocks.'

Hess said, 'Make that two.'

Friedrich looked at him, 'I thought you didn't drink.'

'Normally I don't, but I too have been under a little stress. I won't tell if you don't.'

They both sat in silence for a few moments.

'How are you Friedrich, really?' Hess said.

Friedrich took a sip. Why was Hess was taking such an interest suddenly?

'I'll not always be here and until recently you seemed so focused,' Hess said, 'I just want to make sure you'll be fine, when you're back in charge.'

Friedrich looked at him; he wasn't concerned about him, but the job.

'Work is fine,' Friedrich replied, 'I just thought I'd hand the reins over to you while you are here.'

'Well,' Hess laughed, 'I don't want them; I have other things to do.'

'Oh,' Friedrich was a little confused.

'It must be good though,' Hess said, 'to have Natasha, as support.'

'Yes.'

He didn't want her support; he didn't want her anywhere near him.

'Does she not support you?' Hess casually asked.

'It's not that,' he paused, 'she's very dedicated to the cause, it's just…'

'She's stubborn,' Hess said.

'Yes,' Friedrich said, 'and defiant, and detached.'

He stopped; he didn't want to say too much.

'You're very lucky I think,' Hess said, 'She's an amazing woman. You must be – proud.'

'Hmm,' Friedrich looked at the bottom of his glass, 'It's not that easy.'

'Sometimes I think that you don't really know each other at all,' Hess said.

'Oh, believe me,' Friedrich said, 'I'm getting to know my daughter more day by day.'

'Just as long as you do,' Hess said pushing his untouched glass to Friedrich. 'I thought you might need another.' Hess got up and left.

It was a strange conversation. Friedrich rolled the bottom of Hess's glass on the bar. Bringing it to his lips, he drained its contents. Hess had no idea what he was thinking. How could he? Could he?

***

Goebbels came out of his office and had a look around.

'Where is everyone?' he said looking at Jean.

She looked around. There were three empty desks. Two of them she knew about, the other she could only assume.

'I don't know,' she replied looking confused, 'Is there a holiday, I don't know about?'

'Hmm,' Goebbels said, 'maybe.'

Then he walked back into his office. Jeans hands felt clammy, and she could feel sweat on her forehead. She started to take long deep breaths to calm herself. She put her chin up, relaxed her shoulders, and continued doing her work. She must remember to act as normal as possible. Her hand involuntarily went to touch the scarf around her neck. She pulled her hand back down and put it on the desk.

***

Natasha walked into the dining room yawning. She was still in her dressing gown and had slept in a little longer than she wanted. She got some toast and sat down at the table. Friedrich was reading the paper.

'Good morning,' she smiled.

'Good morning.'

'What are you doing today?' she said.

'Going to work.'

He pushed his chair back and stood up, with his paper.

'If you've finished with that? Could–'

'No.'

He walked out of the room.

She took a bite of the toast. That went well. She didn't feel hungry. Dropping the toast on the plate, she put her elbows on the table and lent her head in the palm of her hands. His behaviour upset her, but she couldn't afford to have distractions now. There was too much happening. Father, please be fine.

***

Jean walked through the door of her apartment with a large smile on her face.

'I survived.'

Wilhelm laughed. 'Congratulations. But I need your help.'

Wilhelm and Michele had been trying to hide her bruising with makeup.

'Leave it to me,' Jean smiled and then looked at Wilhelm. 'I'd love a drink.'

Michele sat patiently in the seat while Jean went to work. Every time Michele tried to talk; Jean would stop her. Wilhelm just looked on amazed at the transformation. By the time Jean had finished Michele looked like new, apart from a slightly swollen lip.

'Thank you,' Michele said.

'My pleasure.'

'It's time for us to go,' said Wilhelm.

'Jean,' Michele ignored him, 'why did you call?'

Jean replied, 'It was about the Russian invasion. But Wilhelm can tell you all about that.'

Michele turned to Wilhelm, 'Oh, can he?'

'Of course,' he smiled, trying to look angelic, 'of course I will.'

Michele turned back to Jean. 'No more information collection for at least a month,' she said. 'Wait till everything settles.'

Jean nodded.

Wilhelm smiled and leaned forward, 'That means no spying.'

Jean rolled her eyes, 'Wilhelm spying is illegal, it's treason. We collect information, that's all.'

'Let's go,' Michele said, and then looked at Jean, 'be careful.'

Michele grabbed Wilhelm's arm as they walked out the door. 'Now why don't you tell me about Russia.'

Jean walked over to the kitchen. Wilhelm had made her a lovely coffee, which she poured down the sink. That wasn't the type of drink she wanted. She opened the cupboard, pulled out a bottle of vodka and poured it into a glass. Throwing it down her throat she looked out the window. Oh, it's good to be alive. She poured herself another.

CHAPTER 18

Oskar could see the train in the distance, slowly working its way towards the station. He waited in the car just opposite the entrance. Jean had phoned warning of Michele's arrival, her fragile state and that she was travelling with someone. She didn't say who. Oskar leaned back in the seat and lit a cigarette.

The train pulled up, he got out of the car and walked into the station, looking for Michele. She emerged from the train slowly; you could tell she was hurt. She smiled and spoke to an elderly lady in front of her. Oskar assumed she was the other passenger. Behind Michele was a German Officer, who carried a satchel, and stood very close to Michele. She looked up and noticed Oskar, then started to walk towards him. The officer grabbed her arm.

Oskar froze. Sharp breath in. What to do? Was she being arrested? He looked around. No other uniforms. Maybe undercover. Act calm or take him on. What to do?

Oskar turned and walked to the car. There was a gun under the seat. Michele wouldn't betray him, no way, she wouldn't. She would lead them away. Distance was good.

***

Michele got off the train slowly. A lady in front of her turned and asked if she was alright, as she struggled with the steps. She thanked her and then started walking along the platform. She looked up and saw Oskar and smiled. Thank you. The last thing she wanted to do was to wait. She started to stride down the platform.

Wilhelm grabbed her arm.

'He'll wait, you know.'

She smiled. 'Yes, he will.'

They started to walk towards Oskar.

Oskar didn't look well at all. Why? Then he quickly turned and walked away. Michele stopped for a moment and looked at Wilhelm. 'I don't understand,' she said. Then it dawned on her, 'Oh, yes I do understand.'

She smiled.

'The uniform?' Wilhelm asked.

'I think so.'

They were at the end of the platform. Michele paused. 'I need to talk to him, alone.'

'I understand.'

Wilhelm let go of her arm. She walked towards the car and indicated to open the window. 'Thank you for picking me up.'

'You all right?' Oskar nodded towards Wilhelm.

'I'm a bit bruised and battered, but I'll live.'

A pause.

'He's a good guy,' Michele said.

Oskar didn't move.

'Hey,' she said, 'listen to me.'

He looked at her.

'When have I ever jeopardised the group? Never, and I don't intend starting now. Do you understand me?'

He nodded.

'Right, we're taking him to headquarters,' she said.

He looked at her in shock. 'What?'

'You heard me.'

'Can I blindfold him?' he said. 'I'd feel better.'

Michele looked at him for a moment. 'Yes. But not here.'

Oskar took a deep breath and nodded.

Michele walked back to Wilhelm. She faced him, and grabbed his hands bringing them together, 'We're going now. Do you trust me?'

He smiled and glanced at their hands and then back to her face. 'Of course.'

'Good,' she replied. 'I want you to know that I trust you. But he doesn't. Not yet. So, when we get into the country, you're going to be blindfolded. Is that alright?'

His face set.

'Sorry.'

'Fine.' Although his tone indicated otherwise.

'I think first you need to change clothes,' she said.

He smiled nodding, and they both walked to the car.

The sun was just creeping over the horizon by the time they'd reached the outskirts of the city. Wilhelm was in civilian clothes, sitting in the passenger's seat, with Michele in the middle. Oskar pulled over to the side of the road. The operations' room was in a different direction, but it was now time to blindfold Wilhelm. They would also need to drive the back roads to avoid anyone seeing.

Michele turned to him.

'I'm sorry,' she said.

'It's alright,' he grumbled, and flicked a quick look at Oskar before a scarf, then a shirt was tied around his head. Michele put a hat on him, so it was harder to see the blindfold.

'This is a bad idea,' Oskar remarked to Michele.

'I may not be able to see,' Wilhelm said, 'but I can still hear.'

Oskar grumbled and started the car. They drove the long way to the farm. Pulling up to the front house, Oskar got out of the car and handed the old woman the keys.

As he arrived back, Wilhelm said, 'Can I take it off yet?'

Before Michele could reply Oskar snapped, 'No.'

'In fact,' he added, 'there is something else we must do.'

Oskar leaned over and put a peg on Wilhelm's nose so he wouldn't notice the farm smells. Wilhelm felt a pinch. He couldn't believe it, he sighed with anger. As if the country air would smell different out of the truck. He tried to imagine what he looked like. A smile grew across his face, and he started to laugh. He knew that would anger Oskar so he tried to stop, but he couldn't. He just couldn't help himself. Oskar turned and stared at Wilhelm. He didn't trust him at all, and now he was laughing. Michele looked at Oskar and thought if looks could kill, Wilhelm would be a corpse. But he wasn't, and his laugh was contagious. She started to giggle. Oskar looked at her in disgust; she tried to calm down, but it just made her worse and she collapsed into hysterics. This infuriated Oskar even more and he slammed the door.

'Don't be so grumpy,' Michele yelled.

Oskar turned and looked really hurt. Michele got out of the car and helped Wilhelm out.

'Just look at him Oskar,' Michele called.

Oskar looked at Wilhelm. He looked stupid. Wilhelm had a shirt tied over his face, on top of the scarf. The collar was covering his eyebrows, and the back of the shirt was hanging off the tip of his nose. This was attached firmly to his nose, by a wooden peg. And he wore a hat. But Oskar was determined not to laugh. So, he gave a large huff and turned and stormed off, before she could see him smile. He wasn't letting them off the hook that easily. They didn't need this guy, why was he even here? They are fine without him. Everything was working well without any outsiders. Natasha had been different. She'd always been there, but no one had known. Yosef would be back soon, and everything would be back to normal. Oskar didn't like Michele's new friend, and he hoped he wouldn't stay.

Michele tried to guide Wilhelm to the barn. He stumbled and the process was slow. He gripped her arm tightly. He hated having to rely on someone else and not knowing what was going to happen. But rightly or wrongly he trusted her.

***

Natasha sat at the table, looking down at a piece of blank paper. She didn't really know what she wanted to say or plan. Hess had said that he hadn't wanted anyone to know what was happening. She had managed to convince him Michele would need to know. It meant that things would have to be done and planned without the rest of the resistance knowing the full story. Natasha didn't mind that. It was something that she was used to, but Michele wasn't. I don't think she'll like it. So, can I really tell her? She looked around as if it was going to make the decision easier.

Anneliese turned to Natasha. 'She should have been here by now.'

Henri said, 'They'll be here soon.'

Natasha smiled.

The bell rang, and Oskar stormed down the stairs. He wasn't happy. Michele came down the stairs, walking backwards. She was guiding someone. The figure, blindfolded with a shirt, and a peg on their nose.

Natasha got up and stared at Michele with anger. She leaned over to Henri and whispered, 'Sit him down, and keep him blindfolded.'

They both walked over to Michele. Natasha grabbed her by the arm and yanked her across the floor, while Henri sat Wilhelm.

'What do you think you are doing?' Natasha whispered angrily to her younger sister. 'You've put everyone at risk.'

'Natasha,' Michele quietly replied, 'It's Wilhelm, surely you know he's on our side.'

'We,' Natasha paused, 'know no such thing.'

'He's been helping,' Michele said, 'We had a situation that he helped with in Berlin.'

'Do not let your personal feelings cloud your judgement,' Natasha whispered sternly. 'Take him back.'

'How dare you,' Michele snarled. 'My life is this cause, don't think that I would jeopardise it. You know nothing about this, and I suggest...'

'Natasha,' Wilhelm called out, 'it wasn't her fault.'

Everyone froze. No one could hear the conversation between the sisters, apart from the last line. How did he know that it was with Natasha?

'I know it's you,' he continued, 'you have to trust me. Please.'

Natasha took a deep breath and set her jaw. She looked at Michele, who looked like she'd just been told off.

'You three out,' Natasha said to the others.

'He's already seen me,' Oskar snarled.

'All right,' Natasha replied, 'both of you wait outside, out of sight.'

Anneliese and Henri left.

Natasha lent on the back of a chair, 'You can take this all off now.'

Oskar looked at her. She nodded a reassurance to him and then looked back at Wilhelm. After blinking a couple of times, he started to look around. The room was an organised operations room. Wilhelm couldn't believe his eyes. Information on Germany and England covered the walls. Wilhelm's eyes wandered over to Natasha and he smiled.

'Of course, you'd be here,' he said.

Michele sat in a chair, looking a little bashful. She was thinking about what Natasha had said. No, it wasn't anything to do with personal feelings. Obviously, Wilhelm was a nice person. He seemed caring, and intelligent and protective and handsome, yes very handsome. Stop. He had also saved both Jean and her, which meant he knew too much. No, it was factual evidence. He's an asset. She sat back in her chair with a defiant gaze. Natasha, how dare you put doubt in my head? I'm being completely rational.

'What happened in Berlin?' Natasha asked.

Wilhelm and Michele recounted the incident, including how they had covered Jean.

'How are you?' Natasha asked Michele.

'Fine.'

'Good,'

Next, they talked about Operation Barbarossa. There had been no definite timing put on it and it still seemed very up in the air. But Wilhelm agreed to keep them posted on any developments.

Natasha surveyed the small group. Whether she liked it or not Wilhelm was one of them now. She wasn't the only one who was unsure. Oskar was sullen during the discussions and his eyes never left Wilhelm.

'Wilhelm,' Natasha said, 'do you think you could teach someone how to fly?'

Michele sat quietly with a little smile on her face. She couldn't wait to learn. It would be so exciting. Wilhelm threw a quick look at Michele and then back to Natasha.

'Of course,' he said, 'it'd be my honour.'

'Great,' Natasha said, 'Oskar, when will you be able to start training?'

All three faces dropped.

'I don't know if—' Oskar began.

'It's settled then,' Natasha said.

'But I want to learn,' Michele said.

'And you can,' Natasha said, 'after Oskar.'

Natasha looked at Wilhelm, who smiled. There was a dare in her eyes. Wilhelm had just been given a chance to win Oskar over. It would be a tough challenge though. He looked at Natasha and nodded. He understood her reasoning, although he didn't understand why someone needed to learn how to fly.

***

Friedrich walked along the streets to the offices. He found himself reminiscing on the days before the war before Helene had left. He stopped outside the bakery. It had always been there for as long as he could remember. Herr Schmidt looked up.

'Hello,' Herr Schmidt asked, 'can I help?'

'I don't think anyone can,' Friedrich said. Then remembering himself he surveyed the selection. 'Can I have a mini apple strudel?'

He reached into his pocket for change.

Herr Schmidt handed it over the counter and said, 'My treat Friedrich, please take care of yourself. I worry about you.'

Friedrich smiled and thanked him. A mirror caught his attention; he briefly thought that he had seen a reflection of Helene. He spun around, but no one was there.

'What's wrong?' Schmidt said.

'I'm seeing ghosts.'

He walked out of the shop towards the headquarters.

***

Helene pressed herself in a doorway in the alley beside the bakery. She saw Friedrich cross the street and enter his office building. Slowly she took a step forward to see if anyone was about. The street was almost empty, so she casually walked into the baker.

'That was very close,' Schmidt said.

'I know,' she sighed and rolled her eyes. 'How is he?'

'Are you concerned?' Schmidt asked.

'Only in a polite way,' she said trying to sound uninterested.

'Fine, I guess,' Schmidt smiled to himself as he cleaned the back shelves, 'would be the polite answer.'

She looked down at the floor for a moment and then said, 'Really?'

Schmidt turned around and took a deep breath. 'No, he's lost. In fact, I think he needs to be watched, if he's of value to anyone. Because I've never seen him like this.'

'Thank you,' Helene said.

She bit her lip, turned and left the shop before Schmidt could see her eyes well up. Poor Friedrich, she thought, you really picked the wrong path to follow.

***

Schmidt shook his head. He'd seen Friedrich and Helene grow up and fall in love. They were the perfect couple, with the perfect family. If only it could've stayed that way. He started wiping down the bench. So many things made him mad. Made him angry. It wasn't good for his health, his heart was old. In a normal world he'd look at retiring. But the bakery kept him sane, alive, available. It was all he had. But everything was messed up. The war, society, even love. How could one person devastate everything so effectively? Hitler had done it perfectly.

***

Natasha walked through the front door and went towards her room. It'd been a long day. The front room light was on, and she opened the door to switch it off. Fumes, wow, fumes hit her, whisky, no, no, brandy. Both? Her father had passed out on the lounge and had knocked over a bottle of brandy, spilling it all over the floor. She tried to clean up what she could and then placed a blanket over him. She looked at Friedrich. If only you knew, if only I could trust you. But I can't, and I'm here, and you hate me. And I'm all alone, by myself, in front you. Her eyes felt watery. I'm not as bad as you think. She knelt on the floor beside him and stroked his hair, crying, wishing things could be different and knowing they wouldn't be.

CHAPTER 19

Natasha sat on the park bench. The air was so cold that she wore not only her coat, but a scarf, gloves and hat, to try and keep warm. She looked like a bundle of black with eyes, peering out. Hess walked over and sat down.

'Good morning,' he smiled.

'Good morning.' Natasha shivered, 'I think we have a problem.'

He looked at her sideways.

'Wilhelm and Michele,' she continued, 'are, shall we say, building a bond.'

'This can be used against them,' he sighed.

Natasha nodded.

'At the moment all they know is that someone else needs to learn how to fly. I haven't told Michele the plan yet. But because of their relationship I think we need to decide whether we tell them both everything or,' she paused, 'nothing.'

They both sat in deep thought for a few moments.

Hess broke the silence, 'Tell them.'

He moved to leave.

'I have a question,' said Natasha. 'You never said why. Why us?'

He smiled, but it was an embarrassed smile.

'You'll think it's strange,' he began, 'I met you a long time ago. I don't know if you remember. You were a child, maybe a little older. It was the day your mother left.'

Natasha took a sharp intake of air. She had not expected it, it was like a side punch that came out of nowhere.

'Natasha, you were never a child, physically yes, but never,' he paused, 'a child.' He flicked his hand dismissively, 'It doesn't matter.'

'Anyway a few days, well nights later I had a dream, or a feeling or I don't know, something that urged me to keep an eye on you.

Natasha sat not knowing how to process the information.

'So, I did. I watched your progress, how you have worked your way into the regime. You are one of the reasons that female positions within the Kripo are being created. You insolence to authority, your self-imposed isolation, it has all helped your reputation. It has made you stand out from the crowd. It reminds me a little of how I view things.'

He paused and looked at her with a warning, 'But be careful. You walk a very fine line with Hitler, and it could get you killed.'

'So, you spied on me,' she replied, 'sounds like a good use of resources.'

'It's worked out well for me,' he replied, 'Wilhelm helped, of course he didn't realise, but he did. All your act and attitude hid something I underestimated.' Again he paused. 'You are quite intelligent. Although I don't know why that was a shock to me.'

'A dream to keep an eye on me started all of this.'

'No, well not exactly. Now here is the crazy bit.'

There was a smile, but some confusion and a little disbelief on his face. 'I had another dream, where I went to England to negotiate peace,' he spoke as if he didn't really believe himself.

'Oh, you top Nazis really believe all this occult stuff, dreams from the other side, I forget. I know it's your belief but I...'

Now he looked annoyed.

'Some people believe all of that, and others believe different degrees of it, I believe... it doesn't matter what I believe. But in relation to this. Think of my dreams not so much as messages from a higher source, prophet, or the other side, but purely from my mind. Juggling all my thoughts and observations into a logical scenario that I wouldn't be able to do if I consciously directed them.'

She nodded, 'Now that I can understand.'

'The enemies of my enemies are my friends. It would be more efficient to make peace with Britain than with Russia. It's as simple as that and you are someone who can look after things when I'm away. You have the skills. You and Michele have the resources and experience to do things.'

Natasha looked at him. There was something he was not saying. Something was not quite right.

'Everyone has skills, it just depends on if they are the right ones for the job.'

He nodded and smiled. He knew this was likely to be a one-way trip. Hitler would mark him a dead man if he returned and a return was unlikely. He would be a prized prisoner for the British. He just hoped something good would come out of it. He hoped that the signs he had noticed were pointing him in the right direction. It was his destiny. Because here there was nothing more he could do. Lebensraum had been his goal. He'd introduced Hitler to it, that was how they had bonded. They both agreed on unification and expansion of Europe to the east. That was the goal. The man had such focus. He had understood they would have to take on the Jewish and the Bolsheviks to do it. Of course, they would, or Germany would be taken over with them, just not…

He smiled with sad eyes as Natasha got up and walked away.

Everyone had a line and Hess was closely approaching his. He did not want to step over it. But if he did nothing he would be forced, and he knew he would never recover from that. He would not allow his Germany to be remembered for the wrong legacy, it would destroy its future potential, it would destroy him. He must save it.

***

Jean had been told to act just like a secretary, for a whole month. She sat at her desk opening mail. Act just like a secretary, where was the adrenaline in that? Act, just like a secretary, only a secretary, I'm going insane. How do secretaries do it? How do they survive, how do they stay sane? When war ends, and if I'm still alive shoot me, if I need to work in a secretarial pool. Where's the adventure, the risk, the mystery or intrigue.

She sat back and thought for a second, I guess you could get to live a little longer, that may be appealing to some. She giggled; no, not to her.

Two new people had been brought in. Jean assumed they were agents to replace those that had been killed. She had asked about the others, but Goebbels just said they'd been transferred.

Until now Jean had just concentrated on collecting information. She had not expanded her network at all. In her mind, expanding a network did not count as intelligence work, it was just socialising with purpose. She needed to get into the special filing cabinet in the corner. But every time she got close; she was stopped by one of the senior staff. She knew she needed to branch out to other departments too if she wanted more information. Later, of course. Although the thought of spending time with the other secretaries didn't really excite her, it would have to happen, it would help. She had watched over the past couple of months how the girls grouped together.

Just before lunch she walked over to Klara, one of the secretaries, and smiled. The girl looked up confused.

'Sorry' said Jean, 'I was wondering if you could recommend somewhere around here that I could get something to eat. I normally bring sandwiches, but I forgot today. Could you suggest anywhere?'

The girl flicked a quick look at her friend who nodded.

'We are going out for lunch today. Would you like to join us?'

'If that is alright with you, I would love to. Thank you' Jean said.

At lunchtime the three of them left the building and walked down the street to a small bakery which had outdoor seating.

The conversation was surprisingly pleasant. Another group of girls sat at a table nearby.

'Hello' they chorused.

The girls that Jean were with smiled and replied.

Klara leaned forward, 'They are from Muller's office, Gestapo headquarters.'

'Really?' said Jean. 'Are we not supposed to talk to each other? You know, department to department.'

'Oh, nothing like that,' Klara said. 'It's just compared to what we do, their job is rather dull. Sometimes there is something exciting. Then they join us, but most of the time it's just boring interrogation typing. Even the resistance ones can be boring, and you'd think they would be exciting.'

'You would think,' Jean said as she took a sip of her coffee.

***

Wilhelm took his coffee from the counter and then walked over to the table. He sat opposite Oskar. Oskar looked at him with distaste.

'What exactly,' Wilhelm said, 'is it you don't like about me?'

Oskar leaned forward, 'Where do I start. I don't trust you.'

Wilhelm sat back, 'that's a shame. You're going to have to get over that quite quickly.'

'No, I don't, you teach me,' said Oskar, 'then I fly.'

'You don't get it do you?' Wilhelm said. 'Do you really think that Natasha would have you trained if only one pilot was needed?'

Oskar sat back for a moment.

'Whatever the plan is, it's you and me up there. Pilots never fly alone; you fly in a group, and you need to trust them because they're protecting you just as much as you're protecting them. And if it's only you and me, you have to trust me. Clear?'

'I still don't trust you,' said Oskar.

Wilhelm smiled, 'You know what? This has nothing to do with trust.'

'I don't need to listen to this,' Oskar said getting up out of the chair.

'This is to do with Michele, isn't it,' Wilhelm baited. 'It is, isn't it?'

'Leave me alone.'

'What do you think I'm trying to do, replace you?' Wilhelm continued. 'Do you have a soft spot for her, was she your girl?'

'It's not like that.'

Natasha walked into the nearly deserted café and quietly sat down to see what was going on. She'd come to see Henri who was serving behind the counter, but this was far more entertaining.

Henri looked at Natasha, she shook her head, and he remained behind the counter. The last customers left. She turned the sign on the door so that it said closed.

'Can't handle the fact that she may rely on someone else for support?' Wilhelm kept prodding.

Oskar turned and walked over to Wilhelm. 'You know nothing about her or me. Don't think you're someone important. She's like my little sister and she always will be.'

'But deep down inside you don't feel important to her anymore, do you?' Wilhelm taunted. 'Do you?'

Oskar didn't even think as he threw a punch, which took Wilhelm by surprise. Wilhelm was soon up on his feet and punched Oskar in the side to wind him. Henri jumped over the counter, but Natasha stopped him from intervening.

'If you want to help,' Natasha said, 'make sure there's no weapons.'

Henri grabbed all the crockery, cutlery and glasses and moved them behind the counter. Natasha and Henri, pulled up a chair, sat back and watched the show. It was like a boxing match.

A fist connected with a jaw, some blocking, another by the eye. Who was who? A duck. Delivery to ribs. Pause, attack. Oskar's fist just below the ribcage. Wilhelm crashed onto the table. Oskar's hands grabbed around Wilhelm's neck. Wilhelm's hand sliced through grabbing Oskar's neck. Both started turning red, but neither letting go.

Natasha got up, walked over, and bent down so that her face was in eyesight of both of them and said, 'I need to talk to you, so can you stop now?'

They both grunted, 'No.'

She grabbed both by the ears and twisted them, pulling them so that they were both sitting.

'Now let go,' she said, 'or I'll break both your arms.'

They both let go and moved away from each other.

Oskar's nose was streaming blood, and he had a cut lip. Wilhelm had a cut on his forehead, which looked like it needed stitches, and his jaw was swelling.

'Why are you both playing when there's so much to do?'

They were both stood to attention in front of Natasha but didn't say a word.

'Do you know what I see?'

Again, there was silence.

'Two egos fighting,' she said. 'I won't waste my time with egos.'

They both diverted their gaze when she looked them in the eyes.

'You've both, really, disappointed me. Shape up or face the consequences, do we understand each other?'

There was silence.

'I said, do we understand each other.'

'Yes Fraulein,' they chorused.

'Now go,' she said.

***

Wilhelm and Oskar walked out of the café. They felt like pupils leaving the principal's office.

Oskar looked down at the ground. 'You have some good moves.'

'You're not too bad yourself,' Wilhelm replied.

'Anyway, I don't think I've formally introduced myself,' Wilhelm said holding out his hand, 'I'm Wilhelm, I work in intelligence.'

'I'm Oskar,' he smiled, 'and officially I'm a farm hand, who is acting assistant resistance leader.'

'Two o'clock tomorrow then.'

'Two o'clock it is.' Oskar agreed and they both walked off to tend to their wounds.

***

Michele was in bed reading a book when Hilde walked in.

'You should be resting, not reading,' Hilde stated.

'I don't want to,' Michele said. 'Anyway, I am bored of sleeping.'

Hilde shook her head and walked back out the door.

'You should've seen her,' Michele muttered. 'She treated me like a child.'

Hilde walked back in and sat at the end of the bed.

'Worse,' Michele paused, 'she treated me like an idiot. And I'm not an idiot. You know I'm not. She put me down in front of everyone. In front of my entire group, my group! How could she?'

Hilde looked at Michele, she looked so upset.

'In front of Oskar?' Hilde asked. 'And Wilhelm?'

Michele looked at the wall and tried not to cry.

'Michele darling,' Hilde asked, 'is it really Natasha you're angry with?'

Michele couldn't help it; a tear ran down her cheek. Hilde gave her a hug. Sometimes even Michele needed support.

***

Wilhelm walked into Hess's office. Hess was looking at his desk. He reached to the side and picked up a pile of papers.

'Can you do me a favour?' Hess said as he looked up. 'Oh, what happened?'

'Nothing much,' Wilhelm smiled.

'I hope the other guy was worse off.'

'It was pretty even actually, anyway, you were saying?'

Hess looked confused for a second and then regained his thought, 'Get these translated into English.'

'My written English is not the best,' Wilhelm protested. 'I'm not the right person for this.'

'Oh sorry, I didn't mean you,' Hess smiled. 'Michele.'

'Alright,' Wilhelm nodded, turned to leave and then stopped. 'Sorry who?' he stuttered.

'You know who,' Hess smiled, 'your new friend. Don't mess this up.'

'Yes sir,' Wilhelm replied.

He walked out knowing that he'd been warned, but also felt that in a strange way his uncle approved. He smiled, as he walked down the corridor. Then stopped, it hurt too much.

***

Natasha yawned as she reached into her pocket for her keys. It'd been another long day. She was hoping there would be no confrontation with her father tonight. They were fighting all the time now, not about anything in particular, just everything. His drinking wasn't helping. She hated the fact that her father was becoming an alcoholic. She quietly crept through the doorway and gently closed the door behind her.

'Where are you going?' Friedrich's voice boomed from the parlour.

'To bed.'

'Come in,' he commanded, 'have a drink.'

She walked into the parlour, 'No, but thank you for offering.'

'What did you do today?' Friedrich asked.

'Nothing.'

'I saw you with Hess this morning, what were you talking about?'

He poured himself whisky and added some ice.

'Not much.'

Friedrich sipped his drink as he looked straight into her eyes. He didn't believe her.

'I don't want you talking to him,' he replied. 'Stay away.'

He finished his drink and proceeded to pour another.

'He's the second in charge, I thought you'd like that,' she replied.

'What were you talking about?' he shouted.

'Nothing.'

'Stay away from Hess.'

'You can't stop me.'

He said, 'Stay away or…'

'Or what.'

He didn't think. The glass he was holding flew across the room towards Natasha. Natasha froze in shock. Then when she could respond, it took all her willpower not to. She wouldn't show fear.

She felt a breeze as the glass passed her and smashed on the wall behind her. The ice rebound against her back.

Friedrich, stone faced, pushed past her out of the room. He slammed the front door.

Natasha took a deep breath and leaned on the chair. She panted and got the shakes. After a few moments, when she had recovered, she started to clean up.

His anger had moved on, this was the first violent action that her father had ever made towards her. She hoped it wasn't the start of things to come.

***

Friedrich was cold, but he needed some fresh air. Up until recently he'd been in control. He was the Administrative Head in charge of Munich, of his daughter, of his life. But now. He had no control. His hands were shaking. He took a deep breath and then a controlled exhale. He'd lost control of his anger and nearly… He took another breath. He hated her. But she was still his own flesh and blood. That glass had almost caught her face, and still she hadn't moved. He sat down in the square. Things were spinning, but stationary. My world is out of control, I don't know what, I, there's no, nothing is stable. There is nothing to hold on to. Helene, save, please save me, he pleaded.

CHAPTER 20

'So where are we going?' Oskar asked.

'Well, let me think,' said Wilhelm as he glanced at Oskar with a mischievous grin.

Oskar looked back suspiciously, 'what are you thinking?'

'I'm wondering whether I should blindfold you and put a peg on your nose or not.'

Oskar punched Wilhelm's arm softly, 'Ha, ha.'

'We're going to an airport; I thought it may be the best place to teach you to fly.'

They drove down a long entrance way and pulled up at some buildings. Wilhelm got out of the car and walked to the main office. Oskar followed closely behind. As they entered, two guards saluted them and then relaxed as they passed.

'How do you get used to that?' Oskar asked.

'I don't,' he said. 'Unfortunately, it comes with the job.'

Oskar grabbed Wilhelm's arm, 'I'm not flying today, am I?'

'Of course,' Wilhelm replied. 'You can drive a car, can't you?'

Oskar nodded.

'I am going to hand you the keys. It's just like driving a car,' Wilhelm said casually.

Oskar's face turned white, he felt sick in his stomach. Wilhelm's lips turned up to a smile.

'Don't worry,' he said, 'I just want to teach you about the inside of the plane today. You need to learn how to parachute out of a plane before you can learn how to fly it.'

They walked over to a plane that already had a ladder available.

'Climb in,' encouraged Wilhelm, 'let the learning begin.'

***

There was a knock at the door.

'Come in,' Michele called.

The door opened slowly, and Hilde walked in. 'Are you still bored?'

'Out of my brain.'

'How's your English?' Hilde enquired.

'It's okay,' Michele said.

'I have some documents that need translating,' Hilde said.

'Sure.'

Normally she would've delegated this job, but she was really bored. Michele sat up in the bed and Hilde handed her the documents.

'Good luck.'

Michele pulled out a notepad and took a deep breath, maybe it would kill a little time anyway. She opened the parcel and started to read. They were handwritten and mainly notes. There were a couple of reports included in the pile. She would start there. They seemed organised. Michele sat back and started to read. Writing on her notebook, she copied the title 'Scientific experimentation proposal.' Fun, she thought, loads of scientific terms that she didn't understand at all. Reading on for a further five minutes, she put down the paper. It wasn't full of scientific terms or words that weren't understandable. Saliva was rushing to her mouth, her stomach felt sick. How could anyone do this to their own people, to any people. She shivered as a chill went down her spine. People didn't run this country, it was run by animals; no, animals wouldn't even do this. No wonder Hess was going to England. Germany needed help to save themselves, from themselves, and these documents proved it.

***

Natasha walked into Hess's office.

'I think we should have a briefing soon,' she said.

'I agree, am I allowed to your secret operations room?'

'How long do we have?' she asked, ignoring the question.

He looked at the calendar, 'Thirty-seven days. Only key personnel.'

'Of course.'

'On Saturday then,' he said, 'just after lunch.'

'Certainly,' she said smiling, 'I'll have the blindfold ready.'

He laughed back. 'You just try.'

***

'Alright, so you see the ground,' asked Wilhelm. 'What do you do?'

'I start running in the air,' said Oskar. 'When I touch the ground, I continue running and I unbuckle and collect up the parachute.'

'If you're in water.'

'Don't run, legs together' Oskar replied. 'Unbuckle and swim.' Oskar looked bored.

'Good,' Wilhelm said. 'Let's go.'

'Let's go where?'

'Jump out of a plane,' Wilhelm said, as he was walking away.

'When it's flying?'

'Yes,' said Wilhelm looking over his shoulder.

Oskar got up. 'Why would I want to jump out of a perfectly good plane?'

'Because it is easier than jumping out of one that's not,' Wilhelm said sarcastically. 'Now let's go.'

'I ask again…' Oskar said but stopped as Wilhelm walked back to Oskar.

'You know all the people that salute me here,' Wilhelm said.

'Yes.'

'They're under my command. They will, if I request, drag you into a plane and throw you out when I tell them to.' Wilhelm continued, 'Now I suggest you grab a parachute while you still have the chance?'

'You are joking, aren't you?' Oskar laughed nervously.

'They would do it; the real question is, would I? Don't tempt me Oskar.'

Oskar picked up the parachute and asked. 'Where is the plane?'

'That's better,' Wilhelm said. 'This way.'

***

Jean looked up from her desk, Klara was getting ready to go. They had gone for a few lunches now, and Jean was becoming more accepted by their small group. She had decided to try something today. In the morning with the filing, she had been given some documents she normally would have handed to the girls to file in the locked filing cabinet in the corner. It was still on her desk. She waited until Klara was in her coat turning to leave and rushed over.

'Klara, I'm so sorry, but this needs to be filed. Could you do it for me? It is quite confidential, and I don't want to leave it out.'

Klara stopped and looked at the documents, she paused for a moment. Jean could see her thinking and then she took a deep breath.

'Don't tell anyone,' she said, 'the key is on a hook behind the filing cabinet.'

Klara brought her finger up to her lips, 'Shh.'

Jean nodded and Klara was out of the door before Jean allowed herself to smile. She turned and walked to the cabinet, sliding her hand along the back until she found the key. The documents would be easily filed but Jean wanted to check what else was in the cabinet. She flicked through the files. Deportations, provincial reports, propaganda ideas, and a few personnel files. The files were on Himmler, Goering, Haushofer, K and Haushofer, A and Hess. Jean flicked through the papers. Most of the information was not very incriminating. There were a few convictions Hess had overturned, lists of friends and contacts, documents Hess has signed and some photographs of some German Blood Certificates that he had authorised. Two of these were for the Haushofers. She pulled out their files. Haushofer, Karl, was married to a mischling, which also made his son a mischling. The information was far more incriminating for Karl. There were notes on meetings that he had with British diplomats and a lot of contacts in Great Britain and Europe. She put it away and then filed her documents. Locking the filing cabinet, she thought, so this is where Goebbels keeps the truth. She would need more time to sort through this.

***

Natasha approached Hess as he was pouring himself a water.

'We need to talk before the meeting,' Natasha said.

'May I take you out for lunch tomorrow?' Hess smiled.

Natasha paused. It was the first time he had ever seen her surprised. She nodded.

'I'll meet you at the bakery across the street,' he said and then walked away.

Natasha watched for a moment and then regained her thoughts. She had things to attend to herself. She walked out into the corridor, almost coming face to face with her father.

'What are you doing?' Friedrich asked.

'Interrogations.'

'I'm doing them,' he replied, 'you can go home.'

Normally he didn't do interrogations unless it was a high-profile prisoner. What was he up to?

'I thought you didn't do interrogations anymore.'

He just looked at her.

'Anyway, there are two, Father,' she said, 'one each.'

'I can do both,' he said.

'No, you can't.'

Natasha and Friedrich walked down the corridor not looking at each other. The pair of them looked formidable to the guards, who jumped to attention. Father and daughter paused outside the two interrogation rooms. The guards knocked on the doors and slowly they opened. Guards walked out then Friedrich and Natasha walked in.

The door closed behind Natasha. There was a man tied to a chair. He was staring back at her. She didn't recognise him. There were three main types of resistance in Munich. There was Michele's resistance to the regime, foreign agents and the Nazis who just didn't like Hitler. Maybe he was the later.

'What's your name?' she asked.

He looked defiantly towards her. They did that. Normally when they saw a female, they felt more relaxed. They underestimated.

'Alright,' she said. 'Quite frankly I don't want to hurt you, but I will, so tell me something I can use,' she spoke softly.

'I just do administration,' he said. 'I'm a true German.'

'Define true German?' she asked. 'If you're a true German; give me a name of someone who is not.'

He would crack easily; he'd spoken too soon. It was also the look in the eye. The eyes were indeed the key to the soul. She wasn't in the mood for games. She picked up the needle.

'What are you doing?' he asked.

'What do you think?'

Imagination was an amazing thing. She knew he would just go into a trancelike state, where she could question him and then he would sleep for about an hour or so, but his mind was running wild about how much pain he would be in. Anything could be in the vial. He tried to move away from her, but he could hardly move his shoulders.

'Please don't,' he said.

She chuckled internally, if only he knew.

'A name.'

She turned to him and eyed his arm. His eyes widened with fear. She looked at him; this guy really was a wimp.

'Alright, alright,' he spluttered. 'I'll give you a name.'

'I am listening.'

'Friedrich,'

Natasha tensed, could he mean her father?

He whispered, as if someone else could hear them 'Olbricht.'

'Thank you,' she said as she pushed the needle into his arm.

He let out a screech and looked at her stunned. Slowly his wide eyes started to glaze over. He gave a little more information and then he drifted into a sleep. She picked up her leather gloves and put them on. She didn't want to injure this man with her bare hands, but he had to look like he had been tortured, even if it was only superficially.

***

Friedrich walked into his interrogation chamber. The door closed behind him. Leaning against the wall, he looked at the prisoner in silence. Slowly Friedrich walked over to him. He lent down and whispered into the prisoner's ear.

'Tell me something; tell me something that cheers up my day.'

The prisoner stared back at him; his jaw locked. This guy wasn't a mastermind. Friedrich pulled over a chair and straddled it, so he was facing the man.

'You know what?' Friedrich said casually, 'I'm having a bad day. No, I'm having a bad month and frankly I don't care if you are going to talk or not. I'm going to take it all out on you. Because I can, and no one cares, what I do. So, I suggest you try and cheer me up.'

The prisoner looked at him slightly confused and swallowed.

'Fine,' Friedrich said. 'Have it your way.'

He got up and kicked the chair aside. Using the back of his hand he punched the prisoner's cheek, with such force that he almost knocked the prisoner over. He walked over to the table and ran his finger over some items. Friedrich picked up the hammer and gently swung it as he walked back to the chair.

'Anything?'

The prisoner didn't move.

Friedrich slowly walked around behind the chair and brought the hammer down on the prisoner's hands. The crack echoed in the room, closely followed by a piercing scream. The prisoner's breath was shaky.

'Stop, please, stop,' he whimpered.

'They're starting a group,' he began.

Friedrich picked up the chair and sat down. The prisoner told him about a resistance group within the Nazi Generals. He didn't know much but mentioned the name Olbricht.

'Thank you.'

He didn't know what exactly to do with this information. The one thing he did know was that he didn't want Natasha to hear it. He turned and placed his hand just behind the prisoner's head. Grabbing his chin, he jerked the neck around until he heard the crack. The prisoner fell forward. Friedrich turned and knocked on the door. He walked out as it opened. There were other's there that would clean up his work for him. Friedrich had a lot of thinking to do.

Natasha met her father in the corridor.

'Anything?' he asked.

'No.'

'Let me try,' he asked.

'The prisoner is unconscious.'

She indicated to his room.

He shook his head, 'nothing.'

'I can.'

'He's dead,' he interrupted her.

Natasha looked at her father, who turned and walked back down the corridor in silence.

***

Jean opened the door to her old flat, to find Michele waiting in the kitchen area.

'I've missed this place,' she said.

'It's good to see you. Thank you for coming back this weekend. So much is happening, and I think you're going to be an important part of it,' Michele said.

Jean put down her bag and sat beside Michele.

'I got in.'

Michele looked quizzically at her.

'I know where the key is, and I got into the other filing cabinet.' She smiled. 'And it's a full cabinet. It's like his truth files.'

Michele smiled, 'Well done, have you had much time to look through it?'

'No. There are files on Himmler and Goering as you would expect.'

'And Hess probably,' Michele said.

'Yes, but not much,' she said, 'but it does show a link between Hess and Karl Haushofer.'

'Hitler's advisor,' Michele asked, 'the professor?'

Jean nodded, 'Hess issued German Blood Certificates to both his wife and son.'

'German what?' Michele asked.

'German blood certificates,' Jean said, 'Meaning they are no longer considered Jewish.'

'He protected them. I was not expecting that,' Michele said. 'Hess did that?'

'And there are documents indicating that Karl has had meetings with the English' Jean said.

'About what?'

'He doesn't seem to know.'

'Karl has been a busy boy,' Michele said.

Jean nodded with a smile.

Michele sat back; she couldn't wait to tell Natasha.

***

Hess walked straight towards Natasha who was outside Schmidt's bakery. She turned to walk inside, but he grabbed her arm and swung her around to face him. He had surprised her for a second time. Hmmm, she didn't like being surprised.

'I think we deserve something special today,' he said.

She looked at him; Hess seemed in a jolly mood. He escorted her into a nearby restaurant. They were shown to a quiet table in the corner. Natasha looked around. There were not many people in the restaurant, about ten, plus staff.

'I don't think I've ever been in here before,' Natasha said. 'Aren't we supposed to be distancing ourselves?'

'Yes,' he replied, 'but one lunch won't make a difference. And it is an unsaid rule not to talk about this place.'

'Oh,' she said blushing.

Hess outlined his intelligence operation to Natasha. He had created a network that stretched through France, Poland and into Russia. No one else knew the full scope of the operation.

'They pass information back to me. But can be used strategically, when required,' he said.

'So not a traditional network. Almost agents for hire,' Natasha said.

'Yes. Look after it while I'm away. From what I have seen you play a similar chess game to me. Although you may receive some instructions from me during this time too. I'll introduce you to the right people.' Hess said, 'Will you be my guest at my birthday?'

Natasha smiled, 'I'd be honoured, even if you didn't need to introduce me to anyone.'

***

'Today we fly,' Wilhelm began.

Oskar nodded, but he was frantically looking around. The cockpit felt small, and he still couldn't remember what all the little dials did.

'Let the fun begin,' Wilhelm said as they taxied down the runway. Oskar felt like his whole body was vibrating with the force of the engines. He muttered under his breath, but no one could hear, in fact he could hardly hear himself. It was different in the cockpit compared to the back when he'd parachuted. A sudden push and then Oskar felt pinned back in the seat, but the vibrating lessened. Wilhelm made it look so easy. He swirled the plane around in the air like a loud butterfly. Oskar looked at Wilhelm, he really was in his element, and he looked so relaxed, as if he was having a great time.

'You miss it don't you?'

'Yes, I do,' Wilhelm said, 'but I don't miss the fighter pilots trying to shoot me down.'

***

Hess walked down the stairs, 'Well I'm really quite impressed. I never thought that you would have organised this level of operation.'

'I didn't,' she said.

She felt so proud of her sister. 'Michele did.'

She walked into the room. There were only six others in the room. Oskar looked at Natasha as she walked in. He leaned forward shaking his head.

'What is wrong with you two?' he demanded. 'I'm lost for words; I don't believe this.'

He looked at Michele then Natasha, 'First you, then you.'

Wilhelm walked over to Oskar, 'he's fine. The girls investigated us well.'

'I hope so.' Oskar said, 'our lives depend on it.'

Everyone was quiet.

Hess walked over to Oskar.

'I'm glad you're apprehensive. It's a good trait. Although, I need you just as much as you need me. Believe me.'

Natasha walked over. 'Shall we begin?'

Everyone sat down and looked towards Natasha. A map of Europe hung on the wall behind her. She briefly explained the mission.

'We only have a small team for this,' Natasha said. 'Each one of you has an important part to play.'

'May I?' Hess cut in.

Natasha nodded.

'It's good to see you again, Jean,' Hess said. 'Goebbels likes to keep tabs on people. He speaks to everyone, including my wife quite regularly. He has a way of using information to get what he wants. And that is where you come in.'

Jean looked nervous, flicked a look at Michele, who smiled. Jean wasn't used to taking orders from the Deputy Führer.

'Jean,' Natasha began, 'we need you to make Goebbels feel like he has to make Hess fly.'

'Goebbels hates me,' Hess smiled almost chuckling.

'If you make it seem like it would be dangerous for Hess to fly,' Natasha said, 'as he may get hurt or–'

'Worse,' Hess said, 'then he would…'

'Do everything in his power,' Jean smiled, 'to make it happen.'

'He hates me,' Hess said absentmindedly, 'makes him easier to manipulate.'

'Not a problem. But why do you want to highlight that fact?' asked Jean.

'So, anything I do around planes won't look suspicious,' Hess said. 'Hitler doesn't want me to fly at all.'

'Goebbels can't make Hitler change his mind,' Jean said almost chuckling. 'I've seen him in meetings.'

'I won't be fighting it though, in fact I am trying to negotiate with Hitler into allowing me to fly,' Hess replied, 'and Goebbels will use the public.'

'So, while Jean is putting the propaganda machine to work,' Natasha addressed the rest of the group, 'the investigation needs to begin.'

The group looked at Natasha; aiming for the sky was a family thing obviously. They could see it in both sisters. It was going to be dangerous for everyone but there was a feeling of ease and confidence.

'Henri,' Natasha said, 'we need some contacts in England.'

'We have Lord Hamilton,' Henri said. 'My contact in Spain is opening up a line of communication with him. I thought it might be helpful after we identified him as a person of interest.'

Hess smiled. 'Good, I've meet him before.'

'I want a backup though,' said Natasha.

'I need to talk to Churchill, we need a meeting,' Hess said.

'Of course, you do,' Henri said sarcastically. 'No problem.'

'Good,' Natasha said, 'that's the plan.'

Henri's face dropped.

'I was joking,' he said. 'I guess because you don't know me and–'

Natasha walked over and smiled.

'I know you better than you realise and that's why I know that if anyone can do it, you can.'

She turned and walked back to the map. Henri shook his head and rolled his eyes but kept listening.

'The whole flight will be choreographed to music,' Natasha continued. 'Certain songs will indicate when planes take off, meet and when phone calls are to be made, also if it's cancelled.'

'How is everyone going to hear the songs?' Wilhelm asked slightly confused.

'They will play on the radio. Hess will be able to tune into certain frequencies to pick them up. I need you to work with Anneliese to organise when things will need to occur. Work out the timings. Jean, find out who oversees scheduling so that we can coordinate. But also find out who can authorise changes and how easy they are to make; in case we need to on the day.'

Oskar called out, 'I thought that we were all leaving from Augsburg.'

'No,' said Natasha, 'Hess leaves from Augsburg, you two will leave from Baden-Baden. An escorted plane leaving any runway will ring alarm bells too early. It needs to look like a normal flight. We need to give ourselves time.'

She pointed out on the map the route they would fly. Hess would go west slightly, and Oskar and Wilhelm would meet, before heading north.

'You'll go right through here,' she said.

'Do you realise that's the most heavily guarded area in Germany?' Wilhelm said.

'Yes, it is,' Natasha replied, 'At another song, Anneliese will phone and ask for a safe passage.'

'It'll either work,' said Oskar, 'or be a suicide mission.'

'Michele,' Natasha said ignoring his comments, 'if anything goes wrong it's down to you to coordinate.'

Michele nodded then looked confused.

'What exactly are you going to do?'

'I'll be socialising with Hess's enemies and apart from that nothing,' she remarked. She needed to set up an alibi for herself, and a dinner was a perfect occasion.

A general discussion broke out. Hess, Natasha and Michele sat in silence. They surveyed the scene and then looked at each other. Michele sat back. It was time the three of them had a meeting.

Natasha looked at her little sister, she was so proud of her, but she also feared for her. After this operation everything would change. The distance between them would increase to its normal size. She just hoped that Michele would be able to handle it. She took a deep breath; in all honesty she hoped she could.

It was not long before the discussion finished, and people started to leave. Michele looked through documents, until Natasha and Michele were the only people present.

'Your silence is deafening. What is it?'

Michele's jaw was set as she looked at Natasha.

'I can't believe you would do this. Welcome Hess into the resistance, introduce him to the members.'

'I didn't exactly invite him in.'

'Yes, you did. They are our friends Natasha. You've put them all at risk. And for some reason I feel like I let you. Why would you put me in that position?' Michele was angry, not just at her sister, but also at herself.

'It was strategic,'

'How dare you. They are people I care about. Not some–'

'I didn't have a choice' Natasha snapped. She leaned her hands on the table and dropped her head slightly.

Michele looked at her sister, she had not seen her like this before. But since her escape, Natasha had lost some of her control, the calm that she normally had. It left Michele disorientated.

'What do you mean?'

'He knows everything, he knows everyone. It was only a matter of time before he followed someone here. Hell, he may already have known. He made me search this location.'

Michele couldn't move. 'We need to warn everyone, we need to leave.'

Natasha sighed and looked up, 'It doesn't matter. This group means nothing to him. He doesn't care. Or they would all be hanging in the centre of Munich by now. People are chess pieces for him. He needs you and me for something.'

'No, he needs everyone,' Michele said, 'or as you said they would dead. Already, right?'

Natasha shook her head. 'He needs your help, which he wouldn't have if something happened to the group. And he needs my help, which I wouldn't give if something happened to you. They are safe for now, while we are needed. But I was not going to let him find this place when he wanted. I needed to take back some control and get him here on my terms. It's strategic.'

Michele wasn't used to thinking like this, it was not where her mind would have gone. She looked up at her sister.

'What if he doesn't need me either. What if it's you, that he needs?'

There was silence.

'Maybe, but that is a lot of lives and a lot of risk for one person.'

'What could he possibly want,' asked Michele?

'We could waste a lot of time trying to work out the way he thinks. We know what he's doing, that's enough for now.' Natasha had focused. 'What we need to do is work out what it is we want.'

There was silence.

'What future do you see?' Natasha asked.

Michele looked at her sister a little confused.

'What will it be like after the war?' she continued. 'Or what would you like it to be like?'

Michele thought for a moment.

'I don't know.' She paused, 'I can't imagine.'

'So why do you do it? What keeps you going?'

'It's not fair,' she started, 'all the fighting. Not just with other countries, but here. Here, we use to help our neighbours, no matter who they were. Now. Now everyone is suspicious of each other. We're so divided. So isolated. Friends and families turning on each other. Each and every one of us feel like we have no power. No choice. The fighting, the anger, the blame and the control needs to stop.'

Michele was angry, 'I won't accept that, I won't lose my friends, I won't look away. I don't accept that this is what the rest of my life will look like.'

'I understand, and I hate it too. But you can't start down this road and have no end goal, or you may create something worse.'

'How can anything be worse? We are disrupting things. We can do more. The regime will fall, the war will stop and there will be peace.'

'Stopping the war does not mean there will be peace. It is not enough,' Natasha said.

'Well doing nothing is not acceptable.' She looked at Natasha. 'What are you trying to say – to do nothing, to give up? We have started, I won't give up.'

'What I am saying is that there's no point in doing something if there is no goal, if there is no plan for after.'

Michele's eyes glistened, 'But I can't see that far ahead, I can't see through this.'

'But maybe the trick is not to look through but start from scratch and work backwards.'

Michele nodded.

'We are caught between two powers and if we are not careful Germany will be absorbed into both. We need a leader.'

'But who?' Michele asked. 'Who would lead the country that Hitler has not already imprisoned or killed.'

'I don't know,' Natasha said, 'and therein lies the problem.'

Michele started giggling and then really started laughing.

Natasha looked at her confused.

Michele took some deep breaths to steady herself. 'I was thinking, just for a tiny moment. You. And if that happened, I would love to see Hitler's face.'

'The expression would be funny,' Natasha giggled, 'but I don't think the country is ready for a female Chancellor. They're only just letting girls into the Kripo.'

'But seriously, who?' Michele asked.

'I don't know. But we need to start looking.'

***

Friedrich walked towards his car. He paused and played with his keys. Sighing he leaned on the car and thought about everything. The world, his head, it was spinning. He was confused, agitated and frustrated. But Helene. Helene was there, at the centre. He tossed the keys in the air a couple of times and then got in the car. He needed to find Helene. It was the only way to reclaim his sanity. He set out towards the border. A couple of days off would be good for him.

He drove along the road towards the Swiss border. Last time he had come this way he had been following someone. However, he knew this territory.

He had first met Helene not far from where her sister lived now. Anita had inherited the family home.

I loved that time. The first time I met you. Ladies' man, yes. And that was him being modest. The village girls were always searching for that tall, chiselled stranger who would marry them and take them away from the quiet life. Easy targets. Oh, Helene, you, you were not interested. You were not looking to get married. Helene was silent and inquisitive, and intriguing, oh so intriguing. He'd been drawn like a moth to a flame. Then her eyes. They penetrated his soul. He had wanted her, he had chased her, proved himself to her. The tables had turned. There was no escape.

He could feel his eyes clouding over. He pulled over to the side of the road. How had he gone from there to this? He had to do it again, prove himself, win her back. He could, he had to. He wiped his face with one hand and reached into his bag with the other. Grabbing his hip flask, he opened it and went to take a swig. Stop, look, think, stop. Was this what he had become? Was this really what he wanted Helene to see him like? He wanted her to know that he had changed, but this? No, not this. He screwed the lid back on and sighed deeply. He would drink later, now wasn't the time. He placed the flask under his seat and started the car. There was a long drive ahead of him.

Friedrich parked on the road a little way from the pathway that led to the house. As he walked, he could feel the breeze as it gently rustled the leaves in the trees. The house appeared through the holes in the foliage. Friedrich walked to the edge of the field. The house was a fair distance away still, but he could see into it vaguely. There was no movement. He moved around the bush line to get as close to the house as possible. Soon Friedrich was running across the field to the backdoor. As he got there, he tried to catch his breath. He wasn't as fit as he used to be. The door was unlocked. He edged it open slowly. He paused. Listened. The house appeared deserted, no sound. He walked around cautiously but couldn't find anyone at all. Walking up the stairs, he found a bedroom. The journey had been draining and he was tired. Friedrich lay down for a nap and drifted off into a deep sleep.

He didn't know how long he had slept for, but a noise woke him. He sat bolt upright and looked around but couldn't see anyone. Friedrich slightly opened the door and peeked out. No one. Walking out the door, he headed downstairs and turned towards the kitchen area. Suddenly the kitchen door swung open, and a woman came running towards Friedrich holding a saucepan yelling. 'Get out, get out!'

'Stop,' Friedrich yelled running back towards the stairs.

He was reaching for his gun. As soon as he had it, he turned around and pointed it straight towards her. She stopped dead and gulped.

'Put down the pan,' Friedrich said, 'put it down and I will not hurt you.'

She lowered the pan and waited.

'Let's sit down.'

He directed her through to the front room.

They sat down and looked at each other.

'I'm looking for someone,' he said. 'I don't want to hurt you.'

She looked at him warily.

'Do you want to give me the pan?' He asked stretching his hand out towards her.

'Do you want to give me the gun?' she said.

He sat back and looked at her. She didn't act or look like resistance. She was nervous and anxious. He could see how scared she was.

'I'm looking for a lady called Helene.'

'I don't know Helene,' she said, a little more relaxed.

'What about Henri?'

'No.'

'Whose house is this?'

'Fraulein Greta's,' she answered. 'I clean it for her.'

He thought for a moment, this girl probably didn't know half the things that happened in this house. He reached into his pocket. She drew back and her eyes widened with fear.

He looked at her and slowly pulled out a photograph. He leaned forward and pointed at the man in the picture. 'This is me.'

She smiled and nodded.

He pointed to the female and asked, 'Have you seen her?'

She smiled, 'Yes, but she has short hair now.'

Friedrich looked confused. 'Are you sure?'

Helene loved her long hair, why would she cut it?

'Yes, oh she had beautiful hair, but she said that it was the only way she could go back.'

'Back where?' Asked Friedrich.

'To Munich.'

He smiled. She's back in Munich. Then he took a deep breath, oh no she's back in Munich. Natasha.

'Are you alright?' she asked.

'Fine,' he said clearing his throat, 'I'm just a little tired.'

She put down the pan and walked over to him.

'Ms Greta will not mind you using the guest room to rest.'

She walked with him up the stairs and indicated the room. She followed him in and picked up his jacket.

'In future, know that this will not get you a good response around here,' she smiled as she exited closing the door.

He was so used to wearing his uniform that he forgot about it. He lay down on the bed. Now he would sleep, tomorrow he would continue his search. He had to find Helene before Natasha got her.

***

Everything was normal Henri thought as the train passed through the tunnel. He used to like traveling to visit his friend before. But that was before, and this was not planned. He was not supposed to be making this trip now. But Hess wanted Churchill. And there was no time, so he was travelling back. Now.

SS walked down the carriage, stopping randomly to see people's papers. He looked up smiled and then looked out the window as casually as possible. Everything is fine. Everything is normal.

They stopped at his row. 'Papers.'

He reached into his pocket and pulled out the papers. They we authentic, but he still felt the panic rise.

'Thank you.' They said handing them back and then they continued to the next carriage.

They would get off before him. But there was always someone watching. One of Hitler's or Franco's spies, you never knew.

Eventually the train pulled into the station and Henri got out. He looked around the platform and finally found his friend, Peter in the distance. He walked over to him. Peter had changed in the past five years. But so had he.

Peter hugged Henri and smiled as he stepped back.

'How are you? It's been a long time, too long.'

'Yes, it has,' said Henri, 'Thanks for this.'

'Yeah, well I don't even know what this is. Come on,' Peter said as he led them to the car.

Henri looked out the window as they drove through the city. He wasn't used to the landscape, the architecture. They were not the square buildings of Munich, no Bavarian decoration. But the buildings seemed to flow like a river, winding around the windows, with rippled walls that made them look like they were out of a cartoon.

'You have strange buildings,' Henri said.

'That's Gaudi,' Peter said. 'He put his stamp on the area with his design. It's everywhere. You should see the bell tower.'

He paused, 'When I told Dad that you were going to visit. Imagine my surprise when he said that he had seen you less than a month ago.'

'You weren't here,' Henri replied, 'but your dad was really kind.'

'He said we could expect to see you on a regular basis. Even said he may find you a reason to travel to us,' said Peter, 'although he did not expect a visit this soon.'

'A reason to travel would be helpful,' said Henri. 'There have been some changes, some developments.'

'When we get inside rest,' Peter said, 'after dinner we can talk.'

'Henri welcomed rest after the long journey. He fell asleep as soon as his head hit the pillow and didn't wake till Peter knocked on the door to say dinner would be served shortly.

It was nice to have a group sitting around a table, talking, and laughing. There was more of a variety of food than he was used to, with seafood and rice, being the main dish. Things just felt lighter, more colourful in Spain. Henri had to remind himself that they too had a dictator controlling them. Although not quite in the same vein as Hitler. Though it was light-hearted here, it may not be the same in every household in the country.

After dinner, the men retired to the sitting room. Peter had left university and got a job with the British embassy in Madrid. Henri had always seen him as more political than his father Terrance. He hadn't wanted to go into his father's steelworks, even though his many factories were profitable, especially now. But it had been his father's contacts from Barcelona, that had helped Peter get his job.

They sat back in the big leather chairs, sipping brandy, reminiscing about student days, and how much had changed.

The doorbell broke the conversation.

Terrance smiled.

'I invited some friends over,' he said. 'They are interested in you and what you represent.'

Peter shot a look at his father and then down at his glass of brandy.

Henri immediately felt uncomfortable. In a split second the atmosphere in the room changed. He put down his brandy and stood up to welcome the visitors. He always felt better meeting new people when standing up. It allowed for more movement if required. He looked at Peter for reassurance, but he too looked confused.

Two men walked through the door. Peter looked even more confused, 'Ian?' Then his jaw clenched as the last man looked at him and then refocused on Henri.

The first gentleman was shaking Terrance's hand. A genuine smile reached across his youthful oval face. He had charisma, but he used it professionally.

'Hillgarth, Alan Hillgarth,' the man said. 'Henri, isn't it?'

Alan's hand glided across to shake Henri's hand.

'Yes,' said Henri. But his eyes were distracted by the gentleman behind, who was looking at Peter. His stare seemed to be a warning more than anything else.

They all sat down, apart from the other man, who leaned on the table, to participate when needed, or to observe perhaps.

'This is my,' Hillgarth hesitated, 'assistant, Fleming.'

Fleming's face slightly flinched but rebounded into an attempted smile. However, Peter's face dropped and looked away from Henri.

Henri sat back analysing everyone. Suddenly, he trusted no one in the room.

'We have been told you work with a group of like-minded people in Munich,' Hillgarth said. 'That this group may have English sympathies and that I may be of help as I have certain…' he paused again as if he was trying to pluck a word from the air '… contacts.'

Henri could feel Fleming's stare but would not acknowledge it.

'I believe our interests are somewhat aligned,' Henri said. 'I think that it may be wise to build a relationship that could be mutually beneficial.'

This is what Henri and Terrance had spoken about last time. Was this what he had meant when he told Henri about connections?

'To create this relationship, we would need to know who we are working with. We would need to investigate your group to ensure there are no leaks,' Hillgarth said.

Henri knew that this could mean that there would be no link to England for the resistance, but he would not compromise them.

'There are no leaks,' Henri replied, 'and if that is a requirement for our relationship, then I'm sorry to have wasted your time.'

Hillgarth's face dropped, he was trying not to look around. He was obviously someone who normally got what he wanted. Peter smiled, but Fleming didn't flinch or maybe his smile looked just a little bit more authentic for a moment.

He pushed himself of the table and walked forward.

'Alan, I'm sure that won't be an issue to developing a relationship,' he said giving him a reassuring squeeze on the shoulder. Hillgarth seemed to shrink a little. Then Fleming walked around and sat down.

Hillgarth regained his composure, 'What would you like? How can we help?'

'We would like information regarding military movements, and we would like to feed information through to you regarding possible targets, that will not only cripple the German war effort but also effect the morale of the people.'

'We couldn't possibly disclose military strategy,' Hillgarth said, 'especially–'

'You want to create a revolution,' Fleming said, 'a civil uprising. Interesting.'

Silence.

Henri cleared his throat. It was now or never.

'We are in contact with a senior official, who is not part of the resistance but in this instance, we are supporting him. The official would like to journey to Britain and have an audience with Churchill.

Terrance, Peter and Hillgarth's faces dropped and they sat back in their chairs.

Again, Fleming didn't react, but his smile did seem more genuine. Henri was starting to admire his control, but doubted he worked for Hillgarth.

'Of course. Let him know that the arrangements have already been made.'

Hillgarth looked uneasily at him and then raised his glass. 'To mutual benefit.'

Everyone awkwardly agreed and took a sip of their drinks.

Henri sat back in his seat. It was a strange group of men, but their relationships were obvious. Hillgarth and Terrance knew each other well and started talking to each other to distract themselves. Fleming and Peter knew each other, but their reaction was vastly different. They tried to put distance between themselves.

Henri got up and excused himself momentarily. When he was returning down the corridor, he heard a noise and paused.

'Henri,' Peter whispered beckoning him into a side room. He looked around to ensure no one had seen, then closed the door.

Henri stood watching Peter pacing.

'This puts me in a very awkward position.' He said, 'I feel like I'm about to betray my country, although I don't know how, but I do feel this way, with what I'm about to tell you and what I'm not telling Ian.'

'I thought his name was Alan?' Henri said, 'I don't want you to do something you don't feel comfortable with.'

'You're my friend, and I trust you. And I know your friends, and who you associate with.'

Peter shook his head as if registering what Henri had said.

'No Alan is Alan, Ian is Fleming. I don't trust him. He would sell out his own grandfather,' Peter paused, 'but for the good of the country. He is ruthless. But loyal.'

'You're not making sense,' Henri said. 'What is wrong?'

'Hillgarth is sort of a spy, a briber, the British contact type person for the area, well actually for Spain.'

'Oh,' said Henri. Made sense.

'But Ian,' Peter said, 'Ian is NID, Naval Intelligence. I don't know exactly what he does. He's high up though, top level. The Churchill comment. Well, my friend. He'll have an agenda.'

Henri nodded looking around.

'Thank you,' Henri said, 'we should get back then before someone comes looking for us.'

Peter nodded and opened the door. He paused, stepped back and then pushed the door fully open. Fleming was standing in the doorway. He stepped forward and then closed the door.

'So, this is where the real discussions are happening,' Fleming said. 'Now, Peter, I believe you have a decision to make. How far down the rabbit hole do you want to go, because now is the time to leave,' Ian paused and lent towards Peter, 'while one can.'

Peter took a big breath. 'I believe sir, I have well and truly jumped in.'

'I didn't think I could count on you to keep your mouth closed in this relationship. You are close friends after all. But in this case, you have not jeopardised anything, it can be our little secret. The start of many. Everything Peter said is correct. Although for the record, I would think twice about selling out my grandfather. But I would.'

Peter went bright red.

'I rather take it as a compliment. I say this so you know that I would not hesitate to do the same to you and your little resistance group. No matter how good I think agents Snake and Serpent are.'

Henri looked up, 'Yes, I know about the sisters. They have quite a reputation, outside Germany luckily. Although a lot of people think it's just one person.'

Henri tried to compose himself. Fleming knew a lot.

'Thank you by the way, for the agents you helped get out of Munich. They gave us valuable intelligence,' Fleming said.

Henri smiled but had no idea what Fleming was talking about.

'What I want to know is what does the resistance want to accomplish by helping Hess. Yes, we know that too. We know what Hess wants, but the resistance. I can't quite work it out. Hess wants to be in Britain, and we want Hess. But what do they want? Why are they involving the resistance in this?'

Henri thought for a moment.

'I don't know, I don't think it was planned. Hess forced it really. He had so much information on us. I don't know if we had a choice.'

'Interesting,' said Fleming. 'There is always a choice. Everyone has an agenda.'

***

Jean felt odd yet invigorated. It was like her mind was awakened. She still felt uncomfortable working with Hess. It seemed wrong, but it did make sense. Hess had given her an invitation to his birthday celebration, for Goebbels. She had to sneak it into the office to give it to him. Hess flying wasn't a normal topic of conversation. When she got to the front door of the building, she took a deep breath. The guard indicated that her bag needed checking. It always did, but today she was nervous. The invitation wasn't exactly treacherous, but there would be queries as to why she had it. The guard looked through the bag, pulled out its contents. A book, a letter opener, lipstick, her identity papers, money and ration book. He checked her identity papers, and then put the rest back in her bag, pausing with the book. He flicked through it briefly stopping at the bookmarked page and read a couple of lines. Jean tried not to look and just smiled as he held the invite she had used as a bookmark in one hand. He looked up at her, placed it back in the book and handed the book to her.

'Is it good?'

She nodded and put the book in the bag.

She walked along the hall to the office and stopped outside the office to show her papers to the guard, who just waved her though. He was a regular and knew everyone.

Jean sat down at her desk and quickly looked around. Taking the invite out of her bag she slipped it on to the desk and grabbed the pile of mail. Taking a deep breath, she relaxed, everything was as it should be now. She opened the mail and stacked it as normal. There was nothing of importance, just the normal correspondence. Walking into Goebbels office, she placed them on the desk and then left. More than an hour went by before she was summoned back into the room.

'Jean,' Goebbels said looking up, 'can you please phone the Munich office and say that I will attend the celebrations.'

He handed Jean his invitation, 'Here is the information.'

She looked down at the card it was Hess's birthday invitation.

'Is it going to be a big event?' she said.

'Quite big,' he said casually, 'there will be music, entertainment, a flyover.'

Jean smiled.

'A flyover?' she said sounding somewhat confused.

'Yes,' Goebbels said, 'his old squadron is saluting him or something.'

'Wow,' she said pretending to leave. It was now or never, 'I didn't know that he used to fly. I bet his wife is relieved.'

Goebbels looked up confused, 'Why?'

Jean went into dumb mode and turned. 'Well you hear about all these planes going down, not just shot by the enemy but even our own people sometimes. I just bet she's glad he's nice and safe.'

Goebbels sat back in his chair; the sides of his mouth were trying hard not to turn into a smile.

'I'm sure you are right,' he said. 'Thank you.'

Jean walked out, closing the door, thank you Hess. This was the first time that Jean had tried to feed information back to Goebbels for the resistance. She wondered how fast he would react, and if he would? Jean felt a surge of excitement. Maybe, just maybe this misinformation thing could work. Goebbels was so used to manipulating people, he didn't consider the chance that he would be manipulated. Small steps. Don't make assumptions yet. Let's see if he does what he was supposed to.

***

Natasha walked down the stairs to the parlour. Her father was sitting down sipping his drink.

'What are you doing?' he asked.

'I'm ready for this evening,' Natasha replied.

'You don't need to go,' he said, 'in fact I don't think you should.'

'I'm going,' she said.

It was a change from their normal discussions only a couple of months earlier. Now she needed to go to build up a rapport and it was her father, who didn't want her to. Why was everything so hard?

It wasn't long before they were at the function, another boring function. She focused on her mission; it was all about making contacts. Networking, being fake, not what Natasha enjoyed. End goal. Think end goal. Natasha grabbed a glass of champagne and started to wander. This was partly to talk to everyone, but mainly to get away from her father.

She surveyed the room. Wilhelm and Hess were talking to a group of uniformed SS. Wilhelm looked up and saw Natasha and gave her a reassuring wink. They had decided to distance themselves, to ensure no obvious connections, for investigation, regarding Hess's mission.

Natasha's ultimate objective was to organise a type of bond with Hitler, or rather a civil relationship with him. Being nice to him suddenly, would arouse suspicion, she needed to use a more subtle way. Also, it had to be in a way that the women at the top of the Reich, would accept her, and not feel that their positions were threatened. There was an order to things. She took a deep breath and walked towards a pillar. This was going to be hard; it wasn't her natural inclination. Come on. Come on, thought Natasha. She was bored already. It had been less than a minute. Her fake timid smile was killing her. Patience wasn't a virtue that she had. She took another deep breath.

***

Wilhelm looked up from his conversation Natasha was standing all alone. She didn't look her normal self, she almost looked overwhelmed. He'd never seen her look so uncomfortable. Wilhelm went to move in her direction, but Hess grabbed his arm.

He lent forward and whispered, 'she's even fooled you, and you know her.'

'She's not acting' Wilhelm said. 'What's she going to accomplish?'

'Well planned,' Hess said almost to himself. 'If she's still like that in thirty minutes you can save her,'

Wilhelm looked at his watch it had been twenty minutes already.

'Ten minutes to go,' Hess said.

'But she–' Wilhelm said.

Hess interrupted, 'The waiting is over.'

Wilhelm looked at him for a moment and then turned around just in time to see Eva walk over to Natasha. He let out a little chuckle and shook his head. He couldn't believe it; so that was the plan.

**

'Hello,' Eva said smiling to Natasha, 'how are you?'

'Good thank you.'

'You're Friedrich's girl, aren't you?' Eva asked.

Natasha nodded.

'Do you know many people here this evening?' she asked.

Natasha dropped the smile and shook her head, looking as timid as she could. 'Not really.'

'Let me introduce you to some people,' Eva said quietly and indicated for Natasha to follow her.

This is what Natasha had counted on, Eva's reputation as a perfect hostess. She had come through. It wasn't long before Natasha was mingling with a group of elderly gentlemen who insisted on giving her a rundown of their exploits. Her smile made her look very impressed. Natasha was mentally writing files on each of the members of the group. Two of the gentlemen in the group didn't really join in the conversation. They were the ones who intrigued her more. They were polite but quiet. They were the group's most powerful men and seemed to be analysing those talking.

Figures, she thought, that's normally the way.

Something caught one of the gentlemen's eyes and he smiled opening the circle with a welcoming arm.

'Karl do join us,' Fromm said. 'You know most of the group, but we are joined by the lovely Fraulein Natasha, Friedrich's girl.'

Natasha smiled as Karl studied her.

'You know Natasha, Karl is the one that introduced Mein Führer to the concept of Lebensraum. Imagine what our world would be like without it?'

Karl took a deep breath.

'Yes imagine' he said before taking a large gulp of his drink.

Then Karl changed the subject, 'I've heard much about you Natasha. You work hard for the cause. Thank you.'

The previous conversation resumed, and Natasha pondered if it was merely a slip of the tongue or the deliberate use of the word cause.

Wilhelm looked towards Natasha; he leaned over to his uncle, 'I don't believe it.'

'She's good,' Hess replied, 'but lady luck was also on her side.'

'It's not every day one gets to talk to Fromm and Halder at the same time,' Wilhelm said.

'They aren't talking though,' Hess said.

Wilhelm looked towards Hess.

'Neither is Natasha.'

Dinner was served in the main dining hall and Natasha found herself between her father and some of the wives. She couldn't relate to anything that they were saying, although they insisted on including her.

By the time the meal was over, Natasha needed air. She made her way out to the balcony. The night sky was beautiful, full of stars and a waning moon.

'Dinner must have been a form of torture for you,' a voice interrupted her thoughts.

'The food was lovely,' she said turning around to see who was talking to her.

'The company,' Karl said, 'did they talk children to you? I imagine it's not what you would normally converse about.'

'Let's say it's not something that I believe I'll be qualified to talk on for a very long time. I have other interests.' She added almost as an afterthought. 'And ways to serve the Reich. You didn't come out here to discuss verbal interactions of females.'

He chuckled, 'I'd heard that of you. What is the word, direct?'

Natasha smiled.

Karl walked over and stood by her, looking out over the railings.

'It wasn't supposed to be like this. The true meaning of it.' Karl's gaze followed the dark horizon as if he were miles away.

Then he looked at Natasha, 'What do you understand about Lebensraum?'

'Germany needs to take over countries so that the German people can spread out and acquire more resources.'

'Well yes, in part,' Karl paused, 'there are large areas of land that people can work, that are currently untouched.'

Natasha looked at him to try and work out what he was saying. She considered for a moment.

'Untouched, or uninhabited?' she enquired.

'Exactly.' Karl's eyes flickered with excitement.

'So strategically it would be good to keep people where they are and add people to areas that are untouched,' she said.

'One would think so,' Karl smiled and looked back over the landscape. 'This continent and Africa are full of minerals and riches, if we have the resource to extract and use them. That's what Lebensraum is about. That's the geopolitics I taught Hess.'

'Everything changes though,' Natasha said. 'Develops.'

'Amalgamates actually,' Karl replied. 'Well in this case anyway. It has been changed into the building of an Empire. An Empire of land mass. The English have the Empire of the sea. Hitler quite admires them for it. Now it's about the Great Aryan Empire. Like the Greeks and Romans before us.'

Natasha thought she could hear a hint of sarcasm in his voice.

'It's just not how I envisage it, my Lebensraum. We all have different ideas, don't we?' He smiled at her, but it was sad. 'Will you excuse me; my glass is empty.'

She watched him walk away and thought, is this what Hess was doing, building an Empire or did he want the basic Lebensraum. Natasha thought for a moment. Was it just a theory, or could it be done? A different way maybe, could Lebensraum be beneficial for all the people. All the things that the land could offer people if they worked together. She looked back out at the landscape. It was too much to think about for the moment. But it was worth thinking about.

***

Oskar looked out the window.

'Is this what a bird sees?'

'Sort of,' Wilhelm said grimacing.

'You alright?'

'Headache from last night.'

'Hang over don't you mean,' Oskar laughed.

Oskar felt sorry for him. The roar of the engines penetrated your bones; he hated to think what it would do to someone with a queasy stomach and headache. They only talked when needed, as you had to shout. Oskar still felt a little crammed in the cockpit. The dials and controls were slowly becoming more familiar to him. Wilhelm was flying it so gracefully and Oskar thought that it would be easy enough to pick up. For their mission he was a follower, he didn't need to really navigate unless something went terribly wrong.

Wilhelm indicated for him to take the control column. He hesitated and then took a deep breath and grabbed it. Wilhelm let go. Oskar lurched forward. The plane started to drop. So heavy, like I'm carrying the plane. He pulled it back towards him, gritting his teeth and straining his abdominals for extra strength. Oskar knew that he looked uncomfortable, mainly, because he was. Every time he tried to relax, the plane's nose dropped, and he had to resume the position.

'You'll get used to it, after a while,' Wilhelm said. 'Let's go back home.'

Oskar waited for Wilhelm to take back control from him.

'What are you waiting for?' Wilhelm asked. 'You're going to do it.'

Oskar rolled his eyes. There were so many things to concentrate on. The turn was a bit wobbly as he struggled with the rudder pedals. Tight thigh, forced calf, too much to the right, going down, going up, aarrgh. His body ached. He felt muscles he hadn't known existed before.

The runway came into sight. Oskar looked up at Wilhelm.

'Are you going to take this back?' he said.

'No,' said Wilhelm, 'not unless you're about to kill us. Watch the runway and keep the nose up.'

Oskar took a deep breath. That was easy for him to say. This was by far the scariest thing that he had ever done.

'How long does it normally take to teach someone to fly.'

'About a month,' Wilhelm said, 'but don't worry you're a quick learner I can tell.'

'I hope so,' said Oskar.

Oskar started the descent. He felt a little clammy and he could feel the sweat dripping down his forehead.

'Don't drop the nose too quickly,' Wilhelm said watching Oskar intently.

Oskar levelled out a little.

'Think about what I said,' Wilhelm said.

Oskar was frantically trying to remember. Wilhelm had said so much. Don't drop the nose, level keep it level. He started taking quick short breaths while he tried to remember.

'Wheels.'

Wheels, of course wheels, very important. Now where is the button, what does it look like? Guess no remember. Come on.

'That's right,' Oskar said with a forced smile.

He reached for the control.

'Not that one,' Wilhelm shouted, 'that other one.'

Oskar flicked the switch and let the wheels down.

'Watch your right wing,' Wilhelm said.

The runway was getting closer and closer. Wilhelm was quite impressed. It was only the fourth time that Oskar had been in a plane. Wilhelm's hand hovered around his control column. If he touched it, it would override Oskar instantly.

'Watch your nose,' Wilhelm said, 'this'll be bumpy.'

The plane hit the runway, jumping a couple of times.

'I can't see, I can't see, I can't see the runway.'

'I know,' Wilhelm said. 'Try and look out the side slightly.'

Oskar stretched his body trying to see where he was going. Last time they had landed, he had watched Wilhelm so intently that he hadn't noticed.

'I hope I don't drive into anything.'

'So do I,' Wilhelm said. 'Keep straight, you're curving to where you're looking.'

Oskar quickly straightened. He couldn't breathe.

'Okay, good, now try to park over to your right,' Wilhelm directed. Oskar nodded and tried to turn the plane. Grunting he tried with all his might, slowly it turned.

'Wow,' he said. 'I thought it was heavy in the sky, but on the ground it's like a tank.'

They came to a stop and Oskar wiped his forehead. Quick breaths. Oskar dropped his head, breathe don't hyperventilate, breathe.

'You did well,' Wilhelm said.

'That's if you overlook the whole forgetting about the need for wheels.' Oskar laughed nervously. He was shaking.

'You can land without them, it's just a whole lot harder,' Wilhelm said. 'Alright let's get this baby refuelled and teach you how to take off.'

Oskar's face dropped, he didn't know if his heart could take it and he couldn't work out if he wanted to throw up or not. He took a deep breath and looked at Wilhelm. He needed a few minutes to prepare himself and to walk on land for a little while.

***

Natasha finished files on the gentlemen she had met the night before. Some of the information was useful. Fromm and Halder, had really intrigued her, and she wanted to find out more about them. She knew that Fromm was the commander of the Replacement Army for the Reich and that Halder was a Generaloberst but was well known to be involved with invasion plans used by the Reich. Hess has told her they would prove useful, but she wanted to work out how. The conversation she'd, had with Karl stood heavy in the back of her mind. Lebensraum intrigued her.

Friedrich came into the front room, and it felt like he looked through her. He continued through to the kitchen.

'Hello, Father.'

No answer. He came back in with a bucket of ice and placed it on the table beside his seat. She watched him grab a glass. Her face set to hide her sadness. She just wanted to reach out to him, to tell him she wasn't who he thought she was, that she could be there for him, that he could...

'Do you not think that it could be a little early for a drink?'

'Do you know what hurts me the most?' he said.

She shook her head.

'You look so much like your mother. In certain ways you act like her, the way you hold yourself,' he said. 'Even the way you socialise.'

Natasha smiled; she was glad that she had her mother's traits.

'But you will never have her depth,' he said, 'you will never have her compassion, the way she loved, who she really was.'

Natasha gritted her teeth, the comments stung. She could feel her eyes sting; the tears were welling up in her eyes.

She breathed deeply to retain control.

'I don't know who you are,' he said, 'because you repulse me.'

It was only a little click, but something snapped.

'I repulse you. I repulse you! You, don't know who I am? Father. Let me tell you. I am exactly what you wanted in a daughter. I am what you brought me up to be. I am a true German, Nazi breed, Aryan. Is that not what you wanted? Is that not what you dreamt of? However, let me tell you what I am not. I am not an alcoholic, who is hiding from his life at the bottom of a bottle. I'm not that weak.'

'Get out of my sight,' he yelled. 'Get out of my sight and stay out of it.'

'Fine.'

Natasha grabbed her things and left.

Friedrich punched the wall. Damn her, damn her. She was right. She was everything he had ever wanted. He had created the monster. Him alone. Now he was trying to hide from it and everything else.

**

Ilse sat back and touched up her makeup. Her compact was open, and she could barely see her face in the dimly lit car, but it would do, it would have to. She looked out the window. Life was occurring as normal; people were going about their menial jobs as usual. She closed her compact to put it away, but something caught her eye. She reached forward to her driver and asked him to pull over. She peered back out the window. A woman had walked out of the university that looked like an old friend, well maybe not a friend, but someone she'd known, almost another lifetime ago. Her hair was shorter, but her face, though deathly thin, was hers. It was Helene. She was holding a pile of papers and was carrying a bag. Not lady like at all, Ilse thought, but she never had been. Ilse leaned forward and whispered to the driver.

'Follow that woman.'

He nodded and drove down the street.

**

Helene walked into the bakery and smiled at Schmidt. He gave her a wink and asked what she wanted.

Putting the papers on the counter she perused the cakes. She bit her lip smiling and pointed to a slice of cake.

'How are you my dear?' he said.

'I'm fine thank you, how are you?'

'Good, very good,' he said. 'I am glad you're alright. It's so good to see you, but don't do too much at once. I think you need to recover a little.'

She smiled at him. Schmidt was an old friend, her anchor. She turned to go.

'Look after yourself,' Schmidt called out.

'You too,' she replied, she walked out of the shop and crossed the road; she had left a car halfway down the street. Now she was going to Hilde's, she felt like a warm bath and then her slice of cake.

***

Natasha crossed the road and walked into the bakery. She waited patiently while it emptied out. He handed her a bag with apple strudel in it and the papers Helene had left her.

'How are you?' he asked.

'Fine,' she replied.

'Really, how are you?' he said. 'You're losing weight, too much weight. Maybe you should start having more cakes.'

She hadn't noticed the weight; it was the last thing on her mind.

'Father and I are having…' she paused, '… difficulties. We don't really talk anymore.'

She felt like she was walking a thin line of control. She was trying to hold on, if she couldn't, she might break. Natasha sniffed, swallowed and got back her façade.

'He doesn't know you,' Schmidt said.

Schmidt had such a caring sincere face, it calmed her.

'I know,' she said gritting her teeth, 'I know… Thank you,' she said changing the subject to regain composure, 'for the strudel.'

'Anytime,' he smiled back. 'You take care of yourself little one.'

259

She smiled, 'I will, you too.'

She turned to go and then looked back.

'You know,' she was barely keeping it together, 'you're the only one who really knows me, that I can see each day. I hope he sees me one day as you do.'

She took a deep breath, looked up and was out the door.

Schmidt watched her sadly; the weight of the world, should not be on your shoulders my dear.

Normally Natasha was very controlled, but now her emotions were all over the place. She needed to regain her composure before she had another outburst. She crossed the street and decided to go for a walk to get some fresh air.

CHAPTER 21

Himmler sat in the chair opposite Hess. He sat as tall as he could, with his chest puffed out and chin up. His stern face hardly flinched as he spoke. Wilhelm stood, leaning on the wall slightly behind Himmler listening. He could see the muscles on Hess's face twitched slightly as he tried to keep a straight face. Hess leaned slightly forward, resting his elbows on the desk and tried to look like he cared about the conversation.

'Thank you for your concerns,' Hess said. 'I'll pass them on.'

The door burst open, and Ilse stood in the doorway.

'I must talk to you,' she said.

The men had all turned to her.

'I've seen her,' she stated.

Her eyes ignored her husband and focused on Himmler.

'Who?' Himmler said.

'Helene, I know all her resistance contacts.'

Wilhelm quickly flicked his eyes to Hess and then back to her. He brought forward a chair.

'Aunt, take a seat and tell us everything you've seen.'

Ilse looked at Wilhelm irritated, then let go of the door and it slammed shut. Hess looked at his wife. A stranger. Then he refocused on the room. Ilse was talking to Himmler.

***

Bang, Natasha jumped. What was that? She strained to listen, Hess, Himmler and Wilhelm talking, and was that, was it a female voice? What a fun meeting that would be. She couldn't make out words, just tones. She'd been waiting for her father, but curiosity was getting the better of her. Pressing her ear to the wall, she tried to listen. No luck. She walked out of her father's office and casually waited by the door with some papers in her hand. Movement indicated that people were getting ready to leave. Natasha quickly paced a few feet away and turned. The door opened and she began walking towards Hess office as if she were reading something. Ilse and Himmler walked by and didn't seem to notice. She saw Hess glance at Wilhelm, who was slightly behind. With a quick sidestep, Natasha and Wilhelm crashed into each other, the papers landing on the floor. The rest of the group continued walking. Wilhelm helped Natasha up.

'They know about Schmidt, Hilde's house and Helene. Get them out.'

Natasha stood still. She was in shock.

'Go,' Wilhelm said firmly. 'Use Hess's office.'

Natasha took a deep breath to calm herself down. Then walked into Hess' office and called Schmidt.

'Hello,' he said.

'Get out now.'

'It's too late.' There was a slight pause. 'I want you to know that you're like the daughter I never had.'

'Run. You can't, I need you. Just run, hide.'

'Look after yourself,' he said.

'I'm so sorry,' she said, a tear rolled down her cheek, her hand was against the window that faced the bakery.

'You can't save everyone.'

Someone yelled in the background. He hung up.

She turned away and then rang Hilde.

'Hello,' Hilde said.

'Get everyone out of the house now,' Natasha said. 'Head for Austria.'

Her voice was starting to break.

'What?'

'You don't have much time. Hide what you can but be gone as soon as possible.'

A shot echoed across the Platz.

Natasha paused and grabbed the window ledge to steady herself. She was shaking.

'Helene was seen and followed,' she said. 'Go. Go now.'

Natasha put the receiver down.

She had to calm herself down. Deep breath in, slow out breath. Her brain started to function. She looked at the phone;

if it was tapped, she would be in trouble. She took another deep breath, but there was nothing else she could have done. She couldn't worry about it now. Now there were things she had to do. She had to buy some time. She grabbed her coat, wiped her cheek, took another deep breath, and strode out of the building to where the shot had come from.

Natasha walked over to Himmler and paused so that her face was no more than an inch from his.

'You idiot.'

She focused on Himmler. If she looked at Schmidt's body, she would lose it.

Himmler took a step back.

'How dare you?'

'You incompetent idiot.'

'Don't talk to him like that,' Ilse said. 'Do you know who he is?'

Natasha turned her head towards Ilse, raised an eyebrow, looked her up and down and then turned back to Himmler.

'What did you find out?' she said.

'He wasn't talking, he didn't say anything.'

A quick realisation flickered across Himmler's face. He tried to explain. He was on the back foot and knew it.

'We know where they live,' Ilse said.

Natasha addressed them both.

'Correction, you knew where they lived. With such a public execution, you have warned those you thought you were going to catch. You have also now lost your only link. I find it hard to interrogate dead men. So, I ask you again, what were you thinking?'

Hess smiled; both Himmler and Ilse were speechless. Natasha had handled this very well. The guards did not know how to react.

'You,' Natasha said to Ilse, 'should not get involved in matters that you know nothing about.'

'Do you know who I am?' Ilse said.

'I don't care. And you,' Natasha directed her gaze to Himmler, 'you should know better. I expect more from you. I hope this was merely a momentary lapse of judgement. Or one might make assumptions as to a reason.'

The shock on Himmler's face said it all. He looked at Natasha and then looked around at the guards.

'Don't start down that path,' he said.

All of Himmler's guards look uneasy and didn't know what to do or where to look. He tried to make himself taller than her to take back control.

She leaned forward to Himmler and said through her teeth, 'I don't trust you. I'll be watching you.'

He scowled at her as she turned and walked off.

Calling over her shoulder Natasha asked, 'Where do you think they'll be?'

Ilse ran off after her. 'Near the old Austrian border.'

Himmler recovered himself and started to organise the guards.

As Natasha passed Hess, she commented loudly enough for everyone to hear.

'I really thought you'd have better taste.'

Ilse stopped short in her tracks; she blushed as she looked at Hess and then looked away. Natasha had known who she was, and she had still treated her with contempt. She hated to admit it, but they had made a mistake, a big mistake and now the element of surprise was gone. She looked back at Hess for support. He turned and started walking away.

Himmler walked over to her. 'Don't worry.'

They walked back to the headquarters together but alone in the group.

Locals had started mulling around the scene. They waited until the guards had gone and then they went to Schmidt's body. Natasha turned to look but stopped herself. No, she wouldn't let herself see. She wouldn't cry, she couldn't cry in public, not in front of them. Schmidt was family, her anchor, he was... No, stop it, seriously stop it or you're going to lose it. You'll lose it all.

***

Friedrich walked into his office and hung up his coat. He had been expecting to see Natasha about some interrogations. Good, not here, maybe she would change career or stay at home. She needed another interest, if he could find one; he might be able to bring her out of this mess. Who was he kidding? She was in too deep.

Friedrich walked over to his chair to sit down. Out of the corner of his eye he noticed a group of people in the square. He turned to the window and looked out. He could see Natasha and Himmler inches away from each other in what looked like a heated discussion.

He walked out of his office and spoke to his secretary.

'What's happening?'

'I don't know,' she said.

He stared at her not budging. This was not the time for games.

'They've discovered some of the resistance,' she said.

She feared Friedrich. He hadn't been his normal self for some time. Friedrich turned and stormed out of the building, just in time to see everyone getting into cars. Natasha was about to get in the front of one of them, when he grabbed her and indicated for her to sit in the back.

Himmler looked over. 'I don't think you should go.'

Friedrich turned. 'Thank you for your opinion.' Then Friedrich got into the car.

Himmler stood there for a minute; everyone was undermining his authority today. He couldn't believe what was happening. This would not occur in Berlin.

He indicated to the guards to stop Friedrich and announced, 'You'll be a liability.'

Natasha opened her door and stepped out

'I believe you have shown yourself to be the biggest liability so far, and you're still going.'

Himmler's face went red he was fuming. He turned and got into his car, and they all headed out.

Natasha sat in the back seat next to Hess. Her father handed her his jacket to hold.

The driver started the car and followed the convoy. He informed Friedrich that it would take about one and a half hours. Friedrich leaned back in his chair and dozed.

Natasha could see Friedrich's gun sticking out between the car seats. She looked at Hess, then back at Friedrich. Keeping her eyes on her father, she slowly eased the gun free. Quietly she removed the bullets and then slowly slid it back into its holster.

She leaned over to Hess.

'You must protect him for me now.'

Hess nodded and wondered how this would all play out.

***

Hilde hung up the phone and managed to make her way to the front room. She paused in the doorway; thoughts were running wild in her head.

Anneliese walked over to her.

'What's wrong, you don't look well, you've turned white?'

Helene looked up from her book. Hilde looked like she had just seen a ghost. Putting her book down Helene crossed the room and slapped Hilde across the face.

Hilde focused. 'We have to leave now. The Gestapo are on their way.'

Helene nodded and focused on organising things.

'Anneliese, get all the documents and information you can think of that is in the house, as well as some bags. Hilde, I need you to find some guns, or any weapons you can think of. I'll get Michele and Oskar. We'll meet at the car.'

'The car's not here,' Anneliese said. 'They took it back to town.'

'Then at the stables.'

They all met half an hour later. Anneliese looked at the pile of documents, 'I didn't realise there were that many. We can't carry them all; we'll have to burn them.'

'They won't fully burn in time, but we can take them with us,' Michele said.

She grabbed the records and put them in the saddle bags of the two horses in the stables.

Michele said, 'Anneliese and Oskar, ride through the woods and head to Anneliese's old house. Don't bury them in the open, but near the trees. Then go to the operations room and wait for us. Take your time and stay off the roads if possible.'

'No,' Oskar said walking towards Hilde, 'I want to stay with you Oma, you may need me.'

Hilde went to her grandson, 'It's better that we split up. I love you; you know.'

She cupped his face in her hands and stood on her toes so she could kiss him on the forehead.

'I love you too, but I…' he started.

'Go,' Hilde said. 'I'll see you soon.'

She tried to sound as confident as possible. He kissed her on the cheek and gave her a tight hug, then turned and mounted his horse. Both Anneliese and Oskar galloped off. Hilde tried to hide the tears, as she watched him disappear.

Michele came over and wrapped her arm around Hilde.

'It's going to be okay, but we have to go now, or you won't see him again.'

She nodded.

They all started walking towards the woods, past the stream. Michele checked that she still had a gun in her pocket. There had been two. She'd given one to Anneliese. They should be fine by horse. One for their group wasn't enough, but it was better than nothing. Now the rest was up to Natasha, but this was a big ask, even for her.

***

As they drove through Mittenwald, the townspeople looked at the official cars, and scuttled into their houses. They didn't know what was happening and they didn't want to know. The cars pulled up at Hilde's house. Natasha looked around. She knew they had already gone. Her discussion with Himmler, had added another twenty minutes onto the time. She just hoped that a couple of hours had given them enough time to clear away any important documents as well. Everyone got out of the cars and waited for the soldiers to search the house.

A soldier came out of the front door and said, 'it's empty Reichsführer.'

Natasha looked at Himmler who just looked away. Ilse had stayed in the car; she was hiding from any more embarrassment.

'Right,' Natasha said, 'Himmler, you and your men go into the forest and head for the old the border and we will go southwest along the stream.'

'No,' Himmler cried out. 'We'll head southwest.'

He leaned over Natasha. 'Men, move out.'

'Wait a minute,' Natasha said trying to stop them, but they had already started moving.

Wilhelm went to stop them, but Hess grabbed him.

Hess turned to her. 'You gave up easily.'

Natasha smiled. 'One has to choose one's battles.'

She then walked over to the car that Ilse was in. Leaning one arm on the roof and bending slightly so she could see inside, she handed Ilse a gun. Ilse looked surprised.

'It doesn't look like you're coming with us, and the enemy may still be around,' said Natasha.

Ilse clenched her jaw and slammed the door.

Natasha and Wilhelm led the small party out, down past the back of the house and stables to the woods.

***

Helene was the only one who did not know the track. Hilde only vaguely knew it from her younger years, so Michele led the way. The house was quite high up, but there was a long way to go. Most of the slope was gradual, but there were the odd places where basic climbing skills were required. Michele tended to move quite quickly. She would pause and then wait for the others; sometimes doubling back to help when needed.

An eight-foot cliff came up in front of them. Michele climbed up first. She lay down on the top and held out her hand to guide her mother. Some crumbling foot holes and embedded stones were in the almost vertical slope. Helene tried to climb up to Michele. She slipped slightly, but Michele grabbed her arm and managed to pull her up most of the way. Helene's foot found a hole and she dug it in. This time it didn't crumble, and she continued her climb.

Next was Hilde. She was feeling weak as it was, but the thought of capture was urging her on. She grabbed a tuft of grass to help her climb. The first foot found a perch. She dug her other foot into the wall. She used her foot to feel for another perch. Michele tried to reach her hand, but her arm was not quite long enough. Hilde moved her hand from the grass, she grabbed a rock and transferred her weight as she felt for something else to grab. Dirt fell on her hand and then the rock moved, it was in the air and then she was falling. Bang, crack, thud. She was on the ground. Hilde looked up. The other two felt so far away. She clenched her teeth. A sharp pain shot through her.

'Both of you go on,' she said.

Michele climbed back down. 'I'm not leaving you.'

She looked at Hilde's leg. Her ankle was red and starting to swell, and it looked bad. Hilde wasn't going to be able to walk far, let alone climb. Michele looked around. She needed something to use as a crutch. She took off her cardigan and used it as a bandage on the swollen ankle. Helene struggled down and they both helped support Hilde.

'This way,' Michele indicated with her head.

There was another way they could go but it would take a lot longer. Michele supported Hilde as they moved along, trying to be as quiet as possible.

***

'I heard something,' one of the officers said. 'This way.'

Natasha and the group started running to the area they had heard the voice. They came to a small clearing that had a steep cliff like incline. Hess indicated for one of the soldiers to go up it.

The soldiers climbed it and called down to the group, 'Someone's been up here recently, but they seemed to have just vanished.'

One of the other guards called out, 'I have footprints this way.'

Natasha took a deep sigh; why do we have the trackers?

***

Michele put her hand up forming a stop sign. They all paused. She looked around. There was no shelter.

'I heard something,' she whispered. 'They're close.'

She walked around and found some small solid branches.

'If any shots are fired drop and grab these as weapons.'

Handing them each a piece of wood, she said, 'There's nowhere to hide. Make a pile of loose dirt near where you are standing, aim for the eyes.'

'Try not to move much,' Helene said to Hilde.

'I love you both you know,' Michele said.

'Don't say that' whispered Helene. 'I know what that means.'

Now all they could do was wait, in silence.

***

'Don't move,' one of the guards called out.

He was up ahead with Wilhelm and Hess. Natasha walked up the track to where the group had congregated. Michele had positioned herself behind the other two. Hilde was leaning on one foot, and her ankle was wrapped. This was not good.

'Hands up,' the guards commanded.

Michele slowly raised her hands. She had tucked the revolver into her mother's belt so she could grab it when she needed to. One guard was standing to the left of Natasha, another was slightly in front of her father and Wilhelm and Hess were flanked by two others. This situation was truly a gamble, she didn't know what her father or Hess would do. Michele looked at Natasha. Natasha had her gun pointed towards Michele but tipped it ever so slightly and let her eyes look left towards the guard.

All the trackers had their guns aimed at Helene. Friedrich's eyes were on Helene. She was slightly shaking her head as if to say no. She knew what he was thinking. She could see the disgust in his eyes. She did not want to lose Natasha, but she didn't know what to do.

Natasha called out, 'Helene, step forward.'

Then everything went in slow motion.

Michele yelled, 'Drop.'

Hilde and Helene dived for the ground as Michele retrieved the gun. Friedrich turned to Natasha and fired his gun.

Helene saw him turn and pull his trigger and screamed. 'No.'

She was already crying as she hit the ground. Hess, Wilhelm and Michele shot their guards almost in unison.

The soldier in front of Natasha paused, looking at the scene. He turned around, slowly comprehending the situation.

Natasha said, 'I'm so sorry.'

She pulled the trigger at the shocked soldier.

The bullet entered the middle of his forehead and then exploded out of the back of his head, with a mixture of blood and brain tissue. Natasha froze, it was the first time she'd ever actually killed someone. Her eyes locked on the point of impact that was now just air with a tree trunk and blood and matter. So much blood. She felt nothing, no breeze, no air, no breath, only a cold that swept over her body. She was shaking, and her face was wet with tears, but she was numb. Natasha couldn't move, her brain couldn't send messages, it shut down, it wasn't reacting. It stopped. She tried to breathe. Where was the air? Tears were pouring out now, harder to breathe. She started gasping and tried to tell herself not to hyperventilate. Breathe.

Friedrich looked towards Natasha. He looked at his gun and opened it. There were no bullets in it at all. He had failed, Helene was on the ground and Natasha was still alive. He looked back at her, she hadn't moved, and she seemed to be shaking.

Michele came running over to Natasha. She took the gun from her hand and started stroking her back, 'It's alright.'

She went to hug her, but Natasha fell on to her knees and started crying and rocking.

Michele said, 'Look at me, come on now. Focus, look at me.'

Michele sat beside her and hugged her.

She started stroking her hair, 'It's alright, it was him or Mama. Remember that.'

She kissed Natasha on the forehead.

'She's human after all,' Hess said.

'She always was,' Wilhelm replied to himself, 'she just couldn't show it.'

Helene raised her head and surveyed the scene. Her precious daughters were still alive. However, she knew Natasha would never be the same again.

Helene stood up and walked over to Friedrich. She slapped him across the face.

'Why could you not believe in her?'

'It's just that...' Friedrich said. He was in shock. 'How was I supposed to know,' he said looking around. 'How was I supposed to know?'

Natasha started to focus. Her stomach. She had to move. She could feel her mouth fill up with saliva. She managed to say, 'Let go of me.'

Natasha ran to another tree and leaned on it as she began to vomit. Helene collected the guns from the dead soldiers. She gave one to Hilde and another to Michele and kept the other two for herself. She sat down on the grass beside the track. What a strange situation this was.

Friedrich whispered, 'Was I the only one who didn't know?'

He looked at Hess.

'I tried to tell you,' Hess said.

'Why you?' Friedrich said. 'Why you and not me?'

'Because I looked, I looked through the façade.'

Friedrich walked over to Natasha and sat down beside her.

'I'm so sorry,' he said as he cradled her in his arms, 'I'm so sorry.'

'It's alright,' she smiled, 'you didn't know.'

'You knew I'd shoot you.'

She nodded. She was slowly regaining her composure. But she felt damaged.

Killing the soldier made her feel sick.

Helene was sitting down with her arms tucked around her legs and her head on her knee staring straight ahead.

'I have to go,' she said, 'don't I?'

Michele looked at her. 'Yes.'

'How do you feel about flying?' said Hess.

Helene looked at him a little confused. Michele and Natasha looked at each other and nodded.

'She'll be fine,' Natasha said.

'We have to go,' Hess said, 'but I'll contact you.'

Wilhelm helped Hilde to her feet. 'Will you be okay?'

'Absolutely fine,' she lied.

'There are a couple of things that need to be done before we go,' Hess said. Wilhelm turned and asked, 'What is that?'

Hess hit him over the forehead with his gun.

Wilhelm staggered a little. There was a trickle of blood from his previous cut.

Natasha scrunched up her face and then opened one eye, 'I'm ready.'

Michele giggled, 'Good.'

She fired the gun so that the bullet just grazed her leg but did no real damage. Natasha held her breath to control the pain.

Friedrich looked at the group; they needed someone really injured. Someone that would need support to come out, instead of continuing to track the others. He walked over to Natasha and gave her a hug. Slowly he grabbed her second gun from her belt and then walked away with his back to the group. He fired the bullet into his thigh. Falling to the ground, he winced with pain.

'You need someone to carry,' he said, 'or it looks suspicious.'

His head was a mess. Everything was wrong. No, he was wrong. No. He was lost. A mess. He had nothing, yet everything now. At least, he could be useful while he sorted out how he felt.

***

Anneliese galloped ahead of Oskar along the foothills. She knew the way well, and so did the horse. Oskar was a little more cautious, he was thinking about his grandmother. He had a bad feeling.

'I don't think–' Oskar said.

Anneliese interrupted him, 'We're about five minutes away.'

They continued riding towards Anneliese's old house. Just before reaching the clearing, they dismounted and tied up the horses.

Anneliese loved the area. The good times here, outweighed the bad. It made her feel peaceful. There was no noise. She walked over the trees near the edge of the clearing.

'Come on,' she said and started to dig.

It took about ten minutes to bury the information.

'I think something's wrong,' Oskar said. 'I just feel it.'

'There is nothing you can do,' Anneliese replied. 'We have to go to the operations room.'

'No,' Oskar said as he got back on the horse, 'I'm going back.'

Anneliese grabbed the reigns.

'No, you're not.'

The horse looked confused as both tried to take control.

'Let go,' said Oskar.

He pulled the reins to turn and dug in his heels. Anneliese was still hanging on. The horse reared. Oskar tried to hold on, but his feet slipped out of the stirrups. The horse reared again and threw Oscar. He sailed off the back of the horse and fell hand first onto the ground. There was a small cracking sound before his head connected with the tree trunk. Anneliese let go of the reigns and ran over to him. She checked for a pulse; it was still strong. Blood oozed from a cut on his head and a bump was rising. She looked at his arm. The bone was protruding slightly, but enough to know that it was a severe break. The horse had settled now and was standing with its head nudging Anneliese. She got up and walked the small distance to the stream. She took off her scarf and put it in the water. Letting it drip she walked back to Oskar and put it on his forehead.

Unbuckling the stirrup, she put it near the protrusion. It was big enough to cover it. She managed to attach it to his arm. It looked ridiculous but it would keep it safe for now.

**

The four of them emerged from the forest. Friedrich was leaning on Hess and Wilhelm. Natasha was limping behind. Himmler was outside the house and his troops appeared to be searching the house for anything of value. He looked up and saw the group approach. He ordered his men to assist. They carried Friedrich back to the car, while both Natasha and Wilhelm were attended to.

'What happened?' said Himmler.

'We were ambushed,' Hess replied. 'The soldiers ahead were killed, we managed to find some shelter. But not much.'

'How many did you get?' Himmler said.

'None,' Hess said. 'Didn't even see them coming.'

Hess walked away.

Ilse came running over. 'Are you hurt?'

'I'm fine,' he replied and walked on.

By the time Hess got to Natasha, she was all bandaged up. She was leaning on the wall of the house, watching.

'How are you?' Hess asked.

'Surface wound,' Natasha replied. 'It'll heal quickly.'

Hess stood beside her as they both looked over the scene. He put his hands in his pockets and glanced at her sideways. 'You know what I mean.'

She took a deep breath and replied, 'You know me, I'm fine.'

She looked up at him; there was an honest concern on his face. His features seemed softer than she had ever seen before. Was that caring in his eyes? She couldn't work him out. His personality was not quite right. She couldn't work it out.

Hess grabbed her by the shoulders, 'It'll get easier.'

'The first is always the hardest,' she whispered.

'That's right,' he lied. 'That's right.'

'You saved them you know,' he said, 'your talk, your fighting, it saved them.'

'Not all of them,' she bit her lip, and her eyes started to water, 'I couldn't save all of them.'

Her lip trembled as she looked down, 'A good man died today. I couldn't save all of them.'

***

'Your mother would kill me,' Ilse said to Wilhelm, 'if anything happened to you because of me.'

'I'm fine,' Wilhelm said. 'I need to walk, don't worry, I'm fine.'

He wanted to check up on Natasha. Wandering around the building, he finally saw her but stopped. Hess was talking to Natasha. Hess leaned forward, said something to her, and then left. Wilhelm had never seen his uncle like that before, maybe only with his son Wolf. His uncle was detached, functional, and didn't waste time on people generally. Wilhelm smiled and thought, so Hess was a little bit human too. He turned and left her in peace.

***

There was still pain in his legs, but Yosef was determined to make it completely down the stairs. He was bored of resting. The steps were wide, so the crutches were quite safe. There were only five more steps to go. He balanced on the left crutch and placed the right on the step below. He continued his challenge as the doorbell rang. The nurse opened the door. Helene and Michele carried Hilde in. Yosef looked up a little surprised at his visitors. He missed the step and lost balance. The nurse came running over to try to stop his fall. She managed to grab him but slipped. They both ended up on their knees. The pain shot through him.

'Ow,' the nurse said, 'are you alright?'

Yosef grunted and took a deep breath. 'Fine.'

She sat him down and then limped over to Hilde. 'Come this way.'

Michele and Helene brought Hilde through.

'I'll call the doctor,' the nurse said and hurried off.

Yosef was getting impatient. He started to crawl up the stairs. He still needed some sort of leverage to get up to use the crutches. Using the banister, he pulled himself on to the crutches and started to follow them.

Michele walked into the foyer, stopped, looked at Yosef and crossed her arms.

'I see patience is a virtue that you still haven't mastered.'

'No,' he said, 'curiosity always gets in the way.'

'Come with me,' Michele said as she walked into an empty room, then sat down. Her mind was focusing on what to do next and where Oskar and Anneliese were.

'Come back,' Yosef interrupted her thoughts. 'Relax for just one moment.'

'You know that if I didn't know you, I would think that was sweet of you,' she said.

'Am I that transparent?'

'Yes,' she said, 'but first weren't you supposed to have a couple more months of bed rest.'

'It was only an approximate time,' he said, 'for normal people.' Smiling he added, 'I was a little bored. Everyone is having too much fun and adventure and I'm just getting bed sores.'

She cringed and shook her head.

'Anyway, it's good to see Helene,' he said. 'It's been so long.'

'Yeah, it's good to see her again,' Michele said, 'but she's going soon.'

'Why? Ah,' he said, 'is it anything to do with this little visit?'

'She's been a bad girl, so I am sending her away.'

Michele smiled, but it was a sad smile.

'Why are you smiling?' Helene said as she walked into the room, 'Have you forgotten what I've done?'

'You didn't mean to,' Michele said.

'Don't dismiss this,' said Helene. 'Let's see a friend is dead, another has a broken ankle and one of the resistance meeting places is now a no-go area.'

Yosef raised his eyebrows.

'If you want to take responsibility,' Michele threw back, 'it was five in total that died. The enemy are only doing their job too.'

'Who died?' Yosef said.

He realised that Annelise was not with them, and a chill went down his spine.

Michele saw Yosef's face drain of colour.

She ran over to his chair.

'It was just Schmidt.'

Helene was in her own little world. 'What do you mean just Schmidt, he was a good friend. He was–'

'Thank God.' Yosef said.

He let out a sigh; relief took over his body and he fought to hold back the tears,

Helene looked around and saw Michele comforting him.

'Oh my God, I'm so, so sorry' she said. 'I didn't even think.'

'I'm sorry to hear about Schmidt,' Yosef said. 'He was a good man.'

They all sat in silence. For all her bravado Michele hated the fact that they'd lost him. He'd been like a grandfather to her. But she had to continue, they all knew the risks and they'd made their choices. She would grieve for him later in her own way. Her mother needed to take some responsibility but now was not the time to dwell. It was time for her to go. She had to leave Germany.

A short scream broke the silence. Helene and Michele ran to the other room. The doctor was beside Hilde's bed.

He looked up. 'She sprained her ankle, but she also dislocated her hip. I had to put it back in place.'

Hilde's face was red.

'I'm okay, just tender,' she said.

Helene looked at the room. She'd been a fool to think that she could change her appearance enough to roam around Munich. But that was home, that was where her girls were. She'd jeopardised everyone. It was time for her to leave. She couldn't be this close and not help. They were right to send her away, enforce distance. But she didn't like it.

A part of her was scared. Here, she knew the places and people. But that was the problem. She needed to step into the unknown, be unknown.

Michele walked back into the parlour.

'I need you to look after Mum, until she leaves.'

'Fine,' Yosef said, 'she can help with my recovery. What's the plan?'

Michele filled Yosef in on everything, then gave him a hug.

'It's good to see you getting back to normal.'

He smiled, 'So when do you leave?'

'That's lovely, I've only just arrived,' she said rolling her eyes. 'Tomorrow, I am a little tired.'

'Oh,' he said, 'so you do sleep? Why don't you spoil yourself, and have some food as well?'

She stood up and pulled a face at him before she walked out the door. She was feeling a little hungry, now he mentioned it.

***

The convoy returned to headquarters. The car that Natasha had travelled in was deathly quiet. Himmler started to walk across the road to the bakery.

'I don't think so,' Hess said. 'You need to file a report, I believe.'

Himmler stared at Hess, then stone faced walked back to the office.

'Come on,' Hess said 'Natasha, let's have a look at the bakery.'

Natasha took a deep breath as they headed across the street. As they approached, they saw blood painted the pavement and the doorway. There was a smashed front window, but there was no body. Natasha paused. She didn't want to walk through the blood, but there was no other way in. Memories were pouring back. She had known Schmidt for as long as she could remember. Her hand ran along the glass on the counter.

'How are you?'

'I've never lost anyone in my care before,' she said. 'Never.'

'There wasn't anything you could do.'

'I can always think of something. I failed.'

'Sometimes failure is less to do with us, than the circumstances,' said Hess. 'You saved others.'

'It doesn't change the fact that I failed him.'

It had been a hard day and Natasha felt broken, so broken. She turned back and pretended to look around. There was nothing of importance here. He'd given her the last pieces of information only a few hours earlier. All the information left was in Schmidt's head and now that would be his secret forever. She did however need to find the body and make sure that that he had a good funeral. She would mourn later, behind closed doors.

CHAPTER 22

Goebbels walked out of his office and stood in front of Jean's desk. She stopped typing and looked up at him.

'Can you ask when Hitler will be free for a meeting?' he said, 'Can you also type these up and hand them to the radio stations.'

He put the notes on her desk.

'Newspapers as well?'

'Yes,' he said, 'I want the press inundated for the next couple of weeks.'

Jean had a look at the press releases. They were small biographies on Hess and added to them almost like an afterthought was a sentence wishing Hess well for his birthday. Jean read it a couple of times. Goebbels had worded it well, at no time did he say Hess would fly, but he indicated constantly how good he was and how victorious he had been. She chuckled to herself. Goebbels, if only you knew.

***

The doctor looked at Oskar's arm.

'You haven't just broken your arm,' he said. 'You've snapped it.'

Oskar looked at it. It had stopped hurting. It was completely numb. He looked at Anneliese.

'I'm sorry,' she said.

'It's not your fault,' he said trying to give her a calming hug with one arm. 'It was just an accident.'

'I have to do some tests,' the doctor said.

'Why?' they both said.

'If I straighten the bone, I could catch a nerve and then you'll have no feeling in that arm at all,' the doctor said. 'Ever.'

'How long will it take to heal?' Oskar said.

'About six weeks give or take,' the Doctor replied.

Oskar grabbed Anneliese with his strong arm and pulled her close enough to whisper in her ear.

'Tell the girls.'

Anneliese nodded and pulled away.

'I have to go,' she said. 'Will you be alright here?'

The doctor nodded. Anneliese smiled at them both, turned and was out the door. Everything had changed. Oskar, Hilde's home, Schmidt. She blinked and looked up at the sky as she absently brushed away a tear. Anneliese took a deep breath so she could think. Taking another deep breath, she smiled and began walking. Henri's house wasn't far away. He was out of the country, but she knew he wouldn't mind her using it.

Anneliese soon arrived and looked around as she took her hair clip out of her hair. She could see no one. She bent down to pick the lock; she knew how now. She turned the door handle and slipped inside closing it behind her. She needed to use the phone.

'Hello, can I please speak to Hess,' Anneliese said.

'I'm sorry, he's in a meeting,' the voice said. 'Can I take a message?'

'No,' Anneliese paused for a second. 'Can I speak to Natasha?'

'No, I'm sorry,' the secretary said, 'she's in the meeting with Hess.'

'Is there anyone else in that meeting?'

'Yes,' the secretary replied, 'Himmler and some SS.'

Her tone had changed, and Anneliese could tell she was getting annoyed.

'Alright,' Anneliese said. 'Can you pass on a message for me please?'

***

Himmler was going through his report to Hess. The cover up on Hess and Natasha's side was easy, Himmler had handed it to them. Hess was picking holes in everything, tying Himmler up in knots. Hess was good at that. Natasha could tell he was having fun. What was more amusing, was the fact that you could see that deep down Himmler agreed with Hess. He had handled the whole thing appallingly. The secretary brought in fresh tea and then started to head out. She paused by Natasha and bent down.

'I have been told to tell you; by a girl who refused to give her name,' the secretary said angrily, 'that she needs to meet you and you'll need to bring some clothes pegs.'

'Thank you,' Natasha said with a smile.

The secretary walked out. Natasha chuckled to herself, and then continued in the conversation. The girl would have to wait.

***

Anneliese gathered a couple of blankets, a pillow, and some food. She drove out to the operations room in Henri's car and handed the keys in at the farm. Walking into the room, she looked around. It was a great operations room, but it wasn't much of a bedroom. She brought a bit of hay down and made a small bed in the corner. She didn't know when Natasha would get here, or if she'd understand the message. Settling down she drifted off to sleep.

The bell rang and Anneliese sat up. It took her a couple of seconds to register where she was. Quietly she got up and moved over to where the detonator was. The roof opened and she saw women's shoes walking down the stairs. It was Michele, who looked a little confused. Anneliese moved out of the shadows towards Michele and gave her a hug.

'How is everyone?' Anneliese said.

'They're safe, Hilde sprained her ankle.'

'Where is–' Michele said.

The bell interrupted them.

'I think this is Natasha,' Anneliese said.

They both waited, leaning against the table.

Natasha walked down the stairs and smiled.

'Did you both think of it?' she said looking at Michele.

'It was me,' Anneliese said. She was looking at them both uncomfortably. 'We have a problem.'

'Think of what?' Michele said looking at Natasha, ignoring Anneliese.

'I'll tell you later' Natasha said. 'What's the problem?'

'It's Oskar,' Anneliese said. 'There was an accident with the horse, and he snapped the bone in his arm.'

'Is he alright?' Michele said.

'He will be in about six or seven weeks.'

Silence. No one said anything. Their brains were trying to reformulate plans, while occasionally being interrupted with the thought, could this get any worse.

'Can't Wilhelm fly?' Anneliese asked. 'He is used to it.'

'He is flying,' Michele replied. 'Hess needs an escort to send the right official message and an escort is made up of two planes.'

'Let's think this through rationally,' Natasha said. 'Michele you could telephone for safe passage and organise Anneliese's tasks and Anneliese could fly the plane.'

Michele leaned on her back leg and crossed her arms. Natasha was ignoring her sister and looking at the map. Natasha could feel her sister's gaze; she knew what her sister wanted. She wanted to fly. Michele was the one person Natasha knew who could successfully learn how to fly a plane in the limited time. But every time she thought about it, she felt bad, a little sick. She turned to Anneliese.

'What do you think?'

Anneliese was white.

'I will do it if I have to,' she said quietly, 'but what about Yosef, his arms are fine?'

'Yosef wouldn't be able to use the pedals in the plane,' Michele said. 'How scared are you?'

Anneliese looked at them both.

'I'm scared of swings in the park.'

Both Michele and Natasha looked at each other.

Anneliese started sobbing.

'I'm sorry, I feel like it's my fault. Oskar was with me,' she said sobbing. 'I stopped him, and the horse reared, he fell. I couldn't stop him and now I can't fly. I'm useless. I'm so sorry.'

Michele walked over and cradled Anneliese with a hug and glared at Natasha. Natasha returned the look. Michele let go and marched towards Natasha. She paused in front of her sister with her arms crossed.

'What is it? Why won't you let me fly?'

'Fine,' Natasha snapped, 'you fly. But I don't like it. No heroics. Do you hear me. No heroics.'

Natasha turned and shook her head; she just hoped her feelings were wrong.

***

Natasha walked through the front door. Everything had changed. She wasn't the same person she had been a couple of days ago.

'Join me,' her father said.

She walked into the parlour and saw her father resting in a chair with his leg on a stool.

'How are you?' she said as she sat down.

'Fine, I've had worse,' he said. 'How are you?'

She shrugged, 'it's just a surface wound.'

Natasha knew her father wanted to talk. But she didn't. She clenched her jaw and looked away to control her breathing.

Friedrich looked at his daughter as she stared out the window. Nothing made sense. How? Where did the lies start?

'What are you thinking about?' he asked.

She didn't move for a second and then lowered her eyes to think, before turning them to look up at him.

'What happens now?'

There was a stilted silence in the air. They were learning how to talk to each other.

'Why would anything change?' he asked, confused.

'It's already changed. I just need to...' she paused, '... I need to plan. I need a plan.'

'But why, I won't tell,' he said. 'I–'

'It's not you,' she replied, 'so much went into making me, me. I didn't realise how much we relied on each other.'

Friedrich sat in silence; he knew she didn't mean him.

'Schmidt was a communication point.'

She took a deep breath trying to steady herself, she still couldn't believe he was dead.

'He passed information on through packets or over the phone. Now he's gone.'

'What do you mean?' Friedrich asked leaning forward.

'If I interrogated a resistance member, I would let Schmidt know where I was taking them by buying certain things in the bakery. He would phone Michele, who would then pick them up.'

Friedrichs jaw dropped, 'Is that all you had to do?'

'Is that all I had to do?' she said rolling her eyes. 'I couldn't go in with a map, could I? It took years to build this up.'

'How many?'

'All of them,' she replied matter-of-factly. 'All of them are living normal lives in other countries, or back here.'

She looked out the window again.

'It can't be, you have killed at least some of them, everyone knows you have. Everyone knows, the guards, the people who work with me, they all know. There must be close to a hundred.'

Friedrich could not focus; he couldn't comprehend what she was saying. He knew, everyone knew.

'It was 127 actually, and I killed no one.' The words caught in her throat.

Her nostrils flared briefly, and her eyes stung. She swallowed, but there was still a quiver in her voice. 'I killed no one, until today.'

Friedrich looked at Natasha. For all the strength she portrayed and the image of the monster she wanted the world to see, she seemed so fragile in this moment. And then he saw her jaw set as she regained control.

Natasha could not afford to lose herself. Not now, not when everything was such a mess.

Friedrich's curiosity got the better of him, he knew now was the time to ask questions, before Natasha refortified herself.

'You passed on information from your interrogations, so why would they trust you?'

She looked at him with mild annoyance.

'I passed you no information from any of the prisoners. I already had the information. We decided what you would get.

I knew what to tell you, so it was enough to prove worth, but vague enough not to allow it to stop things, unless we decided for it to be stopped. Think of it as propaganda.'

'No, I don't believe it, the prisoners, I saw them, the cuts, bruises, broken bones.'

'I never broke bones,' she interrupted. 'I learnt how to make great bruises and cuts, but they were unconscious when it happened. They were for show and hurt only a little. I always worked alone. But the bone breaking that was the others before me. I could never cause those.'

She took a breath and looked down. 'It was hard enough making the marks that I did.'

'You played me.'

'Yes.'

'You didn't need to play me.'

'You have no idea, do you? Everyone hates me. They fear me. It has taken years to make them look at me like a monster, to stay away from me because of the pleasure I take in my work. To think of me as one of the cruellest interrogators, that thinks nothing of life. You think I don't know what they say about me? And I need that to continue. Then I can keep doing what I do, to stay alive. You are part of that, an official in it. It is your duty to get rid of people like me. And I have no doubt that you would. Just like I knew you would kill me today. I have, I need, to deceive everyone, especially you.'

Natasha didn't know when she'd started crying, but her cheeks were warm and wet.

He wanted to save Helene and Michele. He hadn't set out to kill Natasha. But it was her or them. He wouldn't have. But before if he had known, known who she really was, would he? Before everything had happened with Michele and Helene. Before he realised how wrong he was. Would he have killed her? He felt sick. Honestly, he didn't know.

'But if you had trusted me, maybe,' Friedrich started.

'Let's not forget who taught me how to be an interrogator. I learnt from you.'

Natasha stopped. She instantly regretted what she said, but she couldn't take it back.

It stung Friedrich. Not because of the venom in her voice, but because it was true. He had taught her. Why had he taught her? His eyes were stinging, and he couldn't breathe. He tried to focus.

'I can't, I can't even remember the first time,' he said. 'Why would I show you? Why?'

'I remember,' whispered Natasha. 'I remember everything. It was two days before my sixteenth birthday.'

Friedrich looked at her. His face set.

'He was young, around twenty,' she continued softly, while looking out the window. 'It was when Yosef and a small group escaped, the first time. You wanted to know how. You said this was the way people who betrayed Hitler were treated. That they were the lowest of the low. I think you used the word vermin.'

There were tears on Natasha's face, but she couldn't feel them.

'I remember his wrists were bound to the dark varnished wooden chair. It was the only bit of colour in the room and yet it restrained him. Captured him. I remember the whimpering. The sweat dropping from his forehead, as he shook his head and pleaded innocence. The strained breathing. The scream when you broke his kneecaps with the hammer. How he struggled until his wrists bled when you came for his fingers. I had never heard that kind of scream before. That pitch. That intensity.'

Her eyes were starting to lose focus and she closed them as she swallowed, to allow herself time to recompose.

'But then you told me to leave the room.' Natasha shook her head and looked up. It was like she was reliving it. 'And I stood outside and heard the screams, and all I could do was focus on not vomiting. But then there was silence.'

The tears started to flow, and her bottom lip quivered. 'The silence, it was so quiet and that was worse. So much worse.'

She wiped her cheeks and nose.

Friedrich looked at her with tears on his face. Not even a week ago he had considered her a monster. Yet after all he had done to her. After all she had seen. She wasn't the monster.

He was. He couldn't get his memory back to that time, to think why. Why had he not just stopped and thought about it? Why had it even occurred to him to bring his daughter into an interrogation room?

'Why? How can you possibly care for me? Why play the dutiful daughter?'

'I was not your daughter. I have not been your daughter for a very long time. I was your protégé.' She looked at him. 'I don't want your pity. You have no right to pity me. I chose this life. I chose to stay. I could have gone to Mother. But I chose to stay, to know what was happening and to make a difference. You had no choice. You're a follower, not a leader. You were sold a vision and fell into its abyss.'

There was part of him that was angered by what she said. He had worked hard to get where he was. People listened to him; he was a leader.

'We all have to deal with our past. To begin with I hated you. I hated how you made me feel about myself. I hated the things you made me see. The things you taught me. The things you made me do. I used to cry every night, so many tears.' She paused. 'But it made no difference. It changed nothing. So, I stopped. I focused on being hated, detached. I focused on being useful on missions. I am a survivor. I don't need your pity and I don't want it. But now you know. Now we are where we are. You made me do things, I should never have done as a child. But it has made me who I am. Given me the strength to do what I must. But the things that you have done are your demons to deal with. Not mine.'

***

Hess sat in the armchair beside Hitler. The meetings with Goebbels were draining.

'You confuse me,' Hitler said. 'I thought you believed and yet you put up blocks.'

Hess looked at Hitler.

'The Jews conspired against us,' Hitler said. 'They took everything, our land, our pride.'

'Stab in the back,' Hess said. 'I do believe. The Jews, the Communists, the others. They are a plague on our nation. They need to go. Eventually. They will just degrade us, rob us otherwise. This is why the Nuremberg Laws are so important. Maybe we should look at those again.'

'So why not do as Goebbels suggests?'

'I'm a pragmatist. Right now, we need them. Men have been sent to war and more will shortly; women should be breeding. Not working in factories. It also costs too much, employing Germans. The industry needs more money for the weapons they are creating, the tanks. It's pure logic why I disagree with Goebbels. We want to create Lebensraum, the expansion needs support, infrastructure. Obviously, we don't need the weak. But the rest should be used as a resource. Aryans have been limited for so long, we need time to build. Time to rebuild.'

'Hmmm, I see your point,' Hitler said, 'but you push me at times.'

'You lose focus,' Hess said. 'I believe in you and what you can accomplish. Your leadership will make us stronger, Germany stronger. But you must focus. And be strategic. If you annoy too many countries at once, you'll have to fight too many wars.'

'I grow impatient, why do others not see the logic?' Hitler said. 'Hess, you can admit it to me though. It is also a little because it is Goebbels.'

'Maybe,' Hess said smiling, 'he is an idiot after all.'

Hitler went to say something.

'But he too is useful,' Hess said. 'For now, anyway.'

'But it is mostly driven by logic. I would not put my personal feelings above the country's needs. You know that of me.'

'Well while you are feeling so generous,' Hitler smiled at Hess, 'Göring. I have concerns.'

'But why,' said Hess sarcastically. 'He appreciates art and culture.'

Hitler rolled his eyes, 'I said that one time, just one time and I didn't think you would disagree.'

'I don't Adolf, but you said it in front of the press secretary,' Hess said. 'Otto, was always going to make something of it. It'll be in one of Goebbels' files for later use. As primitive as they are.'

'Goebbels' files,' Hitler smirked. 'Does he know where most of the information comes from?'

'Of course not,' Hess dismissed with a wave of his hand. 'He would not be interested in them if he did. And he would start poking his nose around. We can't have that. After all the man also has an appreciation for culture.'

'Hess,' Hitler sighed, 'it's just Göring's house was filled with art, and he seemed like a man who appreciated the finer things in life and your place, your new place, let me add was so-'

'Functional.' Hess said, 'and I believe that in the media it was stated. That you, could not make me your successor as Führer because the house betrayed such a lack of feeling for art and culture. Göring however has a broad grasp of political significance of art. In other words, spectacle before substance.'

'Word for word. You will go to your grave hassling me for that. And it is unfair, you know the real reason he is successor.'

'At the moment,' Hess said, 'and yes, I do, it makes strategic sense. You need the army during a war. But he will be impossible during peace time.'

'He won't be an issue during peace time,' Hitler smiled.

'He's becoming a liability now,' Hess said. 'You praise him for France, which even I could have taken. And then he has no strategy with England. But currently he is controllable. He's an…'

'Idiot?' Hitler smiled. 'Is there anyone you think is not an idiot?'

'Most are idiots, but they are useful. Karl is not. There is one person. And you, of course. If I think of more, I'll let you know.' Hess looked at Hitler. 'And for the record, you are quite right, I have no appreciation for confiscated Jewish art, it does not provide any function, it is not strategic, it is merely to show power, it does not mean you have power. I don't want to be in charge, I want to be exactly where I am. Sitting here having coffee with you.'

***

Anneliese ducked down the Viscardigasse just before the guards stationed on the main street so she would not need to salute the memorial they guarded. Turning out of the alley, she walked right in front of Friedrich. She paused. He looked straight at her. She looked around wondering if he would call someone over.

'It's fine,' he said, sensing her unease.

She tried to sidestep him, but he moved to block her.

'I need to talk to you.'

She looked around again and then looked back at him taking a step forward so no one else could hear.

'There is nothing you can say to me.'

He lent back slightly and paused.

'You're wrong. There is nothing I can say that will change anything,' he said, 'but there are things to say.'

She went to go, and he grabbed her arm. She turned and scowled at him as she pulled free from his grasp.

'I'm sorry,' he said. 'I'm sorry for everything. What can I do?'

Anneliese stepped back and looked at him.

'There is nothing you can do. There is nothing you can change. I hate you; I despise you; you repulse me. I don't know if that will ever change. What you did to my family, to our family; I can't forgive you for.'

'I know, I know, I just don't know what to do.'

'You've done enough,' she said. 'What do you want me to say? It's all okay? Well, it's not. Helene is my compass with you. But don't expect me to forget what you've done or forgive you. You are sorry for yourself. Because you realise what you have lost. Don't pretend that it's anything else.'

She walked away before she started to cry.

***

Wilhelm parked the car behind the hangar. Michele jumped out but hid behind the car until she saw there was no one around.

'What are you doing?' said Wilhelm.

'Nothing.'

She smiled sweetly.

He looked at her with a stern face.

'Well,' she said, 'when we first started snooping around, I may have, flirted with someone here to get information.'

'You flirt with someone,' he said sarcastically, 'to interrogate them?'

'Interrogate is such a nasty word,' she said. 'He was merely relaying information to me.'

'Who?'

'Pardon?'

'Who relayed information to you?'

Michele hesitated.

'You promise he won't get in trouble.'

'Promise.'

'Martin,' she said.

Wilhelm smiled.

'He's a fool for a skirt. Not here today, but we can come back another day and you can be formally introduced.'

'Ha ha,' she said.

She grabbed her bag from the back seat, and they headed inside. Wilhelm was leading the way to show her the inside of the cockpit, but Michele had other ideas.

'Take me through parachuting,' she said

She didn't even try to catch up with him.

He stopped and turned around.

'Do you not want to see the plane?'

'No, that can wait until this afternoon.'

'This afternoon?' Wilhelm said. 'But Oskar...'

Michele walked up to him.

'One would think you would realise by now, that I am not Oskar.'

She smiled at him and gave him a wink. Her hands were on her hips and Wilhelm knew that she wouldn't take no for an answer.

'Parachuting it is then.'

It wasn't long before they were up in the plane. Wilhelm indicated for Michele to come over. She took a deep breath and walked over to the door. Her hands gripped either side of the door. She looked down. Far below her were fields, just to the right she could see the runway. Michele took another deep breath, she had to do this. She reminded herself that in just a few minutes, her feet would be firmly planted on the ground. The noise of the engines was loud. The plane shuddering and she could vaguely hear Wilhelm say something. She took another deep breath.

Wilhelm indicated that it was time to go.

'It's always hard—' he said.

She launched out of the plane.

'The first time.'

He stopped. She hadn't hesitated. He stood stunned for a moment, then realised that he was supposed to be jumping too.

Michele couldn't breathe because of the force of the wind. Her whole body felt like it was vibrating, and her cheeks and eyebrows felt forced off her face. Her bobbing head had a large cheesy smile. Taking the step out of the plane was petrifying. However, the fall was an amazing adrenaline rush. She was supposed to count to ten and then pull the cord. She had counted a few more numbers, but she was enjoying herself too much.

Something hit her head. Then she saw Wilhelm. He was indicating for her to pull the cord. She reached out and pulled the cord attached to his parachute. He was dragged backwards and up as he flew out of her vision. She giggled. The ground was getting closer. Her hand reached down to her parachute cord, her other hand grabbed her strap, and she pulled the cord. She felt the parachute pull her backwards, with the main strain being on her groin. She started running and her feet soon connected with the ground. The connection caught her off balance and she rolled in the grass. Wilhelm landed soon after her.

He stormed over to her.

'What the hell was that?'

'I had so much fun,' she said.

Michele was doing little jumps, bouncing. Her adrenalin was pulsing through her body, and she was buzzing.

'Seriously,' he said grabbing her shoulder harness and spinning her around to face him, 'you could have killed yourself.'

'I was fine,' she said, trying to dismiss his fears.

He leaned over to her so that their faces were a couple of inches apart. Gritting his teeth. He said, 'Don't you ever, do that, again. Do we understand each other?'

She looked at him with defiant eyes.

'Fine'

He turned and strolled off.

She ran to catch up with him.

'Wilhelm,' she said, 'what about training me to fly?'

He stopped and turned to face her.

'I can't even talk to you right now. Leave me alone.'

She stood still and watched him walk away. Looking around she saw a little patch of grass, headed over to it, sat down and waited.

CHAPTER 23

Helene looked out the window. What a mess. Her world had crumbled. In one day, she had opened the resistance up to the Gestapo, lost a friend's house, injured that friend, and killed a father figure. Schmidt. Oh God, I'm so sorry.

She hadn't pointed the gun or pulled the trigger, but she'd been seen, she'd been followed. She had cried so much already; she had no more tears. Now she was consumed by the guilt.

Lunch sat beside her. She wasn't hungry, hadn't even realised that food was there. She just sat still and looked out the window, not seeing anything.

Yosef limped into the room on his crutches. Looking at her, he shook his head. He knew she had to grieve, but she needed to function. She was still mending from the camp. These were dangerous times. He leaned against the wall for a minute, thinking. Then he moved over to the cabinet and opened the drawer.

Yosef threw the gun into Helene's lap.

'Go ahead,' said. 'We'll waste less food.'

She looked at him confused.

'If you're going to starve yourself,' Yosef said, 'we'll keep putting food out. But it will only take one bullet.'

He turned to go and then looked back at her. She was still in shock.

'Do it outside though,' he said. 'I don't want to have to clean it up.'

'Yosef, how dare you?' she said. 'I don't want to commit suicide.'

'Then get a grip of yourself.'

'But you don't understand,' she said, 'Schmidt was like a father to me.'

'And a grandfather to me,' Yosef said. 'I miss him, I grieve. But seriously Helene is this what he would have wanted?'

He looked straight into her eyes.

'Is it?'

She looked away.

'No, it's not.'

'Then pull yourself together,' he said, 'and don't let him have died in vain. Honour his memory.'

He turned and left the room.

***

Wilhelm walked back towards the airfield. Where was she? Buildings, no, waiting room, no. She wouldn't have, would she? He walked towards where he had left her. Pausing he crossed his arms and surveyed the scene in front of him. She was sitting on the ground with her face pushed up against the wall. Her eyes closed, fast asleep. Damn it, how can I be annoyed with someone so damn cute. Taking a handful of her hair, he gently dragged the ends under her nose. Her nose twitched. He repeated the exercise. Her nose twitched again, and she brushed it aside with her hand. Again, he dragged the hair across. Her nose twitched and she frantically used both hands and rubbed her nose until she woke herself up.

Blurry eyed, she looked around somewhat startled until she saw Wilhelm and then she smiled.

'Stop it,' she said.

'You just stayed here?'

'Did a bit of sleeping,' she said, 'waiting for your return.'

'What if I didn't?'

'Then I may have had to bribe Martin.'

She smiled looking at Wilhelm.

'I feel underpaid.'

'I'll double what I'm paying you,' she said. 'Now it's time for you to teach me how to fly.'

Wilhelm paused for a moment to understand what had just been said and then started laughing.

'Let's go. But honestly don't ever do what you did this morning again.'

She nodded and they both walked off towards the hangar.

Michele sat down in the cockpit and put her bag just to the right of her. Wilhelm watched her in disbelief. She opened the bag and pulled out some paper and tape.

'You'll not be able to take notes while I'm flying you know,' Wilhelm said, 'and you can't leave your bag there.'

'I'm not leaving the bag there,' she said, 'and I know that I can't take notes while I'm flying.'

'Good,' he said.

'Now talk me through the instruments,' she said.

Slowly he told her about all the controls and told her what they did. After he had finished each one, she taped a small piece of paper to it with a name. The names were not technically correct, but they were good names. Names she could understand. After he finished, she put everything back in her bag and he wedged it under her seat.

She belted herself in and then said, 'Now talk me through taking off.'

'The first thing,' he said raising his hand to start the engine. She grabbed it.

'Talk me through it, I'm flying.'

He looked at her.

'We don't have a lot of time,' she said. 'I need to be comfortable flying this and I won't be unless I've flown a lot.'

He looked at her, she was right, but he was apprehensive. The only time she had been in a plane was for her parachute jump. She didn't know the feel, how it would handle, or what she would have to do. He also knew there wasn't enough time to coach her the normal way. When he flew a plane, it was as if it was an extension of his body. He had respect for the plane but felt in control of it. She wouldn't feel like that at all, but she needed to get as close as possible to it.

'Fine.'

He reluctantly started to teach her how to take off, although his hand was constantly beside the controls.

Michele couldn't see the runway, so she looked out the side of the plane. Oskar had warned her about this before she'd left, so she would feel prepared and not stupid for doing it. The plane was very heavy to control. Sometimes she had to use all her weight, but eventually it got off the ground. In the air it had a completely different feel. Michele still needed a lot of force, but it was easier.

'Thank you for giving in so easily,' she said.

'Not a problem,' he replied, 'you were right, but don't get used to it, it probably won't happen again.'

Michele laughed and thought, that's what you think.

***

'I don't think I can do this,' Friedrich said.

'What exactly?' Hess asked.

'My job,' he said. 'Everything's changed. My life, it's all changed.'

He was trying to hold his emotions in, but it was difficult.

Hess took a deep breath. Friedrich was right. He wasn't the man he'd been days earlier. How could he be? He was mentally broken, and it would take a long time to heal. But the biggest problem was that Friedrich wasn't someone who was used to hiding things. He didn't have to till now. But now he could jeopardise everything.

'What do you want to do?' Hess said.

'I don't know.' Friedrich said looking down, but not focusing on anything in particular. 'I just don't know.'

'My plane is full.' Hess said, 'and I need you here when the interrogations begin after I leave.'

He waited for a response, but Friedrich did not oblige him.

'After that you can go,' Hess said. 'You'll have to leave the country. You're far too well known.'

'What about Natasha?' Friedrich said.

'Make the most of the time you have with her now,' Hess said. 'She survived before; she'll survive again.'

Friedrich sat motionless. He only just had Natasha back and now he was going to throw it all away. However, he knew he couldn't maintain the façade, he would become a liability, just like his wife.

'I think that's the best option,' he said, 'but please let me tell them.'

Later that evening Friedrich sat in the front room. It felt like it had been such a long time since he had sat in the dusk light listening to the radio. He reached over and grabbed his glass. He took a sip of orange juice and then looked down at the glass. So much had changed. He felt lighter, more positive and he didn't feel the need to drown his sorrows, because now they weren't sorrows, it was about learning, reconciling, it was a new start. But his focus was on everything that was happening, not on himself. He wasn't ready to go there yet, he didn't know how.

The door woke him from his thoughts. Natasha walked over and looked at the glass. Picking it up, she took a sip, put it down and then smiled at her father. She turned to go to her room.

Friedrich called out and she stopped.

'I need to talk to you,' Friedrich said, 'and Michele.'

Natasha turned. 'At the same time?'

Friedrich nodded.

'It's not that easy to safely get us together.'

'You'll be able to do it though,' Friedrich said, 'I have faith.'

Natasha made a deep sigh, shook her head, and walked out of the room. She was smiling but her father couldn't see. Her father was back, no alcohol, no anger, just him. Her eyes started to fill. Seriously, you cry when you're sad, you cry when you're happy. Snap out of it.

***

Wilhelm flew his plane straight in front of hers. Michele pulled to the left to get out of his way. She had gone a long way in the three days he'd been teaching her. He was amazed at her progress. Although it didn't surprise him. She was so determined.

'Let's take it in for landing,' he said over the radio.

Both planes turned back and were soon cruising along the runway. They came to a stop, and both got out.

'I really feel like I know what I am doing up there,' she said. 'I know I still have a lot to learn though, but what a buzz.'

'Do you want another flight today?' he said.

'No,' she said, 'I have to be somewhere. Can you drive me? To the farm.'

She gave Wilhelm a funny little smile, to try to show him that it was a code.

He laughed.

'Not a problem.'

Wilhelm felt like the ops room was his second home. It felt like more of a sanctuary than his home. Everything was clear here. There was no pretence, and he knew where he stood with each of the group.

Michele walked down the stairs ahead of Wilhelm. Friedrich was leaning on the back of a chair, flicking through a file. He looked up and smiled. Putting the file down, he stood up and walked over to his daughter.

Michele ran over and wrapped her arms around her father. He hugged her back, cradling the back of her head and giving her a kiss on her forehead. She felt so protected. It was nice. The cuddle was as much for him as for her. He was a broken man, which helped a little in her forgiving him; but there was still a long way to go.

Natasha smiled and gave a quick wink to Wilhelm, who had sat in a chair. It had been a long time since she'd seen that. She looked down. She was happy to see the reunion, but jealous. It made sense, years of separation. Who was she trying to fool? Her father and her never had that, never had the affection? They had loved each other, that had been enough.

'What did you need to talk to us about?' Natasha broke the silence.

Friedrich sat back in his chair.

'Before I say what I need to say,' he said, as if thinking how to phrase the rest of his sentence, 'I need to fully understand your plan.'

Wilhelm and Natasha swapped a glance and smiled. He was an interrogator through and through. He had no idea what the plan was.

'Well then, let's make sure you don't miss anything. Maybe we should start from the beginning,' said Michele.

Friedrich swallowed and smiled. He'd been caught out.

Natasha and Michele filled Friedrich in on the plan. He listened intently to his daughters. Although it was interesting and well thought out, Wilhelm caught his attention the most.

Leaning forward, his chin resting on his fist, Wilhelm watched Michele intently. His pupils dilated and he had a relaxed smile. He must have heard this plan at least half a dozen times before, but his expressions were of someone who was listening intently for the first time. The girls had focused on their father, so they missed the trance that Wilhelm was in. Friedrich smiled and then focused on Michele. Natasha continued. Friedrich quickly looked at Wilhelm, his stare was the same, but focused on Natasha. Natasha noticed her father's focus. She quickly looked at Wilhelm who blinked but looked alert and attentive. She looked back at her father curiously, before continuing.

'So now you know,' Natasha said, 'what do you want to talk to us about?'

'A lot has changed for me,' he said, 'in the past couple of weeks.'

They all nodded in agreement.

'I've resigned from my post in Munich,' he said, 'it will take effect two weeks after the mission.'

'Why?' Michele said. 'And why two weeks after?'

'I need to be in charge for the interrogations.'

'What interrogations?' Michele said.

'Hess believes that he is the only one that can make peace with Britain, and that they won't take it seriously unless it is in person. He knows that Hitler won't agree, but that he probably wants it. It makes strategic sense. But Hitler will need to save face with the party. Which means he will need to act. That action will be interrogations,' Natasha explained.

'Wilhelm and Natasha will most likely be amongst those interrogated, after Hess's flight because of their connection to him.'

Michele looked at Natasha. 'You can't have her interrogated, she's the safety net there and—'

'I'll make sure they're alright.' Friedrich said.

Michele sat stone faced. She'd not thought about what would happen after. About the fallout. She heard what her father said, but he didn't have the experience. He was new to this. She just hoped that he could protect them.

'Then after that,' Friedrich said, 'I'm leaving Germany.'

Everyone looked at each other. Natasha reached across the table and grabbed his hand.

'I'll miss you,' she said, 'but I think it's for the best.'

'No,' Michele said, 'you can't leave, not yet.'

'Your sister's right,' Friedrich said looking at Michele.

'No,' Michele said, 'I've just got you back.'

She stood up and stormed out. Natasha looked back at her father.

'Michele,' Friedrich said.

'I'll go,' Natasha said, 'you stay here.'

Friedrich watched her disappear. He looked over at Wilhelm who was still staring at the stairs. Wilhelm felt the stare. He looked up at Friedrich.

'Look after my girls,' Friedrich said as he stood up and grabbed his coat.

Wilhelm replied, 'I will, I'll look after them as well as I can.'

Wilhelm headed towards the exit, with Friedrich just behind him.

'You'll have to choose one day though,' Friedrich said just as they approached the base of the stairs.

Wilhelm froze.

'So similar, aren't they, yet so different,' Friedrich whispered into his ear.

'I don't understand.'

'I think you do,' Friedrich said. 'Don't you dare hurt my girls.'

Friedrich walked up the stairs past Wilhelm to catch up with his daughters.

CHAPTER 24

'So,' Rosenburg said, 'you're getting old.'

He laughed at Hess, who politely laughed back, nodding.

He didn't like Rosenburg or what he did. He didn't trust him, how could you trust a thief, even a legal thief? Nevertheless, he was useful.

'My celebration will cost a lot,' Hess said. 'Personally, I would prefer to go out for dinner.'

'We can't have that,' Rosenburg said sternly, 'not for the Deputy Führer.'

Hess sat back as if he couldn't be bothered.

'I'll tell you what, I'll help you out. You know that I can transfer state funds for you. How much do you need?'

'I don't know,' Hess said. 'One of my secretaries is organising it for me.'

'Get me account details and I'll help,' Rosenburg said.

He really wanted to prove his worth to the party. Making friends with Hess, would help his cause.

'If you need more, let me know.'

'Thank you,' Hess said, 'thank you so much. I'll get the girl to contact you.'

Rosenburg made a note in his pad. 'What's her name?'

Hess looked up, 'Anneliese.'

***

Monotony had set in. Jean was tired of being a secretary. Goebbels had played right into their hands. He was pushing any possible stories to help get Hess into the sky. Jean was sick of hearing about it. It would be over soon though. She had arranged for weather reports to go to Anneliese, as she couldn't run the risk of someone finding them within the office.

She was seeing less and less of Hans and had to admit that it was nice having her nights to herself. Her thoughts drifted off into what life would be like after the war. A look of pain went over her face; she would have to do something to keep her adrenalin racing. She took her bag and decided on going for an early lunch.

She needed some fresh air and space. The days were getting warmer and warmer, and she had found a park nearby, where she could sit and read.

She stepped out into the street, and someone grabbed her arm turning her around. Looking up she went to complain and then smiled.

'How are you?' Anneliese said. 'Bored yet?'

Jean smiled.

'You know me too well.'

'I have a little job for you,' Anneliese said.

'Tell me more.'

'We need to open up some bank accounts,' said Anneliese. 'How many IDs do you have?'

Jean looked confused.

'I have a couple.'

'Let's get them,'

They both walked towards her apartment. When Jean returned to the office, she had four bank accounts opened in different names. She didn't fully understand why, but it was part of the plan, whatever that was.

***

Natasha was wearing one of Michele's dresses. They were not quite the same size, but the dress hid that fact. She'd already worn her black dress for too many functions this year, but it was the only one she owned. Maybe she would just raid her sister's wardrobe in the future. Wherever that was. It was easier.

Friedrich and Natasha got out of the car and walked up the front steps of the house. Although they arrived together, they had decided to keep their distance publicly. The front doors opened, and they walked through to the back of the house. Patio doors opened to display a grand, landscaped garden.

Natasha perused the spectacle. Without all the people and the tents, it would look beautiful. Currently it didn't appeal at all; it was heavily decorated and full of people who thought they were somebody. They walked down the steps to one of the bars.

'You know if I had to attend these all the time,' Natasha said, 'I'd be an alcoholic.'

She smiled.

Her father looked at her concerned.

'Don't worry,' she said. 'If I'm not one now, I'll never be.'

She took a glass, smiled at her father, and then walked away. They were late, but they hadn't been interested in the public event, just the official party. She walked through the crowd. A group of people were milling around Hitler and Hess. Poor Eva. People trying to advance their career swamped the area. Their wives, jealous by her position. Eva stood near Hitler, but to the back of the crowd. Natasha smiled; her eyes connected with Hess for a brief second. A mischievous smiled spread over her face. Natasha chose the deepest part of the crowd opposite the two dignitaries. She pushed her way through the crowd towards Hitler. He looked up from his conversation and noticed her. She smiled as she moved forward. He took a deep breath to say hello, just as she passed between Himmler and himself.

'Hello,' Natasha said to Eva.

Hitler's face dropped momentarily. Himmler stood in shock looking at her, while Hess smiled and wondered if he would ever meet someone quite like her again.

'How are you?' Natasha said.

'Good,' Eva said slightly startled. 'How are you?'

Hitler moved around so that he could face her. Himmler tried to stick by his side.

'I haven't heard much from you lately,' Hitler said, 'are you feeling well?'

'I am well,' Natasha said, 'there haven't been many interrogations, that's all.'

'Why?'

'Well, the resistance went cold recently,' she said.

'They've always been tough,' Hitler said, 'down in Munich.'

'Yes, but then someone decided to,' she paused and looked at Himmler, 'to shoot possible suspects before we could interrogate them.'

'There was only one,' Himmler said.

'Maybe you should explain,' Hitler said, turning his attention to Himmler.

Natasha smiled at Hess. 'I hope you're enjoying your birthday.'

'Yes,' he said, 'I'm finding it very entertaining.'

***

'Excuse me, would you like a drink?' a voice called over Friedrich's shoulder.

'Yes,' he said turning to take one.

He looked up to say thank you but stopped in shock.

'Don't act surprised,' Michele said, 'just relax.'

He took a deep breath.

'What are you doing here?'

'Have you ever noticed, how people don't notice the waiters,' she said, 'it can be very informative.'

Friedrich looked around; she was right. Beside most of the important groups, there was at least one waiter.

'Are they all?' he asked.

'I could tell you,' she said, 'but then I'd have to kill you. I need you to introduce Natasha to the influential people here. Can you do that?'

He looked at her and nodded.

'I'll talk to you later.'

He turned and walked away. Michele walked up the steps and turned to face the crowd. She nodded and then went into the house.

***

Henri walked into the kitchen and gently put down the tray. Grabbing his dinner jacket on the way, he walked out of the house and towards a car that had just pulled up at the front door.

'Let's go,' Wilhelm said.

Michele leaned forward and put both elbows on the back of the front seats. 'Did you see everyone?'

'Yes,' Henri said as he got into the car.

They all drove away.

***

'Happy birthday,' Goebbels said, pushing Natasha out of the way.

Ilse who was standing by Hess smiled. Someone finally put that girl in her place, she thought.

'Do you need any more room?' Natasha said. 'Should I step back some more?'

'I'm sorry,' Goebbels said. 'I didn't mean to.'

'No, sorry,' Natasha said. 'I do get a little blunt sometimes.'

They both looked at each other and smiled.

Ilse's face dropped and she folded her arms.

'Let me introduce you both, Natasha,' Hess said, 'Goebbels.'

Goebbels introduced his family and the rest of group. Everyone shook hands.

'Sorry,' Natasha said leaning forward to shake the last girl's hand. 'I didn't catch your name.'

'Jean,' Jean stated. 'Nice to meet you.'

Natasha smiled politely. 'You too.'

Jean was playing the timid overwhelmed secretary very well.

'Hello,' Ilse called out feeling slightly forgotten.

Jean politely included her in conversation. Natasha thought that it was time for another drink. She knew her knight in shining armour wouldn't be able to save her from today's humdrum activities. Not for a little while yet.

***

Michele carried the cake; Henri had a box and Wilhelm had a bag. They walked up the front steps of the SS Headquarters. The guards stopped Henri and Michele.

He looked at Wilhelm. 'Who are they?'

'They're helping me decorate my uncle's office.'

'Your uncle?'

'Herr Hess,' Wilhelm said.

The guards opened the doors, and they went through. They walked into Hess's office and locked the door. Michele put the cake down and grabbed a chair. Standing on it, she knocked one of the loose tiles in the ceiling out of its place. Gripping the wooden beam, she pulled herself into the small space between the ceiling and the second floor. Henri handed her the box and pulled himself into the same space. Handing up the bag, Wilhelm followed suit.

'The light fittings are the best places,' Wilhelm commented.

He showed how to attach them in Hess's office. They split up and took a corridor each. Every office was empty because of the party so it was the perfect time to put listening devices in each room. Hess had supplied them to enhance the intelligence they could gain. It took well over an hour to complete. All rooms were included from the offices to interrogation rooms. They all met back at Hess's office. Scurrying around, they decorated it and then left.

***

'Karl, are you alone this evening?' Natasha asked. 'Where is your wife?'

'She will be attending later,' he said. 'She doesn't feel very…' he paused as though looking for a word, '… comfortable at these kinds of events. But she wanted to come today as Hess is a dear friend.'

Natasha smiled and nodded.

'I was thinking about what you said the other day regarding Lebensraum.' Natasha said.

Karl quickly looked around to see who was in earshot.

'Don't worry' she smiled leaning forward, 'let's have a hypothetical conversation.'

'Hypothetical,' he paused. 'Of course.'

'The concept is sound,' she said, 'but not practical.'

Karl's face set, but he replied, 'Do go on.'

'Who would manage it, or decide where people could or should go?'

'What do you mean?' Karl asked.

'Well land is easy to regulate when it is looked over by one government,' she said, 'which is effectively what Hitler is doing amongst other things.'

Karl went to say something but stopped.

'If the countries being expanded into have no choice, they will not work with the conquerors and war ensues.'

'But England,' Karl said, 'have managed to do that all around the world.'

'Did they?' Natasha asked. 'They do have territories, but how did they get them and how are they managed? I'm of course no expert in geopolitics, you are the professor.'

He looked at her quizzically.

'That is the flaw I think,' she said. 'What is needed is a mutual agreement between countries, which allows for people to move freely without conflict, while the countries still control the land.' She laughed. 'How likely is that to happen, when everyone fears people who look or act different from them?'

'Interesting,' Karl said. 'It's a shame you never attended my classes. That would have been a lively debate.'

'A female studying geopolitics,' she smiled, 'it's not deemed something a good Nazi woman would do.'

'That does not appear to have stopped you from doing anything before,' Karl said.

'I suppose not.'

***

Goebbels leaned towards Jean. 'I want you to do something for me.'

'Certainly,' Jean said, 'what is it?'

'Keep your ears open,' he said, 'if you hear anything of value, let me know.'

'Like what?' Jean said. 'I will try, but I do have a bad memory.'

He looked at her and smiled. 'Any information I might be able to use. Just try.'

This afternoon was going to be fun she thought. She scanned the crowd and saw some familiar faces. The ones from Berlin, like the girls from the Gestapo office she could acknowledge, talk to and laugh with. The others who were in the resistance she could only make eye contact as a greeting. She missed them so much. To have them so close, yet out of reach, felt like such a cruel trick.

***

'Can I get you both a drink?' the waitress said.

Natasha looked up not realising anyone of importance was around. First, she saw Michele with the tray and then turning slightly she saw Wilhelm.

'That was fast,' she said.

'We don't mess around,' said Wilhelm.

'Jean is here,' Natasha said.

'I saw,' Michele said, 'I've told her some things to overhear for Goebbels today. I think it's time you started to mingle more.'

Natasha grimaced.

'There is one thing that Hess has requested we do,' Wilhelm said.

Grabbing Natasha's arm, he led her away.

Michele saw them walk off together. Jealous. No, it was work, right. Maybe. Wilhelm was just a flirt, but Michele felt special around him. Maybe, hmmm, it would be nice. Focus.

When she saw him walk away with her sister, she could see their closeness, their body language, and the tenderness as he guided her through the crowd. It had never crossed her mind that there may be an attraction there. Michele was in shock for a moment. Could they be attracted to each other? She thought, what does it mean? She turned and walked away scolding herself, Natasha was an actor, always had been, always would be. She would have to watch them some more, but for now, until she could conclude either way, it didn't mean anything. Nothing, nothing at all.

***

Somewhat confused, Natasha glanced at Wilhelm. 'So what is this thing that Hess wants?'

'Take a seat.'

Wilhelm indicated a bench and they both sat down.

'I need you to flirt with me.'

'What?' Natasha said, looking around for her sister.

'Do you trust me?' he said grabbing her hands.

'I do,' she said, 'but I don't know about this.'

'Please.'

'Fine' she said, 'but I'm not very good. You're the charmer here.'

'I very much doubt that,' he said. 'Just try.'

Wilhelm moved closer on the bench until their knees touched. He let go of one of her hands and brought his arm behind her and leaned it on the back of the bench while pulling her other hand forward. The whole move happened so fast that Natasha hadn't realised how close they were until she looked up at him. All she could see was his face and his slight smile. But his eyes, looked at her in way that she felt she had been seen for the first time. His intense gaze felt soft, and warm. Her bottom lip dropped as she took a quick breath in. The arm that had been leaning on the back of the bench slid down and around her waist to pull her closer to him. She could feel the heat from his body, his breath on her cheek. And for a moment, just a fleeting moment, Natasha felt safe and protected and sheltered from everything. Don't lose yourself. As his hand traced up her neck to her cheek, her head slightly tilted away, without realising. And there was a moment, a fraction of a moment, where she wanted him to lean forward and kiss her lips. Had she leaned forward, just a little. Maybe.

Wilhelm ran his thumb across her cheek. And she looked back into his eyes. There was a sadness that had crept in.

'You are,' Wilhelm said swallowing, 'really good at this.'

'I have a good teacher,' she smiled.

The words had slightly broken the tension. Natasha reminded herself. It's just an act. He's acting. He likes Michele, not me. Which is for the best. Isn't it?

***

Hess took a sip of his orange juice. He wasn't really interested in any of the goings-on today. But he had to be there. Goebbels was talking intently with Hitler, trying to get small points across. There was no point in Hess trying to stop things now; he wouldn't be able to follow through and he had used up most of his influence. He hoped that he had formed some sort of foundation to guide Hitler. In a few days, he'd be gone. He was nervous. He knew it was the right thing to do. He needed to convince Britain that Russia was a bigger threat. Hitler couldn't do that; he was not the right type of orator, too narrowminded. But Hess was, and if he wasn't, he would probably be a prisoner or dead. But he had to try, it was his duty, his destiny. He took a deep breath to calm himself.

Hitler glanced up from the conversation. Something caught his eye and he started to smile.

'I see the ice queen has started to thaw,' Hitler said.

Goebbels and Hess looked up, slightly confused.

'Your nephew seems to be entertaining,' Hitler said and pointed past Hess.

Hess looked up and his eyes followed Hitler's hand. There in the distance on a bench sat Natasha and Wilhelm. Wilhelm slid a piece of hair behind Natasha's ear, and she leaned her cheek into his hand. Both smiling at each other and moving closer together. Hess's face dropped.

'What's wrong with that?' Goebbels asked looking at Hess's face.

Hess turned to Ilse.

'Get Wilhelm, now,' he said.

Hitler was a little shocked. 'She has attitude, but she's alright on the eye, intelligent and although I hate to admit it, good at what she does.'

'I don't want them getting involved,' Hess said.

'Why?' Goebbels asked again, slightly confused, remembering the earlier encounter.

'I don't trust that girl at all,' Hess said. 'She doesn't act as a Nazi female should, and quite frankly I don't like her.'

'But you always seem so friendly towards her,' Hitler said.

'Keep your friends close,' Hess said, 'and your enemies closer.'

They all smiled and nodded.

***

Wilhelm saw Ilse coming out of the corner of his eye, 'That's all I needed.'

Natasha was a little confused. Ilse grabbed Wilhelm just as he leaned forward to kiss her cheek.

'Your uncle wants you,' she said.

'Can he not wait?' Wilhelm said. 'I'm busy.'

'No,' Ilse said, 'it's because you're busy that he wants you.'

Wilhelm grabbed Natasha's hand, kissed it, and then walked back with his aunt.

Natasha had enjoyed herself, but now she felt used. It wasn't real, remember this is not real. He had made it clear. She wished just a little bit of it would be real. Wilhelm looked at Natasha a couple of times and then turned away. Natasha took a deep breath and stood up, now it was time to socialise. She caught her father's eye and wandered over to him.

CHAPTER 25

Helene grabbed her bag and threw it over her shoulder.

Anneliese looked up. 'Is that all you are taking?'

'Yes,' Helene said.

Anneliese looked at her in disbelief.

'Two reasons,' Helene said, 'there's not much room for cabin luggage.'

Anneliese took a breath to protest.

Helene continued, 'And I don't have many things that are important enough to keep.'

Anneliese relaxed, nodded and then looked at her bag. Most of it was junk if she were honest. She pulled some of it out and then closed the bag.

'I wasn't saying–' Helene said.

'I know,' Anneliese said. 'But maybe you should have, look at it.'

They looked at the pile of things she'd taken from her bag and laughed. Helene thought about what had happened over the last few days. She had loved Schmidt like a father. He had been good to her, and although she was devastated and was still grieving, he had lived a long life. It could have quite easily been her daughters, who were caught through her carelessness. She shook her head trying to dislodge the thought. She was doing the right thing.

'I have to do something,' Helene said.

Anneliese looked up.

'What?'

'I have to say goodbye to my girls,' she said, and then marched out of the room.

***

An hour later a group of guards marched down the otherwise deserted street. It was dark, but the moonlight was bright enough to illuminate the area. Anneliese peered around the corner and waited until the guards had turned. She listened to the silence and then beckoned Helene. They darted across the street. Helene opened the gate; they both ran through and then closed the gate quietly behind them.

'I don't know what to say,' Helene said.

'I'm sure they'll say something,' Anneliese said sarcastically.

'I'm not talking about the girls.'

Anneliese paused; she didn't know how to reply.

'It's alright,' Helene said. 'I'll think of something.'

Anneliese looked around and listened. Silence. She stood up, walked to the door, and knocked on it.

***

Friedrich sat in the parlour. He was deep in thought. Every so often, he could hear the rhythmical march of the patrols, but it only registered in the subconscious. Michele and Natasha were downstairs formulating plans. He was thinking about the future and what would happen. How his world would turn upside down again. A knock at the door broke him from his thoughts. In a trancelike state, he got up and opened the door.

There stood Helene. Anneliese stood still for a little while, until she felt too uncomfortable, and then she discretely walked into the house, past them. She walked down to the cellar. Helene stepped inside, and Friedrich closed the door.

'How are you?' he said.

'Fine.'

She surveyed the corridor.

'I wanted to say goodbye,' she said, 'to the girls.'

'Of course.'

The conclusion of her sentence had wounded him.

'They're in the basement,' he indicated down the hallway.

She walked past him towards the door at the end.

'Helene,' he called after her.

She paused and turned slowly, 'What?'

He looked at her, lost his nerve and lowered his eyes.

'Never mind.'

She turned back around and steadied her breath. They couldn't even have a conversation, even now, when they may never meet again. She stopped herself from thinking about what could have been and walked through the doorway.

'You have visitors,' Anneliese said as she walked down the stairs.

Natasha and Michele looked up.

'What are you doing here?' Natasha said.

'She wouldn't go,' Anneliese said.

'What do you mean?' Michele said somewhat confused.

'Your mother–'

Anneliese didn't get to finish the sentence.

'Are you crazy?' Natasha said. 'This town is on high alert for her, and you bring her here?'

'I'm sorry,' Anneliese said, 'I tried, but–'

The door opened and Helene walked down the steps.

'What were you thinking?' Michele said jumping up with both hands on her hips. 'I mean really, what were you thinking, were you thinking at all?'

Helene froze at the bottom of the stairs for what felt like eternity. There were things she wanted to say, but they scared her. They were fierce in their stance. On one side, she could understand her children's concerns, but on the other, she had to see them one last time.

'I had to say goodbye, just in case,' she said.

She couldn't bear to hear her voice say anything else, not even admit the possibility that she may not see them again. Her face was wet, and she hadn't even realised that she had started to cry.

Michele and Natasha looked at each other. They had been so focused on the mission that they hadn't thought a lot about the future. Anneliese slowly walked up the stairs to let them have some time alone.

'You know I love you,' Michele said breaking the silence.

'Me too,' Natasha agreed. 'We have lost you once before. We're not prepared to lose you again.'

Helene grabbed them both and hugged them.

'I love you both so much.'

Natasha tried to look up and control her breathing, while the other two sobbed.

Helene pulled back so she could see both her daughters.

'You mean everything to me. I'm so blessed to have such special angels for daughters.'

'We'll be alright,' Michele said stroking her mother's cheek, 'and you'll be fine. Hess will look after you.'

'Think of it as a mission,' Natasha said. 'Once you've landed, you'll be given things to do.'

'Henri will be in regular contact with you,' Michele said, 'you'll know exactly what's happening. I promise.'

She looked at them both. They were such good liars. It wasn't that they were lying, it was that they were skirting around most of the important issues. It was probably best that way.

***

Anneliese walked back along the corridor into the parlour. Friedrich was facing a dresser. A glass of ice was in front of him, and his right hand was rocking a bottle of vodka that still had its lid on.

'Friedrich,' Anneliese said softly.

'I love her,' he said.

'The vodka?'

'No,' Friedrich said, 'but it would numb the pain.'

Anneliese looked at him. She could see he was on the edge.

'She's the only thing that hurts now,' he said.

Anneliese grabbed the vodka and indicated for Friedrich to sit down. He gave into her demand.

'I tried to get transferred to her camp,' he said. 'They denied me.'

'The funny thing,' he said, 'was that they thought I wanted to kill her. But I didn't, I wanted to fix her, change her.'

Anneliese didn't know what to say.

'Isn't it lucky I didn't?'

He began to laugh, but it was a sad laugh almost a cry and he shook his head.

'I wanted to fix her. I'm the one who needs fixing. Me. Not her.'

'Can I have the vodka?' Friedrich said.

'No,' Anneliese said.

Tears were seeping down her cheeks.

Friedrich was only a shadow of the man he used to be. She hated him, but she could feel his pain.

'You can't leave it like this,' Anneliese said. 'You can't for your sake.'

You can't for hers, she thought.

Friedrich's bloodshot eyes looked up at her and he nodded.

***

Helene gave her daughters a hug and then turned away from them so they couldn't see her face. Clearing her throat, she called out for Anneliese and walked up the steps. She wanted to get out of the house as soon as possible.

Friedrich saw Helene walk past the parlour. He looked at Anneliese. She encouraged him forward. Quietly he followed Helene. Grabbing her hand, he spun her around and pinned her against the wall.

'I love you,' he said to her as she struggled to push him away. 'I always have, and I always will.'

He tenderly leaned down and kissed her lips. His hands gently held her cheeks so she wouldn't pull away. There was no need, Helene's body melted with his tenderness. She had never stopped loving him, no matter how she tried to hate him. He let go and went to walk away.

'Me too,' she said.

Then she walked out the door.

Friedrich turned around to see Anneliese scurry out after her. Natasha had a little smirk while Michele had her hand to her throat and was all choked up.

'That was so romantic,' she said to Natasha.

Natasha nodded.

'It sure was.'

***

The phone rang and Wilhelm got out of bed. He was still asleep, but he was conscious enough to make it to the telephone.

Picking it up, he said, 'Good morning.'

'I guess you're not a morning person,' Natasha said.

'What do you want?'

'You,' she said. 'I need to talk to you at the house.'

'I'm busy,' he said, 'until this afternoon.'

'That's fine,' she said.

He waddled back to bed thinking, not a morning person. It was still dark, it wasn't even morning yet, what was she thinking? He closed his eyes and drifted off.

***

Yosef wobbled down the corridor with his crutches. He tried not to use them, but they were there just in case. Occasionally he would lean on things to keep his balance. It had been a long time since Rolf had seen Yosef. It was good to see him, but funny to see him so clumsy.

Yosef looked up.

'Hello, what are you doing here?'

'Being a taxi,' he replied.

Yosef looked confused. He hobbled into the room.

'Oh, there's a party,' Yosef said. 'Am I invited?'

Yosef sat down while Oskar relayed the story regarding his broken arm.

'What a great trio we are,' Yosef said. 'So how are you going to fly now?'

'I can't.'

Oskar looked down at his feet. He was so annoyed with himself.

The answer didn't unsettle Yosef; it was its delivery that raised concern.

'Who's flying?' Yosef said.

'Well Anneliese is scared of heights–' said Oskar.

'Who's flying?'

'Michele,' Oskar said. 'Michele is.'

'Who's she leaving in charge?'

Oskar looked at him, he didn't know. It was supposed to have been him, but she had sent him here.

'I guess her Guardian Angel?' Oskar said.

Yosef sat back for a couple of minutes. Natasha could do it, but it would jeopardise too much, she needed minimal contact, she was too well known in the Nazi circles. She was too involved now as it was. But after the flight she would have to create a lot of distance.

'Rolf,' Yosef said, 'can I get a ride to Munich?'

'Yes, but I don't leave until tomorrow.'

Yosef smiled; that would give him some time to prepare.

***

Wilhelm and Natasha were arguing. Friedrich had heard the noise, from upstairs. Then Wilhelm had gone silent. Natasha had won.

Friedrich walked into the room.

'You wanted to talk to me?'

Natasha gave a quick glance at Wilhelm and then took a deep breath.

'After the great escape,' Natasha said, 'Wilhelm and I are likely to be interrogated.'

'Yes,' said Friedrich.

'You may not be able to interrogate either of us, let alone both of us and worst-case scenario you would also be interrogated. Although, you have never really had a close connection to Hess.'

Friedrich sat back in his chair; he didn't think he liked where this was going.

'Pain I can handle,' she said, 'but I don't know about the truth drug, and I think that we should have a practise run.'

Friedrich was shocked, 'You want me to interrogate you, so you can practise?'

She nodded.

'I don't like it either, but she's right,' Wilhelm said.

His face was set, you could tell he hated to agree.

Friedrich couldn't believe what he had just been asked.

'I don't know,' he said, 'I'll need Hess's help.'

***

Jean smiled as the teller closed the third bank account that had been set up for Hess's birthday celebration. The bag she was carrying was now full and extremely heavy. She tried to make it look as light as possible. Normally she would have felt self-conscious walking around, but both Anneliese and Michele were nearby keeping an eye on her.

She crossed the street to the public toilets. One couldn't be too safe. She wanted to make sure she wasn't being followed. Michele and Anneliese entered soon after her and took the cubicles on either side of hers. Michele slipped a bag through, and Jean quickly changed into its contents and removed her black wig. Quickly she divided the money between the two girls and then flushed the toilet. Her bag was now half the size and far lighter and slipped easily into her handbag. When she left the cubicle, there were half a dozen other girls waiting. She brushed her hair and then followed a couple of girls out. Michele and Anneliese left the public toilets separately and went in opposite directions. If someone had been following her, they wouldn't be anymore.

***

Michele pulled her pocketknife out of her bag.

'Nice,' Anneliese said.

She smiled. 'It goes everywhere with me.'

The knife flicked open, and she gently ran it along the lining of the door. It was soon loose enough to remove. She took it off and placed it on the ground. Slowly she filled the cavity with money and then placed the lining back. Before attaching it, Michele held out her hand. Anneliese stopped chewing and handed Michele some gum. She placed it in one corner; removing her own she placed it in the other and then joined the lining. Michele went around to the other door and did the same thing.

'All done,' she said. 'Now be careful.'

***

Natasha and Friedrich walked into Hess's cellar. Wilhelm was sitting in a chair while Hess was organising injections. Something caught Natasha's eye in a dark corner. She couldn't see anything, but she was sure someone was there. As she looked more intently, a figure stepped out of the shadows.

Snapping her head towards Hess she said, 'Who's this?'

Hess didn't even look at her.

'Karl Pintsch, my secretary. He'll report to you from Berlin after the flight.'

She looked at him in disbelief.

'I've heard a lot about you Natasha,' Pintsch said, 'and I trust you.'

'That's not exactly the issue here.'

'I trust you enough for you to interrogate me first,' Pintsch said.

Natasha looked him up and down.

'You better hope you pass.'

Pintsch swallowed and nodded. He sat in a chair in the centre of the room. They tied his arms to the chair and Natasha injected him. Hess started the interrogation with the familiar. He asked about family and friends, what work he did for Hess, the normal questions. Pintsch's answers were short and accurate apart from his duties, where he listed only basics. The goal was to make sure that everything sounded normal, to make sure no information stood out from the rest and that no one was made into an obvious connection.

'Who did Hess socialise with?' Natasha asked.

'Hitler, Himmler, Wilhelm, Göring, Goebbels,' he began.

The list went on but did not mention any of the resistance

'How is Hess connected with the resistance?' Hess said.

'What?'

'How is he connected to the resistance?'

'He's not.'

'Have you ever heard him mention the name Natasha?' she said.

'No.'

'What about Michele?'

'No.'

'Did Hess know Natasha or Michele?'

'I don't know.'

'You don't know?'

'I don't know about everyone he knows.'

'Where's Hess going?' Friedrich said.

'To England,' he slurred.

'Why?' Friedrich asked.

'Because Hitler asked him to,' his speech was becoming more and more slurred.

'Why?' Friedrich said.

'I don't know,' Pintsch answered and then slowly slumped in his chair.

Wilhelm's interrogation followed a similar line of questioning. They had all had previous in-depth training on how to handle it.

Natasha sat down. Pintsch was only just gaining consciousness. Hess was talking to Natasha trying to teach her what to do. She was trying to listen, but she was also petrified.

Hess noticed her breathing and her pulse.

'Calm down,' he said, 'steady yourself.'

Her mind started to focus on her scenario. Make up a world to believe in, to live in. You need to go there in your thoughts.

Keep your answers short, less is good. She felt the pinprick and she could feel her mind start to drift. She tried to retain the scenario in her mind.

But she was losing grip. Stop, stop, and don't say anything. Mouth stop. Her mouth was moving but she didn't have full control. Stop, seriously stop. Slowly she felt her brain drift away and then she blacked out.

Natasha's eyes slowly opened, but they were blurry. Her father was stroking her hair.

'I'm really bad at this,' she said under her breath.

Everyone looked at her but said nothing. She was right. The first two answers had been fine, but the rest had been far too informative, and it was evident she was struggling with the answers. Natasha felt drunk.

'I'm sorry,' she said.

Tears were falling down her face, but she didn't have the energy to sob.

It took half an hour for her to become focused.

'I have to do it again,' she said. 'I have to get used to it.'

'You can't today,' Hess said. 'We'll try tomorrow.'

Hess walked over to clear up.

'I'll make some arrangements,' Pintsch said.

'It won't be necessary,' Hess said. 'She'll be fine.'

'I'll make the arrangements,' Pintsch said grabbing Hess's arm, 'and hopefully we won't need them.'

Hess pulled his arm out of Pintsch's grip and shut the case. Turning away, he walked up the stairs; this wasn't going to plan.

Friedrich edged over to Wilhelm.

'What was that all about?' Friedrich asked.

'I don't know but I hope it wasn't a suggestion for a plan B.' Wilhelm looked towards Pintsch, he needed watching.

CHAPTER 26

The truck pulled up to the farmhouse with a trail of dust following it. It was the first time that Yosef had been out of the house, let alone back in Munich, and he felt energised.

'Where are we going?'

'To the barn,' said Rolf.

He walked over to the house and handed in the keys and then came back to help Yosef out of the truck. Slowly they made their way to the barn and down the stairs into the operations room.

People were crowding around a table and Natasha was leading a discussion pointing at papers and maps.

She paused and looked up. A smile crept across her face as she saw Yosef. He opened his arms slightly, beckoning for a hug.

Natasha rushed past Wilhelm and Hess and threw her arms around Yosef. Wilhelm gave Hess an indignant look. Hess chuckled.

Natasha whispered, 'It's so good to see you.'

There was a general chattering in the room as the resistance group welcomed him back. Then he sat next to Michele and Henri and slowly everyone settled, and the meeting resumed. They gave Jean a list of songs that would be signals during the flight.

'There will be a rehearsal flight on the thirtieth and the fifth,' Natasha said.

Everyone nodded.

'Has all the money been deposited?' Hess asked.

'Yes,' said Anneliese.

'There will be one more deposit on the ninth, then that's it,' said Hess. 'It should help finance your operation for a while and sustain my network.'

Both Anneliese and Jean nodded.

'There is something else to organise,' Hess said. 'One member of my staff knows. The rest need to believe orders have come from Hitler. Any suggestions?'

'Cryptic comments,' said Jean, 'arouse suspicion. Why don't you have one sent from Hitler?'

Hess looked confused. 'I don't want him to know.'

'But he doesn't have to,' Jean said. 'What if someone gave it to you from him.'

'Via your staff,' Wilhelm said. 'Goebbels is wearing off on you, Jean.'

Jean nodded.

Hess thought for a second. 'That may work.'

You could see Hess disappear into thought.

Michele and Henri had been quietly talking at the back of the group. She nudged him forward. 'Let's think about that later, but for now, just mention the meeting.'

Henri stood up and indicated for Hess to join him. Wilhelm also got up to move but Henri shook his head and Wilhelm sat back down.

Henri leaned in towards Hess. 'On the eleventh you have a meeting with Churchill.'

'Good, the eleventh is a favourable date,' Hess said. 'How do I get there?'

'They'll collect you.'

***

'I'm not getting better,' Natasha slurred, 'am I?'

It was the third time she had gone under, and she had revealed more this time than the first.

'No,' Hess said.

He walked up the stairs before anyone could see how sad he was. Hess paced the room. He needed a plan. Natasha was important to... He slammed his fist on the desk. The plan, the plan, Natasha was important to the plan. Nothing could jeopardise that. How can I protect you, no, the mission? She was clouding his judgement. No, it was because she was the only option. He needed to keep her safe for the mission. Hess turned around and saw Wilhelm in the doorway.

'What are we going to do?' Wilhelm said.

'I don't know, she doesn't have time. I should have started this earlier. This is...' Hess said shaking his head, '... this is a real weakness. In the mission. Nothing can jeopardise it. During or after.'

Hess took a deep breath, and they went back down to the cellar.

Natasha was talking to Pintsch. He handed her something and then left the room. She was looking at her hand. Staring at the inevitable. Hess froze, he was not good at this kind of thing. Pintsch was right, but there was a feeling Hess was not used to. Did he... *care*... about Natasha? No. The mission was what he was worried about, feelings got in the way.

Wilhelm walked over to her and went to snatch the pill. Natasha closed her hand before he could get it. Although her lips smiled, her eyes betrayed her sadness.

'It's only a safety precaution,' she said.

Natasha got up and walked out.

Hess sat down. He put his head between his hands and wondered what else could possibly go wrong.

Wilhelm picked up the telephone and called Friedrich.

'Hello.'

'Natasha has a cyanide pill, make sure she doesn't use it, because she will, if she has to,' Wilhelm said, and then hung up.

***

Natasha walked through the door and up the stairs.

'You're home early,' Friedrich said. 'Would you like a drink?'

Normally she would have said no, but today was different.

'Vodka and cola please,' she said.

Friedrich put some ice and vodka in the glass, dropped in a sleeping pill and added the cola. By the time Natasha came back down the pill had dissolved. He handed her the glass and she sat down.

'So how did it go?'

'Not very well,' she said. 'I'm not very good. So please try and interrogate me yourself.'

It felt like she had only taken a couple of sips and her glass was finished.

'Would you like another?' he said. 'So what are you going to do?'

'I have a couple of options,' she yawned. 'I really feel tired.'

He placed the glass in front of her, but she wasn't going to drink it. Her eyelids were slowly drooping. She was trying to fight it, but she was losing. Eventually her eyes closed, and she slid into a horizontal position on the lounge. Friedrich got up and put a blanket on her. He hurried upstairs to her room. Grabbing her bag, he shook the contents out over the bed. A gun fell out with some bullet cases and a purse. He checked in her drawers, and wardrobe. He couldn't find it. He searched through her purse, nothing. Her gun was clean, but fully loaded. He put it down, then it struck him that it shouldn't be loaded. The first bullet case was indeed full of bullets, but the second was empty, apart from a small tablet. He piled everything back into her bag and took the tablet with him.

Friedrich walked down the thin cobblestoned alley and stopped outside a door. The paint was peeling, and the bottom had rotted through. He gave two knocks then paused and then another two knocks. His other hand had his gun poised ready. The door opened slightly and before it could be closed again Friedrich rammed it with his body and walked inside.

'I was going to let you in,' the man said.

He'd been thrown against the wall.

'Honestly.'

He regained his composure and added, 'I'm clean. I'm not doing anything.'

'That's a shame,' said Friedrich raising his gun. 'I guess you're of no use to me then.'

'But maybe I can help you, a friend,' he said.

The short man was slightly cowering but opening his arms in a friendly welcoming gesture.

'I mean, how can I help you?'

'I have a pill, I want to know what it is,' Friedrich said.

Friedrich handed him the pill.

'And I want a harmless or sleeping pill that looks like it.'

The man picked the pill up and looked at it in awe.

'This is a top range Gestapo L pill I think.'

He opened a drawer and took out a syringe. Gently pushing it into the skin of the pill, but then the needle, hit glass.

'Can you put the light on please?' he said.

Friedrich flicked a switch and light flooded the room.

He was now peering down the microscope, looking for the weakness in the glass vial.

'This is definitely cyanide,' he said. 'Come back next week and I'll have a sleeping tablet, which looks just like this.' He was smiling quite pleased with himself.

'Then we have a problem,' Friedrich said. 'You have two hours.'

The smile dropped from his face and his eyes looked like they were going to pop out.

'It's not that simple, I need to make it from scratch or at the very least make a new membrane, reseal the glass vial, test the quality, and make sure it's the right shade. Sleeping pills don't look like this, they are not enclosed in glass.'

He looked at Friedrich who was playing with the safety on his gun.

'Two hours.'

'If I use the glass and this membrane, I might be able to do it,' he said 'but I wouldn't be able to get rid of all the cyanide and whoever has it is going to get sick. Even a little bit left in there can make you sick.'

'How sick?' Friedrich said.

'Not die,' he said, 'but ill.'

Over the next two hours, Friedrich watched him work. Occasionally he would glance at Friedrich, but he didn't really have the time. When he finished, he walked over.

'I take no responsibility for this,' he said. 'I haven't tested it.'

Friedrich went to grab it, but he clasped his hand and pulled it back.

'No alcohol and no other drugs.'

He placed it in Friedrich's hand. 'No responsibility.'

Friedrich went to pay him.

'I can't, I don't know what it will do,' he said.

Friedrich nodded and then left.

***

'This is just like old times,' Michele said.

'But the bed was bigger,' said Natasha.

'No, we were smaller.'

Michele was giggling. Tomorrow she went to Baden-Baden, so they had decided to have a night in. They knew it was dangerous, but it was going to be the last time they would meet for a very long time. So tonight, was all about having fun.

Friedrich stood outside their door and listened. It was great to hear the laughter, but it also made him sad. He'd missed so much.

Michele nudged Natasha. 'So what's happening between you and Wilhelm?'

Natasha looked surprised and pulled a face, but she was reading her sister. She was the interrogator after all. This wasn't just a flippant query.

'Wilhelm and I?' she said. 'Are you joking, he's like my brother and that's just all wrong.'

Her sister relaxed.

'Anyway, the only mushy eyes he has,' Natasha said, 'are for you. And you for him.'

'Me?' Michele said. 'I don't think so.'

'Oh please,' Natasha said. 'Michele likes a boy, Michele likes a boy.'

Michele's bottom lip curled.

'No, I don't. I don't.'

Then her lips turned into a smile.

'I told you, I told you,' Natasha said, jabbing her sister in the ribs.

Michele eventually managed to change the subject.

'Do you trust Hess?' Michele asked.

Natasha looked at her and then up at the ceiling.

'No' she said, 'but now the relationship we have is balanced. We have a common goal. We have enough on him if we need it. But he needs to leave the country and if he can accomplish his mission. It's worth a try.'

'If he can accomplish this?' Michele said, 'I thought that you had confidence in this? If it doesn't work, what happens when he comes back?'

'I understand part of his mission, trying to get England to fight against Russia. That would be a long, bloody war otherwise. But his other plans, whatever they are, I don't think align with ours. So, I hope it doesn't fully work and if it doesn't work, he won't come back,' Natasha said, 'the English won't let him back. I feel though that he knows that too. I'm not sure. There is an arrogance to Hess about this. But there is also a lot that the resistance can get from helping with this plan. I get his network and you strengthen links with Britain. If he comes back, we will need to be careful. He won't need us anymore. We'll be disposable.'

Michele looked at her sister for a moment. 'Natasha, I have to tell you something. But I don't want it to affect anything.'

Natasha nodded.

'Henri said something to me when he returned from Spain, the last time. He said that he had met some people, one of them from British Naval Intelligence. He got mixed feelings from him. He said he felt like he wasn't being told the whole truth. He doesn't want to assume anything, but–'

'He thinks it's a trap.'

Michele nodded.

'Of course, it's a trap. Getting a meeting with Churchill was too easy. It may happen. Either way they will want him alive though. Let's see how it plays out. Then we will know how big a fish we have actually contacted,' said Natasha. 'But I do worry about poor Wilhelm.'

Michele looked a little bit sad, then looked at Natasha.

'Do you trust Wilhelm?'

Natasha smiled. 'Yes, I do. But I trust him more with Hess gone though. He doesn't mean to, but he confides too much in his uncle.'

Eventually Michele drifted off to sleep. Natasha raised herself onto her elbow resting her head in her hand. She started to stroke her sister's hair. She was scared, not just for her but for everyone.

***

Hess walked onto the runway. He was looking forward to today. The plan was to make a quick flight to check the meet up times. The Führer would be travelling in his motorcade. By the time Hitler arrived, Hess would be back on the ground and ready to stand beside him, when Hitler said his speech. Hess had managed to break from the tradition of having the speech in Berlin, saying that by moving location, it included the people working to support the war. He looked at his pocket watch; his contact was supposed to have phoned him by now. He indicated to his aid, who ran into the building. A few minutes later, the aid returned.

'Deputy Führer,' he said. 'Hitler is not making the speech. You are.'

Swearing under his breath, he climbed out of the cockpit.

'Tell Pintsch,' he grumbled and headed back to the hangar.

CHAPTER 27

'Is everything in place?' Hess queried.

'Yes,' Karl Haushofer said. 'You always were so cunning.'

Hess smiled; he couldn't really take the credit for that one.

'Are you scared?' Karl said.

'I would be a fool if I wasn't.' Hess said. 'I owe you so much. You inspired me and him with the vision of what Germany could be. Imagine if I had never been your student. If I had never heard of Lebensraum. We may well have been overrun by the Bolsheviks and well others.'

'We need, no, we deserve, the great German living space for the Deutsche Volk, our culture. It is our right. But this is not as I had expected,' Karl said. 'A vision is only a vision until it is acted on, although sometimes the act can change the vision. But now if we are not careful Rudolf, we will lose everything. I have seen it all fall, I have seen what we could lose. And I have seen what will come if you are successful. Yet again you are leading us in the right direction. You are Hitler's rudder. Although he may not know it.'

'When did we lose our focus, when did it all change?'

'Maybe it didn't,' Karl said, 'maybe we did.'

'Maybe. We just have to be careful that the focus does not undermine the vision.'

They both took a sip of their drinks.

A boarding call for Berlin echoed through the airport and Hess got up. He gave his friend a hug.

Hess whispered, 'Thank you, old friend, goodbye and god bless.'

Before Karl could reply, Hess had turned and left.

Hess turned to his assistant before the boarding gate. 'I'm expecting a message from Karl, you need to stay here and phone Lutz, as soon as you get it.'

The assistant and Lutz nodded.

'When are you expecting the message, sir?' Lutz asked.

'This evening,' Hess replied to his head of security. Hess hoped all his staff would take the bait. That little bit of intrigue.

The flight was a short one and he was soon heading to the hotel.

Hess had waited all day for this. The water was hot around his body, and he could see the steam drifting up off the bath. The heat was relaxing his muscles.

His life felt like an elaborate play. One act following another, all strategically interlinked, yet looking like unconnected events. He was on the right course to tie it all together, to bring it to a climatic finish. His play and the war on the same path, an historic journey. It wasn't for the glory; it was for the idea, the concept, the mission. That was why he had to do this. It was his responsibility. Goebbels and Himmler were show boaters. They did not have the truth, the understanding Hess did. People get in the way of progress. He closed his eyes. Just think of what I could accomplish without having people around. It would be easier. Less complex. There were exceptions. Natasha. Michele. Admittedly even Jean was helpful.

'Hmm,' he said. 'All women. Who would have thought?'

He heard the phone ring. There was no urgency; he knew who it was, and the message. He also knew his security would get it. Right now, he was just making the most of his relaxing time he had to himself.

Eventually Hess came out of the bathroom looking somewhat like a shrivelled prune.

Lutz jumped to his feet, 'Herr Hess, your message.'

'Yes, what is it?' Hess said as he straightened his tie.

'On a scale of one to six, things stand about a three or four and more needs doing,' Lutz relayed, 'and Albrecht will contact you as soon as he returns.'

'Contact Pintsch,' said Hess. 'I must go to the Chancellery immediately.'

'What does it mean?' Lutz said.

'That there is much to do,' said Hess knowingly, 'I have to go.'

Pintsch soon arrived and picked up Hess. Lutz watched the car drive off towards the Chancellery until it was out of sight.

'The city is beautiful by night,' Hess said as they drove along the river.

'Would you like a tour of the city, sir?' Pintsch asked.

'Yes,' Hess said as he sat back and watched the world go by.

It was well over an hour before they returned. Hess walked in the door, straight past Lutz and into his room.

'Where did you go?' Lutz asked.

'To relay the message to Hitler,' replied Pintsch. 'He was not pleased.'

He turned away and smiled as he exited the door.

***

The next day Hess found himself sitting in Hitler's office. He looked around it. The architecture was so big, so grand, it was intimidating to many, but not Hitler, not Hess.

'We cannot defeat them though,' Hitler said. 'They showed us that last year.'

'It was the aircraft that was wrong last year,' Göring said. 'If we change it, we can win.'

'But I want Russia,' Hitler said. 'Your efforts should be directed that way.'

'We need England as our friends,' Hess said, 'but we need to give them something to show friendship.'

Göring and Hitler looked at him.

'Would you be our friends?'

Hitler paced up and down.

'I have a speech to make tonight, and we don't even know what we want.'

'What do you want?' said Hess.

'Russia.'

'Then Russia it is,' Hess said.

Göring looked distastefully at Hess.

'Maybe your speech could highlight that you have no issue with Britain,' Hess said, 'but it is Churchill that is causing the problems, making you react in a way you don't want to. Appeal to the people, to the government. Not Churchill.'

Hitler looked at him.

By the end of the meeting a few points were agreed upon, none were major changes, but they were a start. They ranged from mentioning the previous offer of a twenty-five-year alliance to individually ruled areas. Ultimately, it was just letting England know that the Germans liked and respected the English, they were Aryan after all, empire builders. Hitler would prefer to leave the island and its colonies alone. Most of the discussion Göring had sulked. He did not agree. His belief came from his loss of pride, not from a strategy perspective. Within a couple of hours of leaving Hitler's chambers, Hess was summoned back.

Hess and Hitler set about writing the speech for the evening. An hour into the meeting Hitler broached a subject that he knew Hess disagreed with.

'I was talking to Goebbels today,' Hitler said.

Hess smiled, sat back in his chair, and rolled his eyes. He knew what was coming.

'He thinks we should push on with liquidation of the Jews from Germany,' Hitler said.

'Of course, he does,' Hess said with frustration. 'He's been saying that for the past two years.'

'What do you think?' Hitler enquired.

'You know what I think,' he said. 'I think he's an idiot. A useful idiot, but an idiot all the same.'

Hitler laughed. 'The public are saying–' he said.

'The public are saying what he's telling them to say.' Hess said. 'He hates them so much that he can't think wisely.'

'I hate them too,' Hitler said. 'Why do you protect them?'

Hess said, 'I've told you; the first reason is, it is in Germanys best interests to have as many people work towards the war effort and industry as possible and that includes the Jews.'

'And two?' said Hitler.

'You don't want to set a precedent of Goebbels being able to brainwash the masses so that he can always get his own way,' said Hess, 'because if that's the case, then who is really running the country?'

Hitler grunted and got out of his chair to pace. Hess hoped that his comments would be enough.

Looking out of the window Hitler said, 'I despise them though. I appreciate what you're saying I really do, but I hate them, and I want them gone.'

There was only one more card to play.

'You want Russia more,' Hess said.

Hitler looked at him; Hess had sparked his interest.

'So?'

'You need England,' Hess said, 'on your side.'

Hitler retorted, 'They will still be on my side.'

'No, they won't,' Hess said.

'Yes, they will,' yelled Hitler. 'I'm about to be nice to them.'

'They will not, cannot let you outwardly persecute the Jews.' Hess raised his voice. 'If they die during the war, they are a war casualty. Britain can turn a blind eye to that.'

'You expect me to listen to another country's demands and not my own country's voice?' bellowed Hitler.

'It is not your country's voice,' Hess said. 'It's Goebbels's voice.'

'How dare you?' Hitler yelled back. 'I want them gone.'

'You are playing into his hands,' said Hess.

'I answer to no one but myself.' Hitler said. 'I want them gone.'

'By doing that you commit political suicide in front of the whole world,' yelled Hess, 'and then he does rule Germany.'

Hitler didn't reply, he was analysing what had just been said. Hess took a deep breath and sat back down. He couldn't keep Hitler at bay much longer; he'd made the right decision.

'Once again you are right,' Hitler said, 'but I want them gone eventually.'

'When they are of no use.' Hess said.

They continued writing the speech. Hitler threw his arm around Hess's shoulder as they left.

'Hess you are and always were a terribly stubborn person.'

They both laughed. Hitler walked off to say his speech. Hess waved goodbye to his friend. He turned and walked out the door. He had a train to catch.

***

Hess left his staff to check into the hotel as he wandered into the grounds. Albrecht was soon walking beside him.

'Hello,' Albrecht said.

'I am guessing everything is going well,' Hess said.

'Dissatisfaction is growing in the ranks, sir,' Albrecht said. 'Most of them would easily agree.'

'You only need one not to,' Hess said. 'Don't get overconfident.'

Hess hesitated for a moment on whether to mention Natasha or not and then decided not to.

'Of course,' Albrecht said, 'good luck.'

Hess smiled.

'Thank you and I'll send instructions soon.'

Albrecht turned to leave.

'Take care of yourself and take care of your father. Karl is a good, level-headed man,' Hess said.

Albrecht turned back and nodded.

'Don't try anything till I send word,' Hess said, 'much could be jeopardised.'

Albrecht departed. Hess worried about him; he was very eager, too eager. Hess had the names of the generals he was working on; he would pass them to Natasha to infiltrate, although she had already started with Halder. It was his backup plan. He just hoped it wasn't necessary. A coup was messy, it might destroy Hitler. Hess felt conflicted. Hitler was his friend, he admired him and his vision, but he was becoming too emotional, unpredictable. Peace with Britain had to happen, the other option was not worth thinking about. Hess continued walking around the garden, it was a lovely day for a stroll, but Hess could not enjoy it.

***

'Have you heard back from anyone?' Natasha said.

'The main players will be attending,' Friedrich said. 'There will be about twenty people.'

'Good,' Natasha said. 'The catering is organised.'

'It should go well,' said Friedrich.

'You do realise it's going to feel dreadful?' Natasha said. 'I just hope it distracts us enough.'

'These people are at every function you've ever been at,' Friedrich said.

'I know, I'll mingle as normal,' Natasha said. 'It's just normally... well normally...'

'You have Wilhelm,' Friedrich interrupted.

'Yes,' Natasha said matter-of-factly. 'He's good to converse with.'

'I always thought that you two would end up together,' Friedrich almost spoke to himself. 'You're such a great couple.'

Natasha was lost in thought. 'Some things are just not meant to be.'

Friedrich looked at his daughter. She cared for him, and you could see it in her eyes. She had made her choice. Friedrich wondered what it was like to isolate yourself from the world.

She realised her thoughts had drifted so she resumed talking.

'Or even Addie or Adolf or whatever you want to call him, he amuses me.'

Friedrich shook his head. 'You'll survive.'

She looked up at him.

'Yes, I will.'

***

Hess looked out the cockpit window. He loved flying; it was freeing. The propellers were purring in front of him. He tuned into Kastanie Y radio station to listen to his song. Everyone had chosen a song for their task. His was a farewell song. For although he was giving everyone the impression that it would be a short trip, he didn't believe he would be coming back. Not for a very long time.

The song began and he taxied down the runway.

***

Friedrichshafen wasn't a busy runway; in fact, it was hardly used at all. It had no security, just two men in an office. The office was more of a rundown shack. The problem was that the runway was too short for warplanes. There were tall trees that surrounded it. Only the exceptionally skilled pilots could veer off to the left and use the winds to take off. It was daredevil flying.

Anneliese crouched behind the shed. She had located a small hole in the wall the week before. Putting on her mask, she pulled out a rubber pipe and feed it through the hole. The men inside were talking and laughing which was to her benefit, as it would disguise the sound of the gas. Slowly she turned it on. It had taken a good twenty minutes before the men had fallen asleep. Anneliese turned off the gas and opened the door. It only took a few moments for the room to be clear. Helene turned on the radio and then they both sat on the table between the men with a bottle of ether each. It wasn't long before their song played, and Helene rushed out the door with a white sheet.

***

Hess flew over the airfield once and looked for the signal that everything had gone to plan. He saw white cloth waving in the wind on a grassy patch by the runway. He brought the plane around to land.

He was soon walking across to the office with his briefcase. Helene went to get the truck. Anneliese was still on the table when Hess came in.

'Here, they are' he said. 'Keep them safe for me.'

One of the men started to stir and Anneliese tipped some ether onto the material and shoved it under his nose. He drifted off again.

'The other case is in the truck,' Anneliese indicated. 'Good luck.'

Hess nodded and walked back out. The truck was beside the plane and Helene was sitting on the sideboard.

'Here is the load,' she said, pointing to two sacks, rope and a briefcase.

Hess and Helene managed to push the cargo into the plane. Hess tied the sacks together.

'Are you sure you're that heavy?' Hess said.

'I may be a little lighter, but it is better to be safe than sorry,' she said.

He nodded.

'See you soon,' Helene said.

She smiled, hopped into the truck, and drove away.

Hess put the plane just off the beginning of the runway. Landing was the easy bit. Taking off that would test his skill. He started to taxi. Before he got to the runway, it was a little bumpy, but he managed to gather a little speed. It was going to be tight. He had to lift off before the end of the runway as the ground returned to its bumpy self.

Anneliese and Helene watched the plane.

'Is he going to make it?' Helene said.

Anneliese didn't answer.

Hess felt every muscle in his body working as his limbs tried to overcome the heaviness or the plane. He wasn't as young as he used to be. The end of the runway was fast approaching.

'Please, please, please baby,' he said, 'you can do it. Come on you can do this.'

He felt a slight bump and then he was in the air. He brought his left wing down to dart through the trees and then swung it to the right to use the valley winds. Slowly he breathed out, and then the smile crossed his face. He could feel the adrenalin pumping through his body. This was what he missed most of all, the excitement, the buzz. The next song was heard on the radio. He was a couple of minutes early.

***

Michele had been aching to get into the sky all day. Both she and Wilhelm were in full uniform. They were using older planes that were nearly due for retirement, but that was common amongst high-ranking officers. They tended to not see much action because of their backgrounds. It was like play time practice for rich kids. The workers looked distastefully at the two boys; in fact, they didn't want much to do with them at all. This worked in their favour especially for Michele. From a distance she looked like a boy, but up close you could see that she was female.

A familiar song came on the radio.

'Let's do this,' Wilhelm said.

Michele nodded and they both walked towards the plane and were soon in the air. As they approached the meeting point, Michele looked around.

'I can't see him.'

'Neither can I,' Wilhelm said.

'Because I'm hiding,' a voice said over the radio.

Wilhelm and Michele looked across at each other. Wilhelm looked down and smiled. Hess was below them to the back. Both planes pulled apart and lowered to escort Hess.

'Are the times not right?' Wilhelm asked.

'Perfect,' Hess said. 'I just left a little early and managed to circle once.'

'Having fun?' Wilhelm said.

'Definitely,' Hess laughed.

'Let's fly below the cloud,' Wilhelm said.

They followed his lead. It wasn't long before the second to last song played. They flew for another five minutes and came to the border of the defence area.

'Let's go home,' Hess said.

They all peeled off to their landing zones.

Hess neared the Augsburg airstrip and circled a few times. He dropped the sandbags out of the plane into the paddock.

The parachute opened with ease, and they floated to the ground. The Hess took the plane into land.

***

'Time has gone by so fast,' Anneliese said. 'I can't believe it.'

'To tell you the truth I can't really believe my life,' Helene said. 'I mean, when I was growing up, I never envisaged having a family like this.'

Anneliese said, 'It's a bit crazy. But it's crazy times.'

'When will it all be normal?'

'What is normal?' said Anneliese.

They both looked at each other and laughed. Laughter was such a good stress relief. Deep down both were nervous. They were about to jump into the unknown.

'I have some letters I need you to give out,' Helene said. 'Can you do that for me?'

Anneliese nodded. She handed them over and Anneliese put them in her bag.

'It's going to be alright,' Anneliese said.

'I'm glad you're so sure,' Helene said. 'We can pretend at least.'

She picked up the bottle of wine and poured them both glasses.

***

'Should we really be drinking?' Michele said. 'We have a big day ahead of us tomorrow.'

'Tomorrow night is the big time, not day,' Wilhelm said. He continued pouring wine into her glass, 'We'll be fine by then.'

'So, is it like act like today is your last day?'

Michele giggled and then took a sip.

'Something like that,' he said. 'I don't think I'd be doing this though.'

Wilhelm was momentarily lost in his thoughts and smiled.

'What would you be doing?' Michele had a cheeky smile.

Wilhelm cleared his throat and blushed again he had been caught off guard,

'Just not this.'

'You sure know how to make a girl feel wanted,' Michele said.

'You have no idea,' he said under his breath and then changed the subject. 'Are you excited, scared or both?'

'Both,' she stated.

'To us,' Wilhelm said, raising his glass.

'And tomorrow.'

They both took a sip.

'What will the day after tomorrow be like?' Michele said. 'Everything will be different?'

'Well, no matter what happens tomorrow, know you can always trust me,' Wilhelm said.

'Same,' she replied.

***

Hess looked across the table at Friedrich and Natasha. What an unlikely trio they were. The waiter poured water into their glasses and then disappeared.

'You're not drinking anything stronger?' Hess said.

'No,' Friedrich said, 'I am sticking to the water this evening.'

Natasha smiled. Keeping sober was a problem for her father. He had identified one of his weaknesses and was trying to keep it at bay.

'Have you enjoyed it?' Friedrich said, 'The intrigue and the flying?'

Hess said, 'Yes I have.'

'I bet you'll miss it when it's all over.'

Friedrich laughed and started cutting up his steak.

'Yes,' Hess said with a smile, 'yes I will.'

He looked up straight into Natasha's eyes then looked away.

'But it will be nice to have a boring life for a while.'

'What is going to happen to Mother?' Natasha said.

'I thought I'd throw her out over Scotland,' Hess said.

'With a parachute I hope,' Friedrich said.

'Only if she behaves herself.'

'I'm sorry, have you met my mother?' Natasha said.

Friedrich finished eating and excused himself from the table. Natasha placed her cutlery together and leaned back in the chair.

'You aren't coming back, are you?'

Hess had been poised to take a bite but lowered his fork.

'Hopefully, I'll be back,' Hess said. 'by–'

'Stop,' Natasha said firmly. 'Let's not play games now, it's far too late for that.'

He looked at her stone faced.

'I don't know what's going to happen. But I think I'll be gone for a while.'

'I'm going to miss you, you know,' she said.

'You're going to miss the challenge.'

Hess laughed.

'Of course,' Natasha said. 'What else?'

What else indeed, thought Hess.

'You two look like you are having far too much fun,' Friedrich said as he approached the table.

Hess said, 'You know Friedrich, your daughter is lucky I'm not fifteen years younger.'

'You should be so lucky even if you were,' she said.

Friedrich looked over at them both and shook his head. Thank goodness: the world wouldn't know what hit it.

CHAPTER 28

Germany, 10 May 1941

Hess opened the door and walked over to the bed. He perched on the edge and stroked his son's hair. He loved him so much. Hess could honestly say that. He could admit it to himself. He never got to see Buz anymore. Right now, was an image he wanted to remember forever. Slowly his son's eyes struggled open, and a small hand rubbed its face.

'Papa.'

Hess fondly grabbed his cheek.

'Buz, do you want to go for a walk with me and the dogs?'

A smile crept across the boy's face, and he nodded. Hess winked at him and then got up and left the room.

Hess walked into Ilse's room and started looking through her wardrobe.

'What are you doing?' she said.

Ilse stopped reading and looked up.

'Looking for a book,' he replied.

'What book?' she asked.

'The pilot's book of Everest,' he said. 'I suppose it doesn't really matter, but I really felt like reading it.'

She got up and started looking through a box.

'I don't think it's here,' Ilse said but continued looking. 'If I find it, I'll let you know.'

Hess got up.

'Thank you,' he said.

Beside where she had been reading was a jug of water and a glass. He quickly looked over towards her. She was still searching through the boxes. He reached over and sprinkled some powder into the jug. It looked a bit like dust, but slowly it dissolved into the water. He turned and went to collect Buz for their walk.

Father and son walked down the road hand in hand. Buz always looked so proud walking with his father. They entered the park and Hess unleashed the dogs. Buz looked around for sticks and started throwing them for the dogs to retrieve. The dogs were bouncing around letting off their energy while their mother stuck close to her master's side. Hess sat on a swing and patted her head. Buz ran over and sat on the swing beside Hess.

'How are you?' Hess said.

His son's smile was right across his face.

'Good Papa, good.'

Hess reached over and messed up his son's hair.

'Oh Papa,' he said laughing, 'I'm all messy.'

'You're allowed to be messy sometimes,' Hess said.

'How are you Papa?' Buz said. 'You seem different.'

'I'm fine.'

He squatted in front of his son, who was sitting on the swing. 'So, who is the most important person in the whole world to Papa?'

Hess asked slightly rocking the swing.

Buz bit his lip a little, and then he leaned forward and whispered, 'Hitler.'

Hess smiled a sad smile and shook his head.

'No.'

Buz smiled and sat to attention.

'Me,' he said pointing to his chest, 'I am.'

'Yes, yes you are. But don't tell Hitler, he may get jealous.'

Hess stood up and pushed the swing.

Buz laughed. Moments like these were rare and over too quickly. Soon it was time to collect the dogs.

Before they walked home, Hess lowered himself to Buz's height again.

'Papa loves you very much.'

Buz nodded.

'I want you to remember that Papa has friends who will always look after you, even when Papa is not here,' Hess said.

'Papa, are you going away?'

Buz's face fell, his smile gone.

'I'm on a secret mission,' Hess said. 'You can't tell anyone.'

Buz's eyes were wide, he nodded and put his finger to his lips and said, 'Shhh'

'That's right,' Hess winked. 'They may say some bad things about Papa.'

'Why?' Buz said.

'To cover up the secret mission,' Hess said sternly, 'but always remember the Papa you know.'

'Yes Papa,' Buz said and threw his arms around Hess's neck.

Hess hugged him back and wished he never had to let go. He could feel his eyes getting wet, he couldn't, wouldn't let his son see. He blew out to control his breathing.

It wasn't long before they were back in the house and Hess was preparing for his lunch guest. He walked upstairs to check on Ilse.

'Will you be joining us for lunch?' he said.

'No,' she said, 'my stomach seems to be a little upset.'

She'd been reading. She put the book down briefly and looked at Hess, 'By the way I found your book.'

'Thank you,' Hess said.

She wasn't really listening; she had resumed reading. He looked at his watch, Rosenberg would be here any moment; it was time to get ready. He was soon downstairs for his meeting.

'Thank you for the money,' Hess said.

'Not a problem,' said Rosenburg, 'I gave you a bit of a gift as well.'

'Did you enjoy yourself?' Hess said.

'I should be asking you that question,' Rosenburg laughed. 'But yes, I did. How about you?'

'It was a lot better than expected,' Hess said.

He relaxed for a bit then said very casually.

'Sometimes I wonder what our future will hold and how we'll get there.'

'Very deep,' Rosenberg said.

Rosenberg started to philosophise. Slowly Hess moulded the conversation towards the war. He was sowing seeds of thought in Rosenberg's mind. The conversation flowed onto strategy and strategic planning.

Eventually Hess said, 'I had a feeling that we were a lot alike in the way we think.'

He slowly edged onto the final solution and what other options were available.

'I'm going away for a little while on one of those trips,' he said knowingly to Rosenberg who pretended he understood.

'I need you to support Hitler and advise him while I'm gone.'

'Of course,' Rosenberg said.

Helping Hess, supporting Hitler, this would help his political future.

Hess wound up the conversation and then headed back upstairs.

'So how are you feeling?' Hess asked his wife as she lay on the bed.

'Better.'

Hess picked up the book he had been looking for and turned it over.

He looked down at her.

'Will you be joining me for tea?'

She nodded and slid off the bed into standing position and walked over to the wardrobe.

'I'll meet you downstairs in an hour.'

Hess got up and went downstairs to have a quick nap. He would need all the energy he could get.

Ilse walked into the parlour and sat opposite Hess. Servants buzzed themselves around trying to be inconspicuous. Hess waved and they scurried out the door. Hess leaned over and poured some tea into Ilse's cup.

'Are you feeling alright?' Ilse said.

'You're the one who was feeling unwell,' Hess said.

She didn't answer him but sat back in her chair and eyed him up and down. He was up to something; she just didn't know what. Hess returned her stare for a moment.

'Sometimes I wonder how well I really know you,' Hess said taking a sip.

She raised her eyebrow but didn't reply.

'The other question I ponder is what happened?' he said. 'How did you lose so much of yourself?'

'I don't know what you are talking about.'

Ilse put down her cup and saucer.

'When did you stop thinking for yourself?' he said.

'I think!' she said. 'What are you talking about?'

'When I first met you, I was attracted to your intellect,' Hess said.

'You never loved me,' said Ilse.

'No,' he said, 'but I was attracted to you.'

Stunned she looked away. He had never stated that before. It was so blunt and cutting. Even for him. He leaned over to her.

'Look at me,' he said, 'There are very few things in this world I can truly say I love. I may not have loved you, but I care.'

'You're just saying it now.'

Ilse was being defensive. She didn't really know why it was affecting her so much. He had always been distant, direct, but this was something else.

'If I didn't care,' he said, 'I wouldn't be having this conversation.'

She paused, what he was saying was true.

'If there is one thing that stays with you,' he said, 'it should be for you to be true to yourself.'

'I am true to myself,' she said. 'What are you? Who are you? I don't even know you anymore.'

He hoped that something could sink in, he had to try, but it was only a slim hope.

'Goodbye.'

She looked back confused. Standing up he kissed her on her forehead, walked out of the room and downstairs to Buz, it was time to say goodbye.

Buz was playing with his model airplane, running around the room.

'Brrrrmm,' he roared trying to sound like a plane engine.

Hess bent down and Buz dive-bombed the plane into his arm. He squealed with glee and turned. Hess grabbed his arm before he managed to run away.

'Papa has to go away now,' Hess said. 'I'm going to fly away.'

'Can I go?' Buz said. 'Please Papa.'

'No,' Hess said, 'it's a secret mission, remember.'

Buz nodded. Ilse appeared in the doorway to see Hess hugging his son.

'How long are you going for?' she asked.

'I don't know exactly, perhaps tomorrow, perhaps not,' he said looking up at her smiling, 'but I'll be back by Monday evening.'

He looked and sounded convincing, even if he didn't believe it at all. He kissed her on the cheek and walked down to the car.

Paddocks flew by as the car made its way to Augsburg. Hess's head leaned on the window and his glazed eyes watched the countryside go by. Hess was thinking, but not thinking, in a trancelike state.

Pintsch looked over at Hess. He'd never seen him like this. He was normally withdrawn. But now, it was as if Hess had fortified himself and no one could get through.

Hess wasn't even registering what they were passing. He was thinking about his son. He knew he would be safe no matter what, but he didn't know what he would turn out like, what his character would be like living in this world. If he would pave this own way or go with the masses. His eyes registered to his brain that they had entered the woods area.

'I want to go for a walk in the woods,' he broke the silence. 'Can we stop at the turn-off?'

Pintsch looked sideways at his boss but nodded.

The car turned off the road and parked.

Pintsch walked around and opened Hess's door. Hess stepped out with his briefcase. They both walked towards a path that disappeared into the woods.

'Thank you,' Hess said. 'I'll meet you back at the car.'

Pintsch stood still and watched Hess disappear.

Hess took a deep breath as the woods closed in behind him. He kept walking through the slits of light.

'Hello,' Henri said as he stepped out from behind a tree.

Hess stood still and smiled.

'How are you feeling?' Henri said. 'Calm and collected?'

'Extremely nervous,' Hess said. 'I have some money for you.'

He put down the briefcase and flicked it open with his thumbs. He handed a bundle of notes to Henri, 'I also have a favour to ask you.'

Henri said nothing.

'Look after my son,' Hess said. 'Please.'

Henri nodded and then pulled out some papers and handed them to Hess who put them neatly in his bag.

'Here's a map,' Henri said. 'I have put on the route you suggested, not the one you are flying, and I copied it in your letters.'

'Thank you,' Hess said

He closed the case.

He got up and took the letters that Henri handed to him.

'Take care, and Hess, I will look after Buz,'

Henri melted into the woods.

Pintsch saw Hess emerge from the woods. He ran to the car door and opened it. Hess got inside and leaned his head on the window again. As Pintsch sat down Hess's hand wandered into his coat's top pocket and pulled out a handful of letters.

'Deliver these please,' he said.

He handed them to Pintsch and then resumed concentrating on the countryside.

***

Natasha straightened the glass and bent down so her eye was at table level. The glasses were in place, the entire row hid behind the first stem.

'You need to get ready,' Friedrich said.

She nodded but kept fiddling with the place settings.

'Now,' he said.

She stood up and walked out of the room. Friedrich walked over to the radiogram and turned up the volume.

Natasha dawdled to her room. She didn't want to get ready. She didn't want the party to begin. What she really wanted was time to stop. It wouldn't, not for her, not for anyone.

She slipped into a dress, Michele's dress, and sat in front of her dresser mirror. Closing her eyes, she took a deep breath.

'Control,' Natasha whispered to herself. 'Calm control. Now is not the time to lose control.'

She opened her eyes and smiled. Natasha picked up her hairbrush. I wonder what Michele is doing.

***

She hadn't realised how long her hair had got until she started brushing it to put it up into a bun. Michele had a cap to put over her locks. It only took a few strategic pins before her hair was ready. She stood up and looked at herself in the mirror; the air force uniform almost fit her perfectly. She picked up her pocketknife and put it in her trouser pocket. Then she grabbed her gun, loaded it and put some spare bullets in her jacket pocket. It was better to be safe than sorry. She took a few deep breaths to calm her nerves. It was time to go into mission mode. Concentrating on the mission and its objectives were the most important things.

There was a knock at the door. Wilhelm walked in, he looked uncomfortable. It was probably just nerves.

'Are you ready?'

'Yes,' she said. 'You?'

'Yes. There's one thing I have to do first,' he said.

'What's that?'

His hands grabbed either side of her face, and he kissed her lips, lingering just a little and then he let go.

'Now I am ready.'

Wilhelm turned and left the room.

Michele froze, she couldn't speak. Her index finger ran across her lower lip before she realised what she was doing. Stop it. This is not what she needed before a mission. She took a deep breath; now she had to refocus. Mission mode she kept thinking. She needed to be in mission mode, damn it.

***

Natasha walked into the parlour and collapsed into the chair. Her father was sitting in the chair beside the radiogram.

'Are you ready?' she said.

Her father looked up at the clock and nodded.

'We should turn off the radio,' she said.

'Not yet.'

It wasn't that they thought that they would hear anything about what was happening. It was that they knew what was supposed to be happening with each song.

The doorbell rang and Natasha looked up at Friedrich who grudgingly turned off the sound.

'It's time,' she said, 'to see just how good at acting you are.'

They could hear people in the foyer. Natasha took a deep breath and used her hands to pull herself out of the chair. Friedrich followed suit and they both walked out to greet their guests.

Natasha stood patiently by her father's side. Some of the couples had brought their sons and enthusiastically introduced them to Natasha. She smiled politely and promised to talk with them later. This was going to be a long night. She looked around the room and wondered if she would be able to maintain her patience the whole night.

Friedrich leaned forward, 'a couple of months ago, I would have welcomed this.'

Natasha said nothing.

'Please don't get attached to any of these idiots,' he said.

She raised her eyebrow and looked at him sideways in total disbelief.

'As if you need to tell me.'

CHAPTER 29

Hess walked towards the plane on the runway.

'Are her tanks fully loaded?'

The man walking beside him replied, 'Yes, all of them.'

'That will be all,' Hess dismissed him.

He saluted and marched away. Hess stopped at the base of the ladder and turned. 'It has been a pleasure,' he said.

Pintsch shook his hand.

'The pleasure is all mine. Till we meet again.'

Hess walked up the steps and climbed onto the wing. He saluted Pintsch who returned it with a smile and then pulled away the steps and prepared the plane. Hess took a deep breath and climbed into the cockpit. Today would be a long day. He turned on the radio and made sure he could hear it above the roar of the engine. The song changed and Hess smiled it was time to go.

He turned the plane to face the runway and began to taxi. It wasn't long before he was in the air. The clouds were light, and sight was good. He couldn't have asked for better weather. He headed north for a while until he knew he would be out of sight and then banked left to Friedrichshafen. Hess enjoyed the hum of the engine and even the music felt like silence. There hadn't been much of that in his life for a long time. It was nice and peaceful. He took a deep breath through his nose and smelt the fumes. It was good to be back in the sky.

When Hess landed the plane, Anneliese gave Helene a hug.

'I've been putting this off,' Anneliese said. 'I don't want to say goodbye.'

'Then don't,' Helene said, stroking her hair. 'I'll see you again.'

Helene broke away before Anneliese could see her tears and started to walk to the plane.

Anneliese ran after her.

'Helene, the briefcase.'

Helene looked around red eyed and grabbed the case and then continued walking. Anneliese walked back to the control room to make sure men were still unconscious.

Helene handed Hess the briefcase. She went to climb up the aircraft.

'Wait a minute,' Hess said. 'You need this.'

He threw a bag at her.

'What is it?' she asked inspecting the bag.

Hess shook his head in disbelief, 'It's a parachute.'

'But I don't know how?' she said.

'It's just for your safety,' Hess said, 'if you do need to use it, it will open automatically, and remember to run before you hit the ground.'

Helene still wasn't convinced, but she knew she should have one. She strapped herself in under Hess's supervision.

'Now climb in,' Hess indicated.

She had never been in a plane before and was apprehensive, but she wasn't going to let her companion know. Hess tapped over towards the Gunners area and Helene climbed in. It wasn't the most comfortable of places, but it was only for a short period of time.

'Do you get claustrophobic?' Hess said.

'No,' she replied.

'Good,' he said, 'I need you to duck down as much as you can. No one should see you.'

She nodded and squeezed down until she couldn't see outside.

'Once we have flown across the channel you can wriggle out from there.'

He climbed into the cockpit. Hess felt sorry for her. The radio had replaced the seat and had taken up most of the room she would normally have had. But it was important that it was there.

Helene sat and waited. She felt defenceless and at the mercy of Hess. She knew it was for the best and took deep breaths to calm her nerves. She heard the propellers start to spin and soon the whole area she was in started to shake. There was a movement as the plane turned and then she felt it begin to move down the runway. She could feel the pressure pushing against her back down to her feet, which managed to gain a hold. Helene kept thinking it is not as bad as it seems, and that it just felt worse because she couldn't see.

There was a bump and a loud grinding noise. Then she heard music just above the roar of the engine.

'We're right on time,' Hess yelled above the engine.

Helene just nodded; she wasn't calm enough yet to let out a credible reply.

***

'Oberst?' a short petite secretary called as she ran into the office.

'Yes,' he said turning around.

'Hitler's secretary is on the telephone,' the secretary relayed, 'she wanted to talk to the most senior person here.'

He nodded and walked out.

'Hello,' he said down the telephone.

'Are you in charge today?' Anneliese said.

'Yes. All the plans for this evening's raid are in place. I was just briefing everyone.'

'I am not phoning about tonight, I'm phoning to tell you that very shortly the Deputy Führer and two Bf109 escorts will be flying through your airspace,' Anneliese said. 'Under no circumstance are they to be shot at. Do you understand?' She paused. 'Do you understand?'

'Yes,' he said.

'They are now your responsibility,' she said. 'What is your ID?'

He paused, '1398 B.'

'Thank you,' she said and hung up.

He wondered what was happening. He had never been asked for ID before. That meant he was fully accountable. He rushed into the control room.

'Inform all staff that there is free passage for a plane escorted by two Bf109s,' the Oberst yelled. 'Now!'

Everyone scurried around and started to inform other centres in the area.

***

Michele and Wilhelm were flying above the cloud, the sun was streaming down. It was a gorgeous afternoon. Within an hour the sun would start to set so they were making the most of it.

'It's time,' Michele said, and they both swept down under the cloud.

Just ahead of them they saw Hess. They changed their frequency and edged up beside him. He waved at them both and gave them the thumbs up. They were about to fly into the military zone.

Michele saw a hand slowly wave from the back; it was her mother. She laughed.

'Say hello to her.'

Shortly the wave changed to a thumbs-up and then disappeared. Hess indicated to drop. It was important that the people on the ground correctly identified them.

'We have a gun pointing our way,' Wilhelm said.

'But it's not shooting,' Hess replied.

As they flew by the control centre, Hess rocked his plane as a wave and then continued the journey.

***

'Herr Hess asked me to deliver you a letter,' Pintsch said handing it over to Hitler.

Hitler looked up and grabbed the letter, then sat back in his chair. Pintsch's brow was sweating, but he stood still. Hitler read the letter and smiled. Pintsch relaxed and began to breathe.

'Stay for dinner.' Hitler indicated for him to sit down.

Pintsch hesitated and then obliged him, as if he had a choice. Sitting on the edge of his seat, he looked around. There was no way of getting out.

'Relax,' Hitler said, 'Dinner will be soon.'

Hitler watched as people attended to him and darted around the room. While Pintsch sat patiently, he tried to study Hitler's demeanour. Pintsch was shown to the dining room, with a group of others. Hitler sat and the other guests followed suit. They were served dinner and wine was poured into each of Hitler's guest's glasses. Pintsch looked down at his plate. It looked amazing. Each item placed carefully to create the final masterpiece. Pintsch wasn't really hungry; his stomach was full of butterflies, and he felt sick. He just wanted to leave, go home, and pretend nothing had happened, but deep down inside he knew it wasn't possible. He picked up his knife and fork and started to eat what he thought could be his last meal for a while. He looked at the glass of wine. It was tempting but he would need all his wits about him to survive. Everyone ate in silence as the servants clambered around trying to anticipate everyone's needs. Pintsch place his cutlery down and looked up. Hitler was staring at him, 'Did you enjoy your meal?'

'Yes, thank you,' Pintsch forced a smile, 'and you?'

'Yes, I did,' Hitler said.

Hitler sat back in his chair, looked at his guards and nodded. Pintsch's smile dropped and he took a gulp of air as the guards walked over to him, grabbed him from his chair and dragged him out of the room.

***

Natasha looked at her father across the room. Both were smiling, but it was forced. They had finished dinner and were about to go into the parlour. It was strange but appropriate being back in the old house. It was almost as if the family had a closer bond now than they'd had in a very long time.

The piano had been tuned and dusted. She couldn't remember the last time it had been played, but one of the guests was a pianist of note and would no doubt be tinkering the ivories later in the evening. Staff walked around serving drinks and the group slowly moved into the parlour. Natasha managed to steal a glance at the grandfather clock in the hallway and wondered if everything was going well.

Friedrich perused the room. He hated not knowing and not being able to find out what was happening.

'Thank you for your invitation.' Fromm broke Friedrich from his thoughts. 'You have a magnificent house.'

'Thank you,' Friedrich said, 'I'm glad you are enjoying yourself. Have you met my daughter?'

Friedrich beckoned for Natasha to join them. Fromm was someone she might want to get to know better.

***

So far so good, thought Michele. They were nearing the coast. The plan was to fly to within sight of the English coast, where a final song would play and then Hess would be without an escort.

'We have company,' Wilhelm said.

'Are they friend of foe?' Michele asked.

'I don't know,' Wilhelm said. 'Stay with Hess.'

'You are not authorised,' came a voice over the radio.

'We have authorisation,' Hess said, 'check with ground control.'

'Ground control has requested you land,' the voice stipulated.

'This is Rudolf Hess,' Hess said, 'I have authorisation.'

'I know who you are, Deputy Führer,' the voice commented, 'but you must land.'

Wilhelm peeled off and circled the planes and Michele kept slightly behind Hess.

'If you don't comply,' the voice said nervously. 'I will be forced to shoot you down.'

Michele looked at the plane. If they shot at the wings, it would be fine, and the plane would continue. They were highly unlikely to want to kill Hess, but if they did, they would aim for the tail, with her mother. She couldn't let that happen.

Helene was still pinned in the gunner's area in the tail of the plane. She felt the plane lower but didn't know why. As far as she was aware everything was going to plan.

The planes that were following the trio tried to get behind Wilhelm, but he was ducking around trying to keep them busy. The coastline was almost below them; time was running out.

'Please land,' pleaded the pilot.

'Do what you have to do,' Hess replied.

Hess dropped his plane to as low as he dared. They were flying over the sea now. The other planes tried to follow his lead but were not used to low flying. Michele was behind and slightly above Hess, she was nervous, but she knew she was his only defence. The lead plane swung high and looped to aim towards Hess's plane. Wilhelm knew he wouldn't be able to go too low, but if the aim was right, he wouldn't have to.

'He's going to fire,' Wilhelm said.

Michele saw the fighter plane out of the corner of her eye; she heard the shots fire and turned her plane directly over Hess's. The first few bullets caught her wing. Hess swung to his left and out of the way. The other bullets ripped through the front of the cockpit. Michele felt a sharp pain in her thigh and instinctively winched in pain, making the plane veer up to the right.

Wilhelm had a perfect shot at the second plane that had been following them. He caught the plane with a barrage of bullets. It didn't harm the pilot, but the plane wouldn't be able to fly for long. He smiled it had been a long time. The plane veered off for land and cleared Wilhelm's view, just in time to see Michele's plane jerk to the right and plough through the lead plane's wings. The planes shredded on impact. Then there was an explosion. For a moment Wilhelm forgot where he was.

'Pull up,' yelled Hess over the radio. 'Pull up.'

Something registered in Wilhelm, and he jerked back to life.

'Keep it together,' Hess said sternly.

Wilhelm was in shock. He was struggling to take a breath.

'Are you there?' Hess asked. 'Wilhelm, talk to me.'

'Yes.'

'Go home,' Hess said.

Wilhelm turned his plane and circled the crash site; he flew as low as he dared. Bits of the plane were sinking some were still floating; some still on fire, but there was no sign of life. He couldn't see any bodies, or anyone in the waves. He couldn't see her. It had happened so fast. Had he seen a parachute? No, he wasn't sure, no, he had seen nothing. Where was she? Michele?

'What happened?' Helene yelled out over the engine.

'It's fine,' Hess lied. 'We're safe now.'

***

Natasha tried to mingle as much as possible. She knew now that Hess had gone, she would need to network more. She still got bored with idle women chat. She excused herself and walked towards her father who smiled over towards her.

Halfway across the floor a sharp pain ran through her side. She grabbed the chair for support. Her father's face dropped, and he walked over to her.

'You are not getting out of it that easily,' he said to her.

'I, I don't feel well,' she replied.

She was gulping for air.

'Good try,' Friedrich said.

'No, I need fresh air.'

He looked at her. Her eyes were bloodshot and her face pure white. Grabbing her arm, he helped her to the doorway. Natasha saw the doorway and suddenly darkness crept through it and then she blacked out.

Shock echoed around the room and then there was a flurry of activity. Friedrich picked up his daughter and carried her out of the room.

A gentleman came out of the room and asked if Friedrich needed assistance.

'Can you play the piano? Then keep the party going.' Friedrich said. 'I'll get a doctor.'

The gentleman looked surprised but nodded and walked into the parlour. Within minutes the previous incident was forgotten, and the party continued.

***

Scotland Airbase

'Sir,' a radar operator said, 'a low flying German plane has been detected off the east coast, Sir.'

The Squadron Leader nodded. 'Is it by itself?'

'Yes sir.'

He walked over to the telephone 'Sir, we have a German plane flying towards the east coast.'

There was no reply.

'We await your instructions,' the squadron leader stated.

'Thank you,' said the voice on the telephone, 'Fighter Command is aware of the situation.'

He hung up.

***

'Sir,' the voice said through the receiver, 'he's flying into our airspace, how would you like us to proceed.'

'Who knows about this?' the Duke of Hamilton said.

'The squadron leader who reported it and me,' said the voice.

He paused and then took a breath. 'Scramble a plane from each major base once the plane has passed, they should follow only and wait for commands.'

'Certainly, sir' came the reply. 'What would the commands be?'

'Just swap them if they get too close,' he said. 'Let me know when he lands.'

'Yes' was the reply and then the line went dead.

Hamilton picked up the telephone.

'The Eagle is in the airspace,' Hamilton said, 'the Royals will bring him down to you.'

'NO,' said the voice.

It coughed, then you heard the draw of breath through a cigar.

'I want to see him first. Coordinate it.'

'Yes sir,' Hamilton said.

Hamilton walked out of the office and called a couple of guards.

'Go over to Dungavel and kill the lights.'

Confused the group walked off. Hamilton took a deep breath. He hated when things were changed at the last minute. He just hoped everything would go well.

CHAPTER 30

The sun was setting as Hess approached the east coast.

'Helene,' he said, 'you can come up now.'

Helene shuffled her way into a sitting position. She started punching her legs to get the blood circulating.

'How are you feeling?' Hess said.

'Fine,' she said, 'my legs are a little numb though.'

'I'm glad you're alright,' he said looking out the window.

He tilted the plane off course. Scanning the horizon, he looked for a castle. He looked again at the map on his leg and then looked outside.

Slowly as he flew over a clump of trees, a castle came into view. He checked his belt and then looked outside. A light started to flick on and off in a field nearby.

'Helene,' he yelled back. 'Can you do me a favour?'

'Sure, how can I help?' she shouted.

'There is a small lever above you,' he yelled. 'Can you flick it?'

She reached up and grabbed the lever. It was almost out of reach, but she managed to push herself up to reach it. Finally, she pushed it and it clicked. As soon as it made the noise her glass ceiling flew open.

'I think I broke it,' she yelled pulling a face.

But Hess couldn't hear above the wind.

'Sorry,' he said.

Hess rolled the plane upside down.

He saw her drop out and then he flipped it back over.

Helene had dropped out of the gunner's seat. The wind pushed her face upwards, and her eyes were finding it had to focus. The parachute automatically opened, and it pulled her backwards. Her groin and arms felt like they would come apart with the pull of the parachute and she was slightly winded. The ground appeared suddenly, and she barely had time to think let alone get her legs into action. Her foot hit the ground and she toppled on to her side. The parachute fell on top of her, and she suddenly felt claustrophobic. She grabbed at the parachute trying to find the edge. When she did, she took a deep breath of the cold fresh air.

'Helene.'

She got up, unbuckling herself.

'Yes.'

She looked around to where she thought the voice had come from. Two shadows emerged from the nearby trees.

'Ma'am,' said one of the men. 'My name's George.'

Then he indicated to his right.

'This is Patrick.'

'Ello Lass,' he said with a thick accent.

Helene concentrated hard on what he said. She recognised the greeting but not the next word.

She smiled and said, 'Hello.'

Her English was limited but she had the basics.

'Are you hurt?' George said. 'After the fall?'

She shook her head.

'No.'

She looked at the parachute on the ground and started to laugh.

They looked at her somewhat confused.

'My landing wasn't very,' she said, 'ladylike, was it?'

'No, it wasn't,' said George.

'Wasit ya first time as a Para thun?' Patrick asked.

Helene strained her neck forward so she could hear.

'I'm really sorry I don't understand you; can you speak slower please?' she said.

The men laughed.

'I can't understand him most of the time,' George said. 'Have you parachuted before?'

She shook her head.

'Not bad lass,' Patrick said, 'not bad *atall*.'

Patrick collected the parachute and they all walked off to the car.

***

Hess landed on the ground with the parachute floating down behind him. He turned to see his plane in flames. Knowing that this would cause unwanted attention, he looked around for somewhere to hide. A head of him was a clump of bushes. He took a step forward and fell slightly on the uneven ground. Grabbing his parachute, he walked over and hid in the bushes and waited.

In the distance he could see flashlights waving across the field and men shouting to each other. They were not particularly subtle.

'Mr Hess,' a voice shouted.

'Is that what you are supposed to call him?' asked another.

'I don't know,' replied the first, 'it's better than Rudolf.'

'Gentlemen,' Hess stepped out from under the bush. 'Can we keep it down please?'

'Yes sir,' they both said saluting.

'That won't be necessary,' Hess said.

He felt slightly embarrassed.

'Sir,' one of the men said.

'Hess is fine,' Hess said.

'Yes sir, I mean Hess,' he said looking sideways at his colleague, 'I am McBride, and this is Morris.'

'Nice to meet you,' Hess said, 'but now I am Alfred Horn.'

They started to walk.

'Sir,' McBride replied, 'you're a little off course.'

Hess turned and looked at the soldiers.

'A little,' he said. 'I would've been on course if the runway had any light.'

'It's just that it's made it a little bit difficult,' McBride said.

'I've just crashed a perfectly good plane, so you could find me,' Hess said.

McBride said, 'I know but–'

'Don't lecture me,' Hess said. 'I've had a hard night so far. And I think it's about to get worse.'

'Shh' said McBride.

He could hear someone approaching.

'Damn farmer,' McBride said. 'Act slightly injured. They will have to wait for assistance.'

With that both men disappeared into the shadows.

Confused Hess sat down in the field and waited. It was not long before a tall thin farmer came walking over carrying what looked like a pitchfork. He edged closer to Hess, obviously not sure what to do in the situation.

'Hello,' said Hess.

'You an airman?' the farmer asked.

'Yes,' Hess replied. 'Can you help me.'

The farmer stretched out his arm and helped Hess up. Acting slightly injured was easy. Hess felt like he may have sprained his ankle when he had tripped in the field. He hobbled a little. The farmer seemed to notice, so he helped him along with some support and they made their way to the farmhouse.

When they arrived, Hess bowed as he was greeted by an older woman and a younger woman. Then sat by the table. The farmer made a phone call. Hess just sat and smiled and wondered where McBride and Morris were.

Within five minutes there was a knock at the door, and they entered.

'You were fast,' said the farmer.

'We were on patrol. May I use the telephone?' McBride said.

They indicated where it was located. McBride walked over to it, looked around and then picked up the receiver.

'The package has arrived safe and sound,' McBride said and then hung up.

He had a couple more telephone calls to make.

'Would you like a drink?' the lady in the kitchen asked. 'Tea or something stronger?'

Hess smiled. 'A glass of water would be appreciated.'

McBride walked into the kitchen as the lady opened the refrigerator to get some chilled water. McBride watched Hess's eyes as they followed the lady.

'Water from the tap will be fine,' McBride said grabbing the glass and filling it from the tap in plain view of Hess.

McBride handed the glass to Hess who smiled and nodded. He looked at Hess and wondered what type of society he'd come from.

McBride leaned down and whispered.

'He's been informed.'

Hess took a deep breath and smiled. He liked this guy.

'You aren't as dumb as I first thought,' Hess said. 'That's a compliment by the way.'

'Thank you, I think,' said McBride.

They both sat in silence until a car pulled up the driveway. McBride got up and walked towards the window.

'Great, Home Guard is here.'

He turned to the lady who was waiting patiently in the corner.

'Can you make tea for our new guests please?'

She nodded and set about brewing a pot. There was a knock on the door. No one did anything, so she sighed and went over to open it. McBride stepped over to the pot and dropped in two tiny pills and then added the hot water. He turned and winked at Hess then walked to the other side of the room.

The guards walked in.

'What's your name?'

'Alfred Horn,' he said.

They sat down and tea was handed out for the new additions.

'What happened?' said one of the Home Guard.

McBride gave a rundown of things that had supposedly happened.

'This is now my prisoner,' the guard said standing up. 'Have you got any weapons?'

Hess shook his head.

'No, he's not your prisoner. You can't take him,' McBride said half focusing on the guards and half looking out the window.

'I can and I will.'

The guards indicated for Hess to get up. They quickly patted him down and then all walked out the door. The home guard were starting to be a little sluggish is movement.

Just as Hess was being put in the car another car pulled up.

McBride indicated to Morris to stand behind the guards. One at a time they both collapsed in a deep sleep.

'This is the plan,' said a gentleman who got into the car with Hess. 'Tonight, you will be taken into Glasgow. The lodging is basic but adequate. In the early hours we'll make a switch and then you will be taken to London.'

Hess nodded. The man got out and the home guards were put in the back seat of the car. Someone hopped in the front. Hess wound down the window and reached out to McBride to shake his hand.

'Thank you,' he said, 'only you and I can know about this.'

He wound up the window and the car pulled away. Morris called out to McBride that it was time to go. McBride strolled over to the car and quietly opened his hand. Looking carefully, he saw the object that Hess had handed him in the handshake. It was the Iron Cross. McBride quickly put it in his pocket and got inside.

CHAPTER 31

Winston stood in front of the mirror adjusting his tie. He was going out tonight to see the Blithe Spirit at the Savoy. Although it was the last thing he really wanted to do. He turned and walked towards the dresser. Here he opened his cigar box and chose a cigar, before proceeding through to the lounge. Hate waiting. Hate it. He looked up at the clock, not long to go. He fell into a trance watching time tick by. The phone rang. Winston looked up and then grabbed the phone. It was like waiting for an exam result.

'W,' the voice said.

'Yes?' Winston said.

'The eagle has landed.'

The phone call ended. Winston sighed with relief and a smile moulded his lips. He put down the phone, now he could enjoy the show.

'Clementine,' Winston said, 'it's time to leave.'

'The show will be over,' Clementine said. 'Why could we not go earlier?'

'I was waiting for something,' he said. 'We will be in time for post theatre drinks.'

They walked out to the waiting car, which drove them along the Embankment to the Savoy entrance.

'Do you hear that?' Clementine said.

He looked at her, and then saw spotlights turning on along the south bank of the Thames.

'Stop the car,' said Winston.

'Sir, I should really get you to a shelter,' his driver said.

'Stop the damn car and turn off the lights.'

The driver pulled over to the side of the road. Winston got out and stood against the railings. A plane flew past, followed by another and another.

The first bomb dropped on the nearby bridge and shook the ground. Winston stumbled slightly with the explosion.

This was a strategic bombing. It was full moon, a low tide, which meant reduced water for fires. The targets were infrastructure.

Winston followed the planes as one by one, bombs descended on the House of Commons. The London skyline was alight. Winston was not scared, he was angry.

'Do your worst Hitler and we will do our best!'

He threw his right hand in the air creating a v with his index and middle finger.

'Calm down,' said Clementine. 'You're British, you can't just act like that, people will see you.'

He snorted and then looked at her and smiled.

'Hitler is very angry with us; he has lost something today that we have gained. However, he has managed to do something that Guy Fawkes could not do. Look at our house, our seat of government.'

'Dear, it's happened. You can't change it. Build a new one, give the people a focus, you can shape the new look, and afterwards it will represent who we are and how we act as a nation.'

'Yes, yes, yes, I like that. I think I may use it, change it slightly, but use it all the same.'

'Now can we go to a shelter?'

He looked at her, 'I think it might be good to go to Ditchley for a while, don't you?'

**

Hess yawned as he looked outside the window. He could see nothing. It was too dark. He was nervous, although there was no real point, it was out of his hands now.

They pulled off to the side of the road and stopped. Everyone waited patiently. Ten minutes later a car pulled up. Two soldiers got out of the car and escorted a man about Hess's height to his car. A figure got out of the passenger's side, walked towards Hess's door, and opened it.

'Hello old friend,' said the Duke of Hamilton.

'Not too much of the old please,' Hess said getting out of the car.

'It's good to see you,' Hamilton said.

He gave Hess a hug, then stepped back and looked him up and down.

'You don't look bad in casual gear, not at all.'

Hess nodded.

'Who's this guy?'

'A patient from a psychiatric hospital, poor man, no family no memory,' Hamilton shook his head.

'Brainwashing?' Hess said.

His companion nodded. 'News of your arrival will break in the next couple of days. And you will need to be seen as a prisoner, to have witnesses to that affect. It would delay conversations that we need to have.'

'So, I have doppelganger,' Hess smiled.

'Keep him sedated and uniformed until I tell you otherwise,' Hamilton said to his men.

'We need to go to Ditchley, they are moving from London. Are you ready for a trip?'

Hess nodded and both men walked over to the other car.

The two cars took off in different directions. Hess sat back again in his seat. Always pretending he thought, that was his life, a constant pretence.

'Sorry about the lights,' Hamilton said. 'We had visitors.'

'That's alright,' Hess said. 'Is Helene looked after? She'll be an asset.'

'Yes,' Hamilton said, 'everything is fine.'

Hess took a deep breath, 'No.'

He was looking out the window again.

'Why?' Hamilton said. 'What's wrong?'

'One of my escorts was shot down.'

'I'm sorry,' Hamilton said, 'I'm really sorry.'

'Don't tell Helene,' Hess said. 'Not yet.'

The Duke of Hamilton looked out the window.

He shot his head back.

'Which one?' he said.

'Pardon?' Hess said.

'Which one did you lose?'

'Michele, the head of resistance,' Hess replied reluctantly. 'It was Michele.'

'How does that change things?' he said.

'Hopefully it doesn't,' Hess commented. 'Natasha is strong, hopefully she will manage. She's focused. Strategic.'

Hamilton looked at his friend. He wished he could say he was through the worst of it, but that would be a lie.

***

Water whipped Pintsch's face, bringing him back to consciousness. He opened his eyes just in time to see another bucket of water hitting him in the face. He blinked a couple of times, trying to gain back his vision, but it remained blurred.

'Why am I here?' Pintsch said.

'We need information from you,' a voice said.

'I'll tell you whatever you want to know.'

'Why did Hess fly to England?' the voice enquired.

'Because Hitler asked him to,' Pintsch said.

'That's not what your colleagues said.'

Pintsch knew it was exactly what they said. It was a basic interrogation tool, divide and conquer. The problem for this interrogator was, none of the other's knew anything, so the technique couldn't possibly work.

'That's what Hess told me, that Hitler had asked him to go,' Pintsch said looking a little nervous, 'but I'll say whatever you want me to.'

'I want the truth.'

There was silence.

'I've done my research and I believe out of all of his staff; you would be the one who would know the most.'

'I'm just his secretary,' Pintsch said.

'You've done operations before, in fact, you have even undergone interrogation training.'

Pintsch said nothing. He was trying to adjust his thinking. Pintsch could feel someone breathing in his ear.

'You're very good. It's going to be a pleasure to break you.'

Pintsch just kept on focusing. He heard footsteps walk away. They paused. 'Gentleman, no questions, it is now 6 am, I will be back at 11 am, I want patterns changed every hour.'

The door closed. They put headphones on him, a high-pitched noise came through that triggered a headache straight away. He felt a punch to his side and then to his stomach and to the other side. This was going to be a long five hours.

***

The doctor was holding Natasha's wrist and intently looking at his watch. He placed it back on the bed and felt her forehead.

'What's wrong with her doctor?' Friedrich said.

'I don't know,' the doctor said. 'She seems perfectly healthy, has she been under any stress lately?'

'Not that I am aware of,' Friedrich lied.

'Maybe she just ate something that disagreed with her,' the doctor said. 'She should sleep for another couple of hours.'

Friedrich sighed, he had to go to work like normal. That had been the plan, but this wasn't supposed to happen.

'Should I watch her?'

'She'll be fine,' the doctor replied. 'Just check in with her before lunch.'

He nodded and they both walked out of the room.

***

The sound stopped and someone took off the earphones. Pintsch's head wobbled on his neck. There was nowhere to support it.

'Are you ready to talk?' the voice said.

'I told you everything I know,' Pintsch said.

He was trying to focus, but he couldn't. He felt a pinch in his arm. He wasn't ready, he wasn't fully in control.

'Who was he working with?' the voice said.

'Hitler.'

'Does Wilhelm know anything?' the voice pushed.

'He knows all about science and…'

'Does he know about the mission?' the voice cut in.

'Not that I know of.'

The voice kept hitting him with names. Pintsch could focus just enough. There was a slight pause. Pintsch was trying to refocus to regain control; he wasn't to mention Natasha or Wilhelm.

'Who are Hess's friends?' the voice interrupted his thoughts.

'Ilse,' Pintsch said, 'Buz, Friedrich.'

As soon as he said the Fred, he realised his error.

'His pupils dilated,' said another voice.

'Friedrich eh?' the voice said. 'How does it feel, being broken?'

The hand slapped his face a few times, then he felt a blow to the back of his head, and he passed out.

***

'Another boring day for me,' Jean commented as she pulled apart her pastry. 'How about you?'

'We have been really busy actually,' the girl across the table smiled. 'It's great to have some action.'

'What happened?' Jean asked wide eye leaning forward.

'I'm not supposed to tell,' the girl said, 'but you work with Goebbels, so you're bound to find out soon.'

'What?' Jean said.

She could see her lunch date almost bursting to tell.

'Hess has flown to England,' she blurted looking around to make sure no one could hear, 'without Hitler's permission.'

Jean looked aghast but said nothing. It was important that she looked shocked, but not too shocked.

'Amazing isn't it?' the girl said. 'He left last night and they're already interrogating his staff.'

'Really?' Jean said. 'And have they shed any light on why?'

'Most of them said he was following Hitler's orders,' she said.

The girl took a sip of her tea.

'I thought you said he didn't know about it,' Jean looked confused.

'Maybe that's just the official line,' she said and winked. 'It happens a lot you know, but not normally to such a high-ranking member.'

'How exciting,' Jean said. 'It's a shame they have no other information though.'

'Hopefully, the other officer will be able to help,' she said.

'Who's that?' Jean asked casually.

'Some guy in Munich,' she said. 'I think he looks after the Munich office; they have people on the way down now.'

'Are they not getting the people in Munich to handle it?' Jean said.

'I guess they don't trust them.'

Jean shrugged her shoulders, 'Maybe.'

Jean finished her pastry and took a sip.

'What are you doing this afternoon?' Jean said.

Jean's heart was palpitating, she could hardly hear the girl. It was taking all her concentration to look calm.

'Not much,' the girl said, 'a little baking maybe.'

That was what Jean liked about this girl; she enjoyed talking about herself and her life. This meant she didn't ask Jean many questions at all. Idle chit chat followed, and it wasn't long before lunch was over.

Jean tried to calmly walk back to the office. This wasn't part of the plan. She sat down at her desk smiling as Goebbels handed her some paperwork to do. He was not happy. Patiently she waited until no one could hear her. She picked up the phone and called Natasha.

'Hello,' said Jean.

'Hello,' said Natasha.

Natasha couldn't recognise the voice.

'It's me, Jean.'

'Why are you phoning me?'

'I just found out that your father is not well. I am sorry but he needs your immediate attention.'

There was silence.

'Do you understand?' Jean said.

'Yes, I think I do,' Natasha said. 'Thank you.'

Jean hung up and got back to her work.

***

Natasha walked down the corridor, into her father's office and closed the door. Friedrich looked up and smiled. Natasha stood facing him with a staunch face.

'Are you feeling better?' he asked.

'You have to leave now,' she said not acknowledging the previous question.

'That wasn't the plan.'

'The plan has changed,' she said. 'You can't go home.'

Friedrich solemnly looked at Natasha.

'Do you know where to go?'

'I've been there before,' he said.

Friedrich got up and grabbed some things from his desk and put them in a bag.

'Have you heard anything from—'

'No,' she said. 'I'll call you in the next ten minutes, and you can leave after that.'

And then she was gone.

Friedrich looked around the office. What just happened? No, this was not supposed to happen. Everything was falling apart. He had heard nothing from Helene or Michele. Was the mission successful or not? He started to take deep breaths to try and calm down.

The telephone broke his concentration.

'Hello,' he said.

'I'll see you before you go,' Natasha said.

The line went dead.

Friedrich walked out of the office.

'I'll be away for the rest of the afternoon,' he said to his secretary.

'Yes, sir.'

He walked through the corridor and out the front door for the last time.

***

Natasha waited a couple of hours to allow the Berlin train to arrive, before re-entering the building.

'Where is my father?'

'I, I, I don't know,' the secretary said, 'he said he would be out for the rest of the day.'

Natasha put both hands on her desk and leaned over her.

'That's not good enough.'

'I'm sorry.'

The doors at the end of the corridor burst open. Three Gestapo agents walked in. They weren't locals. The secretary breathed out a relieved sigh. She preferred to deal with the Gestapo than Natasha.

'Well what appointments, does he have? I need to talk to him now.'

'What is happening here?' the officer said.

'Don't worry,' Natasha said. 'It's got nothing to do with you.'

The officer looked at Natasha and then turned to the secretary.

'I am SS-Oberführer Müller. Where is Friedrich?'

'You'll have to wait,' Natasha said. 'I need to talk to him first.'

'Who are you?' asked Muller.

'Natasha.'

He looked confused.

'Friedrich's daughter.'

Good she thought, he has no idea who I am.

'Where is Friedrich?' said Muller.

'I don't know, really I, don't, know,' she said, 'I can't take this anymore.'

She pushed her chair back and ran down the corridor.

'Is this how she normally behaves?'

Natasha rolled her eyes. 'Yes.'

'Why do you need to talk to him?' Muller asked.

'Why do you?'

'We believe he's involved in a plot against the state.'

Natasha let out a laugh and then looked at him slightly confused for a moment.

'My father?'

They nodded.

'I don't think he's capable of that. When I find him, I'll ask him for you.'

'Leave that to the experts.'

'And who would that be?'

Muller's smile dropped.

'Why do you need to talk to him?' he asked.

'Someone has ransacked our house and I want to know why. Was it you?'

He shook his head, then turned towards the two other agents and nodded.

'Show us your house,' he said.

They were soon at the house. A Gestapo agent bent down to inspect the lock. It wasn't forced. Inside there were papers all over the floor, smashed items, and a generally chaotic scene.

'Can I look around?' Muller asked.

Natasha nodded.

'Oberführer,' said one of the agents, 'a broken window.'

Muller went over and to the window. Some glass had fallen on the inside, but the rest had been pushed through to the garden, catching on some of the flowers.

'I want Friedrich found now.'

As they scurried out of the house, Natasha took a deep breath and looked at the clock. That had bought her father some more time. He was now three hours ahead of them. She just hoped that would be enough. She turned around and started to clean the house.

It had taken far less time to create the mess than to tidy it up. So much was happening it was good to focus on something mundane. There were still a couple of rooms to go. Natasha sat down; she needed a break. There was a knock at the door. Typical, thought Natasha. She sighed, got up and walked to the front door and opened it.

Wilhelm stood in front of her. His face set, with pink patchy skin and blood shot eyes. He was silent. He stood in silence.

The silence was deafening. Natasha's smile dropped. She felt a chill cover her like a cloak, and she could feel the hairs on her skin rise in the process. She was cold, she felt like ice.

Natasha's jaw set and her face cemented as she slowly walked backwards down the corridor. She sucked in her cheeks, biting the insides and shook her head. Natasha couldn't continue to look him in the eyes and yet she felt compelled to just in case their message had changed. It hadn't.

Wilhelm walked forward closing the door.

'I'm–'

'No.'

Her left hand made a stop sign to reinforce the word. It was taking all her strength to try and control her breathing. It wasn't working she could feel the tension around her eyes, as she tried to fight the tears. Her hand found a table ledge and she steadied herself.

'I don't believe you.'

For once in her life, her eyes betrayed her. Her head was moving from side to side, and she bit the inside of her bottom lip. Her jaw loosened. He stepped forward to hug her, but she pushed him away. She couldn't breathe, where is the air? Dizzy, I need air. She turned and leaned on the table.

'Go away,' she whispered, 'go, away.'

She turned back to him and screamed, 'Go away.'

By now his face was streaked with tears. In a trancelike state, he walked into the other room and waited.

She couldn't control it anymore. Her eyes blurred and tears dripped from her cheeks. She wiped her face with the back of her hand and slid down the wall, curling into a foetal position.

Why, why, why? Damn it I knew; I knew something would happen. I should have said no. I knew. Oh my God, I knew.

I knew. She curled up even more with her face in her hands and sobbed.

Ten minutes later she walked into the parlour. She didn't look at Wilhelm.

'I'm sorry,' he said.

'What happened?'

Her face was set, but her eyes were bloodshot and puffy.

'We were intercepted off the Dutch coast,' Wilhelm said. 'A fighter plane shot at Hess and Michele managed to shield them.'

'You mean she took the gunfire?'

She could feel her eyes welling up again.

'What were you doing?'

The comment cut like a knife, and she had meant it to.

'Don't talk to me like that,' Wilhelm said. 'You're not the only one that cared for her.'

'I'm her sister.' Natasha paused. 'I had no control over this, damn it. You did, you were there, you were right there. You were right there.'

She clenched her fists, she wanted to hurt him. She knew it wasn't his fault. But she wanted to hate him for not protecting Michele, not looking after her sister.

They stood in silence.

Her mind was trying to come to grips with the fact that she would never see or talk to her sister again. It couldn't be true, it just couldn't.

'Did you see her body?'

'I saw the plane crash into the sea.'

'Did you see her body?'

'I was in the middle of a dogfight,' he said. 'I did a fly by and couldn't see her. I saw the wreckage.'

Natasha got up and walked out of the room. Wilhelm raced after her.

'Natasha, she's dead.'

Natasha paused in the doorway of the study

'You don't know that.'

She turned and walked in.

'Even if she did survive the crash, or the fireball. Do you know how cold the North Sea is?' he said. 'It's cold, and it's rough and she's dead.'

Natasha turned to Wilhelm.

'You can't take away my hope,' she said. She was so close to tears again. 'It's all I have left.'

Natasha punched her fists against his chest and tried to push him away. This time, Wilhelm just pulled her in and cradled her in his arms,

'It's going to be alright.'

'It's not.'

He stroked her head and rocked her, as she sobbed on his shoulder. Slowly his eyes focused on the room he was in.

Without even thinking he said, 'What happened?'

Natasha took a deep breath to calm herself and stepped back.

'Well, I needed it to look like my father had ransacked the house.'

'Why?'

'He had to disappear.'

'Why? There's no ties back to him.'

'That's right,' she said sarcastically. 'Until Pintsch named him this morning.'

'What?'

Wilhelm's face showed his disbelief.

'Yes,' she said, 'I'm having a really good day. So please, please, don't take away my hope. I need—'

She was on the edge of hysteria, fighting the tears yet again. Wilhelm nodded, stepped forward and held her as she crumbled sobbing.

***

Winston looked up.

'Welcome to England. I hope the past twenty-four hours were acceptable to you.'

Hess smiled. 'They were adequate, thank you for organising things, I know you're busy. I have a proposal for you, which I think is in both of our interests.'

'Let's not rush things. Would you like some English tea?' Churchill said.

He nodded to the butler who quickly disappeared.

'Why,' Winston said, 'would Hitler's right-hand man want peace?'

He paused as if waiting for a reply. Hess relaxed in his chair and smiled. Winston continued.

'When although to the rest of the world this looks and will always look like a mission from Hitler, it's actually a joint effort with the resistance. You are effectively turning on a friend.'

'As always Winston, your intelligence is right, although I would've been very disappointed if it wasn't.' Hess said.

Winston smiled.

'Hitler is a good charismatic leader,' Hess said, 'who has simply lost his way.'

'That you can no longer control.'

'Maybe,' said Hess, 'or maybe there are just some aspects of his character that I can no longer suppress. He is losing focus, is emotional and needs to be more strategic.'

Winston noticed Hess's face change. He was lost in thought, in anguish.

'He has too much hate. Too much anger. It controls him, rather than the other way around. He's confused about what is needed, with what he wants. We will lose a lot of Germans and a lot for Germany. I can't condone that.'

Sweat was pouring off Hess's brow. Churchill looked at him. Hess was an intelligent man. He had helped bring Germany out of depression and had a complex intelligence network that the English knew little about. It had all been good for Germany until... Well, there were many untils. Winston was trying to work out what was driving Hess, what had brought him here, what he really wanted.

'There's a problem,' said Winston. 'I can't afford to have peace yet.'

'I could talk him into it. If he thought Britain would stay out of Europe. There are other options,' Hess replied hesitantly.

'Even if Hitler was killed, it wouldn't stop his generals from expanding Germany to the east.' Winston shook his head.

He offered Hess a cigar. Hess declined. Winston cut the end of his. 'Can't do it. Do you not see the problems it would cause?'

'No, I don't,' Hess said. 'You have no idea, do you?'

'No, I think it is you who has no idea,' said Winston.

He banged his fists on the desk making the metal ashtray jump. He leaned forward with a cigar in one hand and his lighter in the other.

'If we declare peace with Germany, we lose any possible alliance with the US and effectively declare war on Russia. We can't afford to do that financially or physically. We do not have the equipment, to take on everyone. And of course, there is the whole reason why we got into the war to start with. Poland, then France and all the other countries you invaded.'

'We were stripped of territory after the First World War. We needed to get it back. They were ours.' Hess retorted.

'Do you know what I see?' Hess questioned. 'Soon as you care so much about the people of Europe. I see millions of Jews, Prisoners of war, Poles and travellers being exterminated, like little more than common vermin. I've seen their plans; I know what they're thinking. I see a nation who loses a generation of youth to death or brainwashing and my son–'

Winston cut in again. 'I see the death of millions of people in Germany, Russia and England. I see nations losing their identity and I see a never-ending war. No one will win. But we do need to limit the disaster.'

Winston lit the cigar and let his comment sink in.

'I've been told about your thoughts on the Bolsheviks and the Jews. Stab in the back theory. You come here and expect me to believe that suddenly you have empathy for these groups of people. The people you think caused Germany to lose the war.'

Hess got up from his seat backing towards the wall.

'I want a greater Germany, and Jews and Bolsheviks will dilute that. They have slowly infiltrated our society and yours. You have the same problems, and your people know it. They do have to go. But there is a right way and a wrong way of doing it. Is that not why you all suggested the Balfour Declaration? You think you should push them to a bit of land you stole. Sorry, govern.'

Winston narrowed his eyes, 'Think very carefully.'

Hess smiled, 'I think they should work for us. For both of our countries. If we could have peace between us, that could be part of rebuilding of the economies, of our cultures. That is something that Hitler could agree with. The right laws would have to be put in place. But it would be beneficial.'

'This is not the way, Hess.' Churchill interrupted, 'it's not strategic.'

Hess had never thought of the fact that Britain needed America's support.

'We're talking about human life, on a huge scale, so many Germans, so many English, I just… there's got to…'

No matter how he analysed the situation, Churchill was right. It was either a slaughter or a larger slaughter, whatever the outcome; blood would be on their hands. He looked at Winston.

'So how do we gain your outcome, keep Germany strong and finish the war as soon as possible? How do we end it?' said Hess.

They both looked at each other. Neither of them knew the answer.

***

Anita opened the door. Natasha and Wilhelm stood on the doorstep.

'Come in,' she said. 'Your father's in the Parlour with Yosef and Henri.'

'Thank you,' Natasha said.

They both walked through. Friedrich got up and hugged her. She looked over her father's shoulder and acknowledged Henri but looked at no one else. Then she stepped back.

'When do you leave?'

'In about an hour's time,' said Friedrich.

She looked quickly at Wilhelm. She couldn't tell her father. She felt guilty that she couldn't deliver the news, but she knew words would fail her. She was finding it hard to hold it together as it was.

'Friedrich,' Wilhelm said. 'Can we talk?'

Friedrich nodded and followed Wilhelm into the kitchen. Anita was busy preparing a salad.

'Can you excuse us for a moment?' Wilhelm said.

Anita nodded and walked into the living room. The kitchen door closed.

'What's happening?' Anita asked.

Everyone looked at Natasha.

'Look at me.' Yosef said.

'Who is going with father?' Natasha asked ignoring him.

'He has directions,' Henri replied.

'No, no' the pained voice penetrated the wall. 'I don't believe you.'

'He can't go by himself,' Natasha said. 'I need you to go with him Henri.'

There was a smash in the kitchen.

Anita looked around and then back at Natasha, she knew something was terribly wrong.

'Why? Natasha, why? Oh my…' Anita paused, '… oh my God, where is Michele?'

Natasha turned away to try to compose herself.

She took a deep breath 'Michele was shot down.'

Natasha tried to fight the tears.

'Is she alright?' Henri asked.

'She crashed into the North Sea,' whispered Natasha.

Wilhelm walked in. There was silence. No one looked at each other.

'Natasha,' Wilhelm said, 'you need to talk to your father.'

She nodded, wiped her eyes, and then walked out of the room.

Wilhelm went over and bent down next to Yosef.

'You have to pull yourself together.'

'She couldn't even look me in the eye,' said Yosef. 'She couldn't look me in the eye.'

Yosef's eyes were glazing over.

'You know her too well,' Wilhelm said. 'I know it's hard, but you have to pull yourself together, this is a dangerous time.'

'I know. I need some air.'

Yosef pulled himself out of the chair and grabbed his crutches. He looked like he was in a trance, as he mechanically left the room.

Anita had disappeared. Henri was in shock. The room felt suffocating; suddenly Wilhelm needed air too.

Natasha walked into the kitchen. There was a trail of salad along the floor and broken glass by the wall.

Her father was sitting on the ground with a bottle of vodka. It shook slightly with the tremble in his hands. Friedrich's eyes were red and his face paler than white.

'I thought we'd stopped this,' she said.

'I've had a hard day.'

'Take your last sip.'

He took a large swig, winced with the taste, and then handed her the bottle.

'Does your mother know?'

'I don't know.'

She looked at her father. It was somehow easier to deflect pain if there was someone to look after, someone else to focus on. 'I'm sorry.'

She sat down beside him and gave him a hug.

'It's not your fault,' he said, 'it began with me, it all began with me,'

He sobbed in her arms like a little boy. He felt like his world had fallen apart and now a very important piece would be missing forever. After a while, he pulled away and took a deep breath. They sat in silence, staring at the kitchen shelves opposite, although neither registered what lay on them. Friedrich turned to say something, and took a breath, then changed his mind. He got up and walked outside.

Natasha stood and looked out the window. Everyone was scattered in the garden, in their own little place, motionless and quiet. There was silence, all Natasha could hear was the wind. When she looked out the window, the world had not changed, it was the same as any other day. The hills were still there, the barn, the sky, everything, it was as if nature had not registered the loss of her sister. It was unfair. It should know, it should show. She looked out the window again. The people. The people she saw, standing in their own little worlds, they would never be the same again. She leaned on the sink and tried to steady herself.

She knew that something had changed in her, and it worried her. She felt calm, maybe it was shock, maybe it was autopilot. She didn't know how long she had stared out the window but wheels on the driveway woke her from her trance. She looked out the front window and then rushed to Henri.

'Your ride is here,' she said.

Henri said nothing but walked outside and chatted to the driver for a couple of minutes then came back inside.

'I need to get my things,' he said.

Natasha walked outside to her father and squatted down so she could talk to him.

'It's time to go,' she said.

He looked at her and reached over to cup her face with his hands.

'Come with me, I want you to come with me,' he said.

His eyes were bloodshot and puffy. She looked at him confused.

'I don't want to lose you,' he paused.

He was on the verge of crying again.

'I can't lose you. Do you understand me?'

She nodded.

'You won't lose me,' she said, 'I promise.'

'I want you safe, with me,' he said.

'We have to go,' she replied.

They both stood up and walked through the house to the front door. Natasha thought about what her father had asked.

Could she do it? Go somewhere where she didn't have to act. Somewhere she would trust people. She sighed. She had acted for so long. She didn't really know who she was anymore. It would be so nice though to have the peace, to find herself, and be a normal girl.

Friedrich started his goodbyes as Henri got into the car. Friedrich got in and moved across the seat, to allow her to get in too.

Natasha had a hand on the top of the door, her elbow leaning on the roof. She looked at her father, then at Wilhelm who was standing opposite her, and back to her father. It was so tempting, just leaving it all behind.

No one said a word.

'What would you stay for?' Friedrich said. 'It's all gone.'

But it hadn't and Natasha knew that.

'I'm sorry, I love you, but I can't,' she bit her lip to control the tears, 'I can't leave yet. There's so much left to do. I hope you understand.'

Friedrich's face dropped and he moved forward to get out of the car. She slammed the door, nodded to the driver, and the car drove away.

Natasha looked up at the sky blinking and trying to catch her breath. Tears were streaming down her face. Everyone was looking at her. She didn't notice. Slowly she regained her breathing. The cool air cleared her nose, and she closed her eyes as she exhaled through her mouth. Calm and controlled she turned to Yosef and Wilhelm.

'Let's go. We have a lot to do.'

They nodded and followed her inside.